The Feminist Architecture of Postmodern Anti-Tales

I0593005

This monograph aims to counter the assumption that the anti-tale is a 'subversive twin' or dark side of the fairy tale coin, instead it argues that the anti-tale is a genre rich in complexity and radical potential that fundamentally challenges the damaging ideologies and socializing influence of fairy tales.

The Feminist Architecture of Postmodern Anti-Tales: Space, Time and Bodies highlights how anti-tales take up timely debates about revising old structures, opening our minds up to a broader spectrum of experience or ways of viewing the world and its inhabitants. They show us alternative architectures for the future by deconstructing established spatio-temporal laws and structures, as well as limited ideas surrounding the body, and ultimately liberate us from the shackles of a single-minded and simplistic masculine reality currently upheld by dominant social forces and patriarchal fairy tales themselves. It is only when these masculine fairy tales and social architectures are deconstructed that new, more inclusive feminine realities and futures can be brought into being.

Dr. Kendra Reynolds received her PhD from Ulster University in Northern Ireland.

Routledge Interdisciplinary Perspectives on Literature

For more information about this series, please visit: https://www.routledge.com

The Feminist Architecture of Postmodern Anti-Tales
Space, Time and Bodies

Kendra Reynolds

Routledge
Taylor & Francis Group

NEW YORK AND LONDON

First published 2020
by Routledge
605 Third Avenue, New York, NY 10017

and by Routledge
2 Park Square, Milton Park, Abingdon, Oxon, OX14 4RN

First issued in paperback 2021

*Routledge is an imprint of the Taylor & Francis Group, an
informa business*

Copyright © 2020 Taylor & Francis

Publisher's Note
The publisher has gone to great lengths to ensure the quality of this
reprint but points out that some imperfections in the original copies
may be apparent.

Library of Congress Cataloging-in-Publication Data
Library of Congress Control Number:2019951765

ISBN 13: 978-1-03-224007-7 (pbk)
ISBN 13: 978-0-367-19312-6 (hbk)

Typeset in Sabon
by codeMantra

Contents

Figures

Introduction

Following a two-day symposium at the University of Glasgow in 2010, Catriona McAra and David Calvin published their edited collection of essays titled *Anti-Tales: The Uses of Disenchantment* (2011). While it was their aim to secure the anti-tale's position in academic scholarship, subsequently little attention has been paid to the anti-tale genre. It appears that, each time the term 'anti-tale' has been brought up historically – namely by Robert Walser (1910), André Jolles (1929), and later in the work of Wolfgang Mieder (1978 & 2008) and John Pizer (1990) – it has not been explored in any kind of depth.[1] Thus, while Calvin and McAra's work has proven seminal in reintroducing the term to fairy tale scholars in the twenty-first century, much is yet to be done to establish it as an essential genre in its own right, particularly as the term has rarely been used since the publication of these essays.

Why is the anti-tale and critical study of it important? Clearly today, fairy tale retellings, particularly 'dark' ones, have a broad commercial appeal. One need only look at the films produced by Disney, or at the range of pop culture novels an Amazon search yields, to appreciate the scope and appeal of this kind of story. Many of these works are perceived to be radical in their narrative digressions from what are considered to be the 'traditional' fairy tales established by Charles Perrault and the Brothers Grimm, and yet most are profoundly conservative and do nothing to challenge the patriarchal and ideological mores of the established male-authored and often misogynist stories. This illusion of false radicalism damagingly endorses the same outdated and sexist ideas conveyed by the traditional, male-authored stories under the guise of post-feminist rhetoric. Further illustrating the popular misconception of the term, Wikipedia's definition of 'anti-fairy tale' currently condones an unhappy or tragic ending as the only necessary requirement for the label.[2] Thus, anti-tale must be seized by scholars as a term that should be used to distinguish between fairy tale retellings (which simply change elements of the story but leave the original morals and ideologies unchallenged) and those reworkings which actually subvert the ideological underpinnings of their patriarchal predecessors.

Calvin and McAra define the term 'anti-tale' as follows: 'rarely an outward opposition to the traditional form itself, the anti-tale takes aspects of the fairy tale genre and reimagines, subverts, inverts, deconstructs, or satirises, elements of them to produce an alternate narrative interpretation, outcome, or morality'.[3] They point out that, rather than rejecting the fairy tale completely, the anti-tale is like a 'shadow' of the older genre, subverting it from within – they are like 'two sides of the same coin'.[4] It is only by acknowledging the anti-tale's affinities with the original genre that it can work within it to subvert the patriarchal fairy tale's prevailing problems. As Angela Carter, the widely recognised queen of the anti-tale, once asserted, 'I am all for putting new wine in old bottles, especially if the pressure of the new wine makes the old bottles explode'.[5] However, this definition by McAra and Calvin is often rejected by critics such as Cristina Bacchilega, who suggests that fairy tales have always constituted an impulse to retell and revise previous stories, 'the anti-tale is always implicit in the fairy tale'.[6] Certainly, fairy tales have often been subversive, containing elements that could be described as anti-tale qualities (such as those by discontented French women writers in the seventeenth-century and oral folk tellers). However, as this book will attest, the anti-tale is not simply a fairy tale retelling or revision, rather the distinction operates at a more fundamental level as the genre possesses its own unique architecture. Therefore, previous backlash on the anti-tale is due to the limited definitions offered by its advocates so far, who, like McAra and Calvin, describe the anti-tale merely as the 'subversive twin' or dark side of the same fairy tale coin. This book recognises the subversive qualities of many fairy tale narratives and how anti-tales seize upon these and enhance them, and I also acknowledge how the anti-tale *does* inherently adopt fairy-tale tropes in a self-reflective manner, but this is all part of their deconstruction which operates at an architectural level making them different and distinguishable from the original patriarchally fossilised fairy tales with their binary-orientated and stifling structures. In essence, this study asserts that it is a genre in its own right, offering an analysis of its unique feminine architecture, based around its structural and conceptual feminisation of dominant notions surrounding space, time, and bodies. In a table of binary traits, Calvin and McAra note that, while the fairy tale is patriarchal, set 'Once Upon a Time', contains a black and white morality, and upholds enchantment, the anti-tale is feminist, often set in a real-world context, contains a grey or murky amorality, and endorses a politics of disenchantment.[7] However, despite being useful in identifying some of the anti-tale's characteristics, their use of binaries to define the term is limited and antithetical to the anti-tale's motivations. My study highlights how problematic this method is, with the anti-tale rejecting such binary constructions of reality. As the chapters to follow highlight, anti-tales complicate our notions of space, time, and bodies altogether in order to expose how we are liberated only when we relinquish the binary-orientated thought processes held up by fairy tales and hegemonic power structures, which deny a space and voice to those who do not fit into either half of dominant dualisms (those regarding man/woman, human/animal, and nature/culture, for example). The anti-tale is much more nuanced and complex than many previous definitions have allowed. As McAra and Calvin's collection of essays provides the only substantial attempt at defining the anti-tale to date, this study aims to move forward from their working definitions and help secure the anti-tale as a crucial, timely term, and a recognised genre, for academic scholarship today.

Furthermore, I am particularly concerned with anti-tales in the twenty-first century. The study of gender in relation to fairy tales took prominence in the 1970s and 1980s during the second wave of feminism and was instigated by Alison Lurie's endorsement of fairy tales as positive stories for female emancipation in a paper titled 'Fairy Tale Liberation' (1970).[8] In the words of Donald Haase, the paper 'sparked a serious and, as it turns out, a lasting debate about the relationship of women to fairy tales'.[9] This was due to Marcia R. Lieberman's 1972 response in her paper 'Some Day My Prince Will Come: Female Acculturation Through the Fairy Tale', which rebuked Lurie's assertions and highlighted the problems with the sexist ideologies inherent in the tales.[10] This debate between the two critics fuelled a heated discourse that would expand into a vital and enduring branch of feminist fairy tale scholarship. At the same time, the 1970s and 1980s also wrought the publication of anti-tales by writers such as Angela Carter, Anne Sexton, and Emma Donoghue, as part of a wider feminist project to rewrite and subvert the male-authored stories. These late twentieth-century texts drew upon the influence of the original female oral folk storytellers, who told stories around the fireside to both children and other adults as a means of expressing communal concerns. These voices were appropriated and sanitised by male collectors (such as Charles Perrault in the seventeenth century and the Grimm Brothers in the nineteenth century). In addition, they also drew upon the often overlooked first female-authored literary fairy tales, which were written by dispossessed French female *conteuses* in the salons of the seventeenth century, whose tales were subtly subversive and only lightly veiled their restlessness and discontent within their restrictive lifestyles.[11] It was, in fact, the most infamous of these French authors, namely Madame d'Aulnoy, who coined the term *contes de fées* (fairy tales). Elizabeth Waning Harries' study *Twice Upon a Time: Women Writers and the History of the Fairy Tale* highlights this history, noting how the more compact or simplistic male stories that dominate our idea of the fairy tale today stripped the complexity and grittiness out of the female folk stories and those of the French *conteuses*, the male collectors favouring simplicity as a means to exploit the fairy tale's didacticism and its usefulness in perpetuating dominant ideologies.[12] Thus, when I refer to masculine tales in this book, I am not erroneously labelling the entire genre as masculine, nor am I trying to tie the fairy tale genre as a whole down to one set of characteristics, rather I am referring to the patriarchally fossilised form of the fairy tale which dominates conventional understandings of the genre, headed by the tales of the Grimms, Perrault, and Hans Christian Andersen, which uphold the social, political, and moral masculine architecture acceptable to conservative societies and power structures. Therefore, the twenty-first-century anti-tales I discuss here are part of a much older, overshadowed female tradition. Yet, while feminist fairy tale criticism, and feminist anti-tales, has been around for decades, and subversive female fairy tales have existed for centuries, scholars have tended to focus on surface elements, such as the depictions of female characters (particularly the 'innocent persecuted heroine trope') and elements of plot.[13] Even now, feminist fairy tale criticism is often guilty of placing a heavy focus upon certain key authors, namely Carter herself, the fairy tale genre's sociocultural history, and the development and origins of the genre which, though crucial in uncovering the extensive female input into the fairy tale's evolution and development, has constituted a kind of mapping of the tales in specific contexts at the expense of close readings of the texts themselves. As Haase noted in his edited collection *Fairy Tales and Feminism: New Approaches* (2004), the modern feminist fairy tale criticism of the twentieth century placed 'its emphasis on the genre's socio-political and sociohistorical contexts' (Jack Zipes, whose prolific publications, including *Breaking the Magic Spell: Radical Theories of Folk and Fairy Tales* (1979) and *The Irresistible Fairy Tale: The Cultural and Social History of a Genre* (2012), provides the most eminent case in point).[14] It is only in recent years that an increasingly theoretical strand of feminist fairy tale scholarship has emerged, which appreciates the great depth within the anti-tales themselves. As Haase stated at the beginning of the twenty-first century, 'what essentially began as a debate over the value of fairy tales based on their representation of females would become a more multi-faceted discussion of the genre's history and a more nuanced analysis of its production and reception, as this collection of essays demonstrates'.[15] While Haase's study moved feminist fairy tale studies forward to discuss such topics as the relationship between women's autobiographies and fairy tales and giving a wider international range of texts to be discussed, it is only in the final essay by Cathy Lynn Preston, 'Disrupting the Boundaries of Genre and Gender: Postmodernism and the Fairy Tale', that the complexity of postmodern fairy tale criticism is introduced. One groundbreaking example of this more nuanced and theoretical appreciation of postmodern fairy tale criticism is Anna Kérchy's edited collection of essays titled *Postmodern Reinterpretations of Fairy Tales: How Applying New Methods Generates New Meanings*, published in 2012. Kérchy's collection opened up a space for a greater in-depth analysis of postmodern fairy tales and anti-tales in which theories of the body, genre mutations, surrealism, narratology, and the creation of fictional realties, emphasised the need to develop an approach to the genres that would do justice to their ever-increasing complexity.[16] It is to this exciting new branch of postmodern feminist fairy tale criticism, with its philosophical and theoretical edge, that this book aims to contribute.

Located within anti-tale and postmodern feminist fairy tale criticism, the narrower conceptual and thematic focus of this study is upon space, time, and bodies. This is not a randomly selected thematic lens. Corporeality, temporality, and spatiality consistently assert themselves in contemporary anti-tales as major components in their feminist subversions. The strategies adopted by feminist anti-tale writers seem to be heavily influenced by postmodern, posthuman, and materialist feminisms, which are currently reconceptualising different ways of conceiving and being in the world. For example, as one of the prominent figures in this project, Elizabeth Grosz, has pointed out, space, time, and bodies must be reconfigured in order to tackle the prejudices inherent in the literal and conceptual 'architecture' of social life (i.e. how we construct, experience, and see the make-up of society).[17] In Grosz's opinion, this striving for a feminist 'Architecture From the Outside', in which women can create alternatives to existing patriarchal realities and logistical frameworks, is dependent upon renewing our understandings of these three fundamental principles. As she states:

> the links between corporeality and conceptions of space and time may prove to be of major significance in feminist research [...] If bodies are to be reconceived, not only must their matter and form be rethought, but so too must their environment and spatio-temporal location.[18]

She goes on to note that

> the project ahead, or one of them, is to return women to those places from which they have been dis- or re- placed or expelled [...] and partly in order to be able to experiment with and produce the possibility of occupying, dwelling or living in new spaces, which in their turn help to generate new perspectives, new bodies, new ways of inhabiting.[19]

At the same time, I investigate how this focus on space, time, and bodies also subverts traditional fairy tales and their sexist ideologies, as well as examine how this trend suggests that the anti-tale is a feminine form, both in terms of its conceptual or philosophical architecture in which it suggests alternative spatial, temporal, and corporeal forms and in its material/textual form. This observation contributes to existing definitions and enhances our understanding of this relatively new genre. Hence, this study is part of postmodern feminist criticism's concern with identity politics that shows how anti-tales today are taking up this project of reconceptualising established ideas about space, time, and bodies in order to liberate women from restrictive patriarchal ways of seeing and being. This field is known as feminist epistemology. For, as Linda Alcoff and Elizabeth Potter have pointed out, feminist epistemologists look at things like 'women's ways of knowing', 'women's experience', or 'women's knowledge', which are alien concepts to traditional philosophers who focused on 'a theory of knowledge in general'.[20] Rather, my feminist epistemological approach is in line with Alcoff and Potter's assertions that:

> this is precisely the premise that feminist epistemologists have called into question. Feminist analyses in philosophy, as in other disciplines, have insisted on the significance and particularity of the context of theory. This has led many feminist epistemologists to scepticism about the possibility of a general or universal account of knowledge, an account that ignores the social context and status of knowers.[21]

In essence, in my study of anti-tales and their revisions of space, time, and bodies, I am focused on how the anti-tales privilege uncertainty, pointing out the political agenda behind the production of knowledges and dominant conceptions of these broad concepts: time being used as a colonial tool to maintain the coloniser's social order, the apparent leakiness or unpredictability of the female body used as a justification for the control of women, the linkage of women and nature as resources to be exploited by men, or the concept of the city as a space dominated by white, heterosexual, and bourgeois males, for example. The anti-tales are keen to exploit the use of pluriperspectivism, weaving competing narratives of marginal identities together, those which do not uphold universal or accepted understandings of the world. Anti-tales ultimately foreground the subjective in knowledge production, exposing how any apparently objective viewpoint is ultimately bound up in its own political agenda, and our conceptions of such fundamentals as space, time, and corporeality are deconstructed, shown to be negotiable, liberating us from the exclusionary politics of the dominant social order and its attempts to establish a limited, universal set of knowledges, modes of experience, or identities.

However, it is also important to clarify what exactly I mean when I refer to the concepts of the feminine and form within this study. First, one might ask whether it is inherently essentialist to utilise femininity at all as part of a feminist argument. This study endorses the approach taken by feminist critics such as Margrit Shildrick, who has stated that her feminism is directed 'towards the possibilities of a feminist take-up of poststructuralism and postmodernism' and 'that it is only that approach which can provide feminism with the tools sufficient to disrupt masculinist philosophy radically and to make a place for a reconceived feminine'.[22] Certainly, this challenge to masculine knowledge is clearly embraced by the authors studied here. Furthermore, I also share the idea of the radical feminine posited by Grosz's revision of cultural scripts, which is 'directed towards the establishment of a viable space and time for women to occupy *as* women' – in essence, it *is* an approach which embraces female difference and experience, rejecting the production of a male universe 'built upon the erasure of the bodies and contributions of women'.[23] However, despite this, such a theoretical position is not essentialist. Rather, my conception of the feminine goes beyond simplistic essentialist dualisms, sharing in Shildrick's assertion that,

> what this entails is the recovery/discovery of a radical sexual difference, a difference that speaks to the feminine *beyond* the oppositional gender binary [...] what is being (re)claimed is not a homogeneous category of women, but rather a multiplicity of fluid positions.[24]

For example, the analyses of feminine knowledges and positions offered by the anti-tales in this study do not exclude male or transgender characters, my conception of the feminine is closely aligned with ideas of queerness; the majority of the characters constituting subversive feminine/queer positions as outsiders, existing in spaces, times, and bodies that seep beyond, and into, the gaps left by restrictive and limiting masculine forms of understanding. This shows the huge potential inherent in embracing radical feminine standpoints and forms of thinking, with Grosz pointing out that:

> Once the universal is shown to be a guise for the masculine and knowledges are shown to occupy only one pole of a (sexual) spectrum instead of its entirety, the possibility of other ways of knowing and proceeding – the possibility of feminine discourses and knowledges – reveals itself.[25]

In essence, feminine constitutes all that is 'other', different, and outside of socially accepted, restrictive norms and ideologies, opening up our minds to a wider spectrum of experience and multiple ways of being in the world. While my book considers a range of outsider positions, I use the phrase 'feminine form' to define that marginality as opposed to 'queer form' due to the fact that my study predominantly focuses on women and deliberately attempts to adopt a meta-critical take on the cultural scripts of 'femininity' currently upheld by patriarchally fossilised fairy tales, which inform, and have informed, the gendered behaviours of women and young girls. Mine is a 'femininity' in quotation marks, a femininity with a difference, which embraces all that is subversive in the notion of female otherness and which attempts to reclaim femininity for feminism rather than allowing its use in dominant cultural scripts to remain unchallenged. Also, although I have used the phrase 'feminist architecture' in my title, this is done to highlight my study's focus on the genre's feminine architecture in relation to the political movement of Feminism, while the use of feminine instead of feminist in the rest of this book indicates that I am not essentualising the formal elements of anti-tale genre, nor am I claiming the genre solely for feminists. Rather, I show how its feminine architecture liberates it from any fixed or limiting structure and illustrate through an analyses of queer and other marginalised identities in the tales, how both feminism and the anti-tale genre can be viewed as combatting multiple forms of oppression in their deconstruction of hegemonic power structures. By referring to the anti-tale's feminine form then, I do not risk universalising the form of the genre, rather this 'definition' ironically embraces the genre's inability to be contained and its openness to multiple meanings and possibilities, as opposed to restricting it to a fixed structure. What this study demonstrates, then, is that the revisions of space, time, and bodies by anti-tale authors all hinge upon this idea of the radical feminine and embracing alternative *forms* of knowing and being, the analysis proving that these tales are highly successful in returning women to, and reshaping, the spaces from which they have been excluded. The anti-tales examined here fulfil Grosz's project outlined above by 'experiment[ing] with and produc[ing] the possibility of occupying, dwelling or living in new spaces, which in their turn help to generate new perspectives, new bodies, new ways of inhabiting'. Such an approach allows for a reconfiguration and reclamation of femininity for feminist discourse, in revising masculine forms of understanding and constructing the world, highlighting a shift from what Anna Kérchy calls 'femininity as masochist entrapment to femininity as feminist self-realisation'.[26]

Therefore, my interest in form is closely aligned with John Frow's definition:

> The concept of form designates those aspects of a text which are recurrent as opposed to those which are singular. It is a relational concept: every formal feature is at another level an aspect of 'content', and every 'content' can be thought, from another perspective, as a dimension of form. As I use it here, it refers primarily to those elements of a text which recurrently shape the material medium of the text and the 'immaterial' categories of space, time, and enunciative position – that is, the most fundamental categories through which the text is organised.[27]

Although my use of form focuses predominantly on what Frow describes above as the 'immaterial categories' that inform the anti-tale's feminine 'enunciative position' in relation to cultural scripts (feminine psycho-geography, negotiable city space, ecofeminist landscapes, physical and symbolical spaces women must experience, and gendered cartographies of viewing), the spatial, temporal, and corporeal elements not only sub-vert the restrictive architecture of masculine knowledges and logisti-cal frameworks upheld by the fairy tale but are also mirrored in those material, narratological elements that shatter the simplistic, heteronor-mative, binary-orientated world of the traditional stories. This is done in many ways: through the anti-tales' material refusal of neat closure, their ecofeminist rejection of the conceptual fairy tale moral framework tagged on at the end of stories, the use of transverbal musicality, the *écriture féminine* of their overlapping story threads, their fragmented narrative styles, the use of body-texts or corporeal narratology, their manipulation of spatial settings, their rejection of established formal motifs such as the 'Once upon a time' trope, or their reconfiguration of temporal orders, and their ever-increasing complexity. Therefore, my conception of form is twofold, encompassing the more abstract concep-tual architecture of the texts in their advocacy of feminine knowledges and their construction of more complex and inclusive societies, while recognising how this is inevitably embodied in the literal or material form and structure of the texts. David Duff also notes this dual aspect when he states that a 'common distinction, central to Romantic the-ory, is between "mechanical" and "organic" form, the former being the fixed, pre-established form imposed by generic rules, and the latter the individual form generated by the internal forces within a literary work'; this is similar to Frow's advocacy of material and immaterial (i.e. content-based) understandings of form.[28] In essence, the spatial, tempo-ral, and corporeal content affects the form of the tale and vice versa. In addition, Frow also noted above how form refers to recurrent aspects in texts, and hence the feminine spatio-temporal and corporeal knowledges that pervade the wide range of anti-tales I discuss here is indicative of a trend which, I argue, needs to be considered as an integral part of the anti-tale's conceptual and literal architecture. Ultimately, my conception of the anti-tale's feminine form embodies Grosz's sense of architecture as the construction of spatial, temporal, and corporeal knowledges *and* the literal architecture of the anti-tales' material elements.

In addition, it is worth noting how these ideas relating to a feminine narratology and stylistics have affinities with New French Feminism's theory of *écriture féminine* (feminine writing style), with Irigaray link-ing the complexity of the female body to the expansiveness of feminine writing that seeps beyond masculine restrictions:

> woman has sex organs just about everywhere [...] Her sexuality, always at least double, goes even further: it is plural. Is this the way culture is seeking to characterize itself now? [...] feminine language

is more diffusive than its 'masculine counterpart'. That is undoubtedly the reason her language goes off in all directions and he is unable to discern the coherence.[29]

Indeed, this quote brilliantly illustrates how the anti-tale narratives in this study also utilise this feminine complexity, through overlapping narrative threads and the use of pluriperspectivism as a major part of their feminine architecture in their revisions of all three concepts of spatiality, temporality, and corporeality, as well as pointing out the power of feminine writing to inspire real cultural change. Thus, the anti-tale genre's feminine approach also relates to Rachel Blau du Plessis' study *Writing Beyond the Ending*, in which she highlights how women writers often attempt to question the traditional structure of narrative forms as a parallel to revising social scripts in real life (fairy tales often ending with a female heroine's marriage, for example). Indeed, we will see this theory of 'writing beyond the ending' in the anti-tales discussed here, with Helen Smith's *Alison Wonderland* beginning after the heroine's marriage has fallen apart, for example. Blau du Plessis' theory of reconceived feminine narratives also includes those texts which accord space to neglected or marginalised voices, a strategy adopted by many of the writers in this study, including Lee's 'Black-Eyed Susan' and its focus on female narratives within the male-dominated city of 1920s Paris.

Before moving on, I would also like to briefly clarify here my reasons for the use of the label 'postmodern' to describe the anti-tales in my title. While the term dates back to the 1960s and is often classed as 'outdated', the feminine architecture of the anti-tale identified here is part of the greater movement of Postmodernism to deconstruct grand master narratives and favour instead, in their deconstruction of limited understandings of spatial, temporal, and corporeal concepts, ideas relating to a plethora of histories as opposed to a singular History, multiplicity, complexity, and hybridity, for example. Although many would argue that we have entered a post-postmodern age, this study operates with the understanding that we have not yet managed to break free from those dominant conceptions of the most fundamental narratives that govern everyday life: regarding space, time, and bodies. The need for the anti-tale's challenge to the fairy tale and its hold on social consciousness is clear evidence of the fact that our society still clings to archaic notions and governing narratives. We are still in the postmodern phase of trying to deconstruct our society's dominant preoccupation with limiting hegemonic frameworks and so I contest that we cannot deem ourselves to be post-postmodern while we are still in the throes of postmodern challenges to dominant narratives, ideologies, and frameworks.

Each chapter in this book adopts a thematic rather than an author-centred approach, and therefore, there are a number of primary texts discussed per chapter. Hence, well-known texts such as Margaret Atwood's *Maddaddam* trilogy and her collection *Stone Mattress: Nine*

Tales (2016), Michel Faber's novel *Under the Skin* (2000), Disney's *Maleficent* (2014), *Into the Woods* (2015), and *Alice Through the Looking Glass* (2016) are discussed alongside lesser known authors and neglected works, including Tanith Lee's *Cruel Pink* (2013), Kate Bernheimer's *How a Mother Weaned Her Girl From Fairy Tales* (2014), Helen Smith's *Alison Wonderland* (2011), Matteo Garrone's art-house film *Tale of Tales* (2015), Betsy Cornwell's *Tides* (2013), Marissa Meyer's *Cinder* (2012), and Nalo Hopkinson's *Skin Folk* (2001), to name a few. Taken together, the works discussed here provide an overview of the subversive use of space, time, and bodies across a wide spectrum of anti-tales, from literary texts to popular culture novels, and from adult to young adult fiction. There is also a wide international scope of anti-tales in this study, ranging from American, British, and Canadian authors to Russian, German, Italian, South Korean, and Afro-Caribbean tales. In addition, while this book is predominantly literary in focus, I have included analyses of some Disney productions and art-house films. This approach is adopted in order to show that the spatio-temporal and corporeal trend my study identifies is one that heavily proliferates and extends across the entire anti-tale oeuvre.[30]

Chapter 1 is titled '"Psycho"-Geographies and Gendered Maps: Reimagining the City in Feminist Anti-Tales'. Here, the history of debates surrounding the city is identified, and the very real problems posed for women, both historically and in contemporary society, are established. This chapter proceeds to outline the portrayal of the city in male-authored literature, noting the absence of women in the city's historical narrative and highlighting the contrasting prominence of the white, bourgeois male *flâneur* figure, who represented a city that is knowable, neat, and easily rationalised – all values upheld by patriarchal Enlightenment writers and thinkers. This chapter argues that Tanith Lee's *Cruel Pink*, with its mentally ill heroine, posits a female *flâneuse* as a subversive counterpart to the patriarchal *flâneur*, with his limited and stifling worldview. In addition, Lee's characters and the female detective heroine in Helen Smith's *Alison Wonderland* – who betray the masculine values of rationality, offer up the idea of a negotiable city, and the impossibility of seeking a unified answer or explanation (inherent in the masculine values of conventional crime fiction) – provide a feminine conception of the city, through the use of psychogeographics, 'magic', and subversive bodies. While these two novels are based in London, Ekaterina Sedia's Russian novel, *The Secret History of Moscow*, provides an excellent example of these radical tactics in another context. They all create a pluralised space that cannot be neatly contained or ever conceptualised in its entirety. Ultimately, the feminine conception of the city offered here shatters the idea of the masculine city and its inherent rational stability, opening it up to feminist revision.

Chapter 2 is titled 'Feminist Journeys "Into the Woods": The Use of Ecofeminist Landscapes in Postmodern Anti-Tales'. Although ecofeminism has been discredited by many critics for its perceived essentialism, it is currently making a return to feminist scholarship. This chapter details the shared oppression of women and nature as victims of man and illustrates how the natural environment is once again reclaimed by anti-tale authors as a feminist space in which women can get beyond the artificial strictures imposed by patriarchy. After all, the woods in fairy tales have always been conceived as a subversive space beyond the remit of social codes – a place for outsiders who refuse to conform to expected standards and behaviours. Issues discussed in this chapter include the use of spiritual ecofeminism as a 'practical magic' and evolutionary storytelling by God's gardener Toby in Margaret Atwood's *Maddaddam* trilogy, the breakdown of artificially constructed species boundaries in Michel Faber's *Under the Skin*, the shattering of patriarchy's binary-orientated worldview in Disney's *Maleficent*, and the subversion of socially constructed hierarchies in the creation of an ecofeminist web of interconnectivity in *Into the Woods*.

Chapter 3, '"Once Upon Many Times": Subversive Temporalities in Feminist Anti-Tales' outlines mechanical time as masculine and patriarchal in its links to social power and control. Examples include the colonial exploitation of feminised native cultures brought under the Western clock's controlling power. This chapter notes how quantum physics and postmodern theories are now conceiving of temporality as feminine, in which time is understood to be non-linear, multidirectional, subjective, and polytemporal. It is this conception of time as feminine that anti-tale authors utilise to undermine the apparent neutrality of the 'Once upon a time' fairy-tale motif and to liberate women from the traditional patriarchal time of the clock. In Disney's *Alice Through the Looking Glass*, rational mechanical Time is literally gendered male – Time being the personified villain of the piece – and this is subverted through Alice's own 'irrational' feminine time-travelling. Tanith Lee's *Cruel Pink* re-emerges as a prime example of the feminist employment of subjective, lived, and polytemporal time frames that liberate characters from heteronormative and restrictive masculine time (her queer characters constantly fail to regulate their lives according to the power of the clock).

In Chapter 4, time is discussed once again in relation to stages of life. Intergenerational warfare is highlighted as a major contemporary problem in that society deliberately pits young and ageing females against each other (a common fairy-tale trope). Kate Bernheimer's *How a Mother Weaned Her Girl From Fairy Tales* is shown to undermine fairy-tale expectations of youth as a time of virtue and innocence, while Atwood's *Stone Mattress* is discussed for its subversion of the fairy tale's portrayal of old age as a time of declining worth. Nalo Hopkinson's Caribbean tales 'Riding the Red' and 'Greedy Choke Puppy' from *Skin Folk* are also discussed for their powerful revisions of age-related fairy tale stereotypes. In these three collections, the authors advocate intergenerational understanding and the coming together of the two groups of women in order to aid in the advancement of feminist strivings for equality.

Chapter 5 is titled 'Embodying the "Inbetween": Subversive Bodies in Feminist Anti-Tales'. The problems and age-old ideologies endorsed by patriarchy about women and their bodies (the fairy tale being a major culprit) is discussed here, and it is suggested that the post-feminist back-lash happening today renews women's sense of corporeal loathing, push-ing the gap between women and their bodies ever wider and negating the achievements made during the sexual revolution. Once again, patri-archy's attempts to neatly rationalise the female body and its 'otherness' is subverted by hyperbolic bodies, with their extreme fleshy baseness and grit, in Matteo Garrone's *Tale of Tales*. The depiction of rebellious bulimic and anorexic bodies in Betsy Cornwell's *Tides* and Han Kang's *The Vegetarian* are discussed for their use of bodies as an alternative corporeal language which loudly voices their oppression, refusing to be silenced due to their inability to be visually ignored. Cornwell's novel also utilises theories around bodies of water, the transformative potential and metamorphoses of selkie (human and seal hybrid) bodies advocat-ing a feminine conception of the world that privileges fluidity and free-dom from restriction. Furthermore, the cyborg-alien adoptee in Marissa Meyer's *Cinder* posits a challenge to patriarchal boundaries while Lee's *Cruel Pink* employs the subversive, self-conscious performances of queer and transgender bodies to redefine which bodies matter.

Through these discussions I aim to contribute to gaps in scholarship and neglected areas of research: these include the concept of time in fairy tales; the potential of ecofeminism for postmodern feminist pro-jects and their revisions of space (I suggest there is a need to reclaim ecofeminism after it was rejected in the late twentieth-century due to charges of essentialism); and I provide analyses of texts that are either relatively new, or that have received little to no critical attention. I il-lustrate how the anti-tales here are a part of the postmodern feminist project to rethink existing configurations of space, time, and bodies in order to free women from the restrictions of patriarchal ways of seeing and being in the world. The anti-tales suggest that, through a renewed understanding of each concept, we are no longer governed by the law of the clock but instead recognise the polytemporal and subjective nature of time for individuals; that we can reimagine the city as a more complex and inclusive space; use the patriarchal essentialist dualism of women's links to nature for feminism's own ends; and shatter the illusion of neat, contained bodies and genders, instead showing that our society's bias towards which bodies matter needs to be broken down in order to create greater inclusivity and equality, beyond patriarchy's limited vision. The revisions of space, time, and bodies by the anti-tales in this study ulti-mately allow us to reimagine notions of gender, sexuality and ways of being in the twenty-first century.

Overall, these discussions ultimately show how space, time, and bodies occupy a fundamental place in the feminist architecture of twenty-first-century anti-tales. I posit that the definition of the anti-tale's feminine architecture, identified in this study, must be added to existing understandings of the term, and it is the genre's feminine architecture that allows it to deconstruct and subvert the masculine structure and ideologies of the patriarchal fairy tale.

Notes

1 See Catriona McAra and David Calvin, 'Introduction' in *Anti-Tales: The Uses of Disenchantment* (Newcastle upon Tyne: Cambridge Scholars Publishing, 2011).

2 'Anti-Fairy Tale' on *Wikipedia* <https://en.wikipedia.org/wiki/Anti-fairy_tale> [accessed 18th June 2017].

3 McAra and Calvin, *Anti-Tales: The Uses of Disenchantment*, p. 4.

4 Ibid., pp. 3, 4.

5 Angela Carter, 'Notes from the Front Line' in *On Gender and Writing*, ed. Michelene Wandor (London: Thorsons, 1983), p. 69.

6 Cristina Bacchilega, *Postmodern Fairy Tales: Gender and Narrative Strategies* (Pennsylvania: University of Pennsylvania Press, 1997), p. 22.

7 McAra and Calvin, *Anti-Tales: The Uses of Disenchantment*, p. 3. Note that it is important to point out how the disenchantment of the anti-tale is not inevitably overwhelmed by the wondrous magic of the fairy tale that many of these texts revise in some way. However, the anti-tale's disenchantment is not a rejection of magic, rather it rejects the use of magic to cover over problematic and patriarchal elements of the fairy tale genre. For example, in Chapter 2, I show how anti-tales disenchant the 'Once Upon a Time' trope by exposing the patriarchal power behind the temporal frameworks that govern the stories. By distancing fairy tales from the real world, the patriarchal messages of fairy tales are allowed to go unchallenged. The anti-tales favour instead magical realism, disenchanting us out of our blindness to the problematic elements of the stories. Anti-tales do not favour the idea that waving a magic wand saves the day, rather their magic is tied into reality, with their 'practical magic' illustrating how it is real action that will inspire change in the real world. For example, in Chapter 2, I discuss the 'practical magic' of ecofeminism through the character of Toby in Atwood's *Maddaddam* trilogy. Toby's ecofeminist ethics and herbal remedies are grounded in reality and her magic is garnered through embracing the power of the natural world. Overall, the escapist and wondrous magic of the fairy tale is disenchanted by anti-tales in order to expose the social ills hidden behind the fairy tale's enchanting veil, but the anti-tale nonetheless embraces its own magic, one that is balanced out through their magical realist approach.

8 See Alison Lurie, 'Fairy Tale Liberation' in *The New York Review of Books* (17 December 1970) < www.nybooks.com/articles/1970/12/17/fairy-tale-liberation/> [accessed 18 June 2017].

9 Donald Haase, 'Introduction' in *Fairy Tales and Feminism: New Approaches* (Detroit: Wayne State University Press, 2004), p. vii.

10 See Marcia R. Lieberman, 'Some Day My Prince Will Come: Female Acculturation through the Fairy Tale' in *College English*, Vol. 34, No. 3 (December 1972), pp. 383–395.

11 See Elizabeth Waning Harries, *Twice Upon a Time: Women Writers and the History of the Fairy Tale* (Princeton: Princeton University Press, 2001) for a detailed account of female fairy tale writings from seventeenth-century France to the works of twentieth-century authors.

12 Ibid.

13 See, for example, Cristina Bacchilega's 'An Introduction to the "Innocent Persecuted Heroine" Fairy Tale' in *Western Folklore*, Vol. 52, No. 1 (January 1993), pp. 1–12, which is part of a whole journal issue on *Perspectives on the Innocent Persecuted Heroine in Fairy Tales*. Also see Jungian critic Marie Louise Von Franz's *The Feminine in Fairy Tales* (London: Shambhala Publications, Inc., 1993) for the structuralist typologisations of female characters.

14 Haase, *Fairy Tales and Feminism: New Approaches*, p. 2.

15 Ibid.

16 See Anna Kérchy, ed., *Postmodern Reinterpretations of Fairy Tales: How Applying New Methods Generates New Meanings* (Lampeter: The Edwin Mellen Press, 2011).

17 See Elizabeth Grosz, *Architecture from the Outside: Essays on Virtual and Real Space* (Cambridge: The MIT Press, 2001).

18 Elizabeth Grosz, *Space, Time and Perversion: Essays on the Politics of Bodies* (London: Routledge, 1995), p. 124.

19 Ibid.

20 Linda Alcoff and Elizabeth Potter, eds., *Feminist Epistemologies* (London: Routledge, 1993), p. 1.

21 Ibid.

22 Margrit Shildrick, *Leaky Bodies and Boundaries: Feminism, Postmodernism and (Bio)Ethics* (London: Routledge, 1997), p. 4.

23 Grosz, *Space, Time and Perversion*, pp. 120, 121.

24 Shildrick, *Leaky Bodies and Boundaries*, p. 9.

25 Grosz, *Space, Time and Perversion*, p. 38.

26 Anna Kérchy, 'Narrating the Nervous, Bulimic Body-Text in Angela Carter's *The Passion of the New Eve*' in *Gender Studies*, Vol. 1, No. 5 (2006), p. 85.

27 John Frow, *Genre* (London: Routledge, 2005), p. 147.

28 David Duff, ed., *Modern Genre Theory* (Harlow: Pearson Education Ltd., 2000), p. xii.

29 Luce Irigaray, *This Sex Which Is Not One* (New York: Cornell University Press, 1985), pp. 28–29.

30 I also want to note here how my explorations of Disney incorporate the concept of dual readership. This refers to 'cross-writing' that speaks to both children and adults. Fairy tales have always been at the forefront of this tradition, with early patriarchal fairy tales written problematically for both children and women as infantilised citizens. But even the subversive fairy tales and folk tales written or spoken centuries ago also voiced communal concerns that crossed age boundaries. This is apt given that boundary-crossing is one of the anti-tale's main strategies of deconstructing dominant hegemonic structures and ideologies. My discussions of Disney look at the sophisticated symbolism and nuances in language that convey deeper philosophical ideas beyond the surface narrative aimed at children. For a detailed account of dual readership, see Sandra L. Beckett's edited collection *Transcending Boundaries: Writing for a Dual Audience of Children and Adults* (New York: Garland Publishing, 1999).

1 'Psycho'-Geographies and Gendered Maps

Reimagining the City in Feminist Anti-Tales

May God forgive London. I do not

– Tanith Lee, *Cruel Pink*[1]

As far as romantic locations go, I've seen better

– Helen Smith, *Alison Wonderland*[2]

Introduction

The city as a subject for literary study has had a rich and varied history; however, there has been a renewed resurgence of interest in the urban space within literary studies, exemplified by the publication of *The Cambridge Companion to the City in Literature* in 2014. Certainly, reading widely around various aspects of the city, the heavy scholarly interest in both the human sciences and the arts is immediately apparent, yet, glaring gaps remain unexplored. For example, this chapter posits the anti-tale as a unique take on city and gender studies. Robert E. Park in 'The City as Social Laboratory' highlights that 'the urban environment represents [humanity's] most consistent and, on the whole, [its] most successful attempt to remake the world [it] lives in more after [its] heart's desire. But if the city is the world which [humans] created, it is the world in which [they are] condemned to live'.[3] Therefore, the city is constantly shifting and being reconstructed according to human desires, reflecting the dominant values and ideologies held by our culture. This is similar to the fairy tale itself, which emerged out of folk stories told by indigenous peoples to reflect upon communal concerns, and it is no coincidence that Jack Zipes's description of the utopian aspect of the fairy tale is similar to Park's reflections on the urban space: the fairy tale

> serv[es] to compensate for the impoverished lives and desperate struggles of many people [...] there was always some sort of hope for a miraculous change. There may still be hope in the fairy tale collisions of their imaginative visions that compel us to re-create traditional narratives and rethink the course our lives have taken.[4]

In essence, both the city and the fairy tale uphold dominant social ideologies. Through the anti-tale then (with its disenchantment and refusal of a detached 'Once Upon a Time', pastoral setting),[5] fairy tales and the city are 're-created and re-designed to counter as well as collide with our complex social realities [... They are] necessary to shake up the world and sharpen our gaze'.[6]

This chapter highlights the urban space as one emerging focus in the postmodern anti-tale's impulse towards achieving this revolutionary vision, particularly in terms of feminist social change. Authors use the city setting to reflect upon the existing architecture of social relations and constructions, both in terms of the physical space itself and what it symbolises, or reflects, about current power dynamics. For, as Deborah L. Parsons notes in *Streetwalking the Metropolis: Women, the City, and Modernity*:

> The urban writer is not only a figure within a city; he/she is also the producer of a city, one that is related to but distinct from the city of asphalt, brick, and stone, one that results from the interconnection of body, mind and space, one that reveals the interplay of self/city identity. The writer adds other maps to the city atlas; those of social interaction but also of myth, memory, fantasy, and desire. That the city has been habitually conceived as a male space, in which women are either repressed or disobedient marginal presences, has resulted in an emphasis in theoretical analysis on gendered maps that reflect such conditions.[7]

Hence, I explore the subversive use of Parsons's ideas of the city linked to 'myth, memory, fantasy, and desire', and 'the interconnection of body, mind and space' in the 'gendered maps' created through Tanith Lee's *Cruel Pink* (2013) and Helen Smith's *Alison Wonderland* (2011). I will also touch briefly on other anti-tales in order to highlight the city as an emerging motif across the genre as a whole and illustrate that this trend extends beyond London into other international contexts, by also discussing the Russian novel of Ekaterina Sedia titled *The Secret History of Moscow*. By first providing a theoretical and literary framework, this chapter opens with a panoramic view of the city as a general source of academic study to the city and gender; the city in literature; and, more specifically, the city in feminist literature, before zooming in on Lee and Smith's adaptations of, and position in relation to, these theories within their stories (including debates around the *flâneur/flâneuse* and bodies/cities). The texts discussed here are prime examples of what Adam Zolkover describes as the emergent genre of 'urban fantasy'.[8] It should be noted that critics often tend to discuss either the city in urban texts *or* fairy-tale elements rather than addressing their complex interactions, therefore this chapter aims to discuss both simultaneously. In addition, Lee, Smith, and Sedia's novels also provide a unique take on the now 'in vogue' concept of psychogeography. The authors even use the idea of 'psycho' literally through mentally ill characters and their relations to the urban environment in order to convey a feminist message: unstable minds reflecting an unhealthy society. A psychogeographical approach, combined with the underground or unseen aspects of the urban environment, and the balance of fantastical and more realistic strands of the stories, draws attention to hidden truths and the transformative potential of what Merlin Coverley dubs, 'the magical realm behind our own'.[9] Certainly, Sedia literally depicts her characters escaping the dreary streets of 1990s Moscow to an underground realm inhabited by mythical creatures, glowing trees, and magic. An imaginative approach to the city can implement the utopian fairy-tale impulse to indicate the possibility of social change. Ultimately then, it is clear that the anti-tales discussed in this chapter utilise London (and Moscow) as much more than a simple backdrop or setting for their stories and, it is argued that, by using feminine outsider positions, bodies, and psychogeographies to construct the urban space of their narratives, anti-tale authors allow an alternative feminine city to emerge in their stories, which shatters the restrictive neatness, rationality, and exclusionary impulses of the existing patriarchal city we inhabit.

Definitions: What Is a City?

First, the question – 'what is a city?' – is not easily answered and the more thought that is given to it, the more difficult it is to find an apt definition – as illustrated in the ongoing nature of the critical debates and discussions around urban space. After all, it is not only modern critics from the late nineteenth century to the early twenty-first century that have contributed to this conversation. As Raymond Williams has emphasised, discussion of the city 'reaches back into classical times', long before the Industrial Revolution and rise of capitalism in the Victorian era.[10] Certainly, Balasopoulos's 'Celestial Cities and Rationalist Utopias' and Susan Stephen's 'The City in the Literature of Antiquity' look back to the ancient cities of 'Athens, Alexandria, Rome, and Jerusalem' in order to emphasise the origins of contemporary ideas about the urban space.[11] In answer to his question – *'What is a city?'* – Balasopoulos notes how

> the question is foundational in a double sense: it is a question about the origins of social and political life, and it is also a question that haunts the very beginnings of the western tradition of thinking about the nature and goals of collective life. It is also, perhaps by virtue of being authentically foundational, an obscure question.[12]

Williams, however, is often quoted as a starting point for anyone approaching, or trying to make sense of, the idea of the city and urban studies. His definition is established through the binaries of *The Country and the City*:

> 'Country' and 'City' are very powerful words, and this is not surprising when we remember how much they seem to stand for in the

experience of human communities [...] On the country has gathered the idea of a natural way of life: of peace, innocence, and simple virtue. On the city has gathered the idea of an achieved centre: of learning, communication, light. Powerful hostile associations have also developed: on the city as a place of noise, worldliness and ambition; on the country as a place of backwardness, ignorance, limitation.[13]

An example of this simple contrast between pastoral fairy-tale world and disenchanted modern cityscape as a feminist method is illustrated in Karen Best's satirical anti-tale 'Blizzard Season'. In this story, a portal opens 'with the first snowflakes of winter' bringing fairy-tale Snow Whites – 'like unassuming plants coming into bloom, they were suddenly everywhere' – into 'the edges of empty parking lots and suburbs-to-be'.[14] These heroines, normally creations of environmental elements (Snow White's mother looking out of a window and constructing her daughter from the white snow and black raven in the Grimms' tale, for example), are now out of place, literally, and part of an artificial and man-made world. This is depicted in Best's parody of the common fairy-tale aesthetic description: 'Hair as black as asphalt, lips like blood. No: Stoplights' (17). She is now a product of the new city space, dehumanised by a material, post-capitalist consumer reality, but also a literal commercial product or walking advertisement: 'Black hair dye and red lipstick sold out in drugstores' (19). Hence, the fairy-tale ideal is once again sold to modern women as the ideal vision of femininity: 'by then it was hard to tell which ones were genuine and which ones were imitators' (19). Yet, as well as utilising Williams's binary definition of natural idealism versus the city as a 'powerful' and 'hostile' space, Best also satirises the 'innocence, and simple virtue', as well as the 'backwardness, ignorance, and limitation' of the pastoral (symbolised by the Snow Whites), in contrasting them to the city as 'an achieved centre of learning, communication, light' (symbolised by the male 'you' the narrator refers to):

> The girls came from a world of soot and straw and iron shoes [...] you let her stay. It wouldn't have been right to make her go back onto the street [...] you grew tired of explaining for the nth time, with the picture of your ex-girlfriend in your hand, that you hadn't painted a picture of your ex; that there were these things called *cameras* and they made *photographs*, while she nodded her pretty head.
> (18–20)

Best details how she (a Snow White) looks out of the window (a parallel to her mother's position at the exposition of the Grimms' story) onto the city and 'tentatively poked at the mini-blinds, you wondered how she was going to survive' (18). While her mother's window scene marks the literal 'birth' of the Grimms' narrative, we certainly do wonder if this Snow White's story can survive so out of context. Exploiting the binaries in Williams's definition, Best is thus able to subvert the traditional 'innocent persecuted heroine' trope as a backward ideal that has no place in the harsh realities of the modern city, while at the same time hinting that there are frightening parallels to the modern female position as an outsider, vulnerable to patriarchal and capitalist ideologies within the urban environment. In summary, Best's story clearly offers an example of how anti-tales can use the city and its contrasts to the pastoral fairy-tale world as a subversive strategy in feminist retellings.

However, the anti-tale novels I discuss here complicate this. Their stories follow postmodern approaches to, and definitions of, the urban space. Feminist and philosophical theorist Elizabeth Grosz offers such a stance, suggesting that the question 'What is a city?' requires a more multifaceted response:

> By 'city', I understand a complex and interactive network that links together, often in an unintegrated and ad hoc way, a number of disparate social activities, processes, relations, with a number of architectural, geographical, civic, and public relations. The city brings together economic flows, and power networks, forms of management and political organisation, interpersonal, familial, and extra-familial social relations, and the aesthetic/economic organization of space and place to create a semi-permanent but everchanging built environment or milieu.[15]

The city is now understood as a conduit of networks and forces that cannot be simply understood solely as a tangible physical space, but must also be thought of as a symbolic one, in which cultural and social ideologies are played out in complex ways. Its 'everchanging' nature is an aspect embraced by feminist writers, as will become evident in a discussion of the novels to follow. These writers have what Peter Preston and Paul Simpson-Housley call a 'post-modernist view of the city'.[16] Refusing to tie the city down to a set of givens or to sum it up with a concrete definition, they leave the urban space open to being shaped and redefined through their stories. The 'magic' or fantastical side to the anti-tale also aids the authors in their postmodern defiance of logical labels and definitions; a feminine fluidity beyond what is often seen as masculine reason.[17] In short, they use the 'spell' of Postmodernism, which R. Boyne and A. Rattansi define as:

> a relatively widespread mood in literary theory, philosophy and the social sciences concerning the inability of these disciplines to deliver totalising theories and doctrines, or enduring 'answers' to fundamental dilemmas [...] and a growing feeling, on the contrary, that a chronic provisionality, plurality of perspectives and incommensurable appearances of the object of enquiry in competing discourses, make the search for ultimate answers [...] a futile exercise.[18]

This idea of a 'plurality of perspectives' is particularly pertinent: anti-tale authors have, as we shall see, women, mentally unstable characters, and social outsiders all express their experiences of the city; feminine or outside views that would normally be excluded from dominant narratives and definitions. Therefore, feminists are the one critical group that is most consistent in its negative critique of existing power relations within the urban environment and among those keen to question and redesign existing relations and attitudes.

Women and the City: History and Problems

Reading widely around various studies into women and the city, it is easy to become overwhelmed by the sheer amount of articles and books written on the subject, which attests to Liz Bondi and Linda Peake's claim about 'the importance of gender relationships in urban politics'.[19] Many of these studies are from the fields of sociology and feminist urban geography, both of which approach the issue through pragmatic and quantitative methods, in contrast to the imaginative interpretations of literary responses. However, it is, of course, beneficial to have an insight into the kinds of problems facing women in the 'real' city before exploring how they are depicted, or reshaped, in anti-tale fiction. The oppression of women in urban environments has been studied from a variety of angles – including the division of private and public space, economics, employment, victimisation from physical violence, rape, and a socially constructed politics of fear – but all are concerned with 'understanding the interrelations between socially constructed gender relations and socially constructed environments'.[20] As Elizabeth Wilson writes,

> The relationship of women and cities has long preoccupied reformers and philanthropists. In recent years the preoccupation has been inverted, the Victorian determination to control working-class women replaced by a feminist concern for women's safety and comfort in city streets; but whether women are seen as a problem of cities, or cities as a problem for women, the relationship is perceived as one fraught with difficulty.[21]

Once again, Best's 'Blizzard Season' aptly captures these ideas and experiences. Best satirises the archaic notion where women were viewed as 'a problem *of* cities' in order to undermine old ideas of what femaleness or 'femininity' should be. For example, 'dressed like she's going to a Renaissance festival', the first Snow White to cross over into the contemporary metropolis marks an infestation of her outdated kind and their passive femininity, as they scurry like vermin into the fast-paced city of the modern day:

> And like that, they appeared all over the city. No one knew where they came from, or even how many there were. Could have just been

a gang of waifish runaways, except they all told the same story [...] People who called talk radio shows said the girls were all drains on the system, and why couldn't they just get jobs instead of asking for government handouts? One group countered with the proposal that what the city needed was an influx of wicked stepmothers.

(17, 19)

The idea of weeding out Snow Whites by the stronger wicked step-mothers is a clever comment on the fact that women who adhere to old outworn values such as the 'innocent persecuted heroine' trope cannot survive the harsh realities of modern urban life. Best tells us that 'You found some clothes that your ex-girlfriend left behind [...] She [Snow White] giggled at the jeans and called them breeches [...] you wondered how she was going to survive' (18). Here the breeches are a symbol of the 'New Woman', a phase bypassed by these Snow Whites in their Renaissance garb. The politics of fear socially instilled in women is embodied by the Snow Whites in mock proportions in order to subvert the notion that all women should be fearful in the public arena:

A girl shivering; lost, flinching. She clutches the leg of your pants as though you're the only person in the world that can help her [...] At least you can get her a cocoa and stay with her until she calms down enough to make sense.

(17)

However, Best simultaneously refuses to undermine the hostility of the masculine space and the threats posed to women in the city. These girls, the ultimate innocent persecuted heroines, might be vulnerable in the extreme, but unfortunately the threats posed are very real and constitute the other half of Wilson's description in which 'cities are a problem *for* women':

Some of the things you'd heard were too awful to contemplate. Better to let the huntsman cut out her heart than see her end up like some of the *Mädchen* did. It made your stomach hurt to know what people would do with a beautiful girl they were sure no one would ever look for.

(20)

Best even references the concern of social critics interested in female employment, women still being underpaid for their work: 'It was said that the girls were good at drudgery, and all they ever seemed to want in exchange were crusts of bread and anonymity' (19). However, Best also rejects what Liz Bondi and Damaris Rose outline as the 'danger of perpetuating an anti-urbanism' and points towards the liberating potential of a reconceived city, as noted by critics in feminist urban geography aiming to provide the scope for radical reinventions of the urban space.[22] For example, Best does hint at the emergence of women from the domestic into the public sphere (Snow White the ultimate and glorified symbol of domestic goddess in the traditional story is, therefore, an apt metaphor): 'The refugees spilled out [...] They all had skills no one needed anymore' (19). This brief overview of the kinds of difficulties arising for women in cities, according to social studies, provides a platform for the following analysis of literary depictions. After all, as Little, Peake, and Richardson state, an awareness of the real issues faced day to day is necessary for any change to take place: 'Once the experiences of women are accepted as valid elements of this process, new truths and different versions of an alternative society become possible'.[23]

Urban 'Performances': The City in Literature

Having established the theoretical background to both city and feminist urban scholarship, we can now hone in on the city in literature. While there is clearly an abundance of quantitative social investigations into women and the city, as Festa McCormick states, fictional 'literature is not of negligible social value':

> We know that sociology itself does not rely merely on cumulative data, and that it does not shun personal interpretations or psychological analysis altogether. It is precisely in these areas that literature can come to the aid of sociology, just as observations of social dealings may initially have inspired, and are eventually found at the core of, the work of art. [...] Art is a purified, unencumbered form of truth, as valid in its restricted presentations of the city as any individual's laboratory research might be.[24]

Significantly, not only literature but also fairy tales, in particular, have been of major interest to sociologists and anthropologists. Their utopian impulse provides just such a 'laboratory' for imaginative social experiments. As Penelope Lively asserts, 'the city is a text, waiting to be read and written or rewritten in literary terms',[25] and this accords with the postmodern notion, outlined by Parsons, that 'There are infinite versions of any one city. The city as a text to be read, the text as a city to be traversed' (1). In this way, cities are built and revised through the words on the page, a radical political method that signifies the possibility of change. The city in literature is sourced in long-standing ideas such as Augustine's City of God and 'The New Jerusalem' from the *Book of Revelation*, both of which are, in the words of Preston and Simpson-Housley, 'types of the ideal city whose perfections only serve to highlight the shortcomings of all the earthly cities'.[26] These fairy-tale-like utopias and

Renaissance ideas of the ideal city-state can, in turn, be traced back to Plato's *Republic*. However, like fairy tales with their conventional gender dynamics and hierarchical power structures, even in these ideal worlds, 'It is rare to find a utopia – even at its most idealistic – that does not specify or imply an element of containment and control'.[27] Thus, literary cities have been structured around an ambiguous response to the urban environment: it is both a site of potential and progress (embodied in the work of French writers from the nineteenth and twentieth centuries in particular), and yet a dominant theme is that of the city as an oppressive force upon individuals (the work of the Romantics such as Wordsworth, and the Victorians, represented by Dickens, being prime examples).

Characters as players in the drama of the city space need not simply be about powerlessness in the face of bigger forces, however. The contemporary metafictional or self-aware nature of the anti-tale genre itself allows for the manipulation of settings for feminism's own ends, turning the Romantic individual in the midst of a hostile city motif on its head. In his tale 'Drawing the Curtain', in which he sets the literal stage for the fairy tale retellings in Kate Bernheimer's *My Mother She Killed Me, My Father He Ate Me* (2010) collection, Gregory Maguire outlines the preparations for the anti-tale performances to follow:

> As for the setting, take a look at the interchangeable flats, the painted scrims, the wing-and-drop sets hoisted in darkness above. Most likely the sets are modest and indefinite [...] That's a lot of world to be stacked backstage [...] The velvet curtains part, side to side, like a parent playing peekaboo.[28]

Authors can manipulate the urban setting in order to convey their particular messages: in their art, they have a certain element of power and control over how the urban space is both portrayed (capturing the hardships faced by women, as in Best's tale) and indicating that it can be imagined differently for the future (new sets waiting to be painted for new worlds).

Also, it is suggested in many anti-tales that characters are no longer simply puppets pulled along by conventional plot movements and expectations (a means of undermining both the patriarchal fairy-tale arc and the power of the city over individuals), but rather they are actors using the city as their stage. Their individual stories can provide a counter-narrative to dominant urban myths and ideologies. They can create the backdrops (like those painted backstage in Maguire's tale) drawing them to tell their own stories and relate their personal experiences. In this way, the city can be seen as a 'landscape [which] encodes stories about its origins, its inhabitants and the broader society in which it is set'.[29] This is certainly the case for the anti-tale novels to be discussed shortly: they contain multiple characters whose lives are played out against the backdrop of the urban landscape (in *Cruel Pink*, for example, one of the characters is literally a disenfranchised actor and London the stage for his various escapades). As Thrift states, 'The city has become even more than formerly, a key storytelling node for the world as a whole, and, as a result, its importance as a spatially fixed centre has, if anything, been boosted'.[30] Yet, as the cover of Smith's novel (with ginger hair parted to either side like curtains revealing an image of the city) suggests, there has been a shift in twentieth- and twenty-first century fiction from thinking solely of the city as a backdrop or *topos* to the city as 'anthropoid – "man-like", "resembling the human being" [...] It becomes quasi-human'.[31] Certainly, Lee herself recently stated that 'It will be obvious to anyone familiar with my writing that large, historical or parallel-historical cities often feature in it, virtually as characters. They have their own [...] life-force', and as we shall see in the forthcoming discussion, the city in these novels is both a backdrop and a central protagonist – it is as changeable and multifaceted as any of the human personalities.[32] Hence, the disturbed psychology of the characters also becomes directly related to, and a product of, the schizophrenic society/ city itself.

The city in literature has clearly had a complex history. Most notable, however, is the fact that the critical lens has been partial to male authors in particular, which is not surprising as female texts were focused more upon domestic confines. This is significant in that, as Festa McCormick notes, 'objects cannot but be seen through given sets of eyes, and the perspective varies with each viewer'.[33] Therefore, in literary depictions, we have often seen through male eyes, giving only one gendered perspective on urban life and containing women observed exclusively through the male gaze. This is all encompassed in the Victorian idea of the white bourgeois male figure of the *flâneur*, who wanders through the city streets, relating his experiences and neatly summing up the city for his reader. Clearly then, it was and is important for female writers to address this discrepancy and add their alternative perspectives and performances within the urban space to the ongoing narrative of the city.

Given the large number of publications in urban studies and feminist criticism on the city space, it might be expected that there is an equally profuse amount of material on feminist urban literature. In fact, there are glaring gaps. For example, in the recent publication of *The Cambridge Companion to the City in Literature*, Kevin R. McNamara remarks that a chapter was commissioned on women and the city but did not come to fruition. This certainly does leave a noticeable chasm within the collection, one that is extended into such scholarship as a whole. Yet, if the chapter had been produced, it ironically would have placed women in a marginal position nevertheless: one isolated category among many others. Even studies dedicated to urban women's writing, such as Parsons's seminal *Streetwalking the Metropolis: Women, the City, and Modernity*, tend only to deal with fiction set in London and Paris and focus solely on women's writing published between 1880 and 1940, during the emergence of the New Woman. These works do bring to the forefront women authors (such as Dorothy Richardson, Jean Rhys, Elizabeth Bowen, and Anaïs Nin) who tend to be overlooked critically in comparison to the urban literature of their infamous French and British male counterparts (including Dickens, George Gissing, Honoré de Balzac, Émile Zola, and Victor Hugo).

It is worth noting that Lee's anti-tale 'Black Eyed Susan', published in *Disturbed By Her Song*, contributes a female perspective on the New Woman and the gas-lit streets of Paris in the 1940s, a kind of writing back to the prominent male-authored urban fiction famous in France at the time of the story's setting and a means of upsetting historical assumptions. Just as fairy tales are palimpsests, each retelling layered on top of the last, female authors contributed their strands to the male-dominated narrative of the city, creating a more complex history. In Lee's tale, for example, the protagonist Esther Garber gets fired from her job as a maid in a hotel called 'The Queen', in which, we are told, the men are 'overridden by the women' (once again a sign of the New Woman's emergence).[34] However, the sexual innuendo of 'overridden' echoes the attitudes of the men that frequent the hotel bar, Esther hinting at the uneasy attempts by men to undermine female dominance and assertion. Far from disappointed by her situation, Esther points out how 'There are few things so liberating, I've found, as being summarily sacked' (18). Her ultimate rejection of taking the safe option and conforming to her seclusion within the hotel's restrictive walls – 'wondering if I should now creep down to the kitchen and sleep Cinderellerishly in the grease by the ovens' – and her preference for rebellion, wandering through the city with her hard-earned financial freedom, marks not only her own emergence but also that of women as a whole from the domestic into the public sphere (11). Enjoying this mobility (gained through her financial independence), she 'stalk[s] out into the town', boldly wearing bright red lipstick and loose hair as a symbol of her freedom and unrestrained sexuality (in comparison to the uniform encouraged in the hotel resembling the modest rags of Cinderella-like heroines) (21). Her story is part of a hidden and alternative lesbian history. In the tale, Esther searches for a love interest who may be a ghost or simply an elusive human whom she christens 'Black Eyed Susan'. Through this ghostly phantom, Lee cleverly plays around with the notion of women as non-entities in the urban space – their presence felt but not fully acknowledged, 'vanishing into thin air at two turning points, a corridor, a street corner [...] But I *had* seen her. She *had* gone by' (31, 23). Lee focuses solely on female characters and their interactions with one another, creating a collective female experience at different levels of city life. From Esther as outsider, to the other hotel maids, Madame Cora the elderly but powerful grandmother of the hotel's owner, the upper-class mistress of her grandson, and the ghost of Susan, all are victims whose stories would otherwise remain unheard within the hustle and bustle of urban life. Asking Madame Cora about the ghostly lady, Esther instead gets the story of the old woman's past: 'the pressure of her sorrows [...] was very great, even overwhelming. Any plan I'd had, gradually to lead her to the elusive subject of the woman called Suzanne, had drained from me as she spoke of her life' (27). Esther goes on the hunt for a woman's story, Suzanne's, but finds many more along the way and ironically the one she seeks becomes the symbol of elusive female histories that fade away untold. At the resolution, Esther is left as the bearer of Madame Cora's true story; only she knows the silent truth behind the old woman's stern evil-queen-like performance that made her a villain (like the fairy-tale figure) to all who knew her:

> Which tragedy then? Oh, that of Madame Cora, who, sitting at her table with her chin propped on her hand, and her eyes wide open, had died in their midst without a sound [...] only that steely, glittering façade was left behind.
>
> (30, 28)

Despite being invisible much of the time, it is this Modernist city depicted by the likes of Virginia Woolf at the start of the twentieth century that dominates much of the discourse surrounding female urban representations, with her remark, 'Why do I dramatise London so perpetually?' indicative of the centrality of the urban within her writing (see, in particular, Susan M. Squire's *Virginia Woolf and London: The Sexual Politics of the City*).[35] She is an author who clearly influenced the two novelists discussed in this chapter, and yet Woolf's claim that as a woman she has no country has been the focus of much debate, similar to Elizabeth Bowen's, 'My darling, my darling, my darling. Here we have no abiding city'.[36] Certainly, as Parsons notes in relation to the late nineteenth century and early twentieth century, and as Lee suggests through the ghostly Black Eyed Susan, there was a tendency to see this peripheral/outsider aspect as a part of 'women's ongoing (non)identity as urban "stranger"' (15). Yet, Woolf did not ultimately reject any notion of women's belonging in the city – her words simply reflect her contemporary position as a woman slowly emerging from the domestic sphere. It is important to note, however, that it was a long time before the concern with space was attributed to Modernist works at all. Andrew Thacker's *Moving Through Modernity: Space and Geography in Modernism* challenges the long-established dichotomy created by critics, which asserted Modernity's preoccupation with time and Postmodernity's partiality to concepts of space. Instead, Thacker highlights how the Modernist concern with history, temporality, and processes of becoming cannot be separated from space and he foregrounds in particular 'the urban character of Modernity' (evident in

Woolf, James Joyce, and Jean Rhys for example).[37] Certainly, Woolf uses the space and setting of London to represent the Modernist concern with temporality and historical progression. Her novel *Mrs Dalloway* is key in this respect: while the clocks do indeed chime the end of a social chapter after the war, she signifies, through Clarissa's daughter Elizabeth's tentative steps, the impending occupation of urban space by women in the new era (the gender of the 'owner' figure apt as she intrudes on a male domain):

> She looked up Fleet Street. She walked just a little way towards St. Paul's, shyly, like someone penetrating on tiptoe, exploring a strange house by night with the candle, on edge lest the owner should suddenly fling open his bedroom door and ask her business [...] she was a pioneer, a stray, venturing, trusting.[38]

Following Elizabeth's example, the idea of women as strangers to the city has shifted in the twenty-first century with women now at least occupying urban space and their histories being added to the overarching historical narrative.

It should also be noted here that those who still float under the radar or male gaze (elderly women, for example) can actually utilise that position of invisibility. However, while this does allow for a freedom of movement or a liberating anonymity (which we will see with the old woman in *Cruel Pink*), as Jacqueline Rose attests in *States of Fantasy*, 'you can't, even as a woman, just float off'.[39] Best's collection *A Floating World* uses a thread motif across the stories to suggest that it is necessary to utilise the freedom that comes with floating between fluid boundaries as an outsider, but that there also need to be threads tying and grounding women in spaces that they have every right to be a part of. This is done through her balance of magical realism, the fantasy permitting a fluidity, and the realism keeping us grounded in the 'real' world. Like Esther in Lee's tale, then, one part of feminism's project is to create a place for women in a hitherto masculine city. As we shall see, Lee and Smith's novels follow in the tradition of earlier female urban writers like Woolf whom Parsons described as

> occupy[ing] a variety of social, economic, political, and sexual spaces, and [whose] urban narratives are very much based in these locations, on the pavements of the city rather than floating detachedly above it. They portray a non-fixed, but also a located city experience. It is this conception of identity in relation to place that I think is manifest in women writers' use of the urban metaphor.
>
> (14)

This is where the anti-tale creates an important means of subversion: we are at once fixed in the real masculine world and also avail of the fantastical possibilities beyond the boundaries and strictures of reason, creating a means for manoeuvre and the creation of new identities and ways of inhabiting a reconceived, or imagined feminine urban space, and work to bring it into being. This approach no longer allows the patriarchal city to remain unchallenged or to keep up its illusion of solidity and neat totality. Hence, like Parsons, I aim to get beyond a simple comparing and contrasting of male and female experiences of the city. Parsons did this for late Victorian and Modernist women writers and I aim to contribute a similar approach to the study of postmodern urban narratives of today, the anti-tale of course being my dominant focus. As Parsons states:

> My aim is therefore to explore the experience of the urban landscape and environment in terms of a fusion of empirical and imaginative perspectives, and to relate this to a gender-related city consciousness. The masculinist ideologies that have dominated the discourses of urban geography and literary modernism are gradually being exposed. But too often the politics of gender difference are concerned with the comparative experience of the male and female subject *in* the city, and overlook their relative foundations *of* the city [...] I have concentrated on those women for whom the city operates as not just a setting or an image, but as a constituent of identity, and who translate the experience of urban space into their narrative form [...] each writer is concerned with representing a female city consciousness alternative to that of the male.
>
> (7)

Finally, then, it should also be noted here that Angela Carter, the inspiration for many disenchanted anti-tale rewritings, has also recently been studied for her use of the city in *Angela Carter: New Critical Readings* (2012), and it is her combination of fantasy and the urban setting that provides the clearest literary predecessor to the authors considered in my study. Carter was aware, in the words of Nick Bentley, that the postmodern city can be seen as 'a space of male construction and female objectification'; however, she also recognised the complexities beyond that, with women now wandering through, and having a more diverse relationship with, the city space without the same restraint as their female predecessors: 'The complexity of contemporary urban space is thereby rendered in the postmodern novel through a pluralisation of space, time, and social discourse, while the alienated modernist observer is replaced by multiple perspectives that produce heterogeneous representations of the city'.[40] Postmodern works are, therefore, extremely complex and multifaceted, their depictions of the urban space now extremely diverse in character and content.

Emerging from the female tradition of ideas and theories outlined in this section, we have the new urban fantasy/anti-tale narratives.

Helen Smith's *Alison Wonderland* and Tanith Lee's *Cruel Pink*

Both British authors, Smith, a new novelist, and Lee, with an established career that stretched across four decades, have been overlooked by academics and have much in common, particularly in their two London anti-tales.

Alison Wonderland tells the story of Alison Temple; a modern-day Alice negotiating the rabbit hole of the contemporary city following the aftermath of a 'not so happily ever after' marriage: 'I used to have this line when people asked me if I'm married. I'd say, "I'm waiting for Mr. Wonderland and when I find him I'll get married. Until then I'm staying single"' (1). In this way, the novel adopts a familiar anti-tale technique in its subversion of marriage as the 'happily ever after' conclusion. Instead the novel uses an anti-tale politics of disenchantment to undermine the simplistic enchantment of fairy-tale sexual politics. Married to a cheating husband, Alison is disenchanted out of her fairy-tale domesticity and becomes part of the all-female detective agency, 'Fitzgerald's Bureau of Investigation', in London. Smith told an interviewer that this private investigation firm is based on one in Singapore and that she liked the idea because it was

> kick-ass and feminist. But the boss of the agency explained that the reality was that they spent most of their time following unfaithful husbands. I love the gap between perception and reality, and I wanted Alison to be doing fairly mundane, routine jobs at the agency until Taron shows up and sprinkles some magic into her life.[41]

Taron is a beautiful but unusual young woman who believes her mother is a witch; she approaches Alison with a strange request:

> I need some statistics about which part of the country babies are abandoned most often, what time of year, and where to find them – outside hospitals or police stations or under hedges or in phone boxes. [...] Lately my mother's become depressed and ill. She's losing the battle against the forces of evil [...] If I find an abandoned baby, it will help her. It can be her apprentice.
>
> (9, 12, 13)

Yet, Taron quickly becomes Alison's best friend along with her eccentric neighbour Jeff, the Madhatter-like inventor who adores Alison but is extremely shy and vulnerable: 'There are times when his poetry makes me want to put on an apron, cook up a storm and hug his brittle body in my womanly arms' (16). Here Alison is the epitome of empowered business woman and Jeff is an emasculated figure who stays at home and writes poetry: an inversion of the female domestic and male public dichotomy, mirroring the shifting gender roles of our time: 'he expresses his love for me in details, particularly domestic ones' (17). In the end, it is Alison who becomes the hero, rescuing Jeff (the damsel in distress) as he gets caught up in a top-secret case Alison is assigned to by Mrs. Fitzgerald. Another agency is covering up illicit activities and perpetuating false trails of information to muddy the tracks: '"Flower", she says, "and Bird, my old adversary. Their services have been retained by Emphglott, a pharmaceutical company that specialises in vivisection and genetic manipulation of animals"' (33). This leads to attacks and pursuits all over London by the hyper-masculine and sexist Bird and his recruits to stop Alison and those associated with her from gaining information on the illegal experiments. The book gives us insights into the discrepancies between illusion – characters as they are seen by each other – and reality – as they actually are inside their heads, an insight available to the reader alone.

Cruel Pink also looks at the mental life of its characters and focuses on the issues of identity experienced by five totally disparate existences occupying the same block of apartments in London. Emenie, a female serial killer (an anti-tale inversion of the 'Bluebeard' story that shifts the conventional gender dynamics) listens to signs from birds and her surroundings as she walks the city streets for prey. For her, it is a ruined and collapsing world and her actions almost seem sane amidst the rubble of the decaying city: 'We each then sadly looked down at the ground, politely mourning Civilisation's end' (29). Rod is a typical businessman from the outside, without friends and drifting through life, only imposed upon by relations. However, he also has a secret: he feels more like a woman and obsesses over the feminine clothing he locks away in the wardrobe. Klova, an attractive young woman, as vulnerable as Smith's Taron (both are like modern-day fairy tale princesses), lives on handouts provided in her almost science-fiction-like existence of liquid silver refreshments in a place where time is measured by 'Zones' and 'The street[s] smell clean and hygiene-brushed' (27). She spends her life going to parties at the 'Leaning Tower' and musing over a lipstick she holds dear from her mother with the initials 'C. P.', which gives the novel its title. Like Smith's anti-tale disenchantment of the 'happily ever after' marriage motif, Klova is a contemporary Cinderella whose attendance at the ball results in disaster. Her prince charming, Coal, turns out to be a literal pollutant in her life, his love burning out quickly and leaving her on the verge of suicide. Irvin is the actor, living in an archaic sixteenth-to seventeenth-century world of duels and philandering; his bisexuality and poverty leave him a hated outsider. And finally, Dawn is an old woman at the end of her life whose mind is failing. Like many anti-tales, her character creates a new and more positive portrayal of the old crone/evil Queen-type figure as her character is given depth and a backstory in order to explain her actions. She only comes into the picture at the end when trivial things in her world, such as the electric fire and pigeons in her roof, draw parallels with the other characters and the events happening for them: Emenie listening to the birds and trying to escape her burning house for example. In the end, mirroring the resolution of Atwood's *The Handmaid's Tale*, we are told by 'Pink', an academic James Pinkerton, that he is doing research on the life of a mad old woman (Dawn Jones) who lived the lives of numerous personalities, dressing up and wandering all over London to the bemusement and ridicule of the public: 'Like a kid dressing up. Fancy dress. Amateur theatrics' (199–200). Yet, despite all of the characters experiencing an awful demise before the academic research draft of Pink, Lee has them resurrected at the end, miraculously surviving against all odds. This subverts the logical fact gathering of Pinkerton (who favours geographical wanderings and interviews to prove what has been); the novel instead privileges Dawn's words of wisdom (her subjective perspective is no less true for its intangibility): 'Just because you can't see things, doesn't mean they're not there' (193). Dawn is aware of her multiple personalities, just as she is aware of the various perspectives and experiences of the city that alter with era, age, gender, sexuality, and class:

> I must finish all of my five lives, for the sake of myself and others [...] One by one, as each, I and they, become ready, we will walk up on to the bridge of steel, or of copper, or of diamond, opal and ruby, or iron-black, or gold and silver, and cross through into the bright mist. And there we will all be one and quite different, so different from anything we have been here, ever, that I can't imagine it. Nor any of us could.
>
> (228)

This is both an equaliser (death as a universal inevitability) and an acknowledgement of the variety of human experience. In this way, both novels allow for alternative, feminine narratives of the city to emerge, privileging those of women and outsiders in particular.

Gendered Cartographies: Judging Books by Their Cover

Even an initial glance at the cover illustrations of the two novels foregrounds the city and gender as the major focus (Figures 1.1 and 1.2).

At the outset of this chapter, Parsons was quoted in reference to 'gendered cartographies of viewing', and the two covers immediately highlight these narratives as gendered and imaginative maps of the city. The image design for *Cruel Pink* is a map reminiscent of the seventeenth or eighteenth century, with 'London' scrawled across it in bold black font, and the focal point is the archaically titled 'River of Thames'. As Howard F. Stein and William G. Niederland's work has pointed out, maps from the seventeenth and eighteenth centuries were more anthropomorphic or symbolic in content, and they often creatively linked the map

Figure 1.1 Helen Smith, *Alison Wonderland* cover (2011). Reprinted under a license agreement originating with Amazon Publishing, www.apub.com.

images to the female anatomy. *Cruel Pink*'s cover image then deliberately plays around with these ideas and also resembles the surrealist maps popular in twentieth-century Paris, which Joan Gibbons described as 'both a remapping and re-experiencing of the city that subverted prescribed or pre-constructed ways of experiencing or knowing the city and replaced them with more open, creative ways of negotiating the urban landscape'.[42] Certainly, *Cruel Pink* and *Alison Wonderland* both creatively map and remap the city and use this subversion to make feminist statements. In addition, blackness blurs the top two thirds of Lee's cover like an x-ray of two cloudy lungs at either side, foreshadowing our insights into the darker elements of the city hidden below its outer skin or façade. This is also reminiscent of London smog. The city is the artificial/man-made space which pollutes, or impacts upon, the feminine/

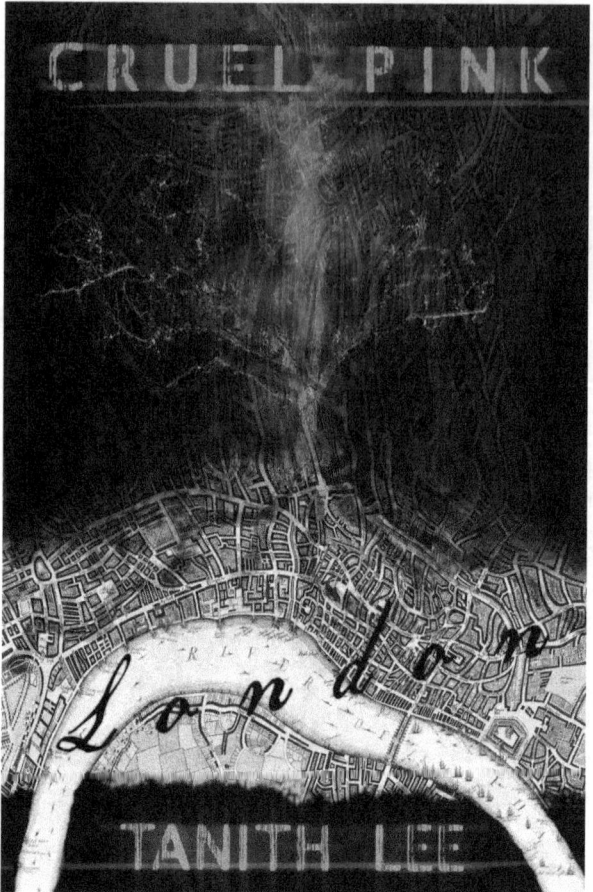

Figure 1.2 Cruel Pink cover (2013). Reprinted with permission of artist John Kaiine.

natural world: femininity symbolised in both the pink font, which mirrors chipped paint but definitely asserts itself as the dominant colour, and the river Thames, is set above the blackness also obscuring the bottom of the map. It is significant that psychoanalyst Sándor Ferenzi has emphasised the well-known symbolism of the river as female (it is linked to such things as fertility – apt since the mystery baby in Smith's tale is found in the sea by Alison and Taron – and the unconscious comfort of being in the mother's womb), while bridges are often associated with masculinity and sexual impotence. Ferenzi suggests that this symbolism is rooted in folk tales, and in both *Cruel Pink* and *Alison Wonderland*, the authors question traditional notions of both masculinity and femininity as well as exploring the complexities of sexuality and identity. As Parsons states, 'this is a blighted landscape, physically, architecturally, spiritually and sexually' (194). Certainly, the equivalent pollution on Smith's cover manifests itself in a black and white photograph of the Thames, the clouds in the sky resembling smoke. The angle of vision is from beneath a dock and highlights the mechanical and man-made grittiness of the bridge's metal structures, emphasising the unnatural harshness of the urban space, whose grey buildings clutter up the background. The long, bright red feminine hair framing this dull image (the city taking the place where a face should be) mirrors the eye-catching 'Wonderland' text while the first half of the title, 'Alison', is black and blends into the city image. This blurring of the name 'Alison' into the urban photograph is a clever representation both of the loss of identity in crowded cities and, in this case, a female identity, while suggesting that there is a potential magic or brighter utopian, alternative or feminine 'Wonderland' that can, or at least could, be found in the urban space. Yet, the stage curtains of hair have loose strands that fall over the picture and resemble ropes, suggesting that the curtains have been pulled on Alison's story; she will no longer remain literally faceless due to the city's precedence over her own self and identity – this novel will allow a woman's urban story to emerge. It is no coincidence then that the female gender (represented by the Thames) is foregrounded on Lee's novel cover also, while the bridge (the male symbol) is almost unnoticed amidst the blue: women are their central focus. However, within Smith's image, the bridge is the focal point of the photograph itself, a balance of feminine and masculine. Does this imply some striving for equality within the urban space? Feminine fantasy and subjectivity invades the cities in both novels perhaps signifying a feminine reconfiguration of the current restrictive patriarchal city. For example, in Simon Goulding's essay on Carter and the city, he writes:

> Consider the role of the Thames in our understanding of London. On any map of the city the eye is drawn to it for two reasons: first, it divides the city into two halves; a northern and a southern and, secondly, we are aware of this because the river is highlighted in contrast to the landmass. This primary geographical feature is recognised as a cartographic sign (component) because of its differentiation in graphical form to the spaces around it; in its function as connotative symbol it serves to delineate the layout and boundaries of the landscape. It suggests that there are two Londons – a north and a south. In some respects this is a perfectly correct analysis, the river splits the city by a, roughly, east/west flow so the division must be north/south. The reality of London is of course not so simple [...] What constitutes the city may not be as simple as considering the ordnance survey maps, A-Z street guides or a listings magazine. The city for Jonathan Raban is not a fixed entity: '[t]he city as we imagine it, the soft city of illusion, myth, aspiration, nightmare, is as real, maybe more real, than the hard city one can

locate on maps'. What we perceive is more important, argues Raban, than that which is offered to us as representation.[43]

The reference to the river as the dominant map sign due to 'its differentiation in graphical form to the spaces around it' is apt. It is the female symbol, and as the theories outlined in this chapter show, women have often been displaced or cut off from the city space; they often felt a sense that they did not belong. The divisions Bentley emphasises also correspond to the 'two Londons' of these novels: the 'Wonderland' (the feminine, subjective, imagined, or hidden city) and that which is the 'real', patriarchal, or culturally accepted city.[44] In addition, as the quotation suggests, these maps are alternative, but they are also the subjective maps of our psyche. They capture more 'truth' than the quantitative measurements of normal cartography, taking into account lived experience (allowing the impact of elements such as gender and class to be considered). Thus, while in Bentley's view the Thames does embody the notion of divisions, and symbolically for Lee and Smith this is useful in mirroring the division of experiences between men and women, all boundaries in their stories are broken down, opening up an opportunity for shared use of the urban space and the invention of new ways of inhabiting the city. As Ferenczi states, 'the bridge may [also] be used as a formal representation of "transitions", "changes of condition" in general'.[45] This foreshadows the feminist impulses inherent in the feminine recreations of London, aimed at social change, and carried in the magical/realistic dichotomy of Lee and Smith's anti-tales.

'Psycho'-Geographies: Subjective and Pluralised Cities

Inherent in this feminisation of the urban environment is the 'in vogue' concept of psychogeography, which Vamik D. Volkan explains is 'not a new discipline but merely a new angle or focus on the complicated and emotional ties between human beings and their physical environment'.[46] Established by the Letterist Group and Guy Debord in 1950s Paris, in which it 'became a tool in an attempt to transform urban life, first for aesthetic purposes but later for increasingly political ends', the term is difficult to define due to its various uses and manifestations.[47] There exist two forms of psychogeography, however: the scientific, used by psychologists (such as Howard F. Stein and William J. Niederland's study Maps From the Mind), and an artistic and subjective perspective for writers (of which Merlin Coverley's book Psychogeography is an example). However, Volkan's definition is useful for this chapter and its focus on gender and space: he asserts that,

Psychogeography is the study of how issues, experiences, and processes that result from growing up in a male or female body become symbolised and played out in the wider social and natural worlds, which serve as 'screens' for inner dramas.[48]

This is apt, given the theatrical metaphors in the anti-tales mentioned earlier. These ideas have clearly been inherent in literature for a long time: the work of the Romantic poets seeing landscape as a metaphor for the speaker's state of mind, or the gothic genre and its sense of the past haunting the present, as well as the hidden tunnels and passageways as negotiations of the mind's unconscious (Alison's reference to the underground maze of London's tunnels as a dark space 'where the things you're scared of can hide' is a prime example of this) (154–155). It is important to recognise, however, that the emphasis on the literary does not overshadow the very real implications of psychogeography, supported in the heavily political writings of Defoe and Blake. Anti-tales as a genre are clearly embracing psychogeography's possibilities. An example beyond the two novels discussed here is Karen Brennan's story 'The Snow Queen' in Bernheimer's *My Mother She Killed Me, My Father He Ate Me* collection. In this tale, the heroine moves back to the city of her earlier years and browses the psychology section of a library before going home with a disturbed friend, and playing out the traumatised memories of her childhood and her son's homelessness. All of this is linked to her mother's readings of Hans Christian Anderson's story when she was a child. The city becomes a psychological landscape which triggers the memories she has hidden in her unconscious: 'I'd just moved back to the city, having been away for a long time [...] when I returned to the city I found everything changed [...] I let my mind wander'.[49] Elizabeth Wilson has pointed out how

> Nostalgia is an accommodation with change. To revisit a city after many years was to be made abruptly aware of change, of the tortoise-like process of slow erosion that normally goes unnoticed to those who tread the same streets day after day.[50]

Nostalgia then can produce an awareness of the possibility of moving beyond that which exists in the present, an idea which is embodied in such anti-tale revisions of the city for women.

The fairy tale has indeed always been studied from a psychoanalytic perspective, as children map out their mental development onto to the narratives in order to resolve conflicts between the conscious and the unconscious (as illustrated in psychoanalyst Bruno Bettelheim's *The Uses of Enchantment*). The two novels discussed in this chapter fall into a category Coverley refers to as 'London Psychogeography'; indeed, Lee's novel is referred to on the back cover as 'psychological fantasy'.[51] Certainly, Alison is like a child when, in her room after the traumatic raid of her home by Bird and Flower, 'Darkness brings back my childhood fears and makes me irrational' (74). It is also true that all of the characters in both *Cruel Pink* and *Alison Wonderland* have had troublesome childhoods or absent parents (the latter a common theme in the fairy tale genre). As well as this, their damaged states of mind mirror the disturbed city they inhabit, hence the pun in this chapter's title. The novels truly reflect a 'psycho'-geography. Dawn literally creates all five of her lives and cities in her mind. Even the buildings in both novels are a projection and material fulfilment of the characters' mental states. Lee's Alison proudly asserts, 'I live in an upside down house', the bedroom being on the ground floor with the door onto the garden; an immediate indication perhaps that this world is on the level of dreams and the mind (the house essentially standing on its head which is on a level with the street) (14). Similarly, the block of flats housing Dawn and her multiple personalities contains an 'attic-loft conversion. Although the way Dimble described it the place sounded as if it had an extra attic on top of that' (217). Dawn takes living totally in her head to a new level. In this way, the novels emphasise how space affects the individual and vice versa. As Stephen Pile states,

> Aspects of identity, or self, develop in relation to place (people make their homes), but places set a brute limit on what individuals can make of themselves (homes make people). The home is not simply an expression of an individual's identity; it is also constitutive of that identity.[52]

Clearly then, psychogeography can be used as a radical political method in literature, and as we have seen in the anti-tales in this chapter, it can allow texts to illustrate the impacts of the city upon women and outsiders – the constraints inhibit the healthy expression of their desires and personalities which instead manifest themselves in the form of mental illness: ill people products of an ill society. This is illustrated by Alison's boss, Mrs. Fitzgerald, whose public and private personae could not be more divergent:

> Mrs. Fitzgerald wonders whether you are supposed to be able to feel something when you're thinking [...] She's outwardly at ease with herself, which is why young women like Alison find her presence reassuring. Mrs. Fitzgerald has the appearance of being able to deal with any matter, domestic or business, with equanimity [...] Mrs. Fitzgerald secretly fears that she's being claimed by madness.
> (23, 25)

Yet, this does not mean that the psychological city maps of these novels are any less real, instead, as Volkan asserts,

> The social consequences of psychogeographic thinking are vividly real [...] The study of the human penchant to construct maps from the unconscious mind illuminates [...] how shared internal representations come to be experienced externally and acted upon as the nature of the real world.[53]

This is precisely symbolised by Taron and Alison's discussion on their road trip:

> 'Have you got the map?' I ask. 'Or is it in the car?'
> 'Do you mean the road map or the mental map?'
> 'What's a mental map?'
> 'It's like a wish list, but it's an actual picture of something you want to happen'.
> 'I mean the road map'.
> 'It's in the car. Do you want to see my mental map?'
> 'I don't know'.
> The mental map is like a primary school art project. She has made a collage by gluing a photo of herself, a photo of me and a picture of a baby cut from a magazine onto an A4 sheet of paper. We're floating together in a disembodied group, superimposed on a view of Weymouth's seaside taken from a tourist leaflet [...] 'This isn't magic, it's just using the power of the mind. You visualize something and make it happen. If you believe, you're halfway to making it real'.
>
> (102, 103)

As well as the term 'disembodied group' being an apt description of women's place in the modern city, this extract summarises the feminist use of psychogeography in both novels and their revisions of the city. As Taron sates, these novels use 'the power of the mind' to 'visualize something and make it happen'; they foreground both the mistreatment and exclusion of women in the urban space, while illustrating that there are alternative ways of seeing and possibilities of being – this city is revisable, not set in stone. Anti-tale authors such as Lee and Price are like Red Riding Hoods straying from the path of traditional urban and fairy tale narratives through the radical use of magical realism. In the words of Parsons, women writers can construct 'cities within the pages of their texts, combining the real and the imaginary to create their own psycho-urban space [...] In so doing they create an urban consciousness modeled on alternative values to those of their male counterparts' (15–16). Hence, as Anna Kérchy points out, this conception of psychogeography 'allows for a significant revision of our sense of space by inviting explorations beyond objective mappings and measurings, and highlighting the affective components of our spatial experience', once again permitting a feminine and subjective reconception of the city, or rather, cities, to emerge.[54]

Flâneur vs. Flâneuse: Subverting the Knowable and Rationalised Patriarchal City

Using psychogeography as a means of producing a feminised, alternative and subjective city consciousness is also related to Lee and Smith's revisions of the controversial figure of the male *flâneur* in urban literature. To give more clarity, the *flâneur* is a nineteenth-century phenomenon coined by Walter Benjamin, and described by Parsons as the motif for

> the writer and writing of urban modernity [...] the expert observer of the urban scene, translating the chaotic and fragmentary city into an understandable and familiar space, and [a figure who] seems to become increasingly detached from his asphalt environment.
>
> (2)

As stated previously, the *flâneur* was almost exclusively a white bourgeois male in previous literature and, in the words of Elizabeth Wilson:

> It is this *flâneur*, the *flâneur* as a man of pleasure, but more, as a man who takes visual possession of the city, who has emerged in feminist debate as the embodiment of the 'male gaze'. He represents men's visual and voyeuristic mastery over women. According to this view, the *flâneur*'s freedom to wander at will through the city is an exclusively masculine freedom, which means that the concept of the *flâneur* is essentially and inescapably gendered.[55]

However, as Parsons states, Michel de Carteau was keen to stress

> the crucial distinction between the urban observer as 'voyeur' and as 'walker'. His contemporary urban walker constructs the space of the city with his footsteps rather than his eyes, which entwines with those of the rest of the urban crowd into a 'poetic geography'.
>
> (9)

This suggests that the texts created in these wanderings are strands of multiple stories walked by other people, creating an accumulative narrative of the city. Yet, if the *flâneur* was predominantly male (women not having the same access or freedoms to literally 'walk' through the urban space in previous eras), the story has clearly been prejudiced and incomplete. As Janet Wolff has suggested, 'there could never be a female *flâneur*; the *flâneuse* was invisible; or rather, did not exist'.[56] However, Lynda Nead's historical study *Myths of Sexuality: Representations of Women in Victorian Britain* outlines the prevalence of prostitutes (literal streetwalkers) during the era. These women were not invisible, often wearing brightly coloured and lavish clothing to attract attention, however, the unusual visibility in the city afforded to these women was also a means of control as 'private and hidden forms of prostitution were defined as a specifically urban vice'.[57] Nead emphasises how the prostitutes were a major part of the visual culture, frequently being subjects of paintings, as keeping them in public site was a means of asserting surveillance and control over a group of women that threatened gender confines through their financial independence, sexual promiscuity, and unlimited wanderings of the predominantly male stage of the city. Good women were invisible women who remained hidden behind the doors of their homes. Yet, as Judith R. Walkowitz's *City of Dreadful Delight: Narratives of Sexual Danger in Late-Victorian London* shows, there *were* more women in the public arena than contemporary history and literary representations highlight: her book includes examples of female participation in public protests (particularly in relation to their rights to the public space, such as access to department stores and music halls), Karl Pearson's 'Men and Women's Club', and the response caused by the infamous case of Jack the Ripper (with an illustration, 'Ready For the Whitechapel Fiend', depicting 'respectable' women who refuse to be labelled victims by arming themselves with guns and knives). Even Flora Tristan's *London Journal* (1842) contains a personal account of a remarkable woman who contributed much to public life through her speeches and writing. As Jean Hawkes writes, Tristan 'grew aware of the forces which had shaped not only her own life, but the lives of all the poor and oppressed, particularly women'.[58] Tristan attended 'political meetings, factories, prisons, schools, slums, a brothel, an asylum and the races, all used as a base from which to investigate the functions of institutions in a repressive society, and the evils they both perpetuate and engender'.[59] Yet, Tristan was indeed a remarkable case, divorcing her husband and struggling with money to remain independent her whole life, and despite the reality of female participation in urban life outlined in such studies as those of Tristan, Walkowitz, and Nead, women's absence from literary representations persisted and their access to urban space was not uncontested. Certainly old women, drably dressed women, and those from the working class who did appear in the streets were generally invisible to the male *flâneur*'s gaze and were, therefore, predominately annihilated from the city narrative. This is still true to an extent today with Lee's elderly Dawn almost obliterated from the urban narrative despite her vast wanderings due to her invisibility. As the character of Pinkerton surmises in *Cruel Pink*:

> The suburbs can be less people-indifferent than inner London, but even so they're not that socially involved. No, despite what a lot of Londoners say, those little clusters of shops and by-ways, where you can meet the same people again and again, are still not like the old villages that, even now, you can come across, in Scotland, say, or the outlands of Manchester. Plenty down here pretend to be arm in arm, and heart in pocket with the rest of their ghetto. But they're not. Again, it's gossip, speculation. If something looks really exciting, or awkward – some gorgeous girl, some dangerous, spiky guy – they may take notice – but even so it's most likely guesswork.

(196–197)

This brings in the male gaze once again: if a girl or woman 'looks' attractive her place in the urban environment will be briefly acknowledged, yet only so far as she is an object for the male observer. This is similar to the Snow Whites in Best's 'Blizzard Season' who, caged in 'Snow Houses' to recover from the trauma of encountering the contemporary city, are like circus animals on display for the men who literally 'walk' the streets to gaze upon them:

> Men who worked nearby just happened to reroute their paths to carry them past the Snow Houses when the girls were out walking in the yard, because one thing that was true about them was that each one was the fairest in the land, and even when you thought you'd seen the prettiest girl, the next one would be inexpressibly more beautiful.

> (18)

While these men prowl around the streets and perimeters of their cage, the Snow Whites are confined to 'walking in the yard' – their footprints are not part of the wider urban story. Pinkerton's observations in *Cruel Pink* undermine the idea that fiction has represented a collective narrative. Rather, it foregrounds the inaccuracies and chasms that have been left unaddressed. After all, Lee's Dawn (the embodiment of the mad old crone stereotype to observers on the street) subversively wanders all over different areas of the city almost totally unseen, or at least left alone because of her strangeness, living out five lives in relative secrecy – even Pinkerton (the researcher) has to go on a hunt to find scraps of information to confirm her existence.

Yet Dawn's wanderings highlight how the absence of the female urban walker has shifted as a result of Postmodernity; the *flâneur* has taken on a much larger and all-encompassing role. The *flâneur* is a term used so widely now that 'he' has imploded upon himself: as Parsons points out, 'this intended agent of demystification has himself become one of the mysteries of the modern city' (2). This lack of stability in role or identity is effectively captured in Dawn's multiple-personality disorder and the identity crises experienced by all of the characters in *Alison Wonderland* in a struggle to logically define both themselves and their environment. The *flâneur*'s rational summing up of the city is thus no longer possible – the *flâneuse*'s alternative feminine story disrupts the previous male figure's realism and certainty. This has, however, resulted in a multifaceted lens that acknowledges the different perspectives of individuals and various social groups. The *flâneur* is no longer restricted to a 'type', a freedom that feminist writers have embraced: 'he is an increasingly expansive figure who represents a variety of "wanderings", in terms of ambulation, nationality, gender, race, class, and sexuality [...] Used to allude to a whole range of urban identities' (3). This shift has led critics such as Zygmunt Bauman to assert that, in Postmodernity, there has been a 'feminization of the *flâneur*'s ways', constituting a feminine fragmentation in contrast to the previous male figure's attempt at mastery over the city through an 'all-knowing' perception (79). Parsons sums up the crucial questions posited by contemporary feminists:

> How are women writers situated, and how do they situate themselves, in the maps of urban location and literature? [...] What is the status of women who trespass upon his [the *flâneur*'s] pavement and his page? Can there be a flâneuse, and what forms might she take? Is the *flâneur* bourgeois or vagrant, authoritative or marginal, within or detached from the city crowd, masculine, feminine, or androgynous? And what does a redefinition imply for theories of women's place in the urban landscape?
>
> (2)

As we shall see, Lee and Smith's narratives make an ingenious, playful experimentation with these ideas and questions.

Previously, Maguire's 'Drawing the Curtain' was mentioned in relation to the city as a new setting or backdrop for fairy-tale performances through the anti-tale genre. This theatrical metaphor is carried further in *Cruel Pink*, in which women and outsiders reclaim their right to the *flâneur/flâneuse* role as urban walkers. Irvin, the dispossessed actor, reflects that,

> It is a fact both women and men become enamoured of the actor kind. And since nowadays women, too, parade on the stage, as in former times they did not, they draw so many admirers they (and I) must sometimes leave the premises by a side-door.
>
> (135)

Irvin is aligned with women in his effeminacy, and both, though still outcasts and once invisible in urban narratives, now take centre stage to perform their lives and experiences before the reader. Rod and Klova are also haunted by a title – *Five of My London Lives* – which surfaces at random in their minds; they are metafictionally aware of their roles in Dawn's psyche (at least at a subconscious level). More broadly, they are aware that their stories constitute part of the larger narrative of London: '*Five of My London Lives*. Not a book, I thought, puzzled. A play, perhaps? Why had I thought of that?' (147). These are the stories that have been buried or are absent from urban literature to date through the exclusionary myth of an overarching narrative of London. There are as many Londons as there are people. Emenie, the female serial killer, claims her right to the urban space by prowling the streets in an inversion of Little Red Riding Hood's negotiation of the forest – 'I'd put on a jumper of dark orchid-red. I sometimes do wear red clothes. Though I don't always dress to kill, red's often my killing gear. *If* I wear red, I am

fairly certain I'll be hunting. (Hunting pink)' (155). Instead, she is a mixture of heroine and wolf, using the city as her 'hunting' ground. 'Hunting
pink' is a metaphor perhaps for her murder of the 'innocent persecuted
heroine' trope embodied in her prey, Micki, who is like 'A Victorian
child, smiling. Innocent, wanting to be good. So many examples in so
much literature' (47). As in Best's tale, discussed earlier, there is no room
for this outdated fairy-tale motif in the contemporary city. Smith's Alison, for example, observes 'dancing princesses' who are vulnerable in
the public arena due to their adherence to the old fairy-tale values:

> The dance floors are full of glamorous, half-naked dancing prin-
> cesses but the harsh lighting in the queues for the toilets transforms
> them into very pale, sweating scarecrows with straggly hair, dilated
> pupils. Most of them are jiggling, either because they need the loo
> and they remember that jiggling helped when they were little girls on
> long cars trips or because the drugs they have taken to make them
> dance can't discriminate between the flaky-paint interior of a toilet
> and the rammed, pulsating dance floor.
>
> (115)

Here they regress to a childlike vulnerability, attempting to stand out
to potential suitors (like the women at Prince Charming's ball in *Cinderella*), unlike Alison who seizes her newfound independence after the
domestic life as wife to her cheating husband: 'I work at the agency now.
I've stopped waiting for Mr. Wonderland. I don't need him anymore' (4).
Refusing to play victim, Alison no longer seeks escape from the perils of
the city and embraces her space within it. As she reflects on her trip with
Taron (the novel's damsel-like figure):

> I have to get back to London and sort things out. Part of the reason
> we came here was to be free of the danger in London but now I just
> want to get home, and bugger the danger. I'll be closer to where
> things are happening and won't feel so powerless.
>
> (147)

This comes back to a point made earlier: women cannot simply reject the
city but must carve out their rightful place within it. The city is the centre
of social ideologies and power networks and remaining outside of it in a
fairy-tale-like escapism will not effect change. Both Alison and Dawn (in
her various personae) continually emphasise their reclamation of 'space'.
Smith highlights the difficulty posed in this task, however, through the
figure of Clive (Mrs. Fitzgerald's brother) who 'haunts the office' claiming
'the phone and spend[ing] too long on the toilet, disturbing the comforta-
ble female environment' (25). Yet, both authors ultimately depict their female characters negotiating the city and claiming a space for themselves.

Sitting on her chair, with the belief that she is about to die, Dawn's final thoughts highlight this preoccupation to the extreme: 'All those pigeons, too, I think they've got into the other part of the house roof. Well. Good luck to them. I don't need *that* bit of space, do I?' (193–194).

The women and outsiders of these anti-tales emerge in the role of *flâneuse,* subverting, through their more complex feminine perspectives, the neat and tidy summations of a knowable patriarchal city endorsed by the white heterosexual bourgeois male *flâneur* that persisted for centuries. Irvin's parting words sum up this triumph, the female and outsider characters having 'walked' their stories into existence: 'My space I had had to walk the stage of this world [...] Man, nor woman, can do no more than that' (192).

Elusive Cities: The Feminisation of Urban Crime Fiction

These anti-tale narratives do much more than substitute women and outcasts into the role of *flâneur/flâneuse,* however. They also totally debunk the idea of any authoritative position and interpretation of the urban environment – one method they use is a feminine reinterpretation of urban crime narratives. Divided up into first-person sections allotted by character name (Emenie, Rod, Klova, Irvin, Dawn), each personality appears in a random order and all are woven together to create the whole (Dawn's self-aware summation at the conclusion versus Pinkerton's 'logical' narrative in his draft 'research' paper). Thus, the complex form of *Cruel Pink* fractures the *flâneur*'s authority as the bearer of all knowledge. Pinkerton's role as knowledgeable urban walker, on his trawls for information relevant to the publication of a commissioned paper on Dawn's 'case', is subverted since we have already been given a detailed insight into her mind and the psychologies of her various personalities. We watch as he flounders with his interpretations of the so-called facts, attempting to squeeze the subjective 'truth' of Dawn's reality into an objective and academic format. This is once again an example of feminine subjectivity and complexity versus masculine rationality and objectivity, suited to the magical realist dichotomy of the anti-tale form. It is also worth noting that he uses the city as his source, following, literally, the footprints of her story to various locations. This is similar to Smith's undermining of Alison's limited perspective and fact gathering in the detective case. As in *Cruel Pink,* the chapters in *Alison Wonderland* vary in order to focus on a particular character's thoughts; however, these are all written in the third-person (apart from Alison who speaks directly to the reader), giving us both a detached perspective and an individual viewpoint. In each case, the reader becomes the *flâneur*'s postmodern counterpart – the 'ragpicker', who gathers scraps of information rather than pretending to have a totalising perspective. The reader thus takes on Alison's role as detective and attempts to piece together a narrative from the fragments of information and sources scattered (like the rubble in Emenie's apocalyptic and decaying London) throughout both texts: 'Only the man at the top ever needs to know everything' (45). These anti-tales subvert the traditional *flâneur*'s authority (embodied in the ultimate literary *flâneur* and detective figure of Sherlock Holmes for example) through an inversion of the rationality and enlightenment at the core of detective and crime fiction.

As Philip Howell's article 'Crime and the City Solution: Crime Fiction, Urban Knowledge, and Radical Geography' points out, the real urban radicalism comes not from summing up the narratives into a coherent conclusion, but in recognising the gaps, chasms, and untidy threads that cannot be neatly tied together and understood. In this way, women writers such as Lee and Smith seem to be involved in a kind of post-modern 'writing back' to previous detective fiction, with feminine complexity and fantasy elements upsetting the genre's masculine concepts of rationality and justice being served. With *Alison Wonderland*, the reader has the overarching perspective, watching in despair as Bird (the representative of brutal male 'rationality') steals Taron's address book believing that, not only is it Alison's, but that the names are all conspirators in her investigation: 'Nevertheless, Bird will persevere until he finds the links he's sure exist' (132). In contrast, Taron (initially labelled 'Mad Cow' by the cynical Alison) has a mind prone to flights of fancy and finds more truth through magic; the magical realism of the novel is played out in these dichotomies: 'When she comes back, I tell her I'll charge her twenty-five pounds an hour for the research. "Good", she says, "that's about the same as the fortune teller is charging me"' (9, 15). *Cruel Pink* also offers an alternative perspective as we start at the level of the criminals/players themselves. Unlike normal crime fiction, here we dig our way to the surface to create a broader context for the abundance of details rather than beginning with an investigative purpose. In this way, Pinkerton recognises the ridiculousness of his attempt to 'know' or understand Dawn's story (playing the role of detective) by questioning people or visiting 'crime scenes': 'Neither the various Geographias nor word of mouth seem to offer up proof of its existence' (207). (It is worth noting that even the name 'Pinkerton' has historical associations, as it was the name of a detective agency in nineteenth-century America founded by a man named Allan Pinkerton.) Some truths are not tangible and concrete; they do not exist in the realist narratives of crime fiction logic. He reaches this awareness, recognising that for Dawn, and for all of us in our adoption of various personae in everyday life, they are '*real*':

> I have a feeling. This 'dry run', dress-rehearsal [of the academic article] – now it's done ... I may just hand over my three hundred pounds to Dimble. And suggest to D.C.W. he find another patsy. Rest in peace. Let it go.
>
> (221)

In addition, the fairy-tale aspect of good versus evil is an ideal medium through which detective stories can unfold and yet the anti-tale genre plays upon these ideas by blurring any easy moral categorisations. It is worth noting that the anti-tale comic book series *Fables: Legends Living in Exile* also uses a detective story in its opening issue, 'Who Killed Rose Red?'. The series follows the exiled inhabitants of the fairy-tale world as they live as citizens of Fabletown alongside New York's inhabitants. Images of nature and fairy-tale excess crowd the borders and separating pages in contrast to the grittiness of the city setting occupying the narrative's panels. Bigby (the Big Bad Wolf) is a detective solving the case of Rose Red's murder along with her sister Snow White (who is Director of Operations, wielding a lot of power despite impinging on male positions of authority). In the revelation scene, Bigby shares the metafictional awareness inherent in Lee and Smith's characters, announcing,

> This is it. In the mystery novels this is called the 'parlour scene', where the clever detective reveals all. If this were a work of fiction, the author would pause the story here to ask the reader if they'd put all the clues together yet.[60]

However, he acknowledges that much of it was based on conjecture; the reader did not have the subjective insights into the minds of the characters as in *Alison Wonderland* or *Cruel Pink*. Instead, the reader only receives a few concrete images and is left with glaring gaps until all of the characters are offered the space to tell their stories and fill in the less tangible truths. Like these two novels, *Fables* also ends without a 'happily ever after' or neat conclusion. Instead we are left with uncertainty. As Howell points out, there is nowadays a pushing of detective fiction to its limits in order to get beyond the idea of the city as a knowable place and to undermine enlightenment and knowledge.[61] This constitutes a radical move of feminine reinterpretations of the city in fantasy works away from the masculine realism inherent in much of the traditional urban writing tradition. Certainly, these narratives could continue in any direction and, despite all of the attempts at rationalisation and understanding, neither us, nor the characters, are any the wiser or better off. Instead, all of the texts ask us to value and recognise the importance of the stories for their own sake and to embrace the feminine plurality of perspectives and experiences hidden in the hustle and bustle of any city, be that the fictional setting of Fabletown or contemporary London.

Feminine 'Magic': The Use of Fantasy in Imagining Alternative Cities

The fairy-tale element of these novels also provides a major means of subversion in this respect: as stated previously, the *flâneuse*'s feminine perspective undermines the *flâneur*'s masculine rationality. For, as Parsons points out:

> 'Masculinist geographers [and writers] are by and large still demanding an omniscient view, a transparent city, total knowledge. Meanwhile, feminist geographers are understanding the contemporary city not as the increasing fragmentation of a still-coherent whole, but rather in terms of a challenge to that omniscient vision and its exclusions'. Benjamin's geography of the city is indeed marked by an obsessive attempt to know the city in its entirety, a surrealist desire to penetrate the fantasies of its phantasmagoria, and a determined project of reacquisition of its fragments [...Instead feminist writers aim for] an understanding of the urban space that is not predicated on the model of the omniscient or exclusionary map.
>
> (7)

Indeed, there is a radicalism inherent in the magical realism created by the convergence of the two genres of fantasy and urban fiction. As Zolkover points out, anti-tales such as *Alison Wonderland* and *Cruel Pink*

> deploy a combination of history, literature, prior fantasy, and legends in order to populate a landscape [this is done very literally in *Fables* and its immigration of fairy-tale legends into the streets of New York] at the border between fantastic and uncanny. And through that combination [...] each functions as a kind of Janus mirror of everyday life: they reflect human worlds both as we hope they might be, and as we fear that they might become.[62]

Thus, the fantastical nature inherent in the anti-tale's magical realism is a clever device in the fulfilment of Parsons's proclamation that:

> the city falls into two extremes; the modernist, geometrically ordered city of Le Corbusier, and the postmodern, informal and flexible city [...] The former is an environment for the rational and purposive figure, the latter for the nomad and lover of the picaresque. The former follows the scopic form of the telescopic panorama, the latter that of the kaleidoscopic myriad. Postmodernism, with its characteristic lauding of that which is disparate as unlimiting, asserts a despotic nature to the ordered city.
>
> (8)

This is symbolised by Smith's psychic postman who communicates telepathically on behalf of Taron's witch mother to warn the young women of the perils to follow: 'the psychic postman writes a message on one of a stack of cheap postcards with views of London he carries with him and he pushes it through Alison's letterbox. DANGER, he writes, BEWARE' – he literally writes the uncanny and magical onto the London of the images (75). It is also interesting that the 'telescopic panorama' and 'kaleidoscopic myriad' viewpoints, mentioned above by Parsons, are illustrated in serial killer Emenie's use of birds as her authoritative, or more rational, information gatherers that give her the generalised picture of London (a literal bird's-eye view) to supplement her own unstable vision (symbolised by the rubble around her on ground level): 'above the wreckage of the suburbs. It would probably be in London inside ten minutes, the bird. Well, in what was left of London, evidently. But for a pigeon that would, I expect, suffice' (9). Anti-tales have always contained this subversive 'Anti-realist, fantastic, political, subversive, allusive, allegorical and anti-romantic impulse', with Angela Carter credited as 'the fairy godmother' to these new authors.[63] Certainly, the city as a major aspect of Carter's work has only recently been acknowledged by critics, despite the vast amount of scholarship focused upon her oeuvre.[64] As Sonya Andermahr states, 'This curious and distinctive narrative style, which moves continuously between historical actuality and magical realism, and seems to be unique to Carter, has in fact been adopted and adapted in different ways by a number of subsequent women writers'.[65] Lee and Best are just such writers who, I argue, use the fairy tale in conjunction with the city as a radical and feminist 'act of conscious mythologizing'.[66]

The 'otherness' of fantasy or the unexplainable and supernatural has always been associated with women, and it has always threatened the championed rationality associated with male enlightenment. As Emenie points out when her house is on fire (as a result of the raging brutish male relative of one of her victims), 'Men love to burn women, they always have. For witchcraft, or heresy, or adultery. I cite Joan of Arc, Mistress Pently, Queen Guinevere – so burn this fucking heretic witch-queen called Emenie. And block her every exit from the pyre' (184). Thus, it is not surprising that fantasy has been embraced by feminist authors as a subversive mode of writing. Smith immediately alerts us to the fact that there are alternative realities below the surface image of the city in her opening chapter 'Crayfish'. Alison is on an affair case following a suspected cheating husband. Despite her assumptions and the overwhelming evidence of his sexual misconduct, he is actually innocent, struggling for money, and going to the secretive location of Clapham Common simply to gather crayfish to sell to restaurants: 'As I was new to the detective game I found the story quite touching [...] I still keep the picture of a crayfish in my wallet as a reminder *that not everything is what it seems*' (6). Therefore, right at the exposition, Smith forces us to acknowledge that hidden truths of the city subvert established assumptions and neat patriarchal narratives of the city space. In both novels, we see the mysterious/magical underside of the urban space – Mrs. Fitzgerald gardening 'when the spirit world is awake and most of London is asleep', for example (28). Klova's late 'night magic' wanderings are another case in point: invisible to the everyday and waking world, 'The city looks very ordinary by day, I think [...] But when it gets dark [...] London looks supernatural' (41).

This idea of hidden locations perceptible only to the female walkers, as outsiders who have an alternative perspective to the tidy narratives of previous male *flâneurs*, is embodied in the 'The Rescue' chapter in which Alison takes on the role of hero rescuing Jeff (the damsel in distress). Having heard the urban myths about underground prisons for MI6 and one hundred Buddhist monks who 'drum for peace under the Peace Pagoda in Battersea Park in shifts, round the clock', Alison and Taron confirm their existence (153). They literally step through the back of a pub's storeroom where they enter a different realm: 'darkness fills the space, wrapping it up and making a place where the things you're scared of can hide' (154–155). The reference to this realm as a 'maze', with its *Alice in Wonderland*-like choice of three red doors (one of which contains the quest-item, Jeff), and as a space where 'Everything's linked', makes it a visual embodiment of the postmodern or feminine city that breaks off in different directions and harbours many secrets yet to be unearthed (154). It is often the fairy-tale components of fantasy and magic that provide a radical fantasy to these urban anti-tale narratives. At the most basic level, Smith uses fairy-tale imagery to draw parallels with male chauvinism in the modern city. Almost caught having an affair, the enemy Bird throws his lover's (Miss Lester's) clothes out into the Thames and puts her in a boat to hide her from his wife. He dehumanises her to the point that she resembles objectified fairy-tale princesses and the parallel is not lost on the victim herself as she transforms London's buildings into fairy-tale prisons: 'The boat passes under the Albert Bridge, its four turrets, with spires on top, just capacious enough for each one to contain a fairy princess, so long as she never lies down but remains standing up or sitting' (136). Again, this raises issues about confinement and female space. Alison, on the other hand, uses the fairy tale/anti-tale as a means of empowerment, inverting the patriarchal objectification of female heroines trapped in the glass coffins of the male-collected stories:

> If I think too much about him I could fall in love with him again, so instead of thinking about him as someone real, alive and difficult to pin down as a slippery silverfish, I've objectified him and trapped him in The Story of the Unfaithful Husband.
>
> (97)

The fairy tale and fantasy genres are often considered to be female art forms, particularly since the former originated in a female folk oral tradition that existed long before the patriarchal literary tale took centre stage because of Charles Perrault and the Grimms. Indeed, Smith high-lights how the fantastical or fairy-tale-like aspects are a feminine subver-sion through 'Taron's experiments with reality' (147). Her imagination is embraced as a female gift in that it literally gives birth to the baby Phoebe that they find in the sea: 'She only exists because we dreamed her and made her appear. It's magic and you'll spoil it if you analyze it' (165). This is an assertion to which Alison 'can hardly protest, considering the powerful magic that brought her into the world' (144). The imagination as a 'powerful magic' is congruent with the point made earlier with re-gard to the utopian nature of fantasy effecting social change. For exam-ple, it is Taron and Alison's imagination that manifests a real baby, the implication being that the imagination can effect a physical and tangible change in the real world. In addition, it is significant that Lee uses Rod to emphasise the fantastic as an alternative feminine perspective since he considers himself a woman despite being reprimanded for this from a very young age. His uncle George's 'advice' is noteworthy:

> 'Take care, your worship, those things there aren't giants, they're windmills. [...] I think you don't quite see life as it is. You see girls as princesses, maybe, and ordinary streets as castle corridors, trains as chariots, for all I know, clouds as camels'. [...] I gazed at him, quite unable to relate this statement to anything at all in my life. What did *I* ever see in such a reckless, mad and *glamorous* manner? My bloody awful job? The irksome train journeys? My lonely, stuck, just-adequate tiny life?
>
> (145)

Here Lee clearly juxtaposes Rod's feminine view of the city with George's traditional and conservative perspective. Rod is locked into a typical ur-ban persona of middle-class businessman; this version of the city is a patriarchal one to which he does not belong. He cannot deal with the rational and enlightened view associated with the traditional *flâneur* and he is only happy in the feminine perspective of the *flâneuse*: 'On went the straight-jacket of maleness. On went the shackles of *learning*, all over again, what *not*, and *what* to do, to want, to hate' (125). It is apt then that these novels use the blend of magical realism found in the anti-tale and its undercurrents of the feminine fantastic to get beyond limiting mas-culine rationality. Alison concludes her narrative by pointing out how it is 'practicalities that crowd all dreams of the future'; it is the magic spell of 'D E L star dot star' given by Taron's mother that ultimately erases all their names from the enemy database (183, 184). Alison's summation, 'we have saved the world, or our bit of it' underscores how Smith's nar-rative privileges fantasy as a means of capturing and envisioning spaces for women in an alternative city, while Lee's Dawn carries out a similar mission in walking the streets and living in a world just slightly skewed from the 'reality' (184). As Pinkerton states, 'Mrs. Jones did a lot of her imagined life-work in *reality*' – she has one foot in the existing London and another in a potential London of her own making (210).

Flesh and Blood Cities

The body also functions as a subversive site of 'otherness' which, like the city, has both a material reality and a host of less tangible symbolic associations. It is important, in the words of Parsons, to acknowledge 'the ways in which women writers have experienced and/or imagined the connection of their bodies and their pens within the specific urban territories they inhabit or seek' (2). As Grosz points out in her essay 'Bodies-Cities', the body, like the city, defies a simple categorisation: 'the term body cannot be contained within a tidy dictionary definition – something always seeps through'.[67] This again incorporates the masculinity, consciousness, and rationality versus femininity, unconsciousness, and irrationality dichotomies. The body and its linkage to cities is not a new phenomenon – ideas such as the 'body politic' having been around for centuries – yet there is now a renewed interest in the body and space, and a greater recognition of 'the body as a socio-cultural artifact'.[68] This is evident in Heidi J. Nast and Steve Pile's book *Places Through the Body*, which aptly uses an *Alice in Wonderland* illustration as its cover in conjunction with *The Wizard of Oz*. It depicts Alice's growing body bursting through a small house and landing (like Dorothy) in a world in which she must find her own way. As the artist Cindy Davies states:

> I began thinking about how our bodies are defined, controlled and more often transformed by our surrounding spaces. Using Alice as a starting point, I began to conceptualize a fantastical drawing that would illustrate these ideas [...] Both Dorothy and Alice were at odds with their spaces. Poor, dreaming Alice, while pursuing the time conscious white rabbit, was either too big or too small for her space, too sane for the Mad Hatter's Tea Party and too outspoken in the Queen's Court.[69]

Certainly, Lee's Alison is 'too sane' at times for Taron's magic, yet she finds a balance that allows her to function in both the existing and imaginative city (the 'Wonderland') of the novel; she is 'too big' in her power over the effeminate Jeff, who is always left feeling embarrassed in her presence; and she does transform herself and find a space in the city, largely owing to the female environment of Fitzgerald's agency. Grosz also makes a cognate point in her essay: since the city can be viewed as the 'body politic', does this mean that the city is gendered? Is it a male or female body politic or an androgynous one? The cover of Smith's novel is a female head of hair surrounding a city face, suggesting that it is female and looks forward through its fantastical and feminine alternativeness. In contrast, although her novel also privileges a feminine perspective of the city space with its pluralisation and complexity, Lee's London also focuses on a depiction of women and outsiders impacted upon by a patriarchal or male city, to emphasise the city's cruelty. Unlike Alison, they never really belong to the city of the novel but exist in their own imagined cities in their heads.

It is noteworthy in Lee's novel that the snobbish Pinkerton not only links politics and the female anatomy but also ridicules it in his sense of being threatened by his nickname 'Pink':

> The last is a slang term too for a certain part of the female anatomy, wonderful part, true, but I've never been that keen on it being applied to me. As a bloke, I'm not, in any other way aside from name, PINK. Not even politically.
>
> (195–196)

The otherness and male fear of the female body threatens rationality and hence the city forces attempt to keep it under control. Lee illustrates this through Klova (the figure supposed to inhabit a progressive futuristic society). On a night out, she notes how she 'had carnal with a male in the Singles Rooms of the Tower [...] Sex is brilliant, and all the exercise' (26, 27). Here the city treats sex in a sterile fashion, allocating it a room at a club, so that sexuality is no longer a private and subversive thing but rather monitored and contained by public surveillance. This sense of control and order is extended in the next line as she walks home: 'The streets smell clean and hygiene-brushed' (27). As Jane Augustine has pointed out, 'The city tries to stamp out the erotic activity they themselves, by their very nature, generate'.[70] Yet, Lee shows us immediately how the body undermines this attempt at social order: as soon as Klova steps through her door the odour of the decaying bodies in Emenie's apartment permeates and cuts through the image of cleanliness: 'But this house, when you step in from the fresh air [...] it stinks' (27). Decaying bodies threaten the clean order of the city in Klova's world and even the rubble of buildings around Emenie in her apocalyptic time period are linked to corpses in her mind, with 'the remains of Mark's and Spencer's, (in the likewise remains of the old High Street)' (15). This is a radical political statement: the death of the current city and all its power dynamics (gendered and otherwise) in the hope of a phoenix-like rebirth from the rubble into a society that no longer inhibits freedom and expression. The very structure of the novel – with its outlines of the brutal deaths of each character as a kind of catharsis for their sudden rebirth at the end – mirrors this. As David Bell *et al.* point out in *Pleasure Zones: Bodies, Cities, Spaces*, queer sexualities are subversive in the urban environment (as noted earlier in relation to Lee's lesbian heroine in 'Black Eyed Susan'). Certainly, Rod and Irvin use their bodies and sexuality subversively: Rod's surface appearance as heterosexual male in a business suit masking his inner femaleness and wardrobe of women's clothing, and Irvin's bisexual affairs. On his way to meet the husband of a female lover, Irvin describes himself as wandering 'into the winding back ways of London's prodigious skirt-hem'; the personification of the city's streets as a female body forms an obvious metaphor for the hidden and 'deviant' sexual lives that lurk below London's orderly surface (109).

Yet, the body is also a prison controlled by social forces; it is dehumanised and becomes a capitalist puppet. After all, ills of cities include being bound up in what Lewis Mumford calls 'purposeless materialism'.[71] In the sixteenth- to seventeenth-century world of Irvin, we are told of an actress, Merscilla, a 'Poor lass. To be a woman, and sold, as she said, to a man she despised', and this is paralleled with the futuristic world of Klova, highlighting how commodification of the female body is not new but rather manifesting itself once again, albeit in a slightly altered form (138). Dying Klova reflects,

> My body is like bones. My skin, just a bit of stuff draped over [...] Then we kissed, the lipstick and I. People leave bruises on you. The lipstick just leaves pink. It's kind and sweet, even though its name is Cruel. C.P. *Cruel Pink*.
>
> (150)

The letters, we are told, correspond to her mother's initials, yet it is a brand name: she is a child of capitalism, allowing it to define her. She preserves her final kiss not for her lover Coal but for the lipstick that has become so much a part of herself: 'Then I dressed and went out. No cosmetics. Like no eyes, no mouth' (82). Her body is literally drawn and shaped by patriarchy in the form of capitalism. Even Rod observes a store called 'Furnished Futures', the implication being that the acquisition of objects is part of the construction of a better life, a way to numb the pain of his gender conflict (38). Pinkerton's name is once again symbolic, being both a detective agency and also a private security firm that sent men to intimidate and eliminate troublemakers from workplaces during the labour strikes of the nineteenth and twentieth centuries. Similarly, as part of her urban narrative, Smith clearly sees this strand of consumerism and economics as a major topic; the title of each chapter is headed by an image of a penny coin below the title and she includes a lengthy discussion between Jeff and Alison concerning the possible invention of a super-advertisement that would sell anything in the world by being the ultimate predator on human desires and insecurities. Ultimately, Smith conveys a positive representation of female triumph over these challenges in the modern city, with Alison's power rooted in her financial independence and employment at a feminist institution. As Festa McCormick states, women 'must find some way of surviving in a [... space] that is largely fuelled by what are seen as male drives of material possession and professional ambition'.[72]

Looking Beyond London: Ekaterina Sedia's *The Secret History of Moscow*

While Lee and Smith's novels centre on London, the radical anti-tale remapping of the city extends into other urban contexts. Ekaterina Sedia's Russian novel, *The Secret History of Moscow*, provides an eminent case in point. Set in the 1990s, Sedia's context is rife with ambition and criminality, its inhabitants living in the new free market, with its illusory promise of freedom and economic prosperity. It is a space where the old 'historical and beautiful' part of the city is destroyed by 'new life in the shape of kiosks, sprung up on every corner – [selling] magazines, cigarettes, books, Tampax, pins, films, booze, eyeglasses, school supplies, handbags and T-shirts, manned by loud people who wouldn't leave the passersby alone'.[73] In this post-soviet society, everything is in chaos, individuals intent on trying to make a quick buck, the novel describing 'the pungent dreams of the new Russians' as 'a misshapen embodiment of lawlessness and despair' (25). Certainly, at the exposition we are introduced to Galina, a young woman who is regularly hospitalised in mental asylums. She is a victim and outsider in a patriarchal world, one that is driven only by a cold and inhumane materialism. As in Lee and Smith's novels, anyone who does not conform is written off entirely. For example, Galina's mother despairs at her daughter's childless spinsterhood:

> I just don't want her to turn into a bitter man-hater, her mother said. Last time when she came home from the hospital I had hope for a while. But now – I don't know if she should just go back or if there's nothing they can do to fix her.
>
> (3)

The plot revolves around the disappearance of Galina's sister, Masha, who gives birth alone in their bathroom before disappearing from sight, having turned into a jackdaw bird. Identical to Lee and Smith, Sedia's novel is a crime narrative, with Yakov, a police detective, investigating Masha's case. In his investigation, Yakov is dragged through a door, reflected in the windows of a moving train, by Foyodor (a seemingly insane street artist) and Galina (desperate to find her sister after seeing the birds enter another realm through a puddle). The three find themselves in the Underground, a space where fairy tale, mythical, and folklore figures reside among glowing trees, ghostly white birds, and mythical forests, alongside humans who have managed to seek refuge here. Significantly, Galina soon discovers why certain people have found this space: "'It's all the same with everyone here, isn't it?" Galina said. "You wanted so badly to escape". "And we don't fit in anywhere else"' (97). Like the novels discussed earlier, Sedia constructs her chapters according to character names, dedicating a space for multiple stories to emerge, privileging individuals who would normally remain invisible in the urban space: Foyodor, the homeless street artist; Oksana, a young gypsy woman (who befriends rats, recognising their shared status as social vermin); David (Yakov's grandfather who had to flee in order to escape persecution for his liberal political views); and even 'The Corpse', traditionally not much more than an instigative plot device in detective fiction, is literally brought to life after being found dumped in a river. The corpse, Sergey, is given his life, name, and identity back, and, although a criminal, we are shown his humanity and vulnerability. Sergey ends up being crucial in catching the power-hungry villain, Slava, his previous boss in a criminal gang, and a racketeer who steals souls for economic gain (aware that nobody will be able to refuse him business if he can not only kill but imprison their souls for eternity). After all, the inhabitants of this city are also under the control of religious structures: 'There is a reason they call it the city of forty times forty churches' (11). Like Lee and Smith, Sedia highlights how power-hungry societies prey on those who are defenceless and voiceless. After the fairy tale and human characters pull together, successfully turning the birds back into people on the streets of Moscow, Foyodor notes:

> the group of people outside, as they looked at each other and shook their heads, trying to remember, and cried silently, he realized what they had in common. The bird people were the ones who did not know how to be loud, in any sense of the word – they only tried to carry on as best they could, holding to the memory of a dignity that didn't seem to be allowed in the new capitalist jungles that sprouted around them, lush and suffocating and seductive but blocking the view of everything but themselves. He felt acute pity for their voicelessness, for their inability to adjust or to turn back time.
>
> (273)

However, by giving each chapter over to disempowered characters, Sedia allows them to gain their voices in relating a more complex urban narrative, one that is inclusive and radical in pointing towards alternative perspectives. This is also achieved in the novel's revelation of how society obscures the existence of those whose do not fit the correct ideological side of history. Elena, or Countess Vygotskaya, is discovered in the Underground by Galina. As one of the erroneously labelled 'Decembrists' wives', Elena has no legacy of her own in a world of renowned folklore figures and is bitter about her comparative invisibility:

> 'You've heard about me, of course', the woman said.
> 'No', Galina admitted in a quiet guilty voice. 'But I'm sure that –'
> 'The Decembrists' wives. I was one of them'.
> Galina nodded. 'I hadn't realized'.
> 'Neither had I', the woman said mysteriously. And added, noting Galina's perplexed look, 'How difficult it is to be an icon'.
>
> (93)

We also discover that she did not accompany her spouse, unlike the other wives who were revered for their selfless obedience and devotion, following 'their husbands into the frozen woods and summers ringing with mosquitoes, to a place away from civilization and any semblance of everything they knew' (93). When asked why she did not comply with this wifely duty, Elena replies, 'Because they expected me to, I suppose. Because I was an appendage. Because it didn't matter what I wanted' (94). Here, Sedia foregrounds the radical history of a rebellious woman who refused to be chained, and at the novel's climax, it is Elena who leads a group of soldiers into battle to save the others and write her own legacy as an active leader and warrior in her own right.

In addition, Sedia's magical realist subversion of traditional crime fiction is similar to that of Lee and Smith, opening up our perception and refusing to tie the world up into a series of exclusionary, neat summations. Yakov, as a police investigator, likes to believe he represents the values of male enlightenment and rationality, refusing to believe his eyes when things turn strange and convincing himself he's dreaming, constantly losing his temper with Galina, whose alternative way of viewing the world allows her to accept the magic around them. Like Lee's academic Pinkerton, Yakov's attempts to piece together the clues in a logical manner is futile. He is forced to recognise that the world is cruel and does not make sense no matter how hard one tries to justify or cohere meaning:

> The world used to make sense; Yakov remembered that much. And yet, here, underground, he couldn't avoid the thought that the apparent sense and order was just a result of his wistful optimism. It also occurred to him that the closer he found himself to evil, the harder it was to maintain the illusion of a sensible universe.
>
> (199)

Ultimately, as in the previous novels, masculine reason is subverted by feminine fantasy, with magic spells saving the day, just as the spell from Taron's mother provided the code for the computer in *Alison*

Wonderland. Yet again, by holding magical realist tensions together, Sedia highlights that the world is changeable not set in stone, that things can be altered, if only one breaks out of the conservative perspectives we are stifled into by social conditioning. After all, Galina's 'psycho'-geographic perspective is not a result of her supposed mental instability, rather, the novel reveals that she simply views the world in a way that is different and socially unacceptable. When Galina asks if Yakov has ever heard of her condition – 'sluggish schizophrenia' – he reflects: 'He did. It was a fake diagnosis for political malcontents, as far as he remembered. A convenient way of oppression that did not require prisons' (212).

Overall, Sedia, like Lee and Smith, asks us to open up our minds to the city as a complex, fluid, and negotiable space, and she adds alternative stories to the existing urban narrative, highlighting that there are many ways to live our lives not contained in current maps and records. All of the characters are extremely discriminatory in the beginning, the city full of hatred between various groups of people: those native to Moscow (Muscovites), gypsies, the homeless, women, those considered mentally unstable, and even the Underground inhabitants are divided into categories that include 'fleshbags' (humans) and 'freaky things' (113, 56). It is only when boundaries are broken down that they realise their connections, and the cruel lie of divisive social categories, that they succeed. In the end, Galina gives her body over as a vessel to her sister Masha, allowing the latter to look after her child, while she moves into the jackdaw body and starts to lose her human memories and sense of self. While this is a tragic ending, Masha's baby girl, like Alison and Taron's adopted baby in *Alison Wonderland*, inspires hope, forcing us to aspire towards a different world, one where the voiceless will be heard, where discrimination is a distant memory and human empathy and compassion triumphs over materialism. The novel forces us to consider: will we allow Galina, and those unconventional lives yet unheard, to have their voices lost in the urban void?

Conclusion

This chapter initially outlined the problems, both historically and in contemporary society, for women in their occupation of the urban space. By illustrating how women have been excluded, both from the physical space itself and from the urban narrative, the discussion then proceeded to highlight how Lee and Smith privilege the experiences of women and outsiders, who assert themselves and their alternative feminine perspectives as part of the ongoing city narrative. The anti-tales use their magical realist elements of fantasy and magic alongside their gritty realism, to subvert the traditions of crime fiction and offer subjective psychogeographies, as well as foregrounding previously censored unruly bodies, in order to undermine the masculine *flâneur*'s rationalisation and portrayal of a knowable, restrictive, neat, and singular objective city. They offer here instead alternative feminine and pluralised cities, acknowledging the diversity of experience and endorsing a politics of equality and inclusion for those currently outside of the patriarchal remit. Going back to Grosz's statement at the heart of this book –

> The project ahead, or one of them, is to return women to those places from which they have been dis- or re-placed or expelled [...] and partly in order to be able to experiment with or produce the possibility of occupying, dwelling or living in new spaces, which in their turn help to generate new perspectives, new bodies, new ways of inhabiting.

It is clear that these anti-tale revisions of the urban space contribute to this project and aim, through their use of the utopian nature of the imagination and fantasy, to envision a new feminine, pluralistic, and subjective model of the city for the future in order to escape existing oppressions.[74] Visiting a statue in an Old English Garden, Alison holds Phoebe (the baby discovered by herself and Taron), who becomes a symbol of the next generation of women, and worries about her new daughter's place in the world: '"Men and women of England/How long shall these things be?" asks the plaque' (189).

Notes

1 Tanith Lee, *Cruel Pink* (Stafford: Immanion Press, 2013), p. 61. Hereafter, page references will be incorporated into the text.
2 Helen Smith, *Alison Wonderland* (Las Vegas: Amazon Encore, 2011), p. 5. Hereafter, page references will be incorporated into the text.
3 Robert E. Park quoted in Kevin R. McNamara, 'Introduction' in *The Cambridge Companion to the City in Literature* (New York: Cambridge University Press, 2014), p. 1.
4 Jack Zipes, *The Irresistible Fairy Tale: The Cultural and Social History of a Genre* (Princeton: Princeton University Press, 2012), p. 155.
5 See table of anti-tale traits in David Calvin and Catriona McAra, *Anti-Tales: The Uses of Disenchantment* (Newcastle upon Tyne: Cambridge Scholars Publishing, 2011), p. 3.
6 Zipes, *The Irresistible Fairy Tale: The Cultural and Social History of a Genre*, p. 136.
7 Deborah L. Parsons, *Streetwalking the Metropolis: Women, the City, and Modernity* (Oxford: Oxford University Press, 2000), pp. 1–2. Hereafter, page references will be incorporated into the text.
8 See Adam Zolkover, '*King Rat* to *Coraline*: Faerie and Fairy Tale in British Urban Fantasy' in *Postmodern Reinterpretations of Fairy Tales: How Applying New Methods Generates New Meanings*, ed. Anna Kèrchy (Lampeter: The Edwin Mellen Press, 2011), pp. 67–82.
9 Merlin Coverley, *Psychogeography* (Herts: Pocket Essentials, 2006), p. 15.
10 Raymond Williams, *The Country and the City* (Herts: Granada Publishing Limited, 1973), p. 9.

11 Susan Stephens, 'The City in the Literature of Antiquity' in *The Cambridge Companion to the City in Literature*, ed. McNamara, p. 31.
12 Antonis Balasopoulos, 'Celestial Cities and Rationalist Utopias' in *The Cambridge Companion to the City in Literature*, ed. McNamara, p. 17.
13 Williams, *The Country and the City*, p. 9.
14 Karen Best, 'Blizzard Season' in *A Floating World* (Orlando: Beating Windward Press LLC, 2012), p. 17. Hereafter, page references will be incorporated into the text.
15 Elizabeth Grosz, 'Bodies-Cities' in *Space, Time, and Perversion: Essays on the Politics of Bodies* (London: Routledge, 1995), p. 105.
16 Peter Preston and Paul Simpson-Housley, *Writing the City: Eden, Babylon and the New Jerusalem* (London: Routledge, 1994), p. 9.
17 See Mary Eagleton, 'Genre and Gender' in *Modern Genre Theory*, ed. David Duff (Harlow: Pearson Education Limited, 2000), pp. 250–262 for a discussion on feminine forms such as fantasy, gothic, and science-fiction (those that subvert or go beyond the boundaries of rationality/reason) in contrast to established masculine forms and what she refers to as 'masculine realism' (p. 253).
18 Roy Boyne and Ali Rattansi, *Postmodernism and Society* (London: Macmillan, 1990), pp. 11–12.
19 Jo Little, Linda Peake, and Pat Richardson, eds., 'Introduction: Geography and Gender in the Urban Environment' in *Women in Cities: Gender and the Urban Environment* (London: Macmillan Education Ltd., 1988), p. 2.
20 Ibid.
21 Elizabeth Wilson, *The Contradictions of Culture: Cities, Culture, Women* (London: SAGE Publications Ltd., 2001), p. 72.
22 Liz Bondi and Damaris Rose, 'Constructing Gender, Constructing the Urban: A Review of Anglo-American Feminist Urban Geography' in *Gender, Place and Culture: A Journal of Feminist Geography*, Vol. 10, No. 3 (2003), p. 230.
23 Little, Peake, and Richardson, 'Introduction: Geography and Gender in the Urban Environment' in *Women in Cities: Gender and the Urban Environment*, p. 2.
24 Festa McCormick, *The City as Catalyst: A Study of Ten Novels*, p. 193.
25 Penelope Lively quoted in Preston and Simpson-Housley, *Writing the City: Eden, Babylon and the New Jerusalem*, p. 9.
26 Preston and Simpson-Housley, *Writing the City: Eden, Babylon and the New Jerusalem*, p. 2.
27 Ibid., p. 2.
28 Gregory Maguire, 'Drawing the Curtain' in *My Mother She Killed Me, My Father He Ate Me*, ed. Kate Bernheimer (London: Penguin Books Ltd., 2010), p. xxvii.
29 Preston and Simpson-Housley, *Writing the City: Eden, Babylon and the New Jerusalem*, p. 9.
30 Thrift, 'Cities without Modernity, Cities with Magic' in *Scottish Geographical Magazine*, p. 140.
31 Jane Augustine, 'From Topos to Anthropoid: The City as Character in Twentieth-Century Texts' in *City Images: Perspectives from Literature, Philosophy and Film*, ed. Mary Ann Caws (Pennsylvania: Gordon and Breach, 1991), p. 74.
32 Tanith Lee, 'Introduction' in *A Different City* (Stafford: Immanion Press, 2015), p. 8.
33 Festa McCormick, *The City as Catalyst: A Study of Ten Novels*, p. 14.

34 Tanith Lee, 'Black Eyed Susan' in *Disturbed by Her Song* (Maple Shade: Lethe Press, 2010), p. 19. Hereafter, page references will be incorporated into the text.

35 Virginia Woolf quoted in Susan M. Squire, 'Virginia Woolf's London and the Feminist Revision of Modernism' in *City Images: Perspectives from Literature, Philosophy, and Film*, ed. Caws, p. 99.

36 Parsons, *Streetwalking the Metropolis: Women, the City, and Modernity*, epilogue.

37 Andrew Thacker, *Moving through Modernity: Space and Geography in Modernism* (Manchester: Manchester University Press, 2003), p. 2.

38 Virginia Woolf, *Mrs Dalloway* (Hertfordshire: Wordsworth Editions, 1996), p. 100.

39 Jacqueline Rose quoted in Parsons, *Streetwalking the Metropolis: Women, the City, and Modernity*, p. 14.

40 Nick Bentley, 'Postmodern Cities' in *The Cambridge Companion to the City in Literature*, ed. McNamara, pp. 185, 186.

41 Helen Smith in an interview with Lucy Walton-Lange, '*Alison Wonderland* by Helen Smith' in *Female First* (28th January 2013) < www.femalefirst.co.uk/books/alison+wonderland-275631.html> [accessed 26th January 2015].

42 Joan Gibbons, 'Mapping and Memory: Contemporary Psychogeographies' in *Public Space: The Battlefield For Public Art*, No. 10 (September 2007), p. 37.

43 Simon Goulding, 'Seeing the City, Reading the City, Mapping the City: Angela Carter's *The Magic Toyshop* and the Sixties' in *Angela Carter: New Critical Readings*, eds. Sonya Andermahr and Lawrence Phillips (London: Continuum International Publishing Group, 2012), p. 187.

44 Haruki Murakami's novel *Hard-Boiled Wonderland and the End of the World* (1985) also alternates by chapter between two settings: the 'hard-boiled wonderland' and 'the end of the world'. The former is best described as a more realistic science-fiction narrative with the latter being more surreal and fantasy-based – similar to the magical realist tensions in Smith's novel.

45 Sándor Ferenczi, 'Bridge Symbolism and the Don Juan Legend' in *Maps from the Mind: Readings in Psychogeography*, eds. Howard F. Stein and William G. Niederland (London: University of Oklahoma Press, 1989), p. 10.

46 Vamik D. Volkan, 'Foreword' in *Maps from the Mind: Readings in Psychogeography*, eds. Stein and Niederland, p. xxi.

47 Coverley, *Psychogeography*, p. 13.

48 Volkan, 'Foreword' in *Maps From the Mind: Readings in Psychogeography*, eds. Stein and Niederland, p. xvii.

49 Karen Brennan, 'The Snow Queen' in *My Mother She Killed Me, My Father He Ate Me*, ed. Bernheimer, pp. 221, 222, 223.

50 Wilson, *The Contradictions of Culture: Cities, Culture, Women*, p. 102.

51 Coverley, *Psychogeography*, p. 27.

52 Stephen Pile quoted in Goulding, 'Seeing the City, Reading the City, Mapping the City: Angela Carter's *The Magic Toyshop* and the Sixties' in *Angela Carter: New Critical Readings*, eds. Andermahr and Phillips, p. 194.

53 Volkan, 'Foreword' in *Maps from the Mind: Readings in Psychogeography*, eds. Stein and Niederland, p. xix.

54 Anna Kèrchy, 'Feminist Psychogeography and Jeanette Winterson's Passions' in *She's Leaving Home. Women's Writing in English in a European Context (European Connections)*, eds. Nóra Séllei and June Waudby (Oxford: Peter Lang, 2011), p. 134

55 Wilson, *The Contradictions of Culture: Cities, Culture, Women*, pp. 78–79.
56 Janet Wolff quoted in Parsons, *Streetwalking the Metropolis: Women, the City, and Modernity*, p. 79.
57 Lynda Nead, *Myths of Sexuality: Representations of Women in Victorian Britain* (Oxford: Basil Blackwell Ltd., 1988), p. 116.
58 Jean Hawkes, 'Introduction' in *The London Journal of Flora Tristan* (London: Virago Press Limited, 1982), p. xv.
59 Hawkes, 'Introduction' in *The London Journal of Flora Tristan*, p. xxiii.
60 Bill Willingham, 'Who Killed Rose Red?' in *Fables: Legends in Exile*, Vol. 1 (New York: DC Comics, 2012), p. 100.
61 This is contained in his paper's attempt to

> develop further the radical critique of crime fiction by thus turning radical geography's interest in urban representation back on itself, arguing for a more (self-)critical analysis of literary representation and the claims to knowledge they contain. It is argued here that some forms of crime fiction develop what can be called "urban knowledges" that are as critical and counterhegemonic, if not more so, than much of what passes for radical urban geography.
>
> (p. 358)

In this way, it suggests that the metafictional awareness of the elusive nature of 'truth' within postmodern crime fiction, and their imaginative representations of urban settings, radically shatters the concepts of enlightenment and reason, traditionally favoured as masculine traits. Instead, the narratives in this chapter favour a disruption of the neat fairy tale and detective fiction arcs – the clues are not all neatly tied up and measurable, and the future for characters is uncertain. See Philip Howell, 'Crime and the City Solution: Crime Fiction, Urban Knowledge, and Radical Geography' in *Antipode*, Vol. 30, No. 4 (1998), pp. 357–378.
62 Zolkover, '*King Rat* to *Coraline*: Faerie and Fairy Tale in British Urban Fantasy' in *Postmodern Reinterpretations of Fairy Tales: How Applying New Methods Generates New Meanings*, ed. Kèrchy, p. 78.
63 Sonya Andermahr, 'Contemporary Women's Writing: Carter's Literary Legacy' in *Angela Carter: New Critical Readings*, eds. Andermahr and Phillips, pp. 20, 11.
64 For an example, see Goulding, 'Seeing the City, Reading the City, Mapping the City: Angela Carter's *The Magic Toyshop* and the Sixties' in *Angela Carter: New Critical Readings*, eds. Andermahr and Phillips, pp. 187–196.
65 Andermahr, 'Contemporary Women's Writing: Carter's Literary Legacy' in *Angela Carter: New Critical Readings*, eds. Andermahr and Phillips, p. 13.
66 Goulding, 'Seeing the City, Reading the City, Mapping the City: Angela Carter's *The Magic Toyshop* and the Sixties' in *Angela Carter: New Critical Readings*, eds. Andermahr and Phillips, p. 191.
67 Elizabeth Grosz quoted in Jon Binni, Robyn Longhurst and Robin Peace, 'Upstairs/Downstairs – Place Matters, Bodies Matter' in *Pleasure Zones: Bodies, Cities, Spaces* (New York: Syracuse University Press, 2001), p. viii.
68 Grosz, 'Bodies–Cities' in *Space, Time and Perversions: Essays on the Politics of Bodies*, p. 103.
69 Cindy Davies, 'The Cover Illustrations: A Word from the Artist' in *Places through the Body*, eds. Heidi J. Nast and Steve Pile (London: Routledge, 1998), p. xii.
70 Augustine, 'From *Topos* to Anthropoid: The City as Character in Twentieth-Century Texts' in *City Images: Perspectives from Literature, Philosophy and Film*, ed. Caws, p. 85.

71 Lewis Mumford quoted in Festa McCormick, *The City as Catalyst: A Study of Ten Novels*, p. 193.
72 Preston and Simpson-Housley, *Writing the City: Eden, Babylon and the New Jerusalem*, p. 12.
73 Ekaterina Sedia, *The Secret History of Moscow* (Canada: Prime Books, 2007), p. 7. Hereafter, page references will be incorporated into the text.
74 Grosz, 'Women, *Chora*, Dwelling' in *Space, Time, and Perversion: Essays on the Politics of Bodies*, p. 124.

2 Feminist Journeys 'Into the Woods'

The Use of Ecofeminist Landscapes in Postmodern Anti-Tales

> Journeys don't start or finish in the woods. They're the bit you have to slip through to get to where you're going: a liminal, in-between place of crossing paths and knotted roots
>
> – Robbie Collin[1]

Introduction: Journeying 'Into the Woods'

Although binaries, including the urban and rural divide, are too simplistic, this chapter provides an interesting counterpart to the former's focus on the city. While the urban space is an unusual setting that literally displaces the fairy tale into an unfamiliar world, the genre is more at home in a pastoral environment, with the briar hedge of thorns and the enchanted forest being among the most prominent motifs that have captured the imaginations of readers. The conventional city space examined in Chapter 1 has predominantly masculine characteristics, valuing rationality, culture, society, and relentless progress, whereas nature has, right back to ancient goddess cultures, been considered both subversive and feminine, the forest depicted as a space outside of social control and expectations. It is easy to see then why anti-tale authors would make use of these associations for the feminist impulses of their retellings. As I will show in this chapter, it is an emerging trend among anti-tale authors to follow a pattern described by Stacy Alaimo as 'transform[ing] nature into a hospitable space for feminism'.[2] After all, Conny Eisfeld states in her book *How Fairy Tales Live Happily Ever After*:

> The woods have played an important role when integrated into a fairy tale. It is the dangerous or even sinister opposite of the safe and well-encompassed village [...] or city. In psychological terms the forest, as seen through the eyes of a man, is a means to explore everything unknown and mysterious about femininity [...] During archaic times, the forest was also a kind of primeval forest, where natural, animalistic forces were set free. Compared to a structured and stable settlement, the forest implies pure chaos, continuing to change and grow uncontrollably. The ones who live in the wilderness

are usually outcasts of society, e.g. witches, robbers and (enchanted) wild animals. Therefore the forest sometimes functions as a bridge or gateway to another, magical world. Common rules are suspended in this realm.[3]

This extract encompasses many of the theories that will be expanded upon in my discussion. These include the essentialist notion of nature as female (including female oral storytelling as an essential and evolutionary activity in social change), an embrace of the 'magical world' or spiritual side of ecofeminism (women's affinity to the environment being related to magic, the occult and the power associated with ancient goddess myths), and boundary-crossing and the breakdown of dualities (such as nature versus culture or men versus women) in order to undermine the simplistic black and white morality of good versus evil synonymous with the fairy tale genre. An exploration of Eisfeld's notion of 'the wilderness' being home to the 'outcasts of society' (namely the concept of women's inherent 'otherness' and subsequent link to animals and nonhuman nature) will also be discussed and, finally, the ecofeminist principles of equality and interconnectedness as a means to level what she calls the 'common rules' (i.e. culturally constructed differences and damaging social divisions).

It should be noted, however, that many of these theories rely on the contentious notion of essentialism: that women are indeed closer to nature. This will be teased out in more depth as the chapter progresses, but it is this trait of ecofeminism that accounts for the lack of literary scholarship in the area. As Greta Gaard states, 'the anti-essentialist backlash against ecofeminism has already taken its toll: feminist graduate students are being advised against undertaking ecofeminist approaches in their dissertations, and scholars are advised against publishing works with the word "ecofeminism" in their titles or keywords'.[4] An example of this backlash occurs in the very title of Lucy Sargisson's 2010 paper 'What's Wrong With Ecofeminism?' with its disheartening exposition, 'Where to begin?'.[5] Yet, even Sargisson admits in her concluding remarks that ecofeminism has its role and that the most valuable contributions tend to be through literature. This is unsurprising. Literature provides a means of using and exploring essentialist notions without holding them up as absolute fact. In this way, anti-tales in particular can utilise essentialism for their own empowering messages and, as we shall see, they even apply them to excess in order to subvert the problematic usage of the women equals nature trope in the traditional patriarchal stories that employ it to naturalise female oppression. As Sargisson points out, literary ecofeminism 'can inspire and subvert and offer [... a] space in which further utopian imagining can occur. The poems, the stories and the imaginings have a place and a function that should not be denied'.[6] Two key primary texts I use in this chapter – Margaret Atwood's *Maddaddam* trilogy and Michel Faber's novel *Under the Skin* – embrace Alaimo's theory of 'playing nature' in order to provide their cultural critiques. In addition, filmic anti-tales have heavily adopted these perspectives, thus Disney's *Into the Woods* and *Maleficent* (highlighting what Elizabeth Bell *et al.* have pronounced as 'the political in the seemingly apolitical world of Disney'), will be taken into consideration in order to support the ongoing ecofeminist narrative that has seeped beyond literary retellings into popular culture and been expressed through various mediums.[7] As Alaimo states, 'whereas feminist theory's flight from nature leaves nature dangerously abject, a remarkable range of women's texts inhabit nature in order to transform it, not only contending with the natures that have been waged against women but writing nature as a feminist space' (13). Thus, these anti-tales, along with my discussions here, do not flee or try to isolate women from nature, instead, as the epigraph from Robbie Collin implies, I show how these authors and directors journey 'into the woods' in order to subvert existing paradigms and to effect feminist and social change.

The Women and Nature Duality: History and Representation

Women and nature have been both linked and exploited for centuries, with the treatment of the two being shaped by the ideologies of different societies according to their shifting values. For example, the scientific revolution caused nature and women to be viewed as passive objects to be controlled, dissected and understood, while the Enlightenment period emphasised the Cartesian mind and body division, resulting in the rationality/culture/male and nature/unruly/female dichotomies. Writing about attitudes towards gender and the environment, Monique M. La-Rocque also provides the example of the Decadent period of the late nineteenth century, stating that it is 'fraught with anti-women and anti-nature sentiments'.[8] Women were denied as fellow aesthetes and considered inferior to male Decadents (many of whom were homosexual). Decadents prided themselves on being superior to debased nature and the bodily needs associated with women. Their lifestyles were instead focused on the cultivation of the mind and an embrace of what they deemed a 'higher' culture. Ecocritic Val Plumwood supplies an apt summation of these problems when she states:

> There are a number of striking initial parallels between the treatment of women and that of nature [...] For instance the traditional role of both women and nature has been conceived as an instrumental one. Both have been valued in terms of their usefulness to others (e.g. to males in the case of women and to humans in the case of nature) who are taken as valuable in and for themselves. Similarly in

both cases there has been an attempt to impose a sharp separation on a natural continuum, in the one case between the characteristics of the sexes, and in the other case between the characteristics of humans and non-human animals, so that the distance between each side is maximized in a polarity.[9]

Unfortunately, this subordination of women and nature has not changed over time: our society continues to be rife with such ideologies. As Bennett states in relation to Atwood's trilogy (set only slightly into the future):

> Violence against nature and violence against animals inevitably leads to violence against women. Animals and women were both once sacred in early societies that believed animals were gods (or sent by gods) and worshipped women for their ability to create life. But once nature loses its sanctity in a society's mythology – as it has in both our society and the society Atwood depicts – it becomes easy to abuse and exploit it.[10]

Women and nature share similarities, including the fact that they have been historically and similarly oppressed. Traditional collected fairy tales have also pointed out the link, yet they've used it to naturalise women's inferiority and subordination. In the quotation from Bennett above, the phrase 'society's mythology' is particularly significant since fairy tales are an integral part of our cultural outlook and a formative part of social ideologies. Therefore, if the women and nature link is used derogatively in fairy tales, this is inevitably extended beyond the stories and shapes the minds of their readers. Certainly, the linkage of the two in the traditional stories is extremely problematic, and an analysis of some examples will make clear the anti-tale genre's purpose for the rewriting of fairy tales in order to create a new and healthier 'social mythology' as regards women and nature. In the version of 'Sleeping Beauty' told by the Brothers Grimm, the 'hedge of thorns' and desperate princes become a metaphor for rapaciousness (the heroine's name 'Briar-Rose' spelling out the fact that she is synonymous with the barrier):

> The story of the beautiful sleeping Briar-Rose, for so the princess was named, went about the country, so that from time to time kings' sons came and tried to get through the thorny hedge into the castle. But they found it impossible, for the thorns held fast together, as if they had hands, and the youths were caught in them, could not get loose again, and died a miserable death.[11]

Not only is this clearly symbolic of male fear of an all-consuming female sexuality, but perhaps more damaging is the way in which the overall story's symbolic sexual awakening of the heroine is depicted through natural imagery: it conveys chauvinistic assumptions about nature as passive resource being linked to female passivity. For example, the psychoanalyst Bruno Bettelheim has been widely criticised by feminists for his reading of this passage in *The Uses of Enchantment*. Bettelheim states,

> while many fairy tales stress great deeds the heroes must perform to become themselves, *Sleeping Beauty* emphasises the long, quiet concentration on oneself that is also needed [...] a long period of quiescence, of contemplation, of concentration on the self, can and often does lead to the highest achievement.[12]

So while male heroes go out and face demanding trails and challenges that initiate their development, women, according to Bettelheim, quietly retreat into themselves and withdraw from the world. In essence, female passivity is naturalised through this imagery. Sleeping Beauty relies on a prince dominating the land (the briar hedge) to initiate her awakening (she too is passively dominated and lacking in agency):

> by this time the hundred years had just passed, and the day had come when Briar-Rose was to awake again. When the King's son came near to the thorn-hedge, it was nothing but large and beautiful flowers, which parted from each other of their own accord, and let him pass unhurt, then they closed behind him again like a hedge.[13]

Similarly, nature is once again linked to female sexuality in the Grimms' version of 'Little Riding-Hood', a story about the perils of men and the consequences facing women and girls who give in to their desires, as summarised in Perrault's seventeenth-century moral: 'Little girls, this seems to say | Never stop upon your way | As you're pretty, so be wise | Wolves may lurk in every guise'.[14] Too brave and punished for her curiosity in her encounter with the wolf – the Grimms noting how she 'was not at all afraid of him' – the Brothers use flowers as a symbol for the young girl's indulgence of her libido that leads her off the 'path' of social conformity:

> so she ran from the path into the wood to look for flowers. And whenever she had picked one, she fancied that she saw a still prettier one farther on, and ran after it, and so got deeper and deeper into the wood.[15]

Here then, the Grimms convey yet another misogynistic idea – that women's link to nature ties them to their bodies and natural impulses meaning they need to be controlled (in this case by the superego policing force of the Woodcutter who cuts her free from the belly of the wolf).

Red Riding Hood's libido has been tamed, she no longer indulges in the nature of the woods but adheres to the orderly path that connects her with social regulations: "'As long as I live, I will never by myself leave the path, to run into the wood". [...] Little Riding-Hood went joyously home, and never did anything to harm anyone'.[16]

Finally, one of the most infamous parallels of women and nature in fairy tales is in the story of 'Snow-White and the Seven Dwarfs':

> A queen sat at a window sewing [...] she pricked her finger with the needle, and three drops of blood fell upon the snow. And the red looked pretty upon the white snow, and she thought to herself, 'Would that I had a child as white as snow, as red as blood, and as black as the wood of the window frame'. Soon after that she had a little daughter, who was as white as snow, [with lips] as red as blood, and her hair as black as ebony.[17]

Once again, nature is depicted as a resource and used to create the perfect heroine, who is both subhuman and objectified; nothing more than a conglomeration of various convenient elements. The passage ultimately provides a male ideal, and an unrealistic vision of 'woman', that is naturalised through the use of environmental imagery. Hence, our society is plagued with false notions of 'natural beauty' when, in fact, the standards depicted here are entirely unrealistic and unobtainable within nature.

Due to the disempowerment of women through their alignment with nature, feminists have generally fought against the linkage of the two in order to combat the naturalisation of female oppression; it has often 'fated' them to a subordinate state. As Alaimo points out:

> Feminism has long struggled with the historically tenacious entanglement of 'woman' and 'nature'. Mother earth, earth mothers, natural women, wild women, fertile fields, barren grounds, virgin lands, raped earths, a 'woman in the shape of a monster/a monster in the shape of a woman', the repulsively breeding aliens of horror films – these creatures portray nature as female and women as not exactly human [...] European cultures have long imagined nature as feminine. By the sixteenth-century, pastorals depicted nature as mother and bride who could soothe the anxieties of men distraught by the demands of the urban world, comforting them with nurturing, 'subordinate', and 'essentially passive' female natures.
>
> (2)

Although it will be studied at length later, Faber's novel depicts this struggle in its heroine Isserley, as she attempts to 'fit in' to a male-dominated workspace by rejecting her true nature or femaleness: 'It was dawn. The physical world did not exist for her, apart from the ribbon of grey tarmac on which she was driving. Nature was a distraction. She refused to be distracted'.[18] Like feminists, then, Isserley creates a severe divide in order to sever herself from nature and its disempowering associations entirely. As Alaimo states:

> Given that 'woman' has been defined in much of Western thought as that which is mired in 'nature', it is no wonder that feminist theory has struggled to extricate her from this quicksand. By attempting to disentangle 'woman' from the web of associations that bind her to 'nature', however, nature is kept at bay – repelled – rather than re-defined. It is not only ironic but deeply problematic that the aggressive, intellectual 'flight from the feminine' that motivated Cartesian rationalism has been followed by feminist flights from all that Descartes attempted to transcend – 'impure' matter, bodies, and nature. The recent rage to purge feminism of all vestiges of 'essentialism', for example, is one of the most striking instances of feminist theory's flight from nature. Working within rather than against predominant dualisms, many important feminist arguments and concepts necessitate a rigid opposition between nature and culture.
>
> (4)

Avoiding nature denies women yet another space and leaves the dangerous misogynistic dualisms to continue existing without critique or challenge. Anti-tale authors, however, are already involved in a project of rewriting old tales and, as I will show, they refuse to shy away from that which has been problematic and turned against women, working subversively with nature in order to rewrite it too as a powerful and feminist space. Nature, in effect, becomes a source of liberation rather than disempowerment. As we shall see, Isserley's awakening once again mirrors the shift of feminist thought in recognising the potential that exists for them in embracing and inhabiting the natural world once again:

> 'It was an indescribable feeling. As if nature was actually trying to nurture me' [...] It was almost cruelly poignant but delightful too, the way Amlis seemed to regard her as the custodian of an entire world, as if it belonged to her. Which, perhaps, it did.
>
> (224, 239)

Hence, there are clear benefits of, and a necessity for, an ecofeminist perspective within academic discourse.

Ecofeminism: Origins and Definitions

Ecofeminism is still a relatively new and untapped academic field, though, as Greta Gaard notes, 'The current interest in "place studies" seems to have pre-empted earlier concerns about bioregionalism and "the nature of home" that have been foundational issues in ecofeminism', and this certainly coincides with the boom of psychogeography discussed in my previous chapter.[19] Yet, while women predominantly felt like outsiders in the masculine city spaces examined in Chapter 1 (their damaged mental states in *Alison Wonderland* and *Cruel Pink* stemming directly from their urban alienation), this chapter will highlight the great sense of psychogeographical belonging felt by female characters within the natural environment. The roots of ecofeminism, however, can be found in the work of French writer Françoise d'Eaubonne, who coined the term in her 1974 book *Le Féminisme ou la mort*. This was followed up with *Ecologie Féminisme: Révolution ou mutation?* in 1978 which directly confronted the joint oppression of women and the environment. D'Eaubonne's main argument hinged on overpopulation and the problematic symbolism of men planting seeds in both women and the earth as a means of claiming ownership over each. This coincided with protests in the U.S. during the 1970s and 1980s in the form of the antimilitarist action movement and protests against nuclear power and weaponry, which consisted largely of female protesters. This, in turn, initiated the emergence of American ecofeminism in the latter 1980s.[20] One of these activists, Ynestra King, held up ecofeminism as the 'third wave of the women's movement' and, as Sturgeon notes, this indicates 'her sense, at one time, that this most recent manifestation of feminist activity was large and vital enough to parallel the first-wave nineteenth-century women's movement and the second-wave women's liberation movement of the 1960s and 1970s'.[21] Certainly, I contest that it is an emerging and prolific trend that many of the feminist theories in both popular culture and literary anti-tale texts convey through their use of nature and of their characters' engagement with the natural world.

While the roots of the theory are relatively clear, finding an adequate definition of 'ecofeminism' is more problematic since it defies any rigid classifications. As Catherine Villanueva Gardner attests:

> it would be a mistake to begin by trying to state *the* ecofeminist ethical perspective. Because ecofeminism entails both a feminist and an environmentalist ethic and because it engages in theoretical philosophy analysing issues that are of central practical importance, ecofeminism contains a wide range of diverse thought. Moreover, a search for *the* perspective implies that there is a single ecofeminist approach or at least one that may be sought.[22]

However, it is widely acknowledged that ecofeminism recognises, in addition to the traditional view of the world as anthropocentric (human-centred), that it is also androcentric, defined by Debarati Bandyopadhyay as 'putting not all human beings, but man only at the centre of the universe, with nature, women, children and all other life-forms at his disposal'.[23] For the purposes of this chapter, it is necessary to garner some working definitions of the term itself. Sturgeon provides the following definition:

> Most simply put, ecofeminism is a movement that makes connections between environmentalisms and feminisms; more precisely it articulates the theory that the ideologies that authorise injustices based on gender, race, and class are related to the ideologies that sanction the exploitation and degradation of the environment.[24]

This plurality of injustices and the fluidity of ecofeminism is all part of its radicalism, in that it is reacting against the simplistic dualisms created by patriarchal culture. In the words of Villanueva Gardner,

> our [ecofeminism's] initial focus must be not on offering a (simplistic) *causal* account of the connections between ecological destruction and the oppression of women, but on exposing and revising the oppressive conceptual framework that sanctions the joint subordination of women and nature.
>
> (this challenge to the patriarchal framework of binaries
> will be shown as a central tenant of the anti-tale texts
> themselves later in my discussion)[25]

Thus, this expansiveness and complexity means that ecofeminism is not only concerned with women and nature as isolated cases; rather, it recognises and 'is also based on, the recognition that these two forms of domination are bound up with class exploitation, racism, colonialism, and neocolonialism'.[26] This means that it has been viewed, 'at a conceptual level', by Karen Warren, as 'a movement to end all forms of oppression'.[27]

Despite the promising nature of ecofeminism, it has faced much backlash due to its apparent essentialism, especially from academic feminist theorists. For example, ecofeminism was deliberately excluded from the journal *SIGNS*, whose editors refused to do a special issue on it.[28] There are certainly key strands of ecofeminist thought that rely on naturalist tendencies. The most prominent is known as spiritual ecofeminism and, as Sturgeon notes, it is a position

> taken by feminists who are interested in constructing resources for a feminist spirituality and who have found these resources in nature-based religions: paganism, witchcraft, goddess worship, and Native American spiritual traditions. Because such nature-based religions historically contain strong images of female power and place female deities as at least equal to male deities, many persons who are searching for a feminist spirituality have felt comfortable with the appellation of 'ecofeminist'.[29]

Another idea is that of women being 'biologically closer to nature'; for example, the moon being linked to menstrual cycles and spiritual experiences in the wilderness, that make women sensitive to the interconnections of everything in the universe.[30] However, as Sturgeon states,

> Essentialism is not a sin nor a permanent mark of unexamined prejudice nor an enduring implication in domination. Though it can certainly have the effect of maintaining positions of privilege, it can also have the effect of producing an 'oppositional consciousness'.[31]

Certainly, as we shall see, Atwood's trilogy highlights the radicalism inherent in spiritual ecofeminism and essentialist ideas through the character of Toby. In addition, there is the ecocritical perspective of women being closer to nature simply as a result of their roles in home management, for example, in which they see directly the problems and damage being inflicted upon the environment. This approach counters the essentialism of biological and spiritual ecofeminism and as Val Plumwood notes:

> The argument that women have a different relation to nature need not rest on either reversal [idealization] or 'essentialism', the appeal to a quality of empathy or mysterious power shared by all women and inherent in women's biology. Such differences may instead be seen as due to women's different social and historical position ... To the extent that women's lives have been lived in ways which are less directly oppositional practices, qualities of care and kinds of selfhood, an ecological feminist position could and should privilege some of the practices of women over men as a source of change without being committed to any form of naturalism.[32]

This highlights the dual nature of ecofeminist thought. On the one hand, we have what Eric C. Otto calls 'cultural ecofeminism' (the theories of women's inherent spiritual and biological links to the environment) and 'rationalist ecofeminism' (the historical and social links).[33] However, I adopt a combination of the two in this chapter, referred to as 'dialectical ecofeminism':

> a vantage point for creating a different kind of culture and politics that would integrate intuitive, spiritual, and rational forms of knowledge, embracing both science and magic insofar as they enable us to transform the nature-culture distinction and to envision and create a free, ecological society.[34]

As will become evident, this dialectal approach fits well with the magical realist tensions inherent in the anti-tale genre.

A 'Practical Magic': Literary Ecofeminism

Having outlined the broader concepts and origins of the theory, my focus in this chapter narrows this to one particular strand: ecofeminist literary criticism. As Gaard and Murphy note, 'if you conceive of feminism as a movement that requires continuous conversation among activists of many kinds, then all available vehicles for communication must be utilised. Direct action is one such vehicle; literature is another'.[35] Yet they have also pointed out that 'the intersection of ecofeminism and literary criticism is largely unmapped'.[36] Ecofeminism is not a totally separate wave of feminism and has 'been present in various forms from the start of feminism in the nineteenth-century, articulated through the work of women gardeners, botanists, illustrators, animal rights and welfare advocates, outdoorswomen, scientists, and writers'.[37] Yet it is only with the emergence of the term 'ecofeminism' that we have been able to gain a different lens, or perspective, through which to recognise and appreciate those elements in existing works. For example, Alice Walker's infamous essay 'In Search of Our Mothers' Gardens' (1974) is clearly ecofeminist in its perspective and yet this has been largely unacknowledged despite its status. Through the concept of thinking back through our 'literary mothers', Walker suggests that it is necessary to re-evaluate texts in light of ecofeminist theory as a means of 'critiquing the traditional canon and the male tradition of nature writing in American literature'.[38] For it is true that,

> Static categories that define nature or individuals can only be distortions. Likewise, definitions of literature, its genres, and its canons that attempt to establish timeless universals by relying on a few male authors and ignoring the contextual, historical, thematic, and aesthetic dimensions of literary production can also only be distortions. Just as women's writing has been marginalised, so too has environmental writing.[39]

Yet, it is promising that Gaard and Murphy have noticed an emerging critical interest in the field:

> Since the 1990s there has been an eruption of ecofeminist literary analysis. Although individuals have been working in this vein for decades, the majority of ecofeminist criticism is being practiced by younger academics [...] Critics are beginning to make the insights of ecofeminism a component of literary criticism. They are also discovering a wide array of environmental literature by women being written at the same time as ecofeminist philosophy and criticism is being developed.[40]

The ecofeminist literary project is now well underway; however, the focus has been on relatively few authors (Barbara Kingsolver being one of the most prominent and recurring names). It should also be noted that the prominent ecofeminist texts have been written in quite a factual and realistic manner, by writers with a scientific background, who use the literary medium to make these facts and ideas accessible to a general readership. This is related to the emerging genre of creative non-fiction, of which nature writing is a dominant category, which allows the subjective and personal to give a deeper understanding of the experience of reality rather than an attempt at an unnatural, objective recording of landscapes and experiences.[41] For, as Gaard and Murphy point out, 'literature can appeal to certain readers who would not otherwise be moved by theory'.[42] The most prominent author in this category is conservationist and marine biologist Rachel Carson (particularly for her novel *Silent Spring*, written in 1962). Certainly, it is clear from reading ecofeminist material that, as Murphy surmises:

> Fiction is probably the terrain in which the least codification of a nature writing canon or mode of representation has occurred. Even so, traditional realism tends to be emphasised, in part due to a penchant for seeing the fiction approximate the factuality of nonfiction nature writing. A major problem with such an orientation is its failure to acknowledge the popularity of different genre conventions across cultures and that 'traditional realism' is largely an Anglo-American invention of the nineteenth-century.[43]

This is extremely important. Due to the fact that 'realism' is the favoured medium of ecofeminist fiction, it inevitably remains tied up in a patriarchal or 'traditional' canon. Despite the fact that creative non-fiction's use of nature writing and those works of fiction by ecofeminist writers blend scientific fact with fiction, anti-tales provide a slightly different ecofeminist take than a lot of those texts that have received ecofeminist attention to date. They are innately radical due to their magical realist form which allows ecofeminism to reach a wider audience (the popular culture industry, Disney being a prime example). A few critics have begun to recognise the potential of magical realist or fantasy texts as regards the expansion of ecofeminist thought and social change.[44] Barbara Bennett, for example, uses the fairy tale 'One Thousand and One Nights' as the overall motif for her collection of critical essays on literary ecofeminism titled *Scheherazade's Daughters: The Power of Storytelling in Ecofeminist Change*, which contains a section dedicated to the magical realism of ecofeminist texts by a range of women writers. This magical realist blend with ecofeminist politics creates what Bennett describes as a 'defiant magic', something of a mini-movement in itself, 'as far as possible from the scientific enquiry [of much ecofeminist discussion ...] but [...], nonetheless, an effective way to disseminate ecofeminist ideals'.[45] Even Theda Wrede talks about the 'Ecofeminist Subversion of Western Myth' (a project with which the anti-tale is particularly concerned), pointing out how male myths are subverted by a female storytelling tradition that adds more complex layers and voices, subverting simplistic narratives (a mirror of the original female oral folk tradition which we will see through the character of Toby in Atwood's work discussed shortly).[46] As Val Plumwood notes, 'the inferiorization of both women and nature [...] is grounded in rationalism'[47] hence fantasy or magic becomes a means for women to subvert existing narratives and ideologies: 'If (masculine) rationalism, associated with an androcentric worldview that opposes relationality, is at the origin of social inequalities, a solution springs from a relational self that is open to all that seems "other"'.[48] In essence, I posit that much of the radical ecofeminism discernible in anti-tale texts stems from tales' magic and the way in which they are uninhibited by pure, and seemingly unquestionable, rationalism. Although anti-tales are disenchanting in terms of subverting pure utopian magic, they nevertheless contain spiritual, quasi-magical elements in order to point towards alternative ways of seeing or viewing the world. They show us that not everything is able to be tied down, summed up, and controlled. This means that they are free to explore, and play around with, essentialist notions, recognising the fluidity of such ideas. They embrace magical realism as a means of carrying out the prominent element of 'transformation', which Gaard and Murphy hold up as a key concept in ecofeminist thought, suggesting alternative social models in their stories in order to effect change to the existing reality.[49] In this way, anti-tales, and ecofeminist literature as a whole, are as important as on-the-ground activism. Even Atwood's scientific genius of the *Maddaddam* trilogy, Crake, tries to erase the storytelling capacity out of his new human-hybrid species – the Crakers – in his recognition of the dangerous and subversive nature of symbolism, art, and storytelling that would threaten the established order. Anti-tales, with their ability to reach large audiences, to transform nature into a space for feminists, to envision alternative societies, and to restructure the very nature of a 'rational', binary-orientated mode of thinking, contain a unique and radical 'practical magic'.

Introduction to Key Texts: Margaret Atwood's *Maddaddam* Trilogy and Michel Faber's *Under the Skin*

Canadian author Margaret Atwood has had a long and varied career that is still ongoing today, with a range of themes expanding and interconnecting across her oeuvre. Despite this diversity, it is widely acknowledged that she is among the most prominent of the fairy tale revisionists, Sharon Rose Wilson's study *Margaret Atwood's Fairy-Tale Sexual Politics* being the prime example. Wilson points out how the last two novels of the *Oryx & Crake*, *The Year of the Flood*, and *Maddaddam* trilogy, in particular, make use of 'legends, fairy-tale allusions, animal folklore,

folk remedies, sermons, stories about the saints and songs as folk allusions or intertexts'.[50] Hence, one of the main tropes is storytelling, with
this medium used to entertain and impart knowledge of the world to
the naïve human-hybrid Crakers. The scene is clearly paralleled with
attentive children sitting around a fire to hear renditions of female oral
folk tales centuries ago. Yet these are not quite fairy tales. Labudova
aptly calls them 'Toby's mock-myth sugar-coated bed-time stories'.[51]
Atwood's trilogy itself is more anti-tale than fairy tale, however, and
has been described as 'a cautionary tale about cautionary tales'.[52] It
has also been called a 'darkly satiric tale of end times', with J. Brooks
Bouson pointing out how the author 'draws on the philosophy of deep
ecology', invoking 'the type of radical environmentalism embraced by
activist green movements like *Earth First!* intent on environmental
consciousness-raising'.[53] Certainly, the books are laden with warnings
of environmental destruction. As Bennett notes, 'Despite books with
varying labels, Atwood is thematically consistent, with certain themes
evident in virtually all of her work, and these common themes have
much to do with ecofeminism'.[54]

In order to carry out an analysis of the texts, it is necessary to understand the complex plot that runs across the trilogy. Beginning with
Oryx and Crake, we follow the story of Jimmy, also known as Snowman in the present apocalyptic 'zero hour' to the Crakers – so named
after their creator.[55] Jimmy is somewhat of an anti-hero, suffering from
panic attacks and self-pity, due to his belief that he is the last survivor
following the extermination of the human race in the aftermath of the
'Waterless Flood' (a cleansing process instigated by Crake who inserted
a horrific disease into pills that were widely distributed throughout
the squalid urban districts known as the Pleebands). The narrative
flashes between Jimmy's present desolation, in which he scavenges for
resources in the ruins of old buildings and districts, and the story of
his past, in which he grew up in the privileged setting of a Compound
(reserved for the elite and upper-classes, consisting of scientists and
world-changers): 'Once upon a time, Snowman wasn't Snowman. Instead he was Jimmy. He'd been a good boy then' (17). Jimmy's mother
and father provide a symbolic manifestation of the male/artificial and
female/nature dichotomy; the former was a 'genographer' (creating unnatural animal gene splices) at the labs of OrganInc Farms – 'It wasn't
really a farm anyway, not like the farms in pictures' (25) – and, we
find out that the latter became a runaway, dissenting from her scientific position for moral reasons, hunted down and killed after being
derogatively labelled an 'ecofreak'.[56] The society of the novel does not
tolerate disobedience. Despite clever heritage, Jimmy is ridiculed by
Crake throughout his school years for his average intelligence. The two,
nevertheless, fatefully become unlikely friends over the entertainment
of extreme computer games and a horrendous online video culture:

'Executions were its tragedies, pornography was its romance' (98). One game, 'Blood and Roses', is clearly symbolic, foreshadowing the inevitable destruction of the earth:

> a trading game, along the lines of Monopoly. The Blood side played with human atrocities for the counters, atrocities on a large scale: individual rapes and murders didn't count, there had to have been a large number of people wiped out. Massacres, genocides, that sort of thing. The Roses side played with human achievements. Artworks, scientific breakthroughs, stellar works of architecture, helpful inventions. *Monuments to the soul's significance*, they were called in the game.
>
> (89–90)

The goal is to see who can obtain the most 'human achievements' by the game's conclusion, as the bargaining with achievements from the 'Rose' side could stop a 'Blood' atrocity from happening (with the Rose player losing points for failing to prevent them). The concept of a 'social mythology' is clearly a poisonous one in the world of the novel, where such games replace things like fairy tales (literature and art being relegated to an inferior status) and represent the general attitudes culturally instilled in young minds. The 'exchange rates' in the game, for example, make very clear this society's priorities:

> one *Mona Lisa* equaled Bergen-Belsen, one Armenian genocide equaled the *Ninth Symphony* plus three Great pyramids – [...] there was room for haggling. To do this you needed to know the numbers – the total number of corpses for the atrocities, the latest open-market price for the artworks; or, if the art-works had been stolen, the amount paid out by the insurance policy [...] trouble was that the Blood player usually won, but winning meant you inherited a wasteland.
>
> (90–91)

Jimmy eventually graduates from a run-down art academy only to be employed in advertising by Crake, who gains employment at the most prestigious RejoovenEssence Compound, where he works on the creation of immortality. Eventually, Crake's real plan comes to fruition. While the human race dies off, Crake ensures his own demise in killing Oryx, a child sex-slave the two saw online when they were younger but who eventually becomes Crake's girlfriend and Jimmy's lover. In an untypically romantic, fairy-tale hero gesture, Jimmy hopelessly tries to avenge his damsel's death by shooting Crake, yet this act is inevitably a fulfilment of the latter's overall scheme. Having already promised both that he would take care of the innocent and pacifist Crakers housed inside the mini-Edenic world of the Paradise dome, Jimmy becomes the reluctant Christ-like protector of Crake's 'perfect' replacement species.

Crake cleanses the world of human destructiveness, or so he believes, and achieves an immortality of sorts in the thriving of his creations. The novel concludes with Jimmy hiding behind a tree in the present, having found other human survivors but not knowing whether to shoot or greet them and creating yet another 'zero hour' – the potential of a new beginning for the human race – an outcome Crake did not bargain for (433).

The Year of the Flood runs parallel to the chronology of *Oryx and Crake*, yet, as a companion piece, it provides the opposite perspective to that of the male world inside the Compounds. Instead it focuses on the outer areas of the Pleebands that lie beyond the Compound walls. The Compounds maintain a fairy-tale-like façade, using the space beyond their borders as a wasteland or dumping ground. Bodies from murders committed by the CorpSEcorps are literally thrown into urban dumpsters, for example. Significantly, it is in this novel and *Maddaddam* that we see more clearly the effects of the damaging 'social mythology' learnt by men such as Jimmy in the first book, and the subsequent first hand impacts on women and the environment. For, as Katarina Labudova states in her essay on 'Power, Pain, and Manipulation' within the novels: 'The three protagonists, Toby, Ren and Amanda, are women. Their compassion, love and friendship [ecofeminist concepts] are in opposition to the emotional detachment of the CorpSEcorps [i.e. those who maintain the social order]'.[57] Toby in the present post-apocalyptic environment is hiding out in the AnooYoo Spa and like Jimmy we learn her story. Leading a difficult life, she is rescued by the eco-group known as the God's Gardeners, from a workplace in which she was being sexually abused by her boss who would have eventually killed her. We learn of the God's Gardeners rituals and natural lifestyle on the rooftop garden where they celebrate various saints' days (the saints being environmental activists and heroes such as Jane Goodall). Much of the book contains chapters of sermons delivered by their leader, Adam One. Ren was also a member of the Gardeners as a child, making friends with and integrating the third protagonist, the strong-willed and resourceful Amanda, into the group. However, her mother, Lucerne, fed up with lover Zeb (brother to Adam One), returns to both the Compound and husband she had initially fled, leaving Ren to find her place in the misogynistic world of the Pleebands. In the present, she is trapped in the isolation room of an upmarket sex club where she had been placed before the 'Waterless Flood' struck. Eventually freed by Amanda, the two women are then rescued, in turn, by Toby from the mentally disturbed rapists known as the Painballers (murderers that where once part of a sick social game in which convicted men could wave their prison sentence by fighting to the death in a *Hunger Games*-type arena). At Toby's confrontation of these men, Jimmy emerges from the trees, bringing the two novels together for *Maddaddam*. The very title itself suggests feminine evolutionary origins – the Edenic Adam being replaced with a play on the word madam, positing women as the ecofeminist, natural and life-giving force – builders of a new world founded on ecofeminist values – (through Oryx and Toby) as opposed to women being regarded as a sub-species born from Adam's rib and hence only sub-players in the masculine society before the fall of civilisation. The final novel details the back-to-nature lives of the Maddaddam group (made up of God's Gardeners and scientists who were exploited by Crake) as they attempt to rebuild some sort of existence alongside the Crakers and their efforts to extinguish the escaped Painballers once and for all. It is notable that Atwood uses gender in her portrayal of environmentalism: positive concepts are conveyed mainly through the environmental consciousness and spirituality of the female, Toby, and are tempered by Atwood's awareness of the fact that the wrong usage of ecotopian principles can also be extremely dangerous, as in Crake's destructive male power-trip of the 'Waterless Flood'. Another key aspect is the interspecies cooperation depicted between the humans and the human brain-tissue-enhanced pigs known as 'pigoons', who also seek revenge on the Painballers for the murder of their own kind. This blurring of the boundaries between 'human' and 'animal' is a key idea shared and developed by Faber's *Under the Skin*.

Under the Skin is marketed as a mainstream text and written by 'Dutch-born, Australian-raised, Scottish-resident', Michel Faber; this varied heritage perhaps constitutes a motivating factor in the creation of his protagonist, the alien outsider Isserley.[58] Like Atwood, Faber is a diverse author whose work cannot be neatly placed into particular categories, though critics have tended to ignore his rejection of labels.[59] Dillon asserts, for example, that, 'Despite Faber's denial [...] *Under the Skin*, with its story of an alien species farming humans on Earth for meat, is clearly science-fiction [...] metamorphosis is effected by surgery rather than by magic or accident'.[60] It is true that Isserley has been given a human body as a disguise in order to carry out her job on earth, collecting unsuspecting men in her van (they are glad of a lift from an attractive woman) for butchering, and is therefore allowed to avoid her own harsh planet. However, while the otherworldly effects in Jonathan Glazier's loose film adaptation (such as alien goo that cocoons her victims in the floor of a house) shift the story closer to science fiction aesthetics, to ignore Faber's rejection of the label is inevitably to deny the entire point of the novel. The text is much closer to an anti-tale (metamorphosis being a prominent fairy-tale trope), or myth (in that Isserley is not an alien per se, originating instead from a dark and cruel underworld called 'The Estates'), or perhaps closer again, in the notion of her original form being a talking wolf-like species, to the category of fable. Even more significant, however, is the fact that in Faber's novel, Isserley is not the 'alien', humans are. Humans are known in the story as 'vodsels'. As Dillon notes, it is a

> third-person narrative predominantly localised through the protagonist Isserley, a member of a race of what the text calls 'human beings' who come from an ecologically ravaged, strictly class-divided planet.

Members of Isserley's race, while called 'human' actually resemble physically 'a sort of cross between a cat, a dog, and a llama'.[61]

Faber's story deals with big questions, namely, what it means to be human. Blurring the boundaries between humans and animals, like Atwood, though in a much more explicit manner, Faber puts us into the shoes of an outsider in order to view our own 'humanness' from a detached vantage point. This provides an important ecofeminist discourse. Just as the meat industry in Atwood's novel uses human flesh in the Pleebands and animals are grown without organs or heads (in order to eliminate waste) in the Compounds, the unethical treatment of the 'vodsels' (humans to us), harvested in the Ablach farm of Faber's novel, raises serious questions about equality, interconnectedness, and empathy. As we shall see later in this chapter, Atwood and Faber use ecofeminist concepts to radically level any distinctions between species and thus collapse existing hierarchies. As the novel states, 'We're all the same under the skin'; whether we be a human or an animal, a man or a woman (164). This is, of course, the main idea behind the story and ultimately leads to tragedy as the protagonist becomes more and more vodsel-like, increasingly vulnerable in her sensitivity and developing consciousness – she loses the cold detachment (an instinctual and animalistic survival of the fittest mentality) that the species division and notion of difference from the vodsels provided and can, therefore, no longer do her job or remain unaffected by the cruelty around her. In addition, Isserley's sense of alienation (as an intruder on earth and as a woman in a male-dominated workplace) is eased as she discovers the beauty of the natural environment. In this way, Isserley encompasses the contemporary crisis facing us all, what ecofeminist Gaard has called

> the alienation from place-attachment that is widely shared across modern cultures. 'Mobility rules Modernity' [certainly Isserley spends the majority of her time travelling in her van ...] producing alienation and exploitation on many levels, local to global. As an anecdote about alienation, Plumwood suggests that we 'belong to the land as much as the land belongs to us', a belonging and identity that is articulated in [...] dialogical interaction.[62]

In essence, in the natural world, Isserley finds this allusive sense of belonging. While Amlis, son of the business' owner, states that 'My father would chop the planet into pieces if he thought there was profit in it' (it's no wonder that the home planet is entirely spoiled), Isserley, in the end, develops an ecofeminist sensibility and a sense of connectedness to the natural world on earth, where she delights in 'the purity of the air, the lushness of everything': 'Men and their little power games! She'd tackle these inequalities soon enough [...] Isserley was part of that landscape too' (235, 242, 259, 279).

'Strategic Essentialism': The Power of Spiritual Ecofeminism and the Magic of Female Natures

As Gaard has pointed out, ecofeminism, particularly in literature, can employ a 'strategic essentialism', utilising the woman and nature link in order to create empowering messages.[63] The anti-tales discussed in this chapter radically break with the factual forms of much ecofeminist writing and their use of magical realism is apt in conveying more of the spiritual and cultural ecofeminist concepts that depend on women's closer alignment with the environment. Atwood immediately asserts the importance of this magical realist tension in the epilogue to *Oryx and Crake*. Initially, Jonathan Swift is quoted, upholding the masculine link to rationality:

> I could perhaps like others have astonished you with strange improbable tales; but I rather chose to relate plain matter of fact in the simplest manner and style; because my principle design was to inform you, not to amuse you.
>
> (epilogue)

This is immediately subverted by a quotation from Virginia Woolf which marks the flights into feminine fantasy that will pervade the texts: 'Was there no safety? No learning by heart the ways of the world? No guide, no shelter, but all was miracle and leaping from the pinnacle of a tower into the air?' (epilogue). While Swift presents the 'Crake' half of Atwood's world, as knowable and there to be understood, Woolf captures the Oryx side, the allusive nature of life that cannot be pinned down, elements beyond the limits of rational thought. It is at the point of veering into fantasy or magic that we can perceive an ecofeminist sensibility entering the trilogy, as it marks a refreshing change in empowering women through their alignment with nature rather than the reverse. This female power is revealed through a dream of Jimmy's in the first novel:

> The field would be green, but it wasn't a pastoral scene: these were girls in danger, in need of rescue. There was something – a threatening presence – behind the trees. Or perhaps the danger was in him. Perhaps he was the danger, a fanged animal gazing out from the shadowy cave of the space inside his own skull. They could be a bait, a trap. He knew they were much older than they appeared to be, and much more powerful as well. Unlike himself they had a ruthless wisdom. The girls were calm, they were grave and ceremonious. They'd look at him, look into him, they would recognize and accept him, accept his darknesses. Then they would smile. *Oh honey, I know you. I see you. I know what you want.*
>
> (307)

Jimmy's subconscious attempts to establish the typical conventions of a fairy tale, with a beautiful 'green' backdrop and damsels in distress to convince himself that 'these were girls in danger, in need of rescue'. Yet his dream quickly twists into a nightmare, an anti-tale, in which this kind of female 'ceremony' to nature places the girls in a position of power, allowing them access, 'unlike himself', to a 'wisdom' beyond his comprehension. This image of a dangerous and powerful nature, as opposed to a passive one – 'it wasn't a pastoral scene' – is triggered by Jimmy's memories of Oryx, once a child sex slave, who holds immense power over those around her due to her allusive and 'ruthless wisdom' – she has experienced the cruelty of the world yet remains a peaceful, forgiving, and caring figure in spite of it. It is worth noting that this links with Faber's novel, in Isserley's unsettling ability to make us look into ourselves through her own developing sense of self (just as Oryx's gentle nature prompts Jimmy to question the misogynistic culture and conditioning that has transformed him into a 'fanged animal'), making us assess our cruelty both to the environment and to women. In addition, the above extract is strikingly similar to the closing scene of Glazier's film adaptation of *Under the Skin*, in which Isserley wanders in the forest, like Little Red Riding Hood, with the 'threatening presence' of the wolf, a woodsman, lurking in the trees. Cutting down the trees, this predator also pins Isserley to the ground and attempts to rape her. However, her alien self is revealed beneath her torn surface skin, causing him to retreat – she has power once again in her natural form and through the 'otherness' hidden beneath a skin of social and cultural conformity. The God's Gardeners in *The Year of the Flood* also have a hymn in *The God's Gardeners Oral Hymnbook* that reminds its followers to 'Recall [the power of] Australopithecus, | Our Animal inside' (65). Despite the fact that the woodsman sets her on fire, Isserley escapes his advances and combusts into smoke – she rises into the air in another form and becomes part of the environment. Similarly, Oryx floats like a phantom on the peripheries of Atwood's books, haunting Jimmy's dreams and appearing to him in visions (Atwood never clarifies whether these spiritual experiences are really happening or a part of Jimmy's declining mental state). Most significantly, however, in *Oryx and Crake*, Oryx comes to encapsulate the 'Mother Earth' figure of the trilogy following her teachings and work with the Crakers, while they are housed inside Crake's controlled, Edenic Paradice-Dome (a mini-ecosystem):

'She's their teacher', said Crake. 'We needed a go-between, someone who could communicate on their level. Simple concepts, no metaphysics'. 'What's she teaching?' [...] 'Botany and zoology', said Crake with a grin. 'In other words, what not to eat and what could bite. And what not to hurt'.

(363)

Following her death, Oryx takes on mythical importance for the Crakers, and they believe she is a powerful goddess or deity watching over them and the animals, which they call 'The Children of Oryx'. Hence, she is immortalised through myth, as is her nurturing and forgiving – 'what not to hurt' – ecofeminist ethic which lives on through Toby's stories. Hence, the pile of bones – a murky mixture of the remains of the title characters – symbolises the blend of realist 'rationality' (represented by Crake) and the fantastical elements (represented by Oryx). This suggests that, in spite of Crake's destruction, Oryx filters in a glimmer of hope that society can be rebuilt from the rubble on a better, and ecofeminist, framework.

While Oryx's representation harkens back to the powerful goddess traditions celebrated by ecofeminists, and represents a 'Mother Earth'-type figure, it is actually Toby who is most clearly aligned with spiritual ecofeminism. The obvious religious link to nature in the trilogy of course resides with the God's Gardeners headed by Adam One. However, ecofeminist spiritualisms are a complete alternative to male-dominated and patriarchal religions, and it is Toby who is the main exponent of a feminine and nature-based spirituality, introduced in *The Year of the Flood*: 'Toby wasn't much for standard religion [...] Nevertheless, Toby had whispered a short prayer over the patio stones: *Earth to earth*. Then she'd brushed sand into the cracks' (33). It is worth noting here how Atwood also provides a telling contrast through Zeb's father, 'The Rev', with his exploitative religion, the 'Church of PetrOleum', which worships the sacredness of oil (stretching readings of the Bible to place it at the heart of God's teachings), and rallies against the 'ecofreaks' who rebel against his exploitation of this natural resource.[64] Even Crake, as shown in the first novel, despite his endeavour to delete human destructive impulses to prevent the ruination of the earth, also sees nature as secondary to man; unlike the female characters, it has no great spiritual significance to him: '"Nature and God". "I thought you didn't believe in God", said Jimmy. "I don't believe in nature either", said Crake. "Or not with a capital N"' (242). In reality, both Crake's attitude and the Rev's religion are the epitome of the male use of the environment as a resource to be exploited (mirroring the Rev's attitude and violence towards women, in both the murder of his wife and his fetish for violent online female beheadings). The Rev steals money from his parishioners and gets rewards from oil companies for his promotion of the industry. In contrast, although nature is also at the heart of Toby's spirituality and feminine magic, it is founded upon a deep respect for its power: in *Year of the Flood*, we are told, 'Nature full strength is more than we can take' (392). As Shannon Hengen notes, 'Not considered a spiritual writer, Atwood nevertheless points towards the soul as a repository of important values, among them a sense of awe at nature's power'.[65] These teachings at the root of Toby's beliefs have been passed on to her from an elderly Gardener, 'old walnut-faced Pilar', with a special interest in botanicals: 'bees and mushrooms – these were Pilar's specialties' (in this regard Pilar is reminiscent of women who were slain as witches for believing in the great 'Medicine Cabinet of Nature') (118, 193). Pilar and Toby's relationship encapsulates theories of female traditions and community, and, by extension, the passing on of literary stories and myths from generation to generation: '"Thank you for all you've taught me", said Toby [...] "Thank you for learning", said Pilar' (215). Toby, in turn, becomes a mentor to the younger women when they need help. It is also relevant that Atwood uses a fairy-tale metaphor, placing Toby in the role of mother sending Ren on her way, equipped with a 'basket' of protection, a symbol of her newly acquired knowledge:

> She [Toby] gave me a basket of AnooYoo products to deliver, as an excuse in case anyone stopped the van and asked where I was going [...] so I had to put on my pink AnooYoo top-to-toe over my work smock and cotton pants and go off with my pink basket, like Little Pink Riding Hood.
>
> (358)

The excessive repetition of the colour pink heightening the sense of it being a female community. In this way, Pilar also resembles one of the elderly female folk storytellers from centuries ago with her 'fund of bee lore'. Pilar teaches Toby her 'magic' and healing remedies, emphasising that it is the power of a female, a Queen bee, that holds a hive together, also explaining that the bees are messengers between this world and the afterlife (132). This emphasises, once again, the ecofeminist subversion of masculine, scientific thought through the creation of a murky borderline. As Toby asks, 'how to distinguish between such illusions and the real thing?':

> Bees and mushrooms went together, said Pilar: the bees were on good terms with the unseen world, being the messengers to the dead. She tossed that crazed little factoid off as if it was something everyone knew [...] Mushrooms were the roses in the garden of that unseen world, because the real mushroom plant was underground. The part you see – what most people called a mushroom – was just a brief apparition. A cloud flower.
>
> (17, 120)

Even after Pilar's death, when Toby delivers the news to the bees, Atwood reveals this fragile border between the realms of fantasy and reality: '"Bees", she said. "I bring news. You must tell your Queen". Were they listening? Perhaps. They were nibbling gently at the edges of her dried tears. For the salt, a scientist would say' (216). Toby uses Pilar's 'magic' to contact her for advice in *Maddaddam*, by drinking an elixir (once again blurring the lines between fact and fiction) and visiting the elderberry tree planted on Pilar's burial place:

> She gazes at the clustered flowers, thinks, *Pilar.* The wizened old face, the brown hands, the gentle smile. All so real once. Gone to ground. *I know you're here, in your new body. I need your help. Amanda. Will she die, will this baby kill her? What should I do?* [...] *Send me a message. A signal* [...] 'Watch it', says the voice of Zeb. 'Stay still. Look slowly. To the left'. Toby turns her head. Crossing the path, within a stone-throw, there's one of the giant pigs. A sow, with farrow: five little piglets all in a row [...] 'Don't shoot', says Toby [...] Her heart's becalmed [...] Life, life, life, life, life. Full to bursting, this minute. Second. Millisecond. Millenium. Eon [...] You've had your vision.
>
> (222–223)

Just like Oryx, Pilar communicates here through animals in what Toby refers to as 'a mystical quasi-religious experience'; the five little piglets appear to suggest that Amanda's childbearing will be safe or is, at least, all part of a larger natural process, causing Toby to feel 'becalmed' (227). The repetition of 'life, life, life, life, life' and the awareness of the overwhelming power of nature, even in a single 'millisecond' or 'eon' also reminds Toby of her own strength in her connection to it. In *Year of the Flood*, Toby reflects that

> Nature full strength is more than we can take, Adam One used to say. It's a potent hallucinogen, a soporific, for the untrained Soul. We're no longer at home in it. We need to dilute it. We can't drink it straight.
>
> (392)

And yet, pure nature is exactly where Toby finds her home and her soul revels here in its undiluted glory: 'Toby breathed herself in. Her new self. Her skin smelled like honey and salt. And earth' (121).

Similarly, in *Under the Skin*, Isserley, 'trapped in a cage of her own bone and muscle' after the surgery to give her a human, or in the case of the novel, a 'vodsel', body, rediscovers her sense of self (buried beneath her cultured disguise) by 'drinking in the beauty of the great uncovered world' (143, 61). Nature has the power to rejuvenate her and like magic it releases her crippled body from its shell of pain. Going out onto a cliff near the beach to do her exercises (necessary to keep her new body functional),

> she assumed the correct positions, extending her arms towards the silvery horizon [...] then, finally, reaching up to the stars. After a long time repeating these actions over and over, she achieved a state of half-consciousness, mesmerised by the moon and the monotony, and

persisted far longer than usual, becoming so limber in the end that her movements became graceful and fluid. She might have been dancing.
(150–151)

While there is nothing fantastical about Isserley's experiences in nature, they are just as spiritual and deep as those experienced by Atwood's characters. Just as Toby goes through 'vigils' where she drinks a concoction of natural ingredients that opens her mind, Isserley's connection to the universe is strong here and she drifts into a semi-conscious and meditative state. Ironically, this is partly achieved through her body and its physical interactions with the environment around her. No longer trapped by it, she begins to formulate a new sense of self. Isserley's link to the beauty of the natural environment is perceived by Amlis who is equally as awed with the beauty of the earth in comparison to his polluted home planet:

It would be very easy to get seduced by this world, Amlis had said, when he touched her arm. It's very, very beautiful. What had he meant? Could he have been meaning to imply that *she* was beautiful, too? Why else would he have touched her at that moment? [...] But no, of course he hadn't meant that. He was seeing an ocean and a snowy sky for the first time, with a mutilated cripple sweating next to him. The charms of her scarred flesh could hardly compete with a naked new world, could they?
(284)

Amlis recognises that Isserley's real inner, natural self is as beautiful as the landscape she so deeply connects with. He also seems to perceive this connection and beauty as an inherent spiritual 'goodness' or moral compass: '"Take care of yourself", he muttered, lowering himself out of the car onto the white ground. "There's a voice inside you. Listen to what it says"' (246). Faber hints at this earlier in the novel too: 'She liked sheep more than any other animal; they had an innocence and a serene intentness about them that was worlds away from the brutish cunning and manic excitability of, say, vodsels'; Isserley shares this innocence and lack of hardened social conditioning and, together with the sheep, 'seen in poor light, they could almost be human children' (150). The power of nature is a strength Amlis sees inside of Isserley too: 'Nothing that happened on the ground could ever compete with the grandeur of what happened above. Amlis had glimpsed this, had stolen an incredulous look at the sky for a few hours, and then had to let it go' (260). Certainly, like Toby, Isserley also recognises and feels the power of nature,

The variety of shapes, colours and textures under her feet was, she believed, literally infinite. It must be. Each shell, each pebble, each

stone had been made what it was by aeons of submarine or subgla-
cial massage. The indiscriminate, eternal devotion of nature to its
numberless particles had an emotional importance for Isserley; it put
the unfairness of life into perspective.

(61)

The use of 'indiscriminate' is extremely important here: as an acting
'vodsel' and, moreover, a female one, she faces discrimination and unfair
treatment at the hands of men (from those she collects in her van, who
make blatant sexual advances, misogynistic remarks, and even attempt
rape, to those she works for; as the only female, she is a commodity
and source of humour). Luckily, like Toby, Isserley also finds comfort
in nature, and it comes to her aid. While she faces the uncomfortable
sexism of one of her hitchers – '"Sex", he explained flatly [...] "On the
brain. I can spot it a mile off. You love it, don't you?" [...] "Actually,
I'm always working too hard to think about it" [...] "Bullshit"' – the
religious rhetoric used to describe her response illustrates the universe's
significance for her: 'the universe at last seemed to have heard her prayer.
The hitcher's eyes narrowed, then shut in what might have been slumber'
(179–180). Most significant, however, is the ending of Faber's novel in
which Isserley crashes her car and is trapped. Unable to stop a woman
from going to get help, she must eliminate all traces of herself. Although
tragic, unlike Glazier's conclusion to the film, Isserley is in charge of her
demise here and she also achieves a spiritual transcendence. Whereas
she recognised earlier in the novel that 'What went on inside houses –
mere specks under the vast sky – was insignificant' and 'Nothing that
happened on the ground could ever compete with the grandeur of what
happened above', on the level of the entire universe Isserley recognises
the interconnectedness of all things and literally becomes part of that
higher plain (260). She lives on in the air, in particles, as a part of the
landscape she loved so much; no longer an outsider, but part of the grand
design, she has found where she belongs and trusts in the connection she
has established to that space:

> The aviir would blow her car, herself, and a generous scoop of earth
> into the smallest conceivable particles. The explosion would leave
> a crater in the ground as big and deep as if a meteorite had fallen
> there.
>   And she? Where would she go?
>   The atoms that had been herself would mingle with the oxygen
> and nitrogen in the air. Instead of ending up buried in the ground,
> she would become part of the sky: that was the way to look at it.
> Her invisible remains would combine, over time, with all the won-
> ders under the sun. When it snowed she would be a part of it, falling

softly to earth, rising up again with the snow's evaporation [...] She would help wreathe the fields in mists, and yet would always be transparent to the stars. She would live forever. All it took was the courage to press one button, and the faith that the connection had not been broken.

She reached forward a trembling hand.

'Here I come', she said.

(295–296)

Isserley reaches a state where her gender, species, and class no longer matter, a space where everything is equal, interconnected, and has its own small but essential part in the workings of the universe.

Hence, nature in these anti-tales comes to the aid of the female characters in the form of a comforting and empowering spirituality, as a kind of magic, and sometimes literally (the bees swarming Toby's abuser Blanco when he tries to kill her). This mixture of more fantastical ecofeminist ideas in Atwood's trilogy and the more practical or realist approach in *Under the Skin*, highlights, in the words of Jeffrey A. Lockwood, that

Ecofeminists do not reject reason; they simply and convincingly advocate balance. They call for us to be fully human by attending to all of our being – feeling as well as thinking. And they understand that there is a place for passion, that even moderation must be moderated.[66]

As an example, in *Maddaddam*, Toby rationally explains her vision to Zeb, holding its spiritual qualities up alongside a more scientific explanation:

I was communicating with my inner Pilar, which was externalized in visible form, connected with the help of a brain chemistry facilitator to the wavelengths of the Universe; a universe in which – rightly understood – there are no coincidences. And just because a sensory impression may be said to be 'caused' by an ingested mix of psycho-active substances does not mean it is an illusion. Doors are opened with keys, but does that mean that the things revealed when the doors are opened aren't there?

(227–228)

Hence, even imaginative events can motivate actions and responses in real time. It is the blend of cultural ecofeminism and rationalist ecofeminism discussed earlier – dialectical ecofeminism – that these texts try to maintain. They play around with nature in interesting ways, yet at their hearts is an impulse to motivate real and lasting social change.

In the anti-tales I discuss here, ecofeminist subversion is achieved through what Alaimo describes as the use of 'postmodern natures' (158). Nature in these texts, as we have seen, is not just

> an unchanging backdrop against which history plays out its drama, but an actor in its own right [...] nature becomes 'social' [...] Indeed, nature can speak back to culture not only shaping but helping to generate the stories we tell [...] I would characterize this depiction of the land as postmodern precisely because it is 'muddied' by history and politics. 'Nature' here – if it can even be termed that – is, in Haraway's terms, 'effected in the interactions among material-semiotic actors, human and not'.
>
> (158, 159, 161)

In essence, the patriarchal 'nature versus culture' divide is broken down by ecofeminist texts, with both the authors and characters interacting with, and shaping, nature to suit their messages and ideologies – nature becomes a part of culture; shaped through, and shaping, texts.[67] According to Alaimo, this concept of 'Playing nature allows feminist [writers] to shift the discursive terrain of nature and the natural, opening up spaces for feminist articulations' and to '"play nature" as a mode of cultural critique' (170–171). Texts can link women to nature without retaining women's separation from cultural life – instead the texts oscillate between culture and nature in a more balanced manner, bringing women back into a cultural discourse from which they have often been excluded. In this way, Atwood and Faber show their characters' powerful engagements with nature both in a spiritual sense and also through a feminine empathy, as illustrated above. However, one important female power remains: the anti-tales also emphasise how the characters can return to nature, go back to basics, a blank canvas, and shape a better culture than the current patriarchy with the perpetuation of ecofeminist ideologies through the 'magic' of storytelling.

Evolutionary Storytelling

Significantly, as Bennett states, 'oral traditions are a part of ecofeminism as well [...] myths can help to create and exaggerate the power of spiritual women, women who may just be more in touch with themselves and their environment'.[68] Certainly, Toby becomes 'the kindly godmother' figure and takes charge of storytelling for the Crakers in *Maddaddam* (11). She notes how the oral tradition is important in itself as a social event: 'It seems to be a ritual [...] They already know the story, but the important thing seems to be that Toby must tell it' (39, 45). Like old women narrating to children around a fireside centuries ago, Toby's interactions with the Crakers harken back to, and remind readers of, this obscured and skilful female art form; one in which the stories are constantly shaped and retold through the addition of other voices in a collective effort:

> Once Toby has made her way through the story, they urge her to tell it again, then again. They prompt, they interrupt, they fill in the parts she's missed. What they want from her is a seamless performance, as well as more information than she either knows or can invent.
>
> (45)

As Jack Zipes has pointed out, fairy tales and folk stories were once used as a means of voicing the communal concerns of primitive peoples and 'their wish to satisfy their wants and needs'.[69] Fairy tales, then, are at the heart of the tradition Toby passes on. One of the ex-scientists, Manatee, also signifies that these enchanting stories are a specifically female tradition within the narrative – one passed from Oryx to Toby (no coincidence that they are the two spiritual ecofeminists of the trilogy), with Donald Haase pointing out how the collective female voice in oral storytelling has historically marked 'women's ownership of the genre'[70]: 'Tell them a happy story [...] Vague on the details. Crake's girlfriend, Oryx, used to do that sort of thing in Paradice, it kept them placid' (44). Yet, far from keeping them placid, in the first novel, Crake himself feared art's subversive power and knew that it could corrupt his obedient and passive species, and potentially create a rebellious streak: '*Watch out for art*, Crake used to say. *As soon as they start doing art, we're in trouble.* Symbolic thinking of any kind would signal downfall' (419–420). Even Toby frets about the impressionable nature of the Crakers – 'They must have listened more carefully than she'd thought last night' – and does not take lightly the power of her own storytelling to effect change:

> Now what have I done? She thinks. What can of worms have I opened? They're so quick, these children: they'll pick this up and transmit it to all the others. What comes next? Rules, dogmas, laws? The Testament of Crake? How soon before there are ancient texts they feel they have to obey but have forgotten to interpret? Have I ruined them?
>
> (36, 204)

Similarly, in the recent Hollywood blockbuster *Into the Woods*, the concluding song warns:

> Careful the spell you cast,
> Not just on children,
> Sometimes the spell may last,
> Past what you can see
> And turn against you.

Careful the tale you tell,
That is the spell,
Children will listen.[71]

These anti-tales thus highlight the conditioning power of fairy tales and the problematic ideologies instilled in children through the dominant patriarchal literary versions perpetuated by those such as the Grimms and Charles Perrault. And yet, they also point out the possibility for rejecting and rewriting the tales in order to offer alternative ideologies built upon feminist and ecofeminist principles. As Elizabeth Waning Harries has pointed out, 'Fairy tales provide scripts for living, but they can also inspire resistance to those scripts and, in turn, to other apparently predetermined patterns'.[72] As Susan Sellers argues,

> For Marina Warner, fairy tale is an inherently feminist genre [...]
> They imagine what might lie ahead and they suggest ways of proceeding: their happy endings are promises or prophecies rather than accomplished conclusions [...] the enchantments of the tales act as camouflage, wrapping brilliantly seductive images round the harsh truths or daring utterances they speak.[73]

Jimmy captures this radical potential for shaping societies through the stories early on in *Oryx and Crake*, though his brief storytelling escapade is much more careless and unthinking than that taken up by the women in the story: 'These people were like blank pages, he could write whatever he wanted on them' (407). The language here is extremely telling. While Jimmy sees himself as the active and powerful agent imposing his own ideologies on the minds of the Crakers, Toby equips them with storytelling and writing capabilities in order to allow them to think for themselves and create their own thoughts and meaning. This is most clearly illustrated in *Maddaddam* through Blackbeard, a young Craker child, who Toby eventually teaches to write. Excited from spelling out his name on a piece of paper, and having given it to one of the Maddaddamites who reads it aloud to him, Blackbeard delights in his newfound magical power: '"It said my name! It told my name to Ren!" "There", she says. "That is *writing*". Blackbeard nods: now he's grasping the possibilities' (203). It is also through Blackbeard that the radical potential of writing as a 'weapon' is foregrounded towards the trilogy's conclusion. While the group are gathering up supplies and sprayguns in preparation for the final battle, 'Blackbeard marches into Toby's cubicle. "I will bring the writing", he says importantly. "And the pen. I will bring those, for us to have there"' (277).

Hence, storytelling is a valuable ecofeminist weapon in Atwood's trilogy. Yet it is not just the natural aspects of the oral tradition, with its ancient roots, that links storytelling to ecofeminist discourses. In the trilogy, Atwood also ties storytelling to nature through the body, and, more specifically, the female body. For example, Toby's reflection on how she should answer Blackbeard's enquiry into why she cannot have children is extremely telling:

> She's about to add, 'I have scars inside me', but she stops herself. *What is a scar, Oh Toby?* That would be the next question. Then she'd have to explain what a scar is. *A scar is like writing on your body. It tells about something that once happened to you, such as a cut on your skin where blood came out. What is writing, Oh Toby? Writing is when you make marks on a piece of paper – on a stone – on a flat surface, like the sand on the beach, and each of the marks means a sound, and the sounds joined together mean a word, and the words joined together mean ... How do you make this writing, Oh Toby? [...] Once you made it with a pen or a pencil, a pencil is a ... Or you make it with a stick. Oh Toby, I do not understand. You make a mark with a stick on your skin, you cut your skin open and then it is a scar, and the scar turns into a voice? It speaks, it tells us things? [...]* No, she should stay away from the whole business. Otherwise she might inspire the Crakers to start carving themselves up to see if they can let out the voices.
>
> (91–92)

Toby's barren state is related to the necessity of selling her eggs in order to survive during her most desperate times, as related in *The Year of the Flood*. In essence, the patriarchal society of the novel has robbed her of this sacred and natural female expression, leaving only a silent scar. Yet this scar, this piece of writing on Toby's body, is as radical as her own journal records and stories. Just as she records the lives of those around her – such as the heroic tales of her lover in 'The Story of When Zeb was Lost in the Mountains and Ate the Bear' for example – her body is a text that records the brutality of a patriarchal culture that failed both her and the scarred environment she worships. Therefore, the scar does indeed 'turn into a voice'; a feminist one. It is a permanent impression of the wrongs committed by a male-orientated culture. Furthermore, child-bearing has often been considered a creative act and, in the third novel, Atwood exploits this link. It is worth noting here that Zipes also uses the evolutionary theories of Dawkins and links them to the fairy tale genre as 'cultural memes', highlighting that they are an integral part of both natural and biological life:

> Just as genes propagate themselves in the gene pool by leaping from body to body via sperms or eggs, so memes propagate themselves in the meme pool by leaping from brain to brain via a process which, in the broad sense can be called imitation.[74]

Certainly, Toby passes on her stories to Blackbeard (her surrogate child) who then continues an 'imitation' of her storytelling process to his own species following her death in the final chapter of *Maddaddam* titled 'Book':

> Toby cannot tell the story tonight [...] So now I will try to tell this story to you. I will tell it in the right way if I can [...] Now this is the book that Toby made when she lived among us. See I am showing you [...] And when I speak these words out loud, you too are hearing Toby's voice.
>
> (357, 385)

Instead of a bible that lays down dogmas and strictures to be obeyed, the Crakers inherit Toby's ecofeminist journal, full of God's Gardeners ideas and chunks of her own spirituality. They have here the foundations for kinder and more inclusive ideologies. Even the birth of three human-Craker hybrid babies at the trilogy's conclusion highlights the beginning of a new chapter – a hyphen between the past and the present (like the hybrid anti-tale form) – and parallels the survival of both the stories and those subjects they allow to live on in their pages. The births and the stories are linked then, as radical female creations that signify change: 'And these new words I made are called The Story of Toby [...] Swift Fox said that if it was a girl baby it would be named Toby. And that is a thing of hope' (387, 390). As Hengen reflects on Atwood's third novel,

> Storytelling, getting the story right, becomes another of our most basic human needs [...] The most natural version of the self must be discovered under layers of culture [just as Isserley connects with the natural world in order to remind her of her real self under the skin] and then the split halves are rejoined in these tales.

Storytelling, then, is necessary in this new world where the space is a back-to-nature blank canvas waiting for the new human-Craker hybrid species to negotiate their own identities and employ better ways of treating the world they've inherited, in contrast to their belated human ancestors.[75] J. Brooks Bouson points out this dual aspect of storytelling – the intertwined nature of selfhood and the environment, where one has a direct effect on the other:

> literature has the potential to help us 'return to the ego' within the 'eco', which is something we need to do in order to 'address the crisis of the imagination' evident in our current environmental crisis. Atwood may offer some comfort to readers as she suggests that storytelling will survive in the culture of the Crakers. But *Maddaddam* ultimately chills us, offering as it does cold comfort to those who would wish for a more hopeful sign that, if the radical

environmentalists are right, humanity itself will somehow survive the coming eco-apocalypse as will the 'ego' within the 'eco' and the 'ego' within 'eco-literature'.[76]

While the human society before the 'Waterless Flood' encapsulated a widespread crisis of identity (literally enacted through the many characters who have multiple personas crafted in the black-market of the Pleebands), where humans lost touch with themselves and thus, in turn, lost their connection to the natural world, Toby's storytelling passes on an ecofeminist search for selfhood in the Crakers, and it is a search that embraces nature as the guiding force on this journey. The survivors gain an understanding of themselves and the environment they live in through the tales, while also shaping and adapting them in order to effect change. As Bennet states, 'Atwood suggests that all people crave a mythology, a belief system that helps them understand their place in the web of life'[77] and the final 'zero hour', in the words of Labudova, 'can be seen as a time to start the redefinition and rewriting of humanity'.[78]

Weaving an Interconnected Web of Equality

Ecofeminism uses the metaphor of the 'web' extensively in its perpetuation of equality. As Gaard and Murphy assert, 'Life on earth is an interconnected web, not a hierarchy'.[79] This philosophy is illustrated in the very form of Atwood's trilogy that, like *Into the Woods*, weaves both the first-person stories of individual characters and the third-person overarching perspective together in order to create a complex tapestry of voices from different areas of the social, gender, and even species spectrum. The actions of characters in the trilogy (and in *Into the Woods*) directly affect the outcome of one another's journeys, with each action having a domino effect in triggering different parts of the overall narrative. This reflects the ecofeminist tenet outlined by Bennett, the belief in the 'interconnectedness of all things: what happens in one part of the world, or in one life, will eventually affect others in the way that all threads reverberate from movement at any spot in a web'.[80] Hengen also highlights this as an important part of Atwood's environmentalism as 'The human heart also figures significantly throughout her work, as do instinctual drives. Human nature is made as much of reverence and compassion, and a capacity to forgive' (illustrated in Toby's refusal to kill the Painballers herself as it contrasts with her gentle ecofeminist spirituality) 'as of lust, greed, arrogance and cruelty' (embodied in Crake's destructive impulses and the treatment of the vodsels by the employees of Vess Incorporated in Faber's novel): 'to deny any part is to lessen the whole. As whole creatures we both affect and are affected by the larger environment in which we evolve, and her work asks us to bear that interconnectedness firmly in mind'.[81] Embracing the theory of the web, these anti-tales stress that no life is more or less important than the next, bringing us to the breakdown of the human/animal duality. This is a central tenant in both Atwood's trilogy and *Under the Skin* and inevitably gestures towards, and has reverberations for, a web of oppressions, including racial, gender, and class equality. Importantly, as Gaard states, in this endeavour of breaking down constructed hierarchies, 'Ecofeminists [also] strive to evolve structures that respect difference without universalizing'.[82]

One key idea shared by both Faber's and Atwood's anti-tales is the depiction of the meat industry. Vegetarianism is a dominant trait among ecofeminists who recognise the problematic symbolism that surrounds eating meat. Bouson points out how, like Angela Carter, Atwood's insights into 'the gruesome world of human cruelty and sexual predator-prey' dynamics illustrate 'how the strong not only "abuse" but also "meatify" the weak' – a concept inherent in the title of Atwood's novel *The Edible Woman*.[83] The meat industries in both texts link the oppression of women and animals, embodied in Carol J. Adams' *The Sexual Politics of Meat: A Feminist-Vegetarian Critical Theory*, in which she stresses how the two are linked to meat both literally and figuratively 'in the language and images of our patriarchal culture'.[84] Toby's employment at 'SecretBurgers' illustrates these ideas. Not only dealing in low-quality meat, the boss, Blanco, uses it as his own type of sexual consumption, using and then butchering female employees ('the SecretBurgers meatbunnies') once he tires of them. Even his language, when he tries to kill Toby for escaping in *The Year of the Flood*, blatantly highlights this link, 'You're meat!' (303). It is no coincidence that Toby is rescued from this job by the God's Gardeners who stress in their teachings that 'Animals are not senseless matter, not mere chunks of meat [...] *Beware of Man, and his evil heart*' (109). Just like the labs in Atwood's novels (including OrganInc Farms), in which animals are grown without heads or limbs in order to be of prime economical value, the 'vodsels' (humans in our sense) are prepared and butchered at Albach farm in Faber's novel. They are given steroids that leave them unable to move due to the constrictions of their bulky flesh. All features are hidden in the mass of meat,

> Monthling vodsels, with their quarter-tonne of stiff flesh, were not so sprightly [...] It had the typical look of a monthling, its shaved nub of a head nestled like a bud atop the disproportionately massive body [...] Its mouth opened wide to show its cored molars and the docked stub of its tongue. 'Ng-ng-ng-ng-gh!' it cried. Esswis shot it in the forehead.
>
> (98, 100)

It is only when Isserley is simultaneously treated like a lump of meat by one of the hitchers who attempts to rape her that she begins to identify with this oppression, plunging her into a deep crisis of identity as she reassesses the human and animal division. Staring at one of her potential victims, she recognises 'there was something deceptively human about it, which tempted her, not for the first time, to reach across the species divide and communicate' (63).

This introduces a major aspect in the challenge to patriarchal dualisms, namely the animal/human divide, through the use of language. Just as language has been used to define and confine women, it has also been used as a means for man to mark his superiority over the nonhuman world. As Carey Wolfe states:

> In the philosophical tradition questions of the relationship between humans, animals, and the problem of ethics have turned decisively on the problem of cognition and, even more specifically in the modern and postmodern period, on the capacity for language. It would be overly simple, but not wrong, to say that the basic formula here has been: no language, no subjectivity. This equation has in turn traditionally laid to rest, more or less, the question of our ethical obligation to creatures who, because they lack language, lack the ability to 'respond' ... in a two-way exchange that is crucial to the ethical relationship.[85]

In essence, the divide between the species is maintained by the ability to communicate through language, and yet this is simply a patriarchal notion that there is one dominant and superior discourse, denying any other modes of expression. Jimmy's pathetic utterances of random phrases and words also highlight his desperate attempt to maintain a sense of superiority over the Crakers. Just as Toby's tales provide her own feminine mode of expression, which she passes on to the human-animal spliced Crakers, the two novelists foreground the 'other' voices in their pages and emphasise that they can indeed communicate in various 'languages'. Animals communicate in an ecofeminist way through dreams to the Gardeners and the pigoons communicate with both the humans and the Crakers through grunts and gestures (Blackbeard's Craker sensitivity allows him to translate this 'language', pointing out that the pigoons are indeed 'speaking' to them). In *Maddaddam*, Toby comes to an abrupt recognition when she asks Blackbeard, '"Why are they talking to you?" Oh, she thinks. Of course. We're too stupid, we don't understand their languages. So there has to be a translator' (270). Toby thus uses her storytelling mode to convey this message in 'The Story of the Two Eggs', subverting also the authority of Crake as the ultimate patriarch who deliberately denied his species the symbolic aspects of language and understanding in order to keep them placid. Toby uses a metaphor, explaining that once the Crakers hatched out of their egg they were hungry and ate up all the words spilt from the second one:

> And Crake thought that you had eaten all the words, so there were none left over for the animals, and that was why they could not

speak. But he was wrong about that. Crake was not always right about everything. Because when he was not looking, some of the words fell out [...] And none of the people saw them. But the animals and the birds and the fish did see them, and ate them up. They were a different kind of word, so it was sometimes hard for people to understand the animals. They had chewed the words up too small.

(290)

In this way, Toby uses her own style of language while granting power to the language of similarly oppressed entities who have also been dismissed and misunderstood.

Even Faber's renaming of humans as vodsels and of Isserley's animal-like species as humans is extremely subversive in

> drawing attention to how the difference between human animals and nonhuman animals is not one of possession *of* language, but one created *by* language [...] In a defiant literary act of renaming, Faber removes this authority from humankind, linguistically placing us back in the ranks of animals over which we have, for so long, practiced linguistic and thus actual domination.[86]

Isserley desperately tries to keep her 'human' status despite having sacrificed her natural body for a 'vodsel' one and she feels the painful discrimination of her own species now she is 'other', along with the additional hardships she faces as a female. Trying to create some kind of power for herself, she aims to convince Amlis of her superiority over the vodsels, hiding from him that they do indeed have a language. This is apparent in a powerful scene where he asks her to translate the word a vodsel is communicating to him:

> Isserley watched, disturbed as the vodsel scrawled a five-letter word with great deliberation [...] on the other side of the mesh.
> 'No-one told me they had a language', marveled Amlis, too impressed, it seemed, to be angry. 'My father always describes them as vegetables on legs'.
> 'It depends on what you classify as language, I guess', said Isserley dismissively.
> [...]
> 'But what does it mean?' persisted Amlis.
> Isserley considered the message, which was M E R C Y.
> [...]
> She considered trying to pronounce the strange word with a contortion of her lips and a frown on her brow, as if she were being asked to reproduce a chicken's cackle or a cow's moo.
> [...]

'It's a scratch mark that means something to vodsels, obviously. I couldn't tell you what it means'.

She looked straight into Amlis's eyes, to add the power of conviction to her denial.

'Well, I can guess what it means', he observed quietly.

(171–172)

Unfortunately, Isserley also comes to recognise the meaning of the word as she tries to communicate to the opposite species herself when she becomes the victim of attempted rape:

> Desperately she searched for the right word, the word that might make him stop. It was a word she knew, but had only ever seen written – in fact, only this morning, a vodsel had spelled it out. She'd never heard it spoken. 'Murky', she pleaded.
>
> (186)

Once again the oppression of animals is linked to Isserley's treatment as a woman; both are subordinate groups connected in their strivings for equality.

'Is it always "or"?/ Is it never "and"?': Challenging 'Maleficent' Binaries and Damaging Dualities

As Villanueva Gardner surmises:

> A key feature of this conceptual framework [of the subordination of women and nature] is the dualistic classification of reality, with the disjuncts not only being seen as oppositional and exclusive (mind/ body, man/woman, human/nature), but as organized on [...] a spatial metaphor (up/down) with a lesser value attributed to the lower. Thus, body, woman, and nature are put 'down' or given a lesser value. Furthermore, the assumption is that the perceived moral superiority of one group over the other justifies the oppression of the 'inferior' group.[87]

Patriarchy, then, is founded upon this binary system and dualistic structure which legitimises the exploitation of those considered to be the subordinate half of the dualism – men over women for example. It is apt then that the fairy tale (the ultimate disseminator of this dualistic ideology) is challenged from ecofeminist perspectives in the morally ambiguous nature of anti-tale texts. As Eisfeld points out,

> The fairy tale world is a metaphor for a world that can be painted in black and white. Everything is good or evil, poor or wealthy and so

forth and there seems to be nothing in between. In the end the good will be sufficiently rewarded and the evil punished.[88]

Even categories of womanhood have been historically divided into a dualistic structure, as evidenced by the angel and monster dichotomy of the Victorian era. Sandra Gilbert and Susan Gubar outline the dangers of these ideologies in *The Madwoman in the Attic*: 'while male writers traditionally praise the simplicity of the dove, they invariably castigate the cunning of the serpent'.[89] Ecofeminism challenges this very framework in order to perpetuate the principles of equality and interconnectedness among all things. It is apt then that, as Merja Makinen points out, '"Nature" is not fixed but fluid within fiction' – subverting any attempt at neat categorisations.[90] While Labudova notes that Atwood's trilogy 'transgresses not only the opposition of rural/urban spaces but simultaneously also genre boundaries, human/alien, human/animal, nature/nurture and nature/culture oppositions', and *Under the Skin* clearly does the same, this section will discuss the ecofeminist subversion of dualisms in the Disney films *Maleficent* (2014), directed by Robert Stromberg, and *Into the Woods* (2015), directed by Rob Marshall.[91]

I want to take a moment to note that this section will also illustrate how these ecofeminist ideas are moving beyond literary anti-tales into popular culture and, in this case, into children's films. As feminist critics Elizabeth Bell, Lynda Haas, and Laura Sells state,

> Disney successfully invites mass audiences to set aside critical faculties. Indeed, because we too are admiring fans who look forward to each new film release or theme park addition, the naturalised Disney text suggests that we as cultural critics should recognise and ask questions about our own pleasures and participation in Disney film.[92]

Hence, I believe it is important to include these works within this study in order to critically assess the extent of Disney's renewed contribution to the anti-tale genre. For, although Zipes has pointed out how Disney has seized the fairy tale from the line of traditional patriarchal literary predecessors – namely Charles Perrault and the Grimms – it is clear that Disney is now attempting to follow the anti-tale impulse of subverting conventional fairy-tale expectations. Although this is no doubt fuelled predominantly by the financial impetus of the company in its exploitation of what is currently on trend, recent films such as *Frozen*, *Maleficent*, *Into the Woods*, and *Alice Through the Looking Glass*, I would argue, genuinely challenge the accepted ideologies of patriarchal fairy tales enough to be given anti-tale status. However, while numerous fairy tale scholars are currently focusing on the fairy tale genre's evolution into film and television mediums, foregrounding their highly successful subversions of the fairy tale, I am fully aware that conservatism still creeps into Disney's oeuvre, which tends to adopt quite conventional cinematic techniques rather than being radically experimental in form.[93] Yet, as McAra and Calvin noted, the anti-tale is like a subversive shadow of the fairy tale, and it is this simultaneous clash between the traditional fairy tale's ideologies and the anti-tale disenchantment that provides the subversive edge. This is particularly pertinent due to the fact that Disney is renowned for its conventionally sanitised and enchanted productions, hence the dark and gritty subversiveness of these new films shock viewers out of passive viewing and place them in a critical position – requiring them to challenge and question the fairy tales they are more familiar with. Hence, while this book is predominantly literary in focus, I include certain pop culture and art-house films throughout in order to illustrate how feminist ideas about space, time, and bodies are invading the full anti-tale oeuvre, as exemplified here in the challenge to masculine dualistic knowledges in *Maleficent* and *Into the Woods*.

The heroine of Disney's *Maleficent*, with her bright red lips, unnatural cheekbones, animal-like horns, and powerful wings, gives us, in the words of Matt Zoller Seitz, 'an image of female otherness as eerie as Scarlett Johansson wading into black goo in *Under the Skin*'.[94] Certainly, in addition to creating this human/other divide, as Alexandra Mărginean points out, 'Although one of the intentions of the film is to overturn binary oppositions, binarism is present initially in the organisation of space in the story'.[95] Clearly, the film sets up a dualistic framework in order to deconstruct it. The film plays this out visually through the sharp juxtaposition in imagery between masculine and feminine spaces. While Maleficent is the fairy queen of the feminine and magic-infused moors, with their enchanting bright colours and gentle interspecies cooperation,

Figure 2.1 Maleficent's otherness. *Maleficent*, dir. Robert Stromberg (Walt Disney Studios Home Entertainment: 2014).

King Stefan's human society beyond its boundaries (a world significantly represented entirely by men) is darkened through black and greys and founded on a lust for power and intolerance. This divide is effectively illustrated in a paradigmatic short scene between a young Stefan and Maleficent. Stefan has stolen a jewel from the moors (reminiscent of the exploitation of nature's resources), and Maleficent asks him to give it back then returns it to the river:

STEFAN: If I knew you'd throw it away I would have kept it.
MALEFICENT: I didn't throw it away, I delivered it home.[96]

Here Maleficent clearly embodies ecofeminist principles and respects the environment she lives in. Threatened by her feminine powers (derived, like Atwood's Toby, from her connection to nature), the previous king cannot die peacefully while Maleficent lives. As the voiceover states, 'She had never understood the greed and envy of men, but she was to learn. For the human king had heard of a growing power in the moors and he sought to strike it down'. Stefan, although having befriended Maleficent as a child (the friendship eventually turning into love), drugs her, in a scene with clear implications of 'date rape', and cuts off her wings (the element that made her feel most powerful) in order to exchange them for the dying king's throne. Hence, as Zoller Seitz states, this transforms the film into 'a conflicted revenge story with an unmistakable feminist undertone'.[97] Here, the villain of the *Sleeping Beauty* fairy tale is given a motive for her actions in attempting to kill Stefan's daughter, Aurora, adding a level of moral complexity that, in itself, subverts the dualisms inherent in the fairy tale genre and its patriarchal framework. The voice-over challenges the viewer's reliance on simplistic narratives right at the exposition of the film:

> Let us tell an old story anew and we will see how well you know it [...] Once upon a time there were two kingdoms that were the worst of neighbours. So vast was the discord between them that it was said only a great hero or a terrible villain might bring them together.

Maleficent ultimately removes the 'or' in this statement, as she is an anti-hero hybrid of the two. As *The Telegraph* reviewer Robbie Collin surmises, 'the game involves returning to a well-thumbed fairy tale muddling the distinction between good and evil'.[98] Maleficent's humour and sarcasm as she watches the ineffectual fairies 'looking after' Aurora endears her to us – 'Oh look the little beast is about to fall off the cliff' – and her growing fondness for the child she affectionately refers to as 'Beasty' reveals the complexity of her character. Even Aurora mistakes Maleficent's role at their first meeting and continues to do the same when she discovers the truth of the curse placed on her – she cannot initially grasp Maleficent's complexity in her fairy-tale search for neat categories:

AURORA: I know who you are.
MALEFICENT: Do you?
AURORA [*squealing with excitement*]: You're my fairy godmother!
MALEFICENT [*in disbelief*]: What?
[...]
AURORA: When were you going to tell me that I'm cursed? [...] No, don't touch me. You're the evil that's in the world, it's you!

The film also subverts simplistic fairy-tale character and gender roles in its climactic scene. While the fairies believe that the Prince is the answer to waking up Aurora, it is only the 'true love' kiss on her forehead by Maleficent that breaks the spell.

Rejecting the masculine violence she resorted to in her revenge, Maleficent tells Stefan 'it's over' and attempts to walk away; however, he falls to his own death trying to attack her once again. As the voiceover states, 'Maleficent brought down her wall of thorns and took off her crown and she invited Aurora to see how the moors had been once, long ago when Maleficent was but a child and her heart was bright'. Here, Maleficent goes back to her ecofeminist self, giving up the powerful position she took up when she was bitter and seeking revenge, instead becoming part of the moors again rather than a ruler over them. Meanwhile, Maleficent's link to nature is emphasised in the fact that the moors are also healed once again along with her own heart. She symbolically places the crown on Aurora's head – 'Our kingdoms have been unified, you have

Figure 2.2 Maleficent's kiss. *Maleficent*, dir. Robert Stromberg (Walt Disney Studios Home Entertainment: 2014).

your Queen' – and Aurora's crossover between the two realms is the final mark of the breakdown of the division between the natural moors and human world binary. Ultimately, the image of harmony between both humans and nature concludes the story.

Into the Woods is a film musical aimed primarily at children (but also contains the much darker and adult themes of the folk tale) that brings together multiple fairy tale narratives into one complex story. As I briefly mentioned earlier, the film weaves together the stories of various characters, cutting sharply from one character's story to the next in order to illustrate how human beings are all interconnected and responsible for one another rather than self-contained and divided individuals. This feminine complexity in the cinematic form which defies any neat, linear, or rationalised structure, and refutes tidy closure, is successful in undermining the simplistic patriarchal arc of the traditional literary fairy tale with its neat moral and narratological conclusion. Indeed, like *Cruel Pink, Alison Wonderland,* and the *Maddaddam* trilogy, *Into the Woods* adopts the *écriture féminine* technique of overlapping story threads which accords with the New French Feminist idea that writing in a feminine style entails this mode of writing that branches off into several strands. In this film, we have a wide network of experiences: from Little Red Riding Hood who is intersected by the Wolf on her way to grandma's house, Cinderella eager to go the ball, and Jack trying to save his beloved cow from the market by climbing up the beanstalk. All are on a journey, both symbolically and literally, through the woods. The narratives are linked together through the story of the kindly baker and his wife who long for a child. However, they discover that the witch put a curse on the baker's father, who stole from her garden, meaning that his offspring would never be able to have children (note that, in her description of the man's intrusion into her garden, she refers to it as a 'rape' of sorts, once again linking a female character with nature). Hence the couple embark on a mission to collect the ingredients for the witch in order to undo her spell (she concedes since it will allow her to regain her youthful appearance once it ends). The opening sequence in the film captures each character's situation in brief scenes, as the camera switches frantically between their isolated situations and their voices join together in one song as they chant in unison 'I wish …', marking the interconnectivity between people of all kinds. These fairy tale characters all gain knowledge in the woods. They adapt, grow, and change in this natural space outside of social expectations and come to a realisation of the complexity of life that cannot be neatly understood in the simple binaries of the fairy tale framework. As the baker's wife sings to her husband, 'There's something about the woods | Not just surviving | You're blossoming in the woods. | At home I fear we'd stay the same forever [...] Let's hope the changes last beyond the woods'. Even Little Red Riding Hood recognises the positives and negatives of her encounter with the wolf after being saved by the baker: 'Isn't it nice to know a lot | And a little bit not'. She has grown in her journey rather than being punished for transgressing her role as innocent child, as happens in Perrault's story. It is also the baker's wife who foregrounds the film's challenge to dualisms and binaries. Lost and on her own as they all hide from the murderous female giant, she bumps into Cinderella's prince. After a brief romantic encounter she is shocked by her actions, questioning whether life can have these moments that cross over divides. The woods provide her with a space to question things beyond social strictures and expectations:

What was that?

Was it wrong?

Am I mad?

Is that all?

[...]

Wake up,

Stop dreaming,

Stop prancing about the woods.

It's not beseeming.

What is it about the woods?

Back to life,

Back to sense,

Back to child,

Back to husband,

Nobody lives in the woods.

There are vows,

There are ties,

There are needs,

There are standards,

There are shouldn'ts and shoulds.

Why not both?

In her frantic search for an answer, she utters the sentence that sums up the entire film: 'Is it always "or"? | Is it never "and"?'. As Catherine Shoard points out, 'her easily swayed heart is sweet and human in a land of cutouts'.[99] This is a very deliberate contrast, marking out the complexity of human nature that cannot be contained within the dualistic framework upheld by patriarchy. The director himself stated that 'the baker and his wife are really us', in that they are human, complex, and fallible.

Accepting her encounter with the prince as 'a moment' of enlightenment, the baker's wife recognises that it is important to have these episodes where we recognise that nothing is fixed, that what we have is only one version of an infinite array of possibilities, though more precious because of this: 'That's what the woods are for [...] Let the moment go | Don't forget it for a moment though. | Just remembering that you've

Figure 2.3 Baker's Wife. *Into the Woods*, dir. Rob Marshall (Walt Disney Studios Home Entertainment: 2015).

had an "and", | When you're back to "or", | Makes an "or" mean more than it did before. | Now I understand | And it's time to leave the woods'. Although she dies before reaching her husband and the rest of the group, she becomes an inspiration for their victory over the giant and her voice echoes in the woods as a guiding force. She shares her lesson with the baker and Cinderella who then pass it on to the children (Little Red Riding Hood and Jack):

> People make mistakes,
> Fathers and mothers.
> People make mistakes,
> Holding their own,
> Thinking they're alone.
> Honor their mistakes,
> Fight for their mistakes
> [...]
> Witches can be right,
> Giants can be good,
> You decide what's right,
> You decide what's good.
> Just remember,
> Someone is on your side,
> Someone else is not.
> While we're seeing our side,
> Maybe we forgot,
> Someone else is not.

This clearly shares *Maleficent*'s subversion of good and evil embodied in the fairy tale form, and the film ends with a warning that we must be careful with such stories that uphold binaries, sung by the voice of baker's wife who guides the remaining characters and viewers on their way: 'Careful the tale you tell | That is the spell | Children will listen'. Having been a character within the film and having gained her new knowledge, she is placed in the privileged position of omniscient voiceover, trying to impart her new feminine understanding onto the remaining characters. This cinematic placing of the baker's wife from the position of player in the human drama to authorial voice illustrates how she refuses to be an actor playing out the usual black and white moral standard usually imparted by the god-like third-person narrator (the male author's voice and ideologies often heard very clearly) in traditional fairy tales. Rather, she takes control of her own destiny and illustrates that no one authoritative voice or perspective is conclusive. Hence, while the patriarchal fairy tales of Perrault had simplistic and summarised morals literally tagged on to the end of the stories, here the baker's wife provides a more complex anti-moral, with her feminine and ecocritical awareness allowing her to recognise that human beings are complex creatures that cannot be assigned to one neat box or another – man/woman or good/evil – as much as patriarchy attempts to do so. It is also interesting how the film uses the transverbal musicality of the baker's wife to deconstruct the closed form of the fairy tale which is usually neatly contained and interpretation closed-off or limited by an authoritative and omniscient voice. Rather, this is an example of what Kérchy calls 'a musicality bursting representational frames', with music articulating emotions and meanings outside of the realm of vocabulary and fixed understandings.[100] As Kérchy has stated, 'I believe that intellectual pleasure is not all prevailing, and is likely to be complemented, even predominated by a sheer pleasure of sounds, vocality, a transverbal musicality, or joy of imagination soaring into unknowns and impossibles'.[101] Thus, by having the baker's wife sing these messages, the film is able, on a narratological level, to heighten that sense that nothing is absolute, fixed, or set in stone, rather life, emotions, and morality are complicated and open-ended.

Overall, the ecofeminist challenges in this chapter all aim to deconstruct the conceptual or narratological frameworks of fairy tales, particularly those represented most clearly in the work of Perrault, with the tagged on morals at the end of his stories. As Villanueva Gardener states, however, such ecofeminist challenges do not simply shatter the old dualistic framework and replace it with another, rather

> there is no one way that ecofeminists arrive at a rejection of the conceptual framework that opposes women and nature, nor (once this framework is rejected) is there only one way that ecofeminists can develop new ways of moral perception.[102]

Instead, 'ecofeminists refer to their relationship with the natural environment as conducive to producing an ecofeminist consciousness', rather than imposing yet another fixed and solid architecture for viewing the world.[103] In this way, Diamond and Feman Orenstein point out, 'Once the critique of such dualities [...] has been posed, ecofeminism seeks to reweave new stories that acknowledge and value the biological and cultural diversity that sustains all life'; in essence, dualisms no longer exist for them as they level distinctions and emphasise both the interconnectivity between all things and, hence, their equality.[104]

Conclusion

This chapter points out how nature is a space in which women like Isserley and Toby seem to have a greater sense of belonging. This is not to say that the urban environment of Chapter 1 cannot be embraced by ecofeminists and women too. After all, as Michael Bennett and David W. Teague's book *The Nature of Cities: Ecocriticism and Urban Environments* and my chapter here point out, ecofeminism is as much about human nature as external physical environments and the inevitable human endeavour and evolutions inherent in the urban environment are natural impulses. Rather, the difference is that the urban space is predominantly structured around masculine knowledges and is male-dominated so the anti-tales of Chapter 1 *reimagine* the city as a more complex and feminine space, whereas feminists themselves rejected women's links with nature because of patriarchy's exploitation of such essentialisms and the anti-tales in this chapter thus *reclaim* that space. This chapter has illustrated how, despite the historical degradation of women through their alignment with 'debased' nature as opposed to 'high' culture, anti-tale authors have taken back this space and radically redefined it as a feminist one. Anti-tale magical realism was identified as a means of conveying both cultural ecofeminist and rational ecofeminist ideas, permitting authors to combine spiritual aspects associated with female power (including ancient goddess myths, Toby's peculiar female nature-lore inherited from Pilar, and the radical use of oral fairy tales as a kind of evolutionary storytelling) with an impulse for realist societal impact. This has been described as a 'practical magic'. Not simply airy and fantastical, these narratives are aimed at lasting social change, imagining and offering feminine alternatives to the existing patriarchal reality outside of the stories. The ecofeminist goal of breaking down the patriarchal use of a dualistic framework that inevitably subordinates women, nature, and animals was then discussed, with *Maleficent* and *Into the Woods* subverting this through their challenge to fairy tales that mirror patriarchal ideological thinking in their notorious black and white morality. I also discussed the extension of these theories to the breakdown of hierarchies, and their replacement with an ecofeminist consciousness of the interconnected web of life. It was shown how the emphasis has shifted not only to equality between humans and non-human animals but also onto the equality of other oppressed groups tangled in the web, including women and their relation to men. The structure of this chapter has taken us on a journey from an explanation of the weaknesses created by patriarchy for women through their alignment with nature, to an appreciation of how the seizure of this link and its transformation into a powerful backlash has led to the breakdown of the patriarchal ideological architecture altogether, and its replacement with ecofeminism's more feminine architecture of acceptance and, ultimately, equality. The success of the anti-tales in this endeavour is epitomised in the lyrics sung in *Into The Woods* by the baker's wife and her husband, who, due to the influence of the woods and its levelling of social distinctions, recognise and accept their equal status:

BAKER'S WIFE: '*We*'? So you're going to let me stay with you?
[...]
BAKER: It's because I'm becoming aware of us each accepting a share of what's there.
[...]
BAKER'S WIFE: Let's hope the changes last beyond the woods.

Notes

1 Robbie Collin, '*Into the Woods*, Review: "Pure Pleasure"' in *The Telegraph* (7th January 2015) <www.telegraph.co.uk/culture/film/filmreviews/11298668/Into-the-Woods-review-Meryl-Streep-Emily-Blunt-Anna-Kendrick.html> [accessed 5th November 2015].
2 Stacy Alaimo, *Undomesticated Ground: Recasting Nature as Feminist Space* (London: Cornell University Press, 2000), p. 2. Hereafter, page references will be incorporated into the text.
3 Conny Eisfeld, *How Fairy Tales Live Happily Ever After: The Art of Adapting Fairy Tales* (Hamburg: Anchor Academic Publishing, 2014), p. 70.
4 Greta Gaard, 'Ecofeminism Revisited: Rejecting Essentialism and Replacing Species in a Material Feminist Environmentalism' in *Feminist Formations*, Vol. 23, No. 2 (Summer 2011), p. 41.
5 Lucy Sargisson, 'What's Wrong with Ecofeminism?' in *Environmental Politics*, Vol. 10, No.1 (2001), p. 52.
6 Ibid., p. 63.
7 Elizabeth Bell, Lynda Haas, and Laura Sells, 'Introduction: Walt's in the Movies' in *From Mouse to Mermaid: The Politics of Film, Gender, and Culture* (Bloomington: Indiana University Press, 1995), p. 2.
8 Monique M. LaRocque, 'Decadent Desire: The Dream of Disembodiment in J. K. Huysmans' *A Rebours*' in *Feminist Ecocriticism: Environment, Women, and Literature*, ed. Douglas A. Vakoch (New York: Lexington Books, 2012), p. 94.
9 Val Plumwood, 'Ecofeminism: An Overview and Discussion of Positions and Arguments' in *Australasian Journal of Philosophy*, Vol. 64 (1986), p. 120.

10　Barbara Bennett, *Scheherazade's Daughters: The Power of Storytelling in Ecofeminist Change* (New York: Peter Lang publishing, Inc., 2012), p. 50.

11　Jacob and Wilhelm Grimm, 'Sleeping Beauty' in *The Complete Fairytales of the Brothers Grimm* (Hertfordshire: Wordsworth Editions Ltd., 2009), p. 249.

12　Bruno Bettelheim, *The Uses of Enchantment: The Meaning and Importance of Fairy Tales* (London: Penguin Books Ltd., 1976), p. 238.

13　Grimms, 'Sleeping Beauty' in *The Complete Fairytales of the Brothers Grimm*, p. 249.

14　Charles Perrault, 'Little Red Riding Hood' in *Little Red Riding Hood Uncloaked: Sex, Morality, and the Evolution of a Fairy Tale*, ed. Catherine Orenstein (New York: Basic Books, 2002), p. 21.

15　Grimms, 'Little Red Riding Hood' in *The Complete Fairytales of the Brothers Grimm*, p. 143.

16　Ibid., pp.146, 147.

17　Grimms, 'Snow-White and the Seven Dwarfs' in *The Complete Fairytales of the Brothers Grimm*, p. 261.

18　Michel Faber, *Under the Skin* (Edinburgh: Canongate Books Ltd., 2000), p. 197. Hereafter, page references will be incorporated into the text.

19　Greta Gaard, 'New Directions for Ecofeminism: Toward a More Feminist Ecocriticism' in *Interdisciplinary Studies in Literature and Environment*, Vol. 7, No. 4 (2010) <http://isle.oxfordjournals.org/content/17/4/643. extract> [accessed 5th November 2015].

20　See Noël Sturgeon, *Ecofeminist Natures: Race, Gender, Feminist Theory and Political Action* (London: Routledge, 1997).

21　Ibid., p. 23.

22　Catherine Villanueva Gardner, 'An Ecofeminist Perspective on the Urban Environment' in *The Nature of Cities: Ecocriticism and the Urban Environment*, eds. Bennett and Teague, p. 192.

23　Debarati Bandyopadhyay, 'An Ecocritical Commentary on the Posthuman Condition in Margaret Atwood's Fiction' in *The Criterion: An International Journal in English*, Vol. 1, No. 1 (April 2011), p. 3.

24　Sturgeon, *Ecofeminist Natures: Race, Gender, Feminist Theory and Political Action*, p. 23.

25　Villanueva Gardner, 'An Ecofeminist Perspective on the Urban Environment' in *The Nature of Cities: Ecocriticism and the Urban Environment*, eds. Bennett and Teague, pp. 192–193.

26　Gaard and Murphy, 'Introduction' in *Ecofeminist Literary Criticism: Theory, Interpretation, Pedagogy*, p. 3.

27　Karen Warren quoted in Villanueva Gardner, 'An Ecofeminist Perspective on the Urban Environment' in *The Nature of Cities: Ecocriticism and the Urban Environment*, eds. Bennett and Teague, p. 193.

28　See Sturgeon, *Ecofeminist Natures: Race, Gender, Feminist Theory and Political Action*, p. 167, for an account of just such an experience shared by prominent ecofeminist Spretnak.

29　Ibid., p. 29.

30　Ibid.

31　Ibid., p. 9.

32　Slicer, 'Toward an Ecofeminist Standpoint Theory: Bodies as Grounds' in *Ecofeminist Literary Criticism: Theory, Interpretation, Pedagogy*, eds. Gaard and Murphy, p. 53.

33　Eric C. Otto, 'Ecofeminist Theories of Liberation in the Science Fiction of Sally Millar Gearhart, Ursula K. Le Guin, and Joan Slonczewski' in *Feminist Ecocriticism: Environment, Women, and Literature*, ed. Vakoch, p. 30.

34 Ynestra King quoted in Otto, 'Ecofeminist Theories of Liberation in the Science Fiction of Sally Millar Gearhart, Ursula K. Le Guin, and Joan Slonczewski' in *Feminist Ecocriticism: Environment, Women, and Literature*, ed. Vakoch, p. 30.

35 Greta Gaard and Patrick D. Murphy, 'A Dialogue on the Role and Place of Literary Criticism Within Ecofeminism' in *Interdisciplinary Studies in Literature and Environment*, Vol. 3, No. 1 (1996), p. 6.

36 Gaard and Murphy, 'Introduction' in *Ecofeminist Literary Criticism: Theory, Interpretation, Pedagogy*, p. 11.

37 Gaard, 'New Directions for Ecofeminism: Toward a More Feminist Ecocriticism' in *Interdisciplinary Studies in Literature and Environment* <http://isle.oxfordjournals.org/content/17/4/643.extract> [accessed 5th November 2015].

38 Gaard and Murphy, 'Introduction' in *Ecofeminist Literary Criticism: Theory, Interpretation, Pedagogy*, p. 7.

39 Ibid., p. 6.

40 Ibid., p. 5.

41 See Robert Root and Michael Steinberg, *The Fourth Genre: Contemporary Writer of/on Creative Non-Fiction*, 6th ed. (New York: Longman, 2011).

42 Gaard and Murphy, 'A Dialogue on the Role and Place of Literary Criticism within Ecofeminism' in *Interdisciplinary Studies in Literature and Environment*, p. 3.

43 Patrick D. Murphy, '"The Women are Speaking": Contemporary Literature as Theoretical Critique' in *Ecofeminist Literary Criticism: Theory, Interpretation, Pedagogy*, eds. Gaard and Murphy, p. 32.

44 Although there isn't much written on fairy tales and ecofeminism, a few works do exist in this area. See Sara Maitland's *Gossip from the Forest: The Tangled Roots of Our Forests and Fairy Tales* (London: Granta Publications, 2012) and Sidney I. Dobrin and Kenneth B. Kidd's edited collection *Wild Things: Children's Culture and Ecocriticism* (Detroit: Wayne State University Press, 2004).

45 Bennett, *Scheherazade's Daughters: The Power of Storytelling in Ecofeminist Change*, p. 151.

46 Theda Wrede, 'Barbara Kingsolver's *Animal Dreams*: Ecofeminist Subversion of Western Myth' in *Feminist Ecocriticism: Environment, Women, and Literature*, ed. Vakoch, p. 41.

47 Val Plumwood quoted in Wrede, 'Barbara Kingsolver's *Animal Dreams*: Ecofeminist Subversion of Western Myth' in *Feminist Ecocriticism: Environment, Women, and Literature*, ed. Vakoch, p. 42.

48 Wrede, 'Barbara Kingsolver's *Animal Dreams*: Ecofeminist Subversion of Western Myth' in *Feminist Ecocriticism: Environment, Women, and Literature*, ed. Vakoch, p. 42.

49 Gaard and Murphy, 'Introduction' in *Ecofeminist Literary Criticism: Theory, Interpretation, Pedagogy*, p. 3.

50 Sharon Wilson quoted in Katarina Labudova, 'Paradice Regained: Post-Apocalyptic Visions of Urban and Rural Spaces in Margaret Atwood's *Maddaddam* Trilogy' in *Eger Journal of English Studies*, Vol. XIII (2013), p. 32.

51 Labudova, 'Paradice Regained: Post-Apocalyptic Visions of Urban and Rural Spaces in Margaret Atwood's *Maddaddam* Trilogy' in *Eger Journal of English Studies*, p. 34.

52 Hope Jennings quoted in Labudova, 'Paradice Regained: Post-Apocalyptic Visions of Urban and Rural Spaces in Margaret Atwood's *Maddaddam* Trilogy' in *Eger Journal of English Studies*, pp. 31–32.

53 J. Brooks Bouson, 'A "Joke-Filled Romp" Through End Times: Radical Environmentalism, Deep Ecology, and Human Extinction in Margaret Atwood's *Maddaddam* Trilogy' in *The Journal of Commonwealth Literature* (13th April 2015), pp. 1, 9 <http://jcl.sagepub.com/content/early/2015/04/13/0021989415573558.abstract> [accessed 8th November 2015].

54 Bennett, *Scheherazade's Daughters: The Power of Storytelling in Ecofeminist Change*, p. 17.

55 Margaret Atwood, *Oryx and Crake* (London: Virago Press, 2003), p. 3. Hereafter, page references will be incorporated into the text.

56 Atwood, *The Year of the Flood* (London: Virago Press, 2009), p. 48. Hereafter, page references will be incorporated into the text.

57 Labudova, 'Power, Pain, and Manipulation in Margaret Atwood's *Oryx and Crake* and *The Year of the Flood*' in *Brno Studies in English*, p. 138.

58 Sarah Dillon, '"It is a Question of Words, Therefore": Becoming-Animal in Michel Faber's *Under the Skin*' in *Science Fiction Studies*, Vol. 38, No. 1 (2011), p. 134.

59 See Agata Buda, 'Destructive Power of Gothic Time and Space By Michel Faber' <www.pulib.sk/web/kniznica/elpub/dokument/Bila2/.../Buda.pdf.> [accessed 8th November 2015].

60 Dillon, '"It is a Question of Words, Therefore": Becoming-Animal in Michel Faber's *Under the Skin*' in *Science Fiction Studies*, p. 134.

61 Ibid., p. 135.

62 Gaard, 'New Directions for Ecofeminism: Toward a More Feminist Ecocriticism' in *Interdisciplinary Studies in Literature and Environment* <http://isle.oxfordjournals.org/content/17/4/643.extract> [accessed 5th November 2015].

63 Gaard, 'Ecofeminism Revisited: Rejecting Essentialism and Re-placing Species in a Material Feminist Environmentalism' in *Feminist Formations*, p. 36.

64 Margaret Atwood, *Maddaddam* (London: Virago Press, 2013), p. 117. Hereafter, page references will be incorporated into the text.

65 Shannon Hengen, 'Margaret Atwood and Environmentalism' in *The Cambridge Companion to Margaret Atwood* (Cambridge: Cambridge University Press, 2006), p. 78.

66 Jeffrey A. Lockwood, 'Ecofeminism: The Ironic Philosophy' in *Feminist Ecocriticism: Environment, Women, and Literature*, ed. Vakoch, p. 134.

67 See Annie Proulx, *Close Range: Wyoming Stories* (London: Fourth Estate, 1999) for an example of how nature (in this case the harsh wilderness of Wyoming) is a character in its own right, directly interacting with the humans in the story and mirroring their equally sparse and emotionally turbulent lives where growth is stunted. Yet the characters are as hardened and determined as the land, standing firm and building lives out of the few resources available.

68 Bennett, *Scheherazade's Daughters*, p. 167.

69 Jack Zipes, *Breaking the Magic Spell: Radical Theories of Folk and Fairy Tales* (London: Educational Books Ltd., 1979), p. 5.

70 Donald Haase, 'Introduction' in *Fairy Tales and Feminism: New Approaches* (Michigan: Wayne State University Press, 2004), p. 26.

71 *Into the Woods*, dir. Rob Marshall (Walt Disney Studios Home Entertainment, 2015) [on DVD]. Hereafter, all passages quoted in reference to *Into the Woods* are taken from this text.

72 Elizabeth Waning Harries, 'The Mirror Broken: Women's Autobiography and Fairy Tales' in *Fairy Tales and Feminism: New Approaches*, ed. Haase, p. 103.

73 Susan Sellers, *Myth and Fairy Tale in Contemporary Women's Fiction* (Hampshire: Palgrave, 2001), p. 15.
74 Jack Zipes, *The Irresistible Fairy Tale: The Cultural and Social History of a Genre* (Princeton: Princeton University Press, 2012), p. 17.
75 Hengen, 'Margaret Atwood and Environmentalism' in *The Cambridge Companion to Margaret Atwood*, p. 78.
76 Brooks Bouson, 'A "Joke-Filled Romp" Through End Times: Radical Environmentalism, Deep Ecology, and Human Extinction in Margaret Atwood's *Maddaddam* Trilogy' in *The Journal of Commonwealth Literature*, p. 12.
77 Bennett, *Scheherazade's Daughters*, p. 49.
78 Labudova, Katarína, 'Cyborg Children, Illuminous Rabbits, Snowman: Margaret Atwood's *Oryx and Crake* and *The Year of the Flood* as Speculative Fiction' in *Postmodern Reinterpretations of Fairy Tales: How Applying New Methods Generates New Meanings*, ed. Anna Kérchy (Lampeter: The Edwin Mellen Press, 2011), p. 310.
79 Gaard and Murphy, 'Introduction' in *Ecofeminist Literary Criticism: Theory, Interpretation, Pedagogy*, p. 3.
80 Bennett, *Scheherazade's Daughters*, p. 5.
81 Hengen, 'Margaret Atwood and Environmentalism' in *The Cambridge Companion to Margaret Atwood*, ed. Coral Ann Howells, p. 84.
82 Gaard, 'New Directions for Ecofeminism: Toward a More Feminist Ecocriticism' in *Interdisciplinary Studies in Literature and Environment* <http://isle.oxfordjournals.org/content/17/4/643.extract> [accessed 5th November 2015].
83 J. Brooks-Bouson, 'We're Using up the Earth. It's Almost Gone': A Return to the Post-Apocalyptic Future in Margaret Atwood's *The Year of the Flood*' in *The Journal of Commonwealth Literature*, Vol. 46, No. 1 (March 2011), p. 12.
84 Carol J. Adams quoted in Bennett, *Scheherazade's Daughters*, p. 95.
85 Cary Wolfe quoted in Dillon, '"It is a Question of Words, Therefore": Becoming-Animal in Michel Faber's *Under the Skin*' in *Science Fiction Studies*, p. 134.
86 Dillon, '"It is a Question of Words, Therefore": Becoming-Animal in Michel Faber's *Under the Skin*' in *Science Fiction Studies*, p. 140.
87 Villanueva Gardner, 'An Ecofeminist Perspective on the Urban Environment' in *The Nature of Cities: Ecocriticism and the Urban Environment*, eds. Bennett and Teague, p. 193.
88 Eisfeld, *How Fairy Tales Live Happily Ever After: The Art of Adapting Fairy Tales*, p. 22.
89 Sandra Gilbert and Susan Gubar, *The Madwoman in the Attic: The Woman Writer and the Nineteenth-Century Literary Imagination* (London: Yale University Press, 2000), p. 28.
90 Merja Makinen, 'Angela Carter's *The Bloody Chamber* and the Decolonisation of Feminine Sexuality' in *Angela Carter: Contemporary Critical Essays*, ed. Alison Easton (London: Macmillan Press Ltd., 2000), p. 24.
91 Labudova, 'Paradice Regained: Post-Apocalyptic Visions of Urban and Rural Spaces in Margaret Atwood's *Maddaddam* Trilogy' in *Eger Journal of English Studies*, p. 27.
92 Bell, Haas and Sells, 'Introduction' in *From the Mouse to the Mermaid: The Politics of Film, Gender, and Culture*, p. 4.
93 See, for example, Cristina Bacchilega, *Fairy Tales Transformed?: Twenty-First-Century Adaptations & the Politics of Wonder* (Detroit: Wayne State University Press, 2013); Jack Zipes, Pauline Greenhill, and Kendra Magnus-

Johnston, eds., *Fairy-Tale Films Beyond Disney: International Perspectives* (London: Routledge, 2016); Pauline Greenhill and Jill Terry Rudy, eds., *Channeling Wonder: Fairy Tales on Television* (Detroit: Wayne State University Press, 2014); Kristian Moen, *Film and Fairy Tales: The Birth of Modern Fantasy: From* The Blue Bird *to* Harry Potter (London: I.B. Tauris & Co. Ltd., 2013); and Anna Kèrchy, *Alice in Transmedia Wonderland: Curiouser and Curiouser Forms of a Children's Classic* (Jefferson: McFarland, 2016).

94 Matt Zoller Seitz, '*Maleficent*: Movie Review' (29th March 2014) <www.rogerebert.com/reviews/maleficent-2014> [accessed 19th November 2015].

95 Alexandra Mărginean, 'Deconstructive Angles in *Maleficent*' <http://upm.ro/cci3/CCI-03/Lit/Lit%2003%2043.pdf> [accessed 19th November 2015].

96 *Maleficent*, dir. Robert Stromberg (Walt Disney Studios Home Entertainment, 2014) [on DVD]. Hereafter, all passages quoted from *Maleficent* are taken from this film.

97 Zoller Seitz, '*Maleficent*: Movie Review' <www.rogerebert.com/reviews/maleficent-2014> [accessed 19th November 2015].

98 Robbie Collin, '*Maleficent*, Review' in *The Telegraph* (30th May 2014) <www.telegraph.co.uk/culture/film/filmreviews/10858663/Maleficent-review.html> [accessed 19th November 2015].

99 Catherine Shoard, '*Into the Woods* Review: Trees Fall in the Forest, Making One Hell of a Sound' in *The Guardian* (17th December 2014) <www.theguardian.com/film/2014/dec/17/into-the-woods-review-meryl-streep-rob-marshall-stephen-sondheim> [accessed 19th November 2015].

100 Anna Kérchy, *Alice in Transmedia Wonderland: Curiouser and Curiouser Forms of a Children's Classic* (Jefferson: McFarland, 2016), p. 26.

101 Kérchy, 'Ambiguous Alice: Making Sense of Lewis Carroll's Nonsense Fantasies' in *Does It Really Mean That? Interpreting the Literary Ambiguous*, eds. Kathleen Dubs and Janka Kaščáková (Cambridge Scholars Publishing: Newcastle upon Tyne, 2011), p. 116.

102 Villanueva Gardner, 'An Ecofeminist Perspective on the Urban Environment' in *The Nature of Cities: Ecocriticism and the Urban Environment*, eds. Bennett and Teague, p. 195.

103 Ibid.

104 Gloria Feman Orenstein and Irene Diamond quoted in Gaard and Murphy, 'Introduction' in *Ecofeminist Literary Criticism: Theory, Interpretation, Pedagogy*, p. 2.

3 'Once Upon Many Times'

Subversive Temporalities in Feminist Anti-Tales

How is it that time, which has no form nor substance, can crush me with so huge a weight that I can no longer breathe?

Simone de Beauvoir[1]

Introduction: The Alarm Clock Sounds

Once upon a time, Simone de Beauvoir expressed the above words while despairing at her advancing years. This is not surprising, given that women are expected to dread the relentless forward movement of time, that great enemy to humankind. But who decided that time was a greater enemy to women specifically? Due to its invisibility, and resultant lack of tangibility, time can often be taken for granted as an inevitable and external entity – out *there* somewhere – and hence appears to be an objective neutral force. However, as feminist scholar Victoria Browne notes in her 2014 publication, *Feminism, Time, and Nonlinear History*,

> Temporal concepts and orders are not neutral or incidental, but rather are inextricably tied to the way that political change and processes are understood, and to the way politics *works*. The coexistence of times and temporalities takes place in contexts of power and domination.[2]

The alarm clock has sounded: feminists have woken up to the threat posed by current temporal paradigms. Furthermore, Browne's book is part of the *Breaking Feminist Waves* series, indicating the growing awareness among feminist scholars of the need to tackle this daunting concept and the problems it poses for women, what Browne headlines as 'The Politics of Feminist Time'. After all, the mechanical, chronological time of the clock created by dominant social forces (and therefore patriarchy) was established in order to regulate social life, maintain order, and provide a method of control, as this chapter illustrates.

More importantly, such patriarchal influences extend to the use of time in traditional literary fairy tales with their infamous 'Once upon a time' motif. I foreground here the problems inherent in the seemingly ahistorical timelessness of these stories which inevitably universalises patriarchal morals across centuries and conditions female behaviour throughout the ages. In essence, by making the morals timeless, fairy tale depictions of women seem to apply to every era, rather than being shown as situated in the past. It is surprising then that no work focusing on time and fairy tales has yet been published. Despite Bacchilega's promising epilogue in *Postmodern Fairy Tales: Gender and Narrative Strategies,* titled 'Peopling the Bloody Chambers: "Once Upon Many Times" and "Once Upon One Time"', she simply refers to the continuing relevance of fairy tale forms for readers and writers today and does not acknowledge the problematic nature of seeing the tales and their lessons as universal at all.[3] In addition, Jack Zipes has published numerous and prolific full-length studies that focus on the socio-historical nature of fairy tales and their relevance to the different societies from which they spring (highlighting that they are not ahistorical but, if read carefully, can be seen to be rooted in political realities).[4] Yet, Zipes, like Bacchilega, does not grapple with the nature of time *in* fairy tale narratives; instead, both focus on the contexts outside of the stories. However, Catriona McAra and David Calvin have noted, although briefly, in a table contained in their edited collection *Anti-Tales: The Uses of Disenchantment,* that while the fairy tale is ahistorical, the anti-tale often utilises 'a real world context' or setting within the tales themselves.[5] While this does not allow for more complex challenges to fairy tale time beyond the mere grounding of tales in specific time periods, it at least records the impulse inherent in anti-tales to challenge the problematic assumption of 'once upon a time'-ness in the traditional stories.

Building on these ideas then, I analyse here the feminist revisions of time in twenty-first-century anti-tales. This chapter builds on my previous research into the use of specific contexts to subvert the ahistorical aspect of the fairy tale mentioned above. In short, further research has revealed the more complex nature of these anti-tale time subversions to not only situate the tales in a specific context but challenge our assumptions about the very nature of time itself. These innovations highlight what Mitchum Huehls terms 'the need to rethink, but not reject, the political value of time'.[6] I analyse how Tanith Lee's *Cruel Pink* does this by positing what, I argue, is a more complicated feminine alternative to simplistic masculine time frames through the privileging of subjective, fluid, multidirectional, and polytemporal depictions of time in her novel (as well as reading a similar challenge to 'rationalised' time structures inherent in Alice's time-travelling from James Bobin's 2016 Disney film *Alice Through the Looking Glass*). In addition, challenges to the seemingly closed 'happily ever after' structure of the fairy tale will be explored. As Huehls points out, 'whenever the temporal form of a text teaches us new ways of producing knowledge, something deeply political is going on' and, certainly, the temporal experimentation and challenges posed in these works contribute to feminism's project of freeing women from the chains of rigid temporal structures and the stifling ideologies they uphold.[7]

'Time Is a *He*?': Quantitative/Clock Time as Patriarchal Weapon

It is necessary to understand the kinds of temporal problems the anti-tales in this chapter are challenging. So, first, what do I mean by masculine time? Alice's surprise expressed in the question, 'Time is a *He*?', from Disney's 2016 film, is extremely telling: Time (Sacha Baron Cohen) is not only personified in the film but gendered male and held up as evil villain to the story's heroine.[8] With his cog-like necklace and ticking clock, situated where his heart should be, it is Alice's disruption of the chronological and patriarchal order of time that threatens his mechanical life and not any kind of flesh and blood mortality.

Chronological and clock time, despite being naturalised, are artificial. As Browne points out, 'temporal measures are not natural measures that simply exist; rather, they are constructed measures that are decided upon and utilised within specific sociocultural situations and arrangements' (100). Although it is based on cosmological time then, 'calendar time does not belong to nature'; it is socially constructed (this is significant given that anything artificial is literally gendered as *man*-made while, in Chapter 2, I examined women's closer alignment with nature and natural processes) (101). Inevitably, then, as Browne notes, 'the institutionalization of a particular calendar depends upon a certain level of political authority to regulate social, cultural, and economic life according to specific calendrical arrangements' – in other words, such temporal measures are inherently related to gender issues, being already 'deeply enmeshed in power relations' (101). This association of time with power is evident even when considering mechanical time's

Figure 3.1 Time. *Alice Through the Looking Glass*, dir. James Bobin (Walt Disney Studios Home Entertainment: 2016).

inception, with modern Western clock time linked to capitalism and related social advances (such as wage labour and modern market relations
in sixteenth- and seventeenth-century Europe, the rise of factories, and
the integration of railways, shipping, and telephonic communication)
(101–102). This concept assumes time to be linear and chronological
and its arrow continually pointing forward due to the relentless ideology
of progress.[9] Following these changes, individuals no longer conducted
their own daily routines and were homogenised under accepted work
and leisure hours; in this way, they were brought under control and integrated into the dominant social order with its numerical times, dates,
and calendars. Clearly, such measures of time are not innocent, but are
invested with the interests of those with social, capital, and patriarchal
authority. Time's paranoia about upholding the regular tick of the clock
in *Alice Through the Looking Glass* is, on one level, an embodiment
of patriarchy's attempts to keep unruly women, like the time-travelling
Alice who disobeys his rules, under control.

Understood in relation to issues of power, it is easy to see then why
such temporal structures are gendered male. This gendered aspect is
made even clearer in the examples provided by Giordano Nanni in his
research into 'the role of time as an instrument in colonial power'.[10] For,
as he notes, 'the histories of western time and western imperialism are
virtually inseparable; for the extension and structural permanence of
western temporalities beyond western European borders remains con-
tingent on the interruption and reform of "other" cultures of time'.[11] Positioned as feminine, indigenous peoples and their unique temporalities
are considered 'other' (like women with their perceived inferiority and
difference) in comparison to the masculine power and clock time of the
coloniser. Thus, as Nanni points out in his paper, 'Time, Empire and Resistance in Settler-Colonial Victoria', it is important to be aware of 'the
manner in which colonization entailed, as well as territorial conquest,
the subversion of conflicting attitudes to time'.[12] In essence, it constituted a colonisation 'of "Aboriginal Time" [...] helping to absorb the
Indigenous presence within the temporal landscape of colonial society',
with the colonisers arrogantly viewing themselves as 'cultural agents of
the clock's regime to clock-less societies'.[13] The most glaring example,
linking time, colonialism, and power, can be perceived in the introduction of Greenwich Mean Time in 1884. As Nanni points out, it was the
'grandiloquent gesture of temporal imperialism par excellence' which:

> at the height of the colonial era, sought to replace the miscellany
> of 'local times' around the world with a single, centralized notion
> of 'standard time'. Computed and calculated at the geographic
> heart of the Empire, GMT's spatio-temporal equation was, and re-
> mains, an unmistakable indication that European expansion in the
> global fields of commerce, transport and communication would be

paralleled by an analogous control of the manner in which societies abroad related to time. The project to incorporate the globe within a matrix of hours, minutes and seconds – a necessary step in securing dominance over an expanding global military and commercial network – demands recognition as one of the most significant manifestations of Europe's universalizing will.[14]

Hence, the idea of multiple temporalities was obliterated in favour of one accepted time frame, and GMT, described above, can be considered masculine in its role of upholding existing power relations and its domination of less powerful countries who are placed in the feminine position. It is this standardised notion of time that helps to maintain the subordination of those considered to be socially inferior – women, indigenous peoples, and the working classes – ensuring that their movements and lifestyles are in accordance with one 'universal will'.

Even the idea of subsuming the 'difference' of indigenous people, and their aboriginal temporalities, into a numerical and orderly system as a way to control that otherness links quantitative time, with its precise measurements, figures, and calendars, to the idea of masculine rationality versus feminine unruliness. Essentially, mechanical time is considered to be a product of Enlightened maleness in which the frighteningly unknowable nature of time (expressed in the meditations of many philosophers (including Saint Augustine's concession that 'I know what time is if one does not ask me about it')) can be denied.[15] In essence, the quantifiable nature of standardised time is an effort to subordinate women and other social minorities through eradicating their alternative temporalities that stray beyond rational comprehension and are not easily explained or categorised, therefore threatening the neatness and stability of the 'single, centralised notion of standard time' Nanni describes. Here lies the key to the temporal subversions of the anti-tales discussed in this chapter, which posit complex feminine alternatives to the standardised masculine time frames in this section. Even Nanni highlights how 'time [despite being a useful colonial tool] also functioned as a means of Indigenous resistance and cultural negotiation'; time then can be a subversive weapon for social minorities too.[16] For example, Nanni outlines how

it [the colonisation of aboriginal time] entailed at best a case of 'dominance without hegemony', as evinced by the fact that the temporal order of settler-colonial society would always rely more on coercion rather than the consent of the Indigenous peoples, thus falling short.

In essence, the colonising power did not succeed in obliterating 'the inward notation of time' (the subjective times held by individuals that did not coincide with the dominant regime).[17]

These ideas will be developed in relation to the primary texts themselves, but, for now, it has been established that the often passively accepted time of the clock, that regulates our everyday lives, is not neutral, rather it is a political weapon, helping to maintain the power of patriarchal regimes. As Browne states, this standardised conception of time needs revision and our use of it 'requires as much care as our use of language' (117).

'Once Upon a Time': Interrogating Fairy Tale Temporality

As I have noted, time, as regards fairy tales, has received very little attention and yet it requires as much care as our acceptance of the standardised clock time previously discussed. Nevertheless, Donald Haase, in his paper 'Children, War, and the Imaginative Space of Fairy Tales', provides a brief section on 'Time and Space' in the genre. Notable is his observation that:

> The formulaic 'once upon a time' stereotypically associated with the fairy tale would seem to suggest that the genre is largely about time – about temporal displacement from the present to a mythical past or to an imaginative time not governed by the laws of everyday life. This is not entirely true. The folktale and fairy tale might be considered in one respect 'timeless', but certainly not in the conventional, sentimental meaning of that word. Socio-historical criticism of fairy tales has more than adequately demonstrated the social, historical, and cultural importance – that is, the temporal aspects – of the genre's production and reception.[18]

There is a lot contained in this passage. The idea that fairy tales temporally displace readers into a mythical past or imaginative time has been, very appropriately, held up as an integral part of their role in psychological development (see Bruno Bettelheim's *The Uses of Enchantment*), particularly for children, allowing them to project their fears and hopes onto the stories and giving the tales their universal appeal.[19] Indeed, much of their content *is* universal – the struggle of individuals against powerful forces, lost or absent parents, and the daunting period of adolescent discovery, for example – meaning that the tales certainly travel well across different time periods, retaining their relevance and appeal. Indeed, a multitude of critics (including myself) have, and continue, to point out the radicalism of literature that is somewhat detached from the reader's context, a world 'not governed by the laws of everyday life' in which a writer can utilise that imaginative freedom to envision alternatives to their own society. Of course, this is done while still holding everyday realities firmly in mind (note Haase's assertion of the simultaneous 'social, historical, and cultural' grounding of the tales lurking behind their timeless façade). Having the freedom of imaginative space and one eye on social reality, writers can project imagined changes onto actual current affairs, allowing for the very real possibility of social alteration. Elizabeth Waning Harries's *Twice Upon a Time: Women Writers and the History of the Fairy Tale* outlines the deployment of such tactics in the proto-feminist stories of French female *conteuses* in their salons in the seventeenth century to critique their social position and treatment at the time, under the guise and pretence that fairy tales are completely detached from contextual matters.[20] Yet, Haase goes on to presume that, despite his acknowledgement of the inherent importance of temporality in the genre, the fairy tale has no *structural* interest in the *passage of time*.[21] This somewhat contradicts his previous observations and constitutes a dangerously passive acceptance of the genre's supposedly neutral 'timelessness', akin to our naturalised adherence to clock time already outlined. It fails to account for the fairy tale's very real paranoia and consistent demonisation of ageing female characters, for example, which points to the passage of time indirectly, and society's fear of this inevitability. Although fairy tale narratives appear to be stagnant, this is simply an illusion (or in the case of 'Sleeping Beauty', time can only stand still for Briar Rose in her death-like slumber, though time beyond her chamber walls continues to pass, which once again makes clear that time is not stagnant even in the fairy tale universe) – one cannot age if time is standing still and after all fairy tales are often about adolescents coming-of-age and entering a new phase of life. Here there is still growth and time is still essentially moving. Just as masculine mechanical time is bound up with notions of power and control, so too is the innocent 'once upon a time' cover of the literary tales an essential patriarchal weapon. By making the tales appear far outside of our world's temporal range, the patriarchal politics of various societies – Victorian Germany for the Grimms and the seventeenth-century France of Charles Perrault, for example – can invade the stories while remaining invisible behind the timeless, apolitical façade endorsed by the traditional opening line. In essence, the stories are inherently political, and condition female behaviour according to the ideologies of different societies in different eras, making them very much *of* their time rather than *out* of time. Far from a 'structural disinterest' in time then, the constructed notion of 'timelessness' around the fairy tale is very deliberate and highly invested with political purpose.

So, in spite of Haase's claims, temporality *is*, very deliberately, at the heart of the structure of patriarchal fairy tales, it is not simply negated. Talking about the work of Paul Ricoeur, William C. Dowling points out that

> in narrative, it is the entire set of conventions signalling the immemorial situation in which someone is telling and listening to a story – as in, again, the 'once upon a time' of fairy tales or Märchen – that projects a world with a potentially limitless set of listeners or readers who may come to join its audience so long as the written work survives the vicissitudes of historical time.[22]

Here, the problems of the 'once upon a time' motif are made explicit: by making the tales appear to portray a limitless world that anyone from any era can 'come and join', the outdated and sexist moralities and ideologies integral to patriarchal stories (think of Perrault's explicit 'morals' tagged on to the end of each tale, for example) are held up as universal and relevant to all women regardless of era. Women today are still indoctrinated into the same ideologies of passivity, beauty equals goodness, rescue by a handsome prince, marriage as ultimate fulfilment, Snow White domesticity, and 'good' behaviour equating with the reward of 'happily ever after', that were written into the stories centuries ago. Fairy tales are renowned for their predictable structures and inevitable 'happily ever afters' that seem destined to repeat themselves for each new generation. (For example, the Queen in Snow White was once 'the fairest of them all' but is rejected after her marriage to the king and replaced by a new, younger maiden; it is implicit that this fate awaits all women, with Snow White eventually to follow in the Queen's footsteps.) Thus, fairy tales often constitute elements of cyclical mythical time in which there are repeated fates and feats (i.e. heroic acts) doomed forever to repeat themselves.[23] This type of temporal structure leaves no room for change, with even the 'ever after' endings negating the idea of a future in stopping the story at its present state of 'happiness' (usually marriage) as if life ends at that point, to remain unchanged forever, before the next story unfolds between its 'once upon a time' and concluding 'happily ever after' parentheses. (Note that some anti-tales subvert this in showing the unhappy futures that can follow the vague 'ever after' camouflage: Dina Goldstein's photographic image 'Snowy' in her collection *Fallen Princesses*, for instance, depicts an exhausted Snow White cradling two demanding infants, with another pulling at her skirt hem, as she struggles to keep on top of her domestic duties while her husband, Prince Charming, lounges in torn tights watching horse racing, oblivious to the domestic battle going on around him.)[24]

The circle of mythical time shared by the repetitious nature of the fairy tale genre must be broken in order to provide a conclusive closure for outdated ideas and to signal the beginning of new conceptions of being. Freeman notes that one way of doing this is through swapping the circular archetypal pattern for the historical line's trajectory.[25] Essentially, by replacing the stagnancy of mythical time, and its continual repetitions, with endings that look to a different and unknowable future, feminist change can take root. Anti-tales, as revisions of the old stories, envision such new beginnings; despite 'retelling' being an implicit element of this genre, they *revise* the tales, recreating them with an emphasis on their difference or break with the original story. Uncritical repetition is no longer an option.

Overall, the temporal aspects of fairy tales have both pros and cons. While those such as the female conteuses in the seventeenth century

Figure 3.2 Dina Goldstein's 'Snowy' (2008).

availed of the timeless disguise the genre afforded by couching their subversive political ideas in tales of fantasy and magic in an intolerant society, this same timelessness allows outdated ideologies to replay across centuries and remain unchallenged. In addition, as well as the problems of 'once upon a time', 'happily ever after' poses its own set of challenges, with time often stopping at the perceived point of patriarchal fulfilment, marriage. As a genre, it has also been noted that the tales share the trait of mythical time's cyclical repetition, reinforcing stagnant ideas rather than advancing new ones. Anti-tales, of course, break this cyclical loop in reinventing the stories.

Having outlined these ideas, I now have a basis from which to illustrate how anti-tales confront these temporal dilemmas and alter the use of time in order to destabilise assumptions about it, both as we accept time in our everyday lives and time as we have allowed it to go unquestioned within the fairy tale genre. The anti-tales I discuss here do not simply replace one conception of time with another, rather they unsettle and disturb any attempts to know time in its entirety, positing instead a willingness to accept its multifarious nature and constantly shifting complexity.

Time for Change: Rethinking Temporality in the Twenty-First Century

Significantly, while the previous two sections outlined the problematic masculine time of the clock and the troublesome patriarchal tactics inherent in some aspects of fairy tale timelessness, in the twenty-first century more complex understandings of temporality have entered into popular consciousness due to their proliferation in philosophic and scientific discourses. In essence, there is a new, more complex, fluid and feminine conception of time in Postmodernity which informs the ideas perpetuated in the narratives of the feminist anti-tale authors discussed in this chapter.

The early twentieth century saw the publication of ideas that included Einstein's General Theory of Relativity (in which there are no absolutes as regards time and space – both being relative and not set in stone), Bergson's dismissal of the division of time – that is, the slicing of time into neat measures – as 'contrary to experience', Emile Durkheim's assertion that it is the nature of time to be 'more qualitative than quantitative', the birth of Quantum Mechanics (which ultimately rejects time as linear) and the emergence of Heisenberg's Uncertainty Principle in which we 'learned to deal with a spectra of probability rather than certainty'.[26] While it is not in the remit of this study to give detailed discussions of these qualitative scientific discourses, their increasingly human awareness of the impossibility of gaining a total objective or quantifiable understanding of time is integral to the treatment of temporalities in the anti-tale texts of our era.[27] Hence, Linda Hutcheon has alerted us to the fact that the general consensus among critics – that Modernity was a period of temporal inquiry whereas Postmodernism is concerned more with spatiality (and is, therefore, ahistorical) – constitutes a glaring error.[28] As Huehls notes,

> Just because postmodern literature fragments time and flattens history does not mean that it lacks a specific temporality or that it has rejected time as a viable mode of experience. To suggest as much is to throw the baby of temporal experience out with the bathwater of teleological thought.[29]

Hence, while Postmodernism does indeed problematise history, it still contends with temporal ideas; it does not disregard time altogether but is, on the contrary, preoccupied with a complication of our understandings of time and increasing our awareness of its multiple layers. Smethurst uses the idea of the 'postmodern chronotope' then to point out the simultaneous investigation of time and space in postmodern thought and literature (Einstein's earlier scientific exploration of the space-time continuum providing the influential scientific link between the two). He also asserted that,

> In Postmodernity, as in Modernity, science has had considerable influence on how space and time are conceived. Where Einstein's Theory of Relativity had considerable impact on modern chronotopes,

postmodern chronotopes are influenced by chaos theory and ideas from theoretical physics concerning non-directional, non-linear and reversible time.[30]

Thus, although Modernist ideas also upset the notion of orderly, quantitative temporal measurements, Postmodernism takes this a step further with notions of the self and time becoming increasingly problematised and fragmented.

One reason for time's increasing complexity is our digital age of information technology in which we are grounded in our transient physical and material reality while simultaneously existing in, for example, the timeless perpetual presents of our social media profiles. Time, like the self, becomes increasingly difficult to pin down and this loss of our temporal place results in postmodern existentialism. As Smethurst states,

the Postmodern world is guided by simulacra, and sometimes this becomes a substitute for measurement and extrapolation. One effect of this is that we suffer from an excess of information, and the more information we have about the status quo, the harder it becomes to establish precisely where we are and where we might be heading [...] Not the end of history, but the end of history as a map to the future.[31]

The predictability of fairy tale 'happily ever after' no longer holds up, with the future and our predictions balancing on very unstable foundations. Postmodernity is, after all, 'against totalizing narratives', privileging pluralism, anti-history, and anti-structure ideas.[32] In the words of Smethurst:

This indeterminacy flows from a connection with Modernism in which the impetus of the parent movement is carried forward and reversed. For some this is no more than a trick, a sleight of hand, but for others, this simultaneous faring forward and faring backwards, like the double helix which underwrites the building blocks of life itself, signals new directions in the structure of space and time with far reaching impact.[33]

Essentially, the crossover between Modernism and Postmodernism mirrors our continual movements as human beings between past, present, and future, time-travelling through our memories, dreams, hopes, fears, and so on. Time then, as the scientific theories mentioned above attest, is relative to the experience of individuals, not one-directional, and is ultimately subjective. For example, we often perceive time to be moving quickly if we are enjoying something and do not want it to end, whereas, when we want something to be over and done with time appears to slow down and drag its feet. This relative and subjective turn in temporal understanding undermines the chronological and linear objectivity of masculine time. Science, philosophy, and contemporary literature now recognise the relativity of time to human experience and that the past, present, and future cannot be neatly separated or catalogued, just as Postmodernism is not easily separated from Modernism; instead we move continually between past, present, and future, creating a lived polytemporal experience.

Ella Price's 2013 anti-tale collection *Silicon Tales: Storytelling for the Digital Age* contains a story titled 'The Stick of Cherry Red Chalk' that sums up some of these ideas. Told from the chalk's point-of-view we learn that:

> it worked out that it was being used in a lecture on culture, pulling themes of philosophy and science and all sorts of artistic endeavours together in a great big blackboard clock face, which started with the ancient world at about one o'clock and ticked right on round to the twenty-first century chiming in at midnight.
>
> The stick of cherry red chalk quickly worked out that it was definitely getting all the good bits. It was liberally scrawled all over the renaissance, had a total hoot dancing around Da Vinci, and 'Digital Age' even got written in red alone so that it shone out like a beacon. So bright it was that it blasted right out across the lecture hall and into the brain of a student who had never even thought about these things. Certainly not in quite that way. Her neural pathways were suddenly ignited and sparked by that trail of red chalk dust in a manner that would make her potentially even greater than Da Vinci, as it was to turn out. Yes, the inspired, creative story of her life would start straight after that lecture, in the time it took for a large cappuccino and a call to her uncle about funding a trip to Rome.
>
> But when the bell rang the stick of cherry red chalk was put back in its box.[34]

The idea of multiple layers of time is summed up here. On the one hand, the order of a 'great big blackboard clock face' structures the material in a quantitative manner with an hour privileged to each 'great' historical period such as 'the ancient world' or the 'Renaissance', with the twenty-first century 'chiming in at midnight'. Yet this passage reveals that time is largely subjective. For starters, this is a biased historical narrative 'given the passion that the lecturer clearly had for his subject'.[35] It is one individual's reading of history that is on display here and it is no coincidence that Price genders him male and the young student as female: while the 'Great Man' theory of history privileged the achievements of men, as the lecturer does here with 'Da Vinci', the student herself is pointed out to be 'potentially even greater', reminding us of the problems patriarchal time and history posed for female artists and writers bypassed by its exclusionary narrative that recorded only the achievements of their male counterparts in previous eras. Price also highlights how the young woman brings together the three phases of time in one instantaneous moment: when her 'neural pathways were suddenly ignited' in the present, she is influenced by the past (Da Vinci's work), and glimpses the future through sparked hopes and aspirations (her sudden realisation of an artistic vocation). This is a clear example of the fluid nature of our subjective temporal experience in which we cross multiple temporal planes in any given instant, something that the limited measures of the clock cannot account for. In addition, the added complexity of our technological era's impact on time mentioned earlier is summed up in the fact that 'Digital Age' even got 'written in red alone so that it shone out like a beacon'. While historical eras and achievements are scribbled onto different hours on the board, the 'Digital Age' cannot be situated in any specific hour or in any temporal framework, floating free of the blackboard clock's structure – it pulls all of the material together, breaking down the constructed divisions and illustrating that we have reached a period in which time no longer simply moves forwards or backwards or can be arranged into a coherent chronological order – to repeat Smethurst's idea mentioned earlier, in the digital age of Postmodernity, we no longer know where we are nor can we predict where we are going. These ideas are extremely important to feminists, for as Huehls surmises, and as the anti-tales discussed in this chapter demonstrate, 'no single panel of time – future, present, or past – sufficiently grounds politics'.[36]

It is significant that Price's chalk notes that the above 'lecture on culture' pulls 'themes of philosophy and science and all sorts of artistic endeavours together', for this is exactly what this section of my chapter is doing. Science, philosophy, and art are now all bound together and overlap with one another. The outlined turn to more qualitative, relative, and subjective aspects of science and philosophy means that they are now more closely aligned with the arts and humanities, with literature expanding these ideas into popular consciousness. This is exemplified in Sonia Front's 2015 publication *Shapes of Time in British Twenty-First Century Quantum Fiction*. While Front writes about texts clearly interested in Quantum Mechanics, she recognises that literature is 'not constrained by scientific accuracy' and can freely utilise scientific ideas such as 'the shifting shapes of time', the idea of the 'multiverse', and 'the many worlds interpretation'.[37] Note that, while I would not classify the anti-tales to be discussed here as quantum fiction, due to the implied use of magic in some and there being no explicit references to science in any of the texts, the interpretations stem undoubtedly from scientific discoveries and influences. As Smethurst states, like in Modernity,

> in the Postmodern, scientific theory seems to influence social and cultural theory again, with the Big Bang Theory, Chaos theory and the possibility of non-directional (non-linear) time exercising the imagination of the authors of postmodern novels. Leading them to experiment with form again.[38]

The main idea that literature explores is the idea of time and its manifestations on the subjective level of individual experience (think of the use of 'stream-of-consciousness' in Modernist literature, for example). Although literature has a certain amount of poetic licence that science does not have, it does not signal a move away from reality; rather, literature simply changes the way reality is understood and plays out these scientific ideas about time as they relate to human beings and their subjective realities. In this way, such temporal experimentation in postmodern literature becomes, as Smethurst states, 'a political act', in that postmodern texts 'are designed to problematize scientific, social and cultural constructions of time, constructions that are associated with western concepts of reality. Non-linear time in particular has a number of political and ideological implications in the postmodern novel'.[39] Such strategies are used by the authors studied in this chapter as they employ more fluid and 'feminine' interpretations of time to cut across fixed masculine and patriarchal time frames. In the words of Smethurst, the postmodern text is 'a political text, and one that recognises time as a persuasive social construction rather than the hard-edged and incontrovertible reality that supports the tyranny of the clock'.[40]

The shift in temporal understandings brought about by increasingly non-absolute, qualitative, scientific, and philosophical discoveries in the last two centuries has resulted in a more fluid and, as I argue here, a more feminine conception of time which foregrounds subjectivity and privileges non-measurable aspects of temporality such as memories, ghosts from the past, and physical and mental time-travelling. The temporal experimentations in these anti-tales may turn Alice's question on its head; perhaps now the question could be asked if 'Time is a *She*?', given its growing 'irrationality', feminine complexity and ability to get beyond any objective or rational comprehension. As Browne surmises, there now exists the realisation that 'Time is complicated and multifaceted, existing and operating at many different levels' (143).

Feminism and Time: Developing Alternative Models

Feminism has always taken an interest in time (with the publication of works such as Julia Kristeva's renowned 1981 essay 'Women's Time', for example); however, in general, feminist interest has focused more on the idea of history as exclusionary.[41] For example, there has been concern for women writers lost in the Atlantis of patriarchal literary traditions, as expressed by Elaine Showalter in her book *A Literature of Their Own*,[42] and Alice Walker's command to go 'In Search of Our Mothers' Gardens'[43] in order to rescue women from historical obscurity. In essence, women had to begin carving out their own spaces and to reassert their existence in male-dominated chronologies that appeared cohesive, absolute, and set in stone. In addition, Browne has recently recorded this feminist project of 'gendering history', 'premised upon the principle that differently positioned subjects experience and make sense of historical shifts and events in different ways', yet this difference was obliterated in favour of a neat and unambiguous conception of the past (10). Browne describes the feminist strategy in which women writers:

> 'release into the space' occupied by dominant histories, and political processes, a wider spectrum of existing life practices and temporal frameworks [... In this way] History 1 [the grand narrative of History] is continuously interrupted and modified by affective, specific histories or 'History 2s', which cannot be contained or sublimated into History 1. These 'beckon us to more affective narratives of human belonging where life forms, although porous to one another, do not seem exchangeable through a third term of equivalence'. Hence, History 2s 'act as our grounds for claiming historical difference'.
>
> (42–43)

Tanith Lee's *Cruel Pink* employs such tactics, offering the stories and histories of those considered to be unimportant – namely women and those with alternative sexualities – even going as far as setting these within archaic periods, such as seventeenth-century London, in order to convey a sense of forgotten voices and existences who subvert the privileged neat History 1 described above.

Before moving on, another example of an anti-tale that adopts this theory is Afro-American writer Andrea Hairston's story 'Griots of the Galaxy', which resides in the collection *So Long Been Dreaming: Postcolonial Science Fiction and Fantasy*, edited by Nalo Hopkinson and Uppinder Mehan. This collection is important to mention as it understands that the idea of going to distant lands and colonising the natives is an aspect of science fiction that is problematic for writers of colour, being on 'the wrong side of the strange-looking ship that appears out of nowhere'.[44] However, just as fairy tales are deeply laden with patriarchal ideologies, this collection embraces the anti-tale project of revising such science fiction narratives, radically turning the genre's oppressive elements on their head. As Hopkinson points out in the collection's introduction: these are

> stories that take the meme of colonizing the natives and, from the experience of the colonizee, critique it, pervert it, fuck with it, with irony, with anger, with humour, and also, with love and respect for the genre of science fiction that makes it possible to think about new ways of doing things.[45]

Earlier I pointed out how time was used as a colonial weapon to rob native people of their own temporal and cultural rhythms in order to bring them under the regime of the coloniser, with the colonised being placed in the feminised and subordinate position. Hairston's story plays upon the concepts of time, history and colonisation, embracing the idea of foregrounding the importance of small individual 'history 2s' making up a more inclusive and complex collective blanket of History, one that acknowledges the importance of remembering painful narratives in order to bring about a more 'noble' and equal future.

Hairston's tale opens with the following epitaph: 'The Griots of West Africa are musicians, oral historians, praise singers negotiating community. They stand between us and cultural amnesia. Through them we learn to hear beyond our time and understand the future'; foregrounding the importance of recording the stories of those on the margins, on the wrong side of history, not letting us forget that those colonial science fiction narratives are not fantasy but non-fiction, their violence and wrongs only too real and watered down by the grand narrative of History privileged by the powerful.[46] Hairston's protagonist, Axala, is a griot from a far galaxy, colonising various different bodies on Earth and absorbing the memories and feelings of each person she embodies in order to feed back information to the mother ship, giving an overall narrative of earthly life:

> My new life was calling. I had to get on with it. Body historians, griots of the galaxy, we didn't diddle ourselves in jungle paradises, we inhabited flesh to gather a genealogy of life. We sought the story behind all the stories. Collecting life's dazzling permutations, however sweet or sour, was our science, religion, and art – nothing nobler in eternity.
>
> (27)

However, despite being the coloniser (gathering artefacts of earthly lives and absorbing them as part of their own griot culture), Axala comes to recognise that each individual human story is valuable in itself, that eternity and grand, deep time often forgets the stories of small lives which are so precious and important in themselves. Axala no longer wants to just be a 'gig slut' gaining an overarching perspective of life by collecting or stealing stories to download for the mother ship, rather, she wants both her own story, and the lives she has embodied, to be heard and acknowledged. While she states that, 'Body historians didn't usually reveal themselves or get involved, certainly not with pure natives. Just grab the dead miracles and run', she comes to empathise with those whose lives she has colonised and begins to recognise their individual struggles (35). Significantly, the real turning point occurs when she encounters the boyfriend of her current embodiment, Renee. We learn that,

> In Juba, Renee's man, a coward who had abandoned her, who trembled in the shadows while six terrorists violated her, fell on his face

after the first explosion. The terrorists scattered past him, grabbing more weapons and screaming. After the second explosion he crawled towards Renee. When he reached her she was barely breathing. He scooped up her broken body and carried her through the desert to safety [...] Everybody said it was a miracle she got out alive. And he was a hero.

(40)

Axala recognises Renee's pain as a women, betrayed and abandoned, wronged by those with more privilege and power who pervert the historical narrative to suit themselves. But she also recognises the pain of Jay who carries the guilt of his cowardice and wishes he could change the past (the false heroic history created for him) – a clear political message in the recognition of responsibility. Certainly, the boundaries between the colonisers and the colonised are extremely murky in this story: the griots literally colonise earthly bodies, obtaining stories, pieces of culture, and wisdom, but they themselves are like colonised people too, described as

a Diaspora of ghosts living only in borrowed bodies, collecting the wisdom of others, slaves to their appetites, lost to ourselves. After twice ten thousand years on this watery outpost, we were so full of life, the past broke out all over us. Earth had made us aliens to our former selves. We had no desire to be spirits in perpetual exile; we longed to make Earth our story.

(40)

Axala's inability to remain uninvolved in the lives and stories she has collected becomes overwhelming and aspects of all of the previous selves start spilling out at random moments; native stories that would otherwise have been subsumed:

Jay Silver Feather [...] Your great-grandfather was a Seminole, a black Indian, and he told you swamp stories, about stealing slaves into freedom, hiding with trees, making new world communities from the swamps to ... across the border, and never letting white folk catch you at anything. He called you Silver Feather, because you had a spirit that nobody could beat down. I remember your stories, even if I didn't live them. Your spirit is safe with me.

(41)

Axala reaches a designated rendezvous point and finds a video recording of Dr Perez, who states that she is actually Axala when she was housed in one of her previous bodies. Dr Perez/Axala details, in the recording, how 'deep memories' of the lives she'd embodied had started breaking out, no longer just 'Edges' of memories, and that she 'couldn't do it, couldn't separate us [griots] from the body of Earth, couldn't send us on our endless journey. I just didn't have the heart to blast millennia of living into nothing' (44). Therefore, Dr Perez/Axala hired Jay and Renee to explode herself and the other griots in order to 'release [them] from life on earth [...] One blast and we body historians are free to download the burden of Earth and start again' (45). Therefore, Axala realises that Renee and Jay were on their way to the rendezvous point in order to fulfil this task; however, the body of Dr Perez perished and Axala moved into the body of Renee. Having been altered by her new encounters, Axala now acknowledges, 'Each body changes us. We are the sum of all the bodies we have joined', and she is no longer willing to abandon or obliterate the Earth, wanting to fix its problems (45). She chooses to dedicate herself to the future of the Earth, its stories, lives, and histories, in order to contribute towards a better future:

> My left hand hovered over ESCAPE – one touch would blast us to the mother ship. Two right hand fingers rested on ENTER – one touch and we were Earthbound. Paralyzed, I flashed on the forest of ancestors holding Jay and me, on hot milk flowing, humming birds flying backwards [...] and miles of roots holding up a mountain. After twice ten thousand years I wanted to do something impossible, something noble. Instead of chasing down infinity, we could contribute our souls to Earth. A blessing on this future, not now or nothing. The voice and the body and history.
>   Axala of Earth.
>   ENTER.
>
> (45)

While these rescues of individual stories, and the challenges posed to the idea of a singular narrative of the past, are immensely valuable and necessary, feminism often fails to question the equally simplistic ideas surrounding *time* itself; they do not tackle it head on, but instead focus on its product – History. When researching for this chapter, I was surprised by the lack of feminist publications directly addressing time as a concept. Even more telling is the fact that mine does not appear to be an isolated query, with other feminist critics, such as Emily Apter, noting that, at a feminist discussion forum at the Whitney in 2009, 'I was struck by the fact that while temporal references abounded (labour time, the biological clock, intergenerational tensions in the women's movement), nobody addressed the problem of *time* as such'.[47] In the twenty-first century, this chasm is now starting to be bridged, however, with Browne noting the 'time boom' currently taking place in feminist scholarship (2). Elizabeth Grosz, the philosopher-theorist (whose idea of 'space, time and bodies' as the central 'architecture' of postmodern feminist discussion is integral to this study), has turned her attention most obviously to the temporal aspect of this architectural trio in recent years, *Becomings: Explorations in Time, Memory, and Futures* (1999); *The Nick of Time: Politics, Evolution and the Untimely* (2004); and *Time Travels: Feminism, Nature, Power* (2005) constituting some of her most recent book-length publications. Grosz's aim is in line with that of other feminists: to 'develop alternative models' of time that are less restrictive than its historical, chronological, and mechanical, or masculine, conceptions.[48] Grosz focuses specifically on a more 'feminine' revaluation of Darwin's evolutionary ideas (and to some extent on those of Nietzsche and Bergson) in order to counter absolutist conceptions of time. Therefore, while Darwin is often regarded as essential to notions of scientific determinism (due to the Victorian use of his discoveries to support ideological notions of progress and advancement), in actuality, Grosz's reinterpretations of his work reveal a closer alignment with contemporary science and non-determinism. Darwin actually stressed the randomness or 'pure accident' inherent in evolutionary processes, and the anomalies that evade the 'survival of the fittest' idea, but these aspects of his thinking did not adhere well to the British sense of colonial and evolutionary superiority in the nineteenth century, and so, like unruly female or queer histories, these elements were trimmed or ironed out in favour of a neater and more simplistic idea of Darwin and his work.[49] Her reading of Darwinism thus supports the multiplicity of time and:

> problematizes the central position accorded to determinism and to virtues of science or knowledge contained by and at the mercy of the imperative of predictability as one of the defining concepts within sciences, recognizing that determinism is the annulling of any concept of temporality other than one structured by the terms and conditions of the past and present. Determinism annihilates any future uncontained by the past and the present.
>
> More positively, [her reading] affirms time as an open-ended and fundamentally active force – a materializing if not material – force whose movements and operations have an inherent element of surprise, unpredictability, or newness.[50]

In this way, Grosz supports a temporality that is unrestrictive and points towards the idea of an open future full of possibility rather than expounding the dominantly accepted assumptions about evolution (with its notion of a future that is already predicated and is a foregone conclusion). Hence, Grosz describes a similar temporal consciousness to that of Browne, in which feminist change can really take root and provide hope for the future, uninhibited by the chains of the past, an existence 'where the many different paths leading from ambiguous pasts intersect in a complex present, to produce multiple interpretations and possibilities that stretch into the future' (40).

As this section outlines, feminists have finally initiated discussions over the problems with current temporal paradigms and are starting to promote new polytemporal and complex understandings of time that are inclusive, accepting, and non-discriminatory. Yet, as Browne notes, it is important to point out that 'On its own, the claim that there are "multiple times" does not get us very far, as it does not address the question of how different times and temporalities coexist and interrelate with one another' (38). This chapter highlights how these ideas are played out in twenty-first-century anti-tale narratives and what purpose they serve for women today. Overall, while feminists have provided new theories and conceptual understandings of temporal frameworks, these theories and philosophical ideas now need to be extended into various fields and their relevance to real women concretised by an illustration of their liberating potential – literature is one medium that has taken up this task in displaying these alternative temporalities at work in our everyday lives, constituting a subversion of patriarchal time and its inhibiting restrictions.

'We're All Mad Here': The 'Rational' Masculine Clock vs. 'Irrational' Feminine Time in *Alice Through the Looking Glass* (2016)

Having discussed the idea of clock, or mechanical, time as a product of Enlightened maleness, and the contrast of fluid alternative times as unruly and feminine, I now wish to show how these theories have entered subversively into mainstream culture, in this case, through James Bobin's 2016 anti-tale film, *Alice Through the Looking Glass*. The film received very poor reviews, with *The Telegraph*'s Tim Robey echoing many reviewers in his assertion that 'The whole business, this time, is passable eye candy without being any kind of brain candy'.[51] Despite such assertions and the fact that it is also a Disney movie, it appears that critics have failed to pick up on the key point of the film, with Bobin himself pointing out in an interview that it is less about narrative and more about concepts and ideas (like Lewis Carroll's second book upon which the film is loosely based).[52] Critics have failed to grasp the film's depth, with Bobin's feminist message hinging upon his explorations of time and space rather than on simple narrative content. Bobin notes that Alice would have been born around the 1850s and the film is set in 1875, 'the time of the suffragettes', conveyed in Mia Wasikowska's depiction of Alice's restless spirit. Here, then, I wish to explore the use of time as integral to the film's subversive feminism that goes beyond the mere simplistic depiction of Alice as a progressive ship's captain and action heroine.

The film depicts Alice returning home to London from her travelling adventures in foreign lands full of hope and excitement, ready to do further exploring in order to find out more about foreign lands and different cultures. Her rejected suitor from Tim Burton's previous film, Hamish, is now in charge of the company, with Alice's mother (Mrs. Kingsleigh) having sold Alice's share and the bonds of their home (which they will only receive back in return for signing over her father's ship, the 'Wonder'). He informs her that he will not have a female in a captain's role but will 'generously' offer her employment as a clerk instead, the entirely male business cohort chuckling along with his, 'I'm sorry. But this is all we can do for you. No other company is in the business of hiring female clerks let alone ship captains'. Through Hamish, Bobin depicts the financial dependence and vulnerability of women who had no choice but to rely on men economically in the Victorian era (especially those in Alice and her mother's situation who no longer have a father or husband to support them): 'Show up to work on Monday morning and you will receive a salary and a pension. Otherwise we cannot help you'. Alice's interrogation of her mother (who has internalised the patriarchal ideas of her era) introduces the first explicit reference to the theme of time within the film:

ALICE: How could you sell our shares?
MRS KINGSLEIGH: Alice, everything I do is for you, so you can make a *decent* start in life.
ALICE: Five minutes ago I was a sea captain!
MRS KINGSLEIGH: A sea captain is no job for a lady! *Time* is against you and you're being careless with it! You can't just make things how you want them to be. Every woman must face that, Alice. I've had to.

Here Mrs. Kingsleigh endorses the idea that time is the enemy of women specifically and, her idea that as a female 'you can't just make things how you want them to be', perhaps refers to the stifling and immovable nature of patriarchal clock time, which straightjackets women into socially acceptable roles. The heroine is running out of time to fulfil her conventional expectations, according to her mother. Alice's actions in the rest of the movie prove, however, that you can indeed make things how you want them to be, breaking down the seemingly impassable regime of the clock and following her own time-travelling adventures outside of established temporal rules. At the outset of this chapter, I demonstrated how patriarchal clock time is inherently linked to colonialism, with colonisers deploying their Western conception of time in other cultures as part of the process of eradicating alternative temporalities and anything considered to have a threatening 'otherness'. Thus, Alice's role as the ship's captain at the beginning of the film, at first glance, appears to be problematic in aligning the heroine with colonial exploitation and power when she approaches Hamish with her 'business proposition'. Here, it might also be implied that the film's feminist message takes such precedence that Alice's roles are endorsed in favour of female empowerment over the exploration of colonial exploitation. In fact, Bobin does exactly the opposite in emphasising instead Alice's respect for the 'otherness' of the cultures she has seen, the heroine on returning appears to have been willingly colonised by the countries she has visited. For example, she attends the ball in an exotic dress much to the dismay of her conventional mother: 'If it's good enough for the dowager, Empress of China, it's good enough for the Ascotts'. (It should be noted, however, that Alice's outfit appears to be that of the Chinese ruling classes and those in power, yet nevertheless it shows Disney moving some way towards aligning Alice with foreign cultures; Disney, of course, being historically infamous for its problematic racial and cultural depictions.) She also attempts to discuss her discoveries with the men in the business, displaying her empathy, and attempts to create a genuine bond and understanding with those other cultures she'd like to do trade with. Alice's open-mindedness is comically highlighted to be in sharp contrast to the British colonial arrogance and narrow vision represented in Hamish's new wife in the following exchange, in which the latter assumes that the entire world can be summed up in a single sentence:

LADY ASCOTT: Well, how was it?
ALICE [*baffled*]: The world?
LADY ASCOTT: Yes.
ALICE: Highly enjoyable, you should try it sometime.

Here then, Alice is aligned with the otherness of foreign cultures and their alternative temporalities early in the film, with the teaser poster also symbolically depicting her treading carefully over cogs and parts of clockwork machinery trying to negotiate her own way in a world that is stifled by such rules and absolutes. Here then, just before she re-enters Wonderland to escape such regulations, Hamish clearly introduces the seedling of an idea that will take shape throughout the rest of the story: that of masculine rational clock time versus alternative or 'irrational' feminine time. As he explains to the businessmen once she has left the room: 'She spent months up river dressed like she'd gone native. Of course it's said to have done strange things to a man's mind let alone a woman's'.

After escaping through the looking glass, Alice discovers that the Mad Hatter is dying from grief after being reminded of his family's tragedy years ago when they were supposed to have died after an attack on the village by the Red Queen's dragon; a historical event in Wonderland known as Horunvendush Day. Seemingly insane, the Hatter asks Alice to bring his family back (a small hat he made for his father was found in the field where they were supposed to have perished and, in his mind, this is enough proof to suggest that they are alive). Having been freshly conditioned by her mother to believe that 'you can't make things how you want them to be', Alice believes that this is impossible due to the irreversible nature of death and the insurmountable rules of time that prevent this. Having lost her 'muchness' (that is, her belief in the impossible and the excess of spatio-temporal abundance), the Hatter throws her out of his home, accusing her of not being the 'real Alice', 'my Alice would believe me'. Indeed, this Alice has been damaged by social rules in her recent patriarchal encounters. It takes this conversation to awaken Alice's old beliefs in the possibilities of life beyond 'rationality' or rules, and she agrees with the other Wonderland characters that she will 'travel back in time' to put things right and save the Hatter's family. It is only Alice who can do this, as the film shares an idea posited in physics, with the White Rabbit explaining that, 'We cannot use it [a time-travelling device known as the chronosphere] because we have already been in the past and if your past self sees your future self ...'. Being from an alternative universe, Alice is able to do the time-travelling without this worry, and although they do not know the consequences of what would happen if someone was to see himself/herself, they imagine 'everything would be history'. The chronosphere, as the White Queen humorously points out, is 'in the hands of Time. It's his':

ALICE: I'm sorry, Time is a *he*?
WHITE QUEEN: He lives in a void of infinitude, in a castle of eternity. Through here [*points to a large grandfather clock*], one mile past the pendulum.
CHESHIRE CAT: And do try not to break the past, present or future.

We soon discover that Time is a mechanical entity with a matter-of-fact coldness. He has rooms titled 'Underlandians: Living' and 'Underlandians: Dead', which contain pocket watches hanging from the sky with the names of individuals engraved upon them; human beings literally reduced to faceless clocks. He then decides whose time is up and moves them to the dead room, placing them, of course, in alphabetical order (mechanical time's categorical nature being mocked here): 'Who has stopped? Who has ticked their last tock, tocked their last tick?'. Time here is depicted as loving the sadistic power he wields and, tellingly, although he is fearful when he senses an intruder, upon discovering Alice, he is no longer threatened – 'Oh, it's a girl' – and rejects her attempt to, as he puts it, 'disintegrate history' through the use of his 'invincible machine'. The association of Time with corruption is embodied in the fact that his lover is the Red Queen who states that if he gave her the chronosphere as a gift 'we could rule the past, present, and future'. Time's reluctance to exploit his influence highlights that perhaps time itself is not the problem, rather it is the uses of time in power relations that needs to be tackled. Certainly, despite his flaws, we do see a more human side to Time; valuing Alice's wit before she leaves – 'Thank you for your you, Sir' – he smiles and offers her a piece of advice, the significance of which will become clear shortly: 'Young Lady, you cannot change the past but you can learn something from it'. Nevertheless, Alice, instead of leaving, steals the chronosphere (a kind of locomotive machine with ship controls) and voyages across 'the great ocean of time' to save her friend, the Hatter. The fact that Bobin uses this imagery of the sea of time for Alice's time-travelling visually equates this alternative temporal fluidity with femininity, feminine language (or *l'écriture féminine*) being something in which, as Hélène Cixous points out, 'we often find images of the spring, of liquid, of water'.[53] It is a literal and visual illustration of time's fluidity. Feminine temporalities, like Alice, constantly escape mechanical Time's grasp.

Alice discovers in the past that the Red Queen has been the source of constant ridicule due to the fact that her sister lied about hiding crusts of her mother's freshly baked tarts under her bed and pins the blame on her. Upset, the Red Queen runs into the street and hits her head which then swells up to an enormous size. It is this anger that causes her to inevitably carry out the crimes of Horunvendush Day that killed Hatter's family. As well as being an example of the familiar anti-tale technique of giving villainesses the space to reveal the motives behind their actions, her failure to prevent these events, including Hatter's arguments with his father, means that Time's advice – 'You can't change the past you can only learn from it' – now rings true for Alice. Visiting Horunvendush Day itself, the heroine discovers that the Red Queen did not actually kill Hatter's family, rather she kidnapped them. At this point, Time catches up with her and Alice is forced to escape once again back out of a looking glass and into the human world. It is here that rational male clock

Figure 3.3 The sea of time. *Alice Through the Looking Glass*, dir. James Bobin (Walt Disney Studios Home Entertainment: 2016).

time versus unruly feminine time is made most explicit; particularly in the film's juxtaposition of the human world (painted in very plain, dark colours and containing solid urban structures) and Wonderland (with its bright colours and nonsensical, dream-like landscapes). With Time's raging proclamation – 'You cannot escape time' – still ringing in her ears, Alice wakes up staring at a ceiling whose structure is reminiscent of a clock face and discovers that she is lying on a bed inside a mental institution; told by her mother that 'Hamish had you brought here'. For her meddling with the order of time, and her refusal of its rigid rules and conventions, Alice is deemed to be mad, with the doctor observing: 'excitable, emotional, prone to fantasy: textbook case of female hysteria'. It is no coincidence that once Alice escapes, with her mother's support, we see her run past patients that are all female: women who stray outside of society's established order or who question authority (as Alice has done with Time, his servant stating, 'She's here, Sir. The girl who tricked you and made you look a complete idiot'), they are condemned. It is telling then that Alice embraces the subversive unruliness of her own alternative time and lifestyle, exemplified when she steals a horse and carriage to escape the hospital, calling back, 'I plead insanity!'.

Getting back to Wonderland, Alice, Time, the Wonderland characters, and Hatter's family (whom they have liberated from the Red Queen's ant farm) are outwitted when the Red Queen steals the chronosphere and travels back to the past to the incident where she was blamed for her sister's stealing of her mother's tarts. She bursts in on the scene, sees her younger self, and so the universe starts to unravel. As Robey states, here 'Bobin unleashes easily his film's most impressive set-piece: the clockwork nerve-centre of the universe is stricken with a space-time disturbance,

Figure 3.4 Wonderland rusts over. *Alice Through the Looking Glass*, dir. James Bobin (Walt Disney Studios Home Entertainment: 2016).

and begins rusting over. It's like a fast-spreading termite attack on all the film's shiny surfaces and faces'.[54]

The film suggests here then that beneath the artificial 'shiny' exterior, the order of time and the universe can be subverted and unravelled. However, it is only when Alice restores the chronosphere to its rightful place that Wonderland is saved in the nick of time, Hatter reconciled with his family, the White Queen apologising to her sister, and the Wonderland characters all reunited. Hence, the film re-establishes the order of time at the end and, in fact, highlights it as a necessity, with Alice explaining to Time that, 'I know you tried to warn me but I didn't listen. I'm sorry. You see, I used to think time was a thief stealing everything I love but I see now that you give before you take and every day is a gift'. Upon saying this, Alice gives him her father's broken pocket watch to hang up with the others; time has let her grieve. Rather than constituting a conservative ending, however, with the return to orderly time, I would suggest that the film's exploration of time as negotiable and fluid has done enough in subverting the idea of it as an absolute lawgiver. Hatter also introduces the idea of alternative time again to remind the viewer of this before the movie closes when he answers Alice's concerns over their meeting again: 'My dear, Alice, in the gardens of memory, in the palace of dreams, that is where you and I will meet'. Both memories and dreams, of course, defying accepted temporal laws. Returning home, Alice rejects Hamish's simplistic assertion to her mother that 'Time is money', stating that 'Time is *many* things, Hamish, but he isn't money. Nor is he our enemy, mother'. Here Alice reclaims time for women: we no longer need to fear it, rather, we need to manipulate it to suit our wishes and needs. In this way, her mother's assertions of time as enemy and 'you can't make things how you want them to be' as a woman in the world are shattered, Mrs. Kingsleigh now realising that, 'Alice can do whatever she chooses and so can I'. The women sign over the ship (they have grieved for their father and husband) and start up a joint business of their own – 'Kingsleigh & Kingsleigh' – setting sail at the film's close to compete with Hamish's patriarchal company on their own terms: 'Time and tide wait for no man, or indeed, woman'.

'Time Is *Many* Things': Lived/Subjective and Polytemporal Times in Tanith Lee's *Cruel Pink*

Just like Alice, the characters in Tanith Lee's *Cruel Pink* struggle with the tight restrictions of patriarchal clock time. Rod, for example, was brought up as a girl by parents keen to have a female child, which he happily endorses until he is orphaned, and his new guardian is outraged by the unconventional upbringing he has received. The language Rod uses to describe the revelation of his maleness is extremely telling: 'And next I was cast in a new mould very strange to me [...] On went the straightjacket of maleness. On went the shackles of *learning*, all over again, what *not*, and *what* to do, to want, to hate'.[55] Here the pressures of social conditioning and expectations imprison him in a gender not of his own choosing, and most significantly, his paranoia at measuring up to patriarchal expectations is symbolised in his strict adherence to the masculine time of the clock. Preoccupied with time, he is infuriated when his watch refuses to work:

> it was about twelve forty-five, a quarter to one. I say about, my watch was playing up. It tends to do that on or after a train journey, even of twenty minutes. Most machines play up when I use them. At work it's our department's running joke.
>
> (16)

Clearly this emphasises that his feminine nature is out of sync with mechanical time, and his adherence to the clock and conventional masculinity is entirely artificial.[56] Rod even describes his alarm clock as a 'watchdog' that controls his existence and uses an adherence to precise numerical measurements as a means of keeping his subversive desire to indulge in feminine clothing in check:

> I did have one quick look in the wardrobe. Only *one* look. My second, though, if I counted this morning. No worse than the drinks I thought. Half a glass of white wine at lunch and a double vodka in the evening. Half a minute's morning wardrobe-look, and two minutes' look at night. That was enough, and not too much.
>
> (81, 23)

His whole life is kept in order by his clockwork precision and measuring of any kind of indulgence, as though he is a recovering addict of some sort. The controlling force of clock time is also evident at the conclusion of the actor, Irvin's, narrative. Due to the fact that he is bisexual and sexually promiscuous in the sixteenth or seventeenth century, his desires are brought under control by his final conformity to social institutions, including the tick of the clock:

> I shall freeze out from myself the glorious sins of my flesh until I too am stone, both cold and grey, my own fine tower clamped in chastity, and my own bold heart clock-timed to a sedentary *tick*. Starved, flailed and chained. I am to be a priest.
>
> (227)

It is important to consider, then, how the novel challenges such stifling temporal forms.

Two major aspects of the politics of feminist time inherent in *Cruel Pink* are, what Browne calls, 'lived temporalities' and the idea of time as multiple or polytemporal, with the two strands being heavily interlinked (3). *Cruel Pink* is an extreme example of subjective time at work. The five characters, as Chapter 1 highlighted, are discovered at the resolution of the novel to be constructs of the subjective mindset and multiple-personality disorder experienced by an old woman, Dawn:

> While I am myself I can still recall, at last, very clearly, that I am also, a young murderess [Emenie], and a man who has retired early to his childhood home to keep a horse and read books [Rod], and a young girl who dances and makes love in a world of futuristic dreams [Klova], and a proud male actor who will now become a proud and sombre priest [Irvin].
>
> (228)

The theory discussed previously, of postmodern time's increasing fragmentation resulting from the further deconstructions of notions of selfhood in our era, is clearly embodied here in Lee's novel, with Smethurst pointing out that,

> Currie links schizophrenia with postmodern culture because this is a condition in which the subject loses any sense of himself in time, and he is unable to ground his identity in a stable passage of time from past into future.[57]

Thus, Dawn's mental disorder symbolises the radical breakdown of fixed understandings of history, time, and space in contemporary culture. It is similar to *Alice Through the Looking Glass*'s use of irrational feminine time to get beyond the stifles of rationalised temporal frameworks. As Freeman notes,

> a conception of the personhood that is congruent with the complexities of human temporality just identified [... is the idea of] 'multiphrenia', which refers to 'the splitting of the individual into a multiplicity [...] with the demise of a view of life marked by "rational coherence"'.[58]

Hence, Lee's novel also points towards a temporality that gets beyond empirical or scientific measurements of the world towards a philosophy of lived time, creating a complex feminine temporality in which all boundaries are negotiable. Emenie notes that 'The main room and the bedroom seemed warped out of true, their angles all wrong', and Irvin points out, once all of the characters' sense of self begins to unravel at their realisation of the artificial nature of their apparent stability, that 'the clocks began to chime, all out of time and tune with each other as ever' (155, 173). There are as many 'clocks' or times as there are people, all ticking at their own inconsistent pace. For example, Emenie subverts the social clock, measuring time in her own unique way by the bodily decay of her latest victim, with the following passage also providing a clear link to grandma's protesting bones rattling under the bed at Little Red's sexual indulgence in Angela Carter's 'A Company of Wolves':

> There was a kind of half-musical balance for a few seconds, the upper melody of the engines overhead, and me lying on my grandmother's bed – the central theme – while below the darkened strings of my latest victim's deadness formed the base, the percussion, steady and solid as an ancient ticking clock.
>
> (16)

Killing is Emenie's taboo pleasure and with it she lives her own alternative existence outside of time and social acceptability. In addition, Klova's life revolves around beauty and cosmetics and so her clock is 'the tick-tick of my slenderest totter-heels on the milk-light-washed pavement' (26). In essence, time is relative to the individual. In addition, Dawn, suffering from Alzheimer's, inevitably experiences time differently; it is not linear but instead she glimpses snapshots of her past and constantly moves back and forward between these memories and the present. This is an example of what Freeman dubs as the further complication of temporal understanding in 'the numerous and complex "shuttlings" between various modalities of time operative in memory' – we are even taken back in Dawn's mind to the Second World War at one point.[59] Yet, even the simplest statements like, 'Time flies, doesn't it. It was only August a minute ago, or so it seems. And tomorrow it'll probably be Christmas Eve! I'm joking. But it seems that way, to me', destabilise the idea of an objective time, showing us how subjective our experiences of temporality are everyday (152). While it moves quickly here for Dawn whose husband died thirty years ago, at the same time, in a different consciousness, that of Rod, time appears to be stagnant or standing still as he awaits his escape to a house in the country: 'Maybe I will get out. I'm growing edgy after all [...] given the way time is elongating' (169).

To move on slightly from the radical complexity of lived or subjective time, as Browne states,

> historical time should be understood as *polytemporal*. It is an internally complex, 'composite' time, generated through the interweaving of different temporal layers and strands. As such, there is no 'one' historical time or temporal structure within which diverse histories are all embroiled. On the contrary, there will always be multiple, shifting patterns of historical time, as different histories have their own mixes of time and their own temporalities.
>
> (2)

In essence, by viewing historical time as polytemporal, feminists can undermine the idea of a single, coherent chronological history that can be contained within one unified narrative; each individual will have different conceptions or experiences of historical events. *Cruel Pink* focuses very deliberately on characters who are on the margins of society, isolated and absent from dominant historical records due to their alternative gender identities, sexualities, or habits; they subvert the homogeneous nature of historical accounts, instead adding contradictory strands to a once tidy blanket of history that covered over their problematic digressions from the norm. As Browne states,

> The peaks and valleys of historical time [...] may appear in very different places, depending on who is looking and whose fortunes are being tracked across the centuries. Accordingly, we cannot presume that there is a single unified 'space of experience' or 'horizon of expectation', nor one narrative configuration that could draw together and express diverse historical experiences within one encompassing temporal structure.
>
> (86)

Hence, polytemporal time is a necessity in order to account for every individual, rather than patriarchal time's tendency to record only the experiences of those whose lives accord with dominant trends.

This is evident in the very structure of the novel. Smethurst points out that 'postmodern narrative reinscribes difference by reinserting the gaps and silences between different histories and forms of knowledge, and a linear narrative would suppress these breaks and intrusions'.[60] Certainly, Lee's novel embraces such ruptures. While these characters not only live separate lives but also occupy entirely different eras (Rod living in the contemporary world, Klova existing in a sci-fi future of liquid silver drinks and artificial flowers, Emenie surviving in a crumbling apocalypse-scarred London, and Irvin representing the sixteenth or seventeenth century), they still manage to spill over, interrupt, and echo in each other's narratives. For example, the smell of the dead bodies from Emenie's ground floor flat haunts the other characters, despite the fact that they never actually see or know of each other's existence. Rod summarises this when he reflects:

> Yet – how to explain this? I had, now and then, felt an *awareness* of another person – or people – evinced by nothing I could call up as proof – but nevertheless inhabiting both the opposite flat and the rooms above. It – they – scentless, noiseless, unlit, and having no visible form, yet I had a vague awareness of having – *glimpsed* them – without seeing.
>
> (91)

In this way, they are literally ghosts haunting one another's present, with the sci-fi Klova once glimpsing a physical manifestation of the archaic Irvin in her window:

> I didn't want to be there, but where else? I didn't want to be any-where. Not even under the river in case, then, all I could be would be *memory, remembering.*
>
> But I looked up at the flat-house [...] Then I saw there *was* a light. In my social room.
>
> I stood there, looking over, staring. I was amazed, and my true misery I forgot [...] Up to the inside of the window came this old, *old* man. And he stood quite still, and as I stood looking up at him, he looked down at me. He held a funny glass in his hand, like glasses were centuries ago that you see in museums on quick-view. And in the glass was a red drink he was drinking very fast. But he paused a moment, and waved at me.
>
> He waved.
>
> The old, old man.
>
> At me.
>
> From inside my flat.
>
> (84)

Here, the ghosts of the characters function as time travellers and this constitutes a powerful part of the novel's feminist message. This relates to what Browne calls the 'time of the trace' in which

> the politics of the present are inextricably entangled with ideas about 'what really happened' in the past, and there is a commitment to 'tell the truth' about past and present realities [...] What is excluded or forgotten exists as a trace or an echo, with the potential to disturb.
>
> (53, 66)

In Lee's novel then, 'traces from the past "spill forwards into the pres-ent"' allowing the reader to become aware of both alternative histo-ries and the lack of change in our society as regards social minorities (namely women and men with fluid sexualities) (50–51). After all, every character in the novel, regardless of era, experiences mistreatment and social scorn for living outside of societal expectations. Thus, Klova's glimpse of Irvin in her window briefly lifts her out of her own despair, and they are linked in their loneliness and seclusion, reaching out across time to acknowledge one another. This is similar to Front's reading of *Sputnik Caledonia*, in which she argues that the protagonist, 'Robert's, parallel lives, which he glimpses in quantum consciousness, become in Goethe's terms "multiplicity in unity", that is, "One in the form of many and many which are One"'.[61] This creates a kind of shared time or interconnectedness that can be viewed as a radical unification of those who are oppressed in *Cruel Pink*, the reassurance that they are not alone, while still respecting difference and the individual's story. As Dawn concludes the novel:

> One by one, as each, I and they, become ready, we will walk up the bridge of steel, or of copper, or of diamond, opal and ruby, or iron-black, or gold and silver, and cross through into the bright mist. And there we will all be one and quite different, so different from anything we have been here, ever, that I can't imagine it. Nor any of us could.

(228)

And yet, the characters choose for the meantime to linger on in a ghostly limbo, haunting the reader and reminding us of the unstable nature of both self and time, and the liberating potential in the acceptance of the multiplicity and fluidity of both. Like Rod, we are liberated from the straightjackets of gender expectations and patriarchal time, instead appreciating our subjective control of both. There is no predictable or closed 'happily ever after' here, Dawn noting that she 'can't imagine it', the future, in an embrace of Grosz's feminist wish, outlined previously, to view the future as open, unpredictable, and full of potential.

Conclusion

In this chapter, I provide an outline of how time is not a neutral force but rather is informed and shaped by dominant power structures and used as a means of policing behaviour and maintaining social control (colonialism was posited as one example, with feminised aboriginal times being dominated by the standardised masculine time of the coloniser). I detailed the means by which postmodern anti-tales subvert and challenge such traditional patriarchal uses of the clock, and the guise of fairy-tale 'Once upon a time' timelessness, through the creation of more complex and fluid feminine temporalities that cannot be neatly contained by numbers and quantitative measurements. In essence, as the polytemporality in Lee's *Cruel Pink* highlights, there is no such thing as a single coherent time, but rather as many different temporalities as there are people, time being subjective and relative to experience. In addition, the rational objectivity of enlightened maleness, associated with mechanical time, is subverted in Bobins's film *Alice Through the Looking Glass*, with Alice's time-travelling constituting a rejection of the personified male Time's authority as she plays around with ideas of 'irrational' femininity to show the negotiable nature of both space and temporality. What all of the sections in this chapter reveal is that time is a valuable political tool for rethinking the social architecture of hierarchies and power relations, and its feminine revision constitutes a necessary step in feminist progress. As Browne states:

> It can help us to understand feminism as polytemporal, nonlinear, and internally complex, and to develop a historiography that does justice to the vibrancy and variance of feminist histories and temporalities. By unlocking our feminist pasts and presents, we may yet bring about feminist futures.
>
> (146)

Certainly, *Cruel Pink* and Hairston's 'Griots of the Galaxy' posit alternative stories which undermine the exclusionary grand narrative of History, with the characters haunting one another's presents in order to create a shared time, highlighting the interconnectedness of their status as oppressed peoples, despite occupying entirely different eras. Here, the barriers of time collapse and allow them to constitute a collective and powerful voice of the dispossessed, looking forward, and committed to, a new and radically unknown future, constituting what Huehls dubs as a 'qualified hope in the political value of time'.[62] And, as we have seen, the anti-tale is one genre that is currently pushing such ideas, with Browne noting that,

> When the interpreter reflects on the conditions of interpretation, 'the return [to the world after reading the tale] is not so much a turn back as it is a turn forward to the conditions as they are considered in the present ... in view of something projected (hoped for, feared, awaited ...)'.
>
> (81)

In essence, we can use these stories to pave the way for, and envision, a better time, or rather, times, for women in the future.

Notes

1 Simone de Beauvoir quoted in Lynne Segal, *Out of Time: The Pleasures and Perils of Aging* (London: Verso Books, 2014), p. 6.
2 Victoria Browne, *Feminism, Time, and Nonlinear History* (Hampshire: Palgrave Macmillan, 2014), p. 143. Hereafter, page references will be incorporated into the text.
3 Cristina Bacchilega, *Postmodern Fairy Tales: Gender and Narrative Strategies* (Pennsylvania: University of Pennsylvania Press, 1997), p. 139.
4 See any of Zipes's work included in the bibliography for a socio-historical reading of the fairy tale genre.
5 Catriona McAra and David Calvin, 'Introduction', *Anti-Tales: The Uses of Disenchantment* (Newcastle upon Tyne: Cambridge Scholars Publishing, 2011), p. 3.
6 Mitchum Huehls, *Qualified Hope: A Postmodern Politics of Time* (Columbus: The Ohio State University Press, 2009), p. 1.

7 Ibid.

8 *Alice Through the Looking Glass*, dir. James Bobin (Walt Disney Studios Home Entertainment: 2016) [on DVD]. Hereafter, any material quoted in relation to *Alice through the Looking Glass* is taken from this text.

9 'Time's Arrow' is related to the Second Law of Thermodynamics. This pertains to the idea that the energy dispersed with the Big Bang causes increasing entropy and the descent into chaos, with the universe working to equalise the distribution of mass and energy – a state where there is no free energy left to cause chemical reactions or sustain life, bringing the universe to a still equilibrium eventually. This asymmetry of time, in which natural processes are understood as being irreversible, provides direction for Time's Arrow, helping us to distinguish between the past, the present, and the future it pulls us towards, as the universe works through its stages of entropic chaos.

10 Giordano Nanni, 'Time, Empire and Resistance in Settler-Colonial Victoria' in *Time & Society*, Vol. 20, No. 1 (2011), p. 6.

11 Ibid., p. 6.

12 Ibid., p. 5.

13 Ibid., pp. 5, 6.

14 Ibid., p. 6.

15 Quoted in Paul Smethurst, *The Postmodern Chronotope: Reading Space and Time in Contemporary Fiction* (Amsterdam: Rodopi, 2000), p. 31.

16 Nanni, 'Time, Empire and Resistance in Settler-Colonial Victoria' in *Time & Society*, p. 6.

17 Ibid., p. 26.

18 Donald Haase, 'Children, War, and the Imaginative Space of Fairy Tales' in *The Lion and the Unicorn*, Vol. 24 (2000), p. 362.

19 Bruno Bettelheim, *The Uses of Enchantment: The Meaning and Importance of Fairy Tales* (London: Penguin Books Ltd., 1976).

20 Elizabeth Waning Harries, *Twice Upon a Time: Women Writers and the History of the Fairy Tale* (Princeton: Princeton University Press, 2001).

21 Haase, 'Children, War, and the Imaginative Space of Fairy Tales' in *The Lion and the Unicorn*, p. 362.

22 William C. Dowling, *Ricoeur on Time and Narrative: An Introduction to Temps et récit* (*Notre Dame*: University of Notre Dame Press, 2011), p. 14.

23 See Mark Freeman, 'Mythical Time, Historical Time, and the Narrative Fabric of the Self' in *Narrative Inquiry*, Vol. 8, No. 1 (1998), pp. 27–50.

24 Dina Goldstein, 'Snowy' in *Fallen Princesses* <http://www.fallenprincesses.com> [accessed 7th September 2016].

25 See Freeman, 'Mythical Time, Historical Time, and the Narrative Fabric of the Self' in *Narrative Inquiry*, pp. 27–50.

26 Smethurst, *The Postmodern Chronotope: Reading Space and Time in Contemporary Fiction*, pp. 32, 104.

27 For accessible outlines of these scientific ideas I recommend reading Sonia Front's *Shapes of Time in British Twenty-First Century Quantum Fiction* (Cambridge: Cambridge Scholars Publishing, 2015). Front not only explores these ideas but proceeds to apply the theories to her readings of literary texts. See also Paul Smethurst's *The Postmodern Chronotope: Reading Space and Time in Contemporary Fiction*.

28 See Linda Hutcheon, 'The Postmodern Problematizing of History' in *English Studies in Canada*, Vol. XIV, (4th December 1988), pp. 365–382.

29 Huehls, *Qualified Hope: A Postmodern Politics of Time*, p. 6.

30 Smethurst, *The Postmodern Chronotope: Reading Space and Time in Contemporary Fiction*, p. 19.
31 Ibid., p. 84.
32 Ibid., p. 23.
33 Ibid, p.28.
34 Ella Price, 'The Stick of Cherry Red Chalk' in *Silicon Tales: Storytelling for the Digital Age* (Bristol: Silver Wood Books, 2013), p. 106.
35 Ibid., p. 106.
36 Huehls, *Qualified Hope: A Postmodern Politics of Time*, p. 6.
37 Sonia Front, *Shapes of Time in British Twenty-First Century Quantum Fiction* (Newcastle upon Tyne: Cambridge Scholars Publishing, 2015), pp. vii, 1, 14.
38 Smethurst, *The Postmodern Chronotope: Reading Space and Time in Contemporary Fiction*, p. 105.
39 Ibid., p. 175.
40 Ibid.
41 Julia Kristeva, 'Women's Time' in *Signs*, Vol. 7, No. 1 (Autumn 1981), pp. 13–35.
42 Elaine Showalter, *A Literature of Their Own: British Women Novelists from Brontë to Lessing* (Princeton: Princeton University Press, 1977).
43 Alice Walker, 'In Search of Our Mothers' Gardens' in *Making Sense of Women's Lives: An Introduction to Women's Studies*, eds. Michèle Plott & Lauri Umansky (Oxford: Collegiate Press, 2000).
44 Nalo Hopkinson, 'Introduction' in *So Long Been Dreaming: Postcolonial Science Fiction and Fantasy* (Vancouver: Arsenal Pulp Press, 2004), p. 7.
45 Ibid. p. 9.
46 Andrea Hairston, 'Griots of the Galaxy' in *So Long Been Dreaming: Postcolonial Science Fiction and Fantasy*, eds. Hopkinson and Mehan, p. 23. Hereafter, page references will be incorporated into the text.
47 Emily Apter, '"Women's Time" in Theory' in *Differences: A Journal of Feminist Cultural Studies*, Vol. 21, No. 1 (2010), p. 2.
48 Elizabeth Grosz, *The Nick of Time: Politics, Evolution and the Untimely* (Durham: Duke University Press, 2004), p. 3.
49 Smethurst, *The Postmodern Chronotope: Reading Space and Time in Contemporary Fiction*, p. 109.
50 Elizabeth Grosz, *Becomings: Explorations in Time, Memory, and Future* (London: Cornell University Press, 1999), p. 4.
51 Tim Robey, '*Alice through the Looking Glass* Makes Wonderland Look Good Enough to Eat' in *The Telegraph* (26th May 2016) <http://www.telegraph.co.uk/films/2016/05/26/alice-through-the-looking-glass-makes-wonderland-look-good-enoug/> [accessed 25th September 2016].
52 James Bobin in an Interview with Stefan Pape <https://www.youtube.com/watch?v=O2yOy4C0R8g> [accessed 3rd October 2016].
53 Cornell, 'Hélène Cixous and *Les Etudes Féminines*' in *The Body and the Text: Hélène Cixous, Reading and Teaching*, eds. Wilcox et al., p. 39.
54 Robey, '*Alice through the Looking Glass* Makes Wonderland Look Good Enough to Eat' in *The Telegraph* <http://www.telegraph.co.uk/films/2016/05/26/alice-through-the-looking-glass-makes-wonderland-look-good-enoug/> [accessed 25th September 2016].
55 Tanith Lee, *Cruel Pink* (Stafford: Immanion Press, 2013), pp. 121, 125. Hereafter, page references will be incorporated into the text.
56 See Judith Halberstam, *In a Queer Time and Place: Transgender Bodies, Subcultural Lives* (New York: New York University Press, 2005) where the

author emphasises how 'Queer uses of time and space develop, at least in part, in opposition to the institutions of family, heterosexuality, and reproduction'. She also notes that

> Obviously not all gay, lesbian, and transgender people live their lives in radically different ways from their heteronormative counterparts, but part of what has made queerness compelling as a form of self-description in the past decade or so has to do with the way it has the potential to open up new life narratives and alternative relations to time and space.

(pp. 1–2)

Indeed, *Cruel Pink* emphasises this possibility of there being multiple temporalities and a diversity of temporal experiences, paving the way for a radical assertion of 'queer' times that liberate her characters from the straightjacket of masculine, heteronormative clock time.

57 Smethurst, *The Postmodern Chronotope: Reading Space and Time in Contemporary Fiction*, p. 85.
58 Freeman, 'Mythical Time, Historical Time, and the Narrative Fabric of the Self' in *Narrative Inquiry*, p. 43.
59 Ibid.
60 Smethurst, *The Postmodern Chronotope: Reading Space and Time in Contemporary Fiction*, pp. 86–87.
61 Front, *Shapes of Time in British Twenty-First Century Quantum Fiction*, p. 69.
62 Huehls, *Qualified Hope: A Postmodern Politics of Time*, p. 29.

4   Intergenerational Time
Feminist Revisions of Youth and Ageing in Postmodern Anti-Tales

In addition to the temporal subversions of the previous chapter, anti-tales also revise time in terms of life stages, considering important aspects of generational time which are so integral to fairy tales, inherent in their oft-employed binary of young versus old (as well as the implicit generational warfare created by such ideas and still dangerously perpetuated in the media today). After all, women are taught to fear getting older because, like the ageing queen in the Grimms' Snow White, they decline in social worth and are forced to move aside to make way for younger, prettier Snow Whites. Yet, while patriarchy privileges youth, as fairy tales illustrate, our society still likes to maintain control over young women, patronising them with morals and stories designed to keep them on the right social 'path'; like Little Red Riding Hood, punished for her straying sexual impulses. Therefore, in this chapter, I examine how anti-tales are now reclaiming generational time for feminism in positing it, not as a one-directional and authoritative power structure, but rather as a rich source of knowledge that passes backwards and forwards, creating intergenerational ties: in other words, these tales, in the words of Victoria Browne, do 'not conform to a fixed pattern. Generational orders have flexible and complex meanings and temporalities, operating within the orbit of multiple symbolic logics, cultural imaginaries, and historical resonances'.[1] The anti-tales discussed here perform these subversions by revising notions of 'biological time'.[2] Kate Bernheimer's *How a Mother Weaned Her Girl from Fairy Tales*, for example, challenges the notion of naivety and innocence associated with youth and in doing so highlights how younger generations have their own inherent wisdom. This also allows her to undermine the black and white fairy-tale morality of good and evil within her collection, instead positing a grey, murky, ambiguous amorality that has become a major feature of the anti-tale genre. Meanwhile, Margaret Atwood's short story collection *Stone Mattress: Nine Tales* challenges the fairy tale, and indeed societal, worship of youth and the tendency to equate old age with evil, degradation, and powerlessness, in depicting the vivid inner lives of her characters and once again challenging the idea of linear time in showing the youthfulness of her characters still shining from within, through their memories and dreams. Two of Nalo Hopkinson's Afro-Caribbean tales, 'Riding the Red' and 'Greedy Choke Puppy', from her *Skin Folk* collection, will also be discussed for their subversion of age-related stereotypes. The collections analysed here not only challenge conventional understandings of youth and ageing but also expose the artificial construction by the media of a generational war that pits young against old, revealing that boundaries between the generations are socially constructed illusions designed to make us complicit in our own oppression. Youth and old age are seriously undermined stages of life, but these anti-tales posit both as potentially powerful and subtly subversive.

Breaking 'Waves': Feminist Theory and Revisions of Generational Time

Generational time is a major aspect of feminist temporalities. After all, women's studies has focused on rescuing forgotten histories of female role models and Walker urged us to 'go in search of our mothers' gardens' in order to discover female traditions and garner lessons from the experiences and teachings of older women. These 'generational anxieties' are, of course, a major component in the original folklore tradition before literary fairy tales were recorded by male authors: in centuries gone by, female storytellers used the oral storytelling tradition to warn, inform, and educate younger audiences about their societies and the hardships of the adult world, and this is being taken up by feminist anti-tale authors once again in the twenty-first century as they explore and challenge the patriarchal society their readers currently inhabit. As Browne notes,

> Generational time is a relational time, enabling sociocultural and political transmission between people of different ages and eras. It is manifest not only in the quantitative of births, ageing, and deaths, but also in the construction of symbolic generational orders and metaphors, not only *literal mothers* but the metaphor of *literary mothers*.
>
> (119)

Therefore, generational time must be seen as more fluid than mere biology and constitutes concepts such as inherited memory which can shape our approaches to the future by learning from the past. While this is indeed a rich and necessary part of feminism's project, it is problematic too on other levels. For example, this label of 'mothers' for female predecessors has been challenged for being patriarchal and heteronormative and for reinforcing the belief that women's ideas are always passed down in a patronising manner onto younger generations. In this way, some young feminists resent the sense of being 'told what to do' and this has, at times, created divisions and ruptures between older and younger generations rather than supporting the ideal of feminist solidarity for the female cause. Browne succinctly surmises that,

> the idea of a 'generational succession' can conjure images of feminism as a singular, one-way journey, where feminism is 'passed on' or 'handed down' from one generation to the next. As such, generational paradigms can seem inevitably aligned with linear, patriarchal concepts of historical time, steeped in logics of endowment and debt.
>
> (119)

Therefore, Browne proposes a less scientific and more humanistic, or subjective, approach to time and history in which:

> historical time is understood as a form of lived time. This gives us a solid basis for claiming that historical time moves in more than one direction, because what accounts of lived time consistently demonstrate – whether they are phenomenologically, hermeneutically, or sociologically orientated – is that ways of living time do not conform to a straightforward past-present-future chronology.
>
> (2)

This is highly important in negating the idea that time follows a linear arrow that constantly moves forwards, in favour of a multidirectional temporality. In essence, Browne supports the idea of time as lived, subjective, and polytemporal (as we have seen with *Alice through the Looking Glass* and *Cruel Pink*) in that it cannot be pinned down in any singular or absolute way, time always being relative. This chapter is also informed by many of these ideas and provides literary examples of this new feminist direction that seeks 'to develop nonlinear concepts of historical time, and explore its different dimensions as a traced time, a narrated time, a dated time, and a relational time' in a 'reconstructive' project (3). Browne's specific challenge was in deconstructing the problem of imagining feminist history in 'waves' or 'phases' which she views as a result of damaging 'classificatory typologies' (like the categorising and masculine time frames discussed before) coined by feminist theorists from the US and Europe in the 1980s (13). Browne sees this as a very masculine process of division and rationalisation which causes much damage, with its inherent implication that each new wave is somehow 'better' or more radical than the last (first-wave feminism is made to seem minor, or tame, in the wake of the sexual revolution of the second wave, for example). As Browne states, this is a logic of 'sequential negation, when accounts of teleological progress are presented as a "*graduated* progression", and where a "series of successive determinations" are organised into ascending order as each one negates and overtakes the former' (18). The result is 'that perspectives and approaches derived at earlier times necessarily become redundant and "out of date"' and they are essentially relegated to the 'dustbin of history' (19). This inevitably leads to generational discomfort, with younger feminists scorning what they believe to be the comparatively 'modest' gains made by their older counterparts or ridiculing their life choices. It should be noted that these aspects of 'generational time' constitute a large part of Browne's discussion and are analysed in this chapter with regards to youth and ageing within anti-tale narratives. In addition, the intergenerational cooperation and radicalism inherent in the young and old coming together, particularly in our era with its persistent paranoia about maintaining such generation gaps, is integral to many of the recent stories I am concerned with here. As I illustrate, anti-tales are fundamental in countering the backlash and blatant media projection of the myth that today's dispossessed youth have been robbed by a 'greedy' and rather derogatorily labelled 'baby boomer' generation. Browne reshapes temporal paradigms to counter this tendency to negate earlier feminist achievements, taking 'a reconstructive approach that seeks to articulate a multi-directional, multi-linear model of historical time as a basis for thinking and constructing feminist histories differently' (23). By asserting that feminists from previous generations can bring the past to bear upon, and inform, current feminist movements, she highlights how the past can be used in the present to inform the future. Browne notes how more fluid, multi-directional views of time help in the creation of a community of acceptance and solidarity and can have a profound, and indeed a necessary, impact upon current feminist strivings and discussions. Generational time is, therefore, held up as a major contemporary concern, and it is imperative that its distortions by patriarchy are revealed and healed. I will now illustrate how Kate Bernheimer, Margaret Atwood, and Nalo Hopkinson revise the patriarchal and fairy tale stereotypes of youth and ageing, in order to expose the political agenda behind instigating generational wars between different generations of women thus negating a potentially radical feminist solidarity.

Disenchanting Youth in Kate Bernheimer's *How a Mother Weaned Her Girl from Fairy Tales*

Kate Bernheimer is both a fairy tale critic and revisionist, having edited non-fictional works such as *Mirror, Mirror on the Wall: Women Writers Explore Their Favorite Fairy Tales* while simultaneously publishing numerous works of fairy tale fiction. It stands to reason then that her retellings are imbued with her knowledge of scholarly criticism and her awareness of the major feminist project of fairy tale revisionism. Certainly, she provides, within *How a Mother Weaned Her Girl from Fairy Tales*, 'takes on the classical idea of the fairy tale and injects contemporary life into the mix', making women her central focus.[3] It is no

coincidence that the epilogue page marks the feminist crossing of generational boundaries, highlighting how women can reach out across the
divides of time, and even planets, in order to connect:

> Girl from another planet, I'm yours. Your planet is small and diffi-
> cult, but what planet isn't? I like your suit and your hands of metal
> flowers. I have always wanted a friend like you, you know. Also, I
> can hear the vibrations come out of your helmet. That is the song
> I have always wanted to hear: the song of our friendship, and the
> song, also, of time. We will stay together here for a great while, I
> think – until someone finds us, I think. Girl from another planet,
> thank you for visiting us. It was unexpected, and nice.[4]

Here, Bernheimer invites the reader into the 'planet' of her collection,
to reach out to other women in solidarity and friendship, in order to
hear their stories/'songs', and ideas/'vibrations' from their minds/'hel-
mets'. This is also indicative of the vibrations of generations of female
stories rippling through the 'song of time' to impact on women of different eras and ages. The fact that she highlights how our planet is
'small and difficult' immediately introduces the political unease and
challenges women face today – we are like aliens from the future with
our 'hands of metal flowers' entering into the old tradition of the fairy
tale and bringing our contemporary concerns to bear upon the stories,
making them new and relevant. In essence, the collection is a mixture
of the old fairy tale tradition with an infusion of contemporary life and
problems, with older women passing on their traditions and stories to
be taken up and reinterpreted by younger generations in an advancement of the feminist cause while reclaiming and reaching back to the
voices constituted in the original ownership of the genre by female folk
tellers. Bernheimer seizes the fairy tale from patriarchy and offers it
back to women in the revised anti-tale form as a useful feminist and
political weapon. In addition, this image of female companionship is
contrasted with society's construction of generational opposition in her
story 'Professor Helen C. Andersen' (a gender play on the male author
Hans Christian Andersen, whose name is often associated with the
fairy tale genre). In this story, Bernheimer exposes the social barriers
constructed to counter the image of female solidarity that opens the
collection. Helen tells us that:

> The new fabulist moved into her office this week. It's next to my
> office. I asked my chair to assign her an office at the other end of
> the building, because I am a very private person, but he assigned
> her the office next to mine. My chair claims I will be a good mentor
> for her. He has put a one-way mirror between us so she can observe
> me. But why would I be a good mentor for her? She has streaky

blonde hair with pale pink highlights; she wears three-inch heels and straight-legged jeans. Why would she need mentoring from me?

(45)

Helen is the mother of a young librarian from another tale in the collection and so, as the ageing female here, with her 'entire forty-three years', her employer deliberately plays the young woman off against her, conjuring up a choking paranoia for Helen through the young woman's gaze in the 'one-way mirror' (46). There is a clear parallel here to the patriarchal judgements that are conveyed by the mirror to the queen in 'Snow White', dubbing her to be inferior to the younger woman, 'the fairest of them all', with Helen asserting that 'I stare in the mirror a lot' (51). It is worth noting that it is not Helen's skill and wisdom that she sees as the worth of her mentoring, but cosmetic appearances. Clearly, she has internalised the social idea of female worth lying in beauty, the socially idealised woman represented by the young intern tottering around in her heels and her symbolic pink hair which constitutes an external sign of her gender conformity, as well as her 'new collection of stories about flying ponies' (50). This is the ideal young female taken straight from the pages of a patriarchal fairy tale. In contrast, the older woman constantly asserts herself as 'a realist': she is a rebel who doesn't fit the fantasy female prototype society expects her to be, and who doesn't fabricate the truth enough or fulfil such a 'fabulist' or extortionate feminine ideal (47). This is made explicit in the following passage:

One of my problems is that when I sit down to write, I do not write about flying pink ponies. My stories do not come to me through telepathy, as the new fabulist says her stories come directly to her. 'They appear on my forehead and I read them in the mirror', she told me, her eyes brimming with tears.

(50)

Here the artificial nature of the girl's femininity is exposed: she is literally a page upon which society writes, and she simply reads this script written on her flesh in the mirror and tries to channel it into a successful social performance. The women's very existence is a lie, an artificial construction; they are not real beings, as their job as fabulists suggests. In essence, the rivalry here is socially constructed, a manipulation of the vulnerability of the older woman's sense of inferiority and the young woman's impressionability, in order to pit the two women against one another and to profit from the competitive strivings of both. Just as in 'Snow White', the older woman may be expected to step aside in order to let the younger woman take her place. Helen lets it slip that this female rivalry isn't new, rather it is engrained in the very fabric of our culture: 'one must help the town's newest women fit in ... it isn't easy for them.

The women in this town can be ... how to put this ... so cold. My other daughter was a real victim of them' (48). Despite her assertions of help, the ellipses here betray her – her hesitations result from her own complicity in society's game:

> How do you stay so thin, I asked the new one over lunch just today, in an effort to mentor her. Is it natural, or do you have a problem? I asked her. People in town may start to think you have a problem, I told her, if you do not gain weight.
>
> (49)

She is like the typical fairy-tale witch trying to cast a spell in the form of a mind game. And yet, there are no winners here, only women who are victims, made neurotic because of social pressures. Nobody wins this generational war, there is only mutual self-destruction:

> My new project is to find things out about her to expose the new fabulist as an imposter. For example, did you know she was once hospitalised for attempted suicide? I mean who does she think she is? One of my daughters? Or me?
>
> (52)

As this generational focus and the 'song of time' reference in the epilogue attests, James R. Gapinski points out that, 'this is a collection about time, about growth. This book is a series of coming-of-age stories [... in which] Bernheimer seamlessly moves from childhood to teenage angst, and eventually adulthood'.[5] Certainly, the opening story, titled 'The Old Dinosaur', introduces this temporal theme and is, in the words of Gapinski, 'a meditation on time passing, eras ending, and new ideas emerging'.[6] It is no coincidence that this is the first full-length story. Here we are immediately introduced to age as a key factor in the collection and significantly it puts an older character's story first, and not just any character but the only male protagonist in the entire collection. For this old dinosaur is the last survivor or representative of patriarchy, which should be extinct and constitute no place in the contemporary world. We are informed that the old dinosaur is displaced in the contemporary world with his prehistoric values and traditions: he 'lived in a big city [...] alone and forsaken. He was sad at heart – yes, that is the saying' (note how Bernheimer deliberately uses a stale and exhausted cliché here to heighten the sense of an outdated mindset) (3). The dinosaur dreams that he walks into his church and the rows are filled with humans, 'They all held photographs: the photographs were of his relatives, the ones mentioned before, who had died' (6). The dinosaur's archaic nature is represented in the old-fashioned elements that pervade his dream in which, 'The people were dressed in beautiful vintage clothing – the fabrics elegant, dusty and dark' and he sees his great aunt walk towards him, 'dressed, now, in the manner of humans [...] In her hands, she held a photograph of herself torn out of a children's history book' (7, 8). Most significant is the fact that she asks him to:

> 'Look at that altar [...] You will see your two daughters'. And he did: he saw one hanging from gallows, the other tied to a wheel. 'You see', said his great aunt. 'That would have happened to them, if they had lived. The innocent children'. Her eyes misted over. They stood there for a long time.
>
> (9)

Here we are reminded of the cruelties practised on women in previous eras who were condemned as witches or were in some way 'other' to societal expectations. Yet, most importantly, Bernheimer suggests that this has not changed in the contemporary world: his daughters would still have been executed today had they lived, for being monstrous or 'other' – society, despite the passage of time, is still unaccepting of difference. The old dinosaur believes that he has 'seen mercy' since his daughters avoided such horrific fates and so we are told that 'he lay down and died'; however, this does not augur well for the women in the stories to follow as, although 'He was the last dinosaur', and Bernheimer hints that it is the beginning of a new age, patriarchy is not dead, it has just manifested itself in different forms (here in the form of the human species) and lingers on (10, 11). The women in the ensuing stories suffer the cruel treatment the old dinosaur envisioned his daughters receiving in our era at the hands of an unaccepting species/ social order.

Opening her collection with a dying era and the dawn of a new age (albeit one still haunted by sexism), Bernheimer's collection focuses on the younger generation and their development. Even the form of the book implies a childish playfulness, as Gapinski notes:

> This book is a series of coming-of-age stories, but the stories aren't always sure they *want* to grow up. The physical book even looks somewhat like a kid's book, featuring just one block paragraph per page, punctuated by Catherine Eyde's occasional illustrations. Bottom line, if you're willing to suspend disbelief and reconnect with your inner-child, your inner-adult will still have plenty of high-brow complexity to chew on.[7]

For Bernheimer, childhood is not a time of blissful ignorance; rather, the children in her collection are complex beings who subvert fairy-tale expectations. She plays upon the notion that fairy tales are stories that easily socialise children and teach them moral lessons. It is true that, as Cristina Bacchilega points out, 'children are the primary intended market for fairy tales and many classic tales feature children as protagonists',[8] and, in the words of James R. Gapinski:

> She's aware that most people associate fairy tales with children (thanks, Disney), and she doesn't ignore this preconception. In some stories, Bernheimer's sense of childhood wonder is readily apparent – readers are swept away into stories of witches, modern dinosaurs, and talking dolls, and our rational minds don't stop to question these absurdities. In others, the childish perspective is subtler. For example, the main character in 'The Librarian's Tale' manages the circulation desk by day and sleeps in a secret library room at night. It seems a bit odd at first, unless you think back to grade school. In this innocent mindset, the librarian *must* live at the library. It only makes sense. Why wouldn't she live there? There's an internal logic to the illogical veneer.[9]

In this way, Bernheimer's collection traces the inherent wisdom and workings of the young, maturing mind in order to subvert notions of childhood naivety. As Gapinski states,

> although these stories are often innocent, don't mistake them for naïve. Of course, Bernheimer's title story is about weaning girls from magic and wonder rather than encouraging such pursuits. This collection pairs youthful innocence with sobering realities [...] the innocence in her stories is often overturned. Preconceptions of naïveté quickly unravel to showcase complexity [...] layers of meaning emerge amid simpler ideas.[10]

Indeed, youth is generally privileged in the fairy tale genre as a time of virtue, innocence, goodness, and beauty, but anti-tales tend to expose the dark elements of disillusionment behind the genre's veneer of enchantment. For example, childhood, despite our dominant preconceptions, is not always positive, even in fairy tales: Hansel and Gretel's stepmother abandons them in the forest and Snow White's father is an absent figure, while her stepmother tries to murder her. Anti-tales foreground these ideas in order to utilise disenchantment to shatter the hold fairy tales have upon the minds of their readers. Every character in *Cruel Pink*, for example, has a problematic past in which their parents either died young or didn't constitute any place in their lives (Klova treasuring a lipstick and, with it, a self-created lie that the initials engraved upon its case represent her mother's name). One of the brief image passages positioned between stories in Bernheimer's collection depicts a young girl holding male and female heads, representing her parents, on sticks, one in either hand. We are given an insight into the girl's haunting thoughts:

> I'm yours. I will hold you to the sky until my arms get tired and then I will hold you some more. You are very serious. I understand that. It is nice how you gave me my outfit, the one with the knee socks and belt. Also I like to wear the slippers that match the stick hands when we go out. People might wonder why we do this – it is not the usual custom. But we so like to be together: you two gazing off into the distance, me loving you best. We will have each other for always: my legs and your sticks. We have serious eyes; some people think we have problems.
>
> (23)

The motif, 'I'm yours', repeats itself throughout the book and suggests the need for children to pledge allegiance to the adults in their lives, to confirm their adherence to social expectations. And yet, this idea of childhood obedience is subverted by Bernheimer: the child holds her parents on sticks like puppets; it is her eerily controlling them – age does not equate with power. This entire collection undermines the fairy-tale glorification of youth as an enchanting time in one's life and exposes the genre's responsibility for instilling unrealistic expectations and optimism in the minds of children, especially young girls. The child here desperately tries to create such optimism by asserting that 'we so like to be together' and yet this is juxtaposed with the image of melancholy expressions on the faces of her parents; their cold eyes, as the child knowingly observes, 'gazing off into the distance'. It is like she is constantly (and literally!) juggling her parents and their expectations – 'I will hold you to the sky until my arms get tired' – with the 'outfit' they have given her representing the socialised role that she must adopt as the 'good girl' with its restrictive 'knee socks' and 'belt'. Overall, the young girl is both a victim and an oppressor: she is a victim of social and parental pressures and, at the same time, she literally plays her parents like puppets. The extract suggests that the child/parent dynamic is a more complex power struggle than is often imagined. Age is just a number, and such quantitative measurements, as we have seen with clock time, belie the realities.

In this way, as Gapinski points out, 'Bernheimer inserts layers or moral relativism into a genre that modern audiences associate with clear-cut Disney narratives of good and evil'.[11] Essentially, the radical use of a disenchanting vision of youth allows Bernheimer to shatter the simplistic absolutes of fairy-tale morality. Certainly, in the collection's 'Hansel and Gretel' retelling, 'Babes in the Woods', we are introduced to the familiar scenario of a seemingly evil stepmother who abandons two children in the woods. Yet, at the witch's house we are introduced to her daughter: 'This girl wore a white dress and a white bonnet and high, lace-up white boots. She had white hair and was smoking a rose-colored cigar' (107). The excessive repetition of white mocks the fairy-tale ideal of absolute innocence and goodness, while the cigar undercuts the entire image with a 'new woman' vibe. Her actions also subvert the illusion of goodness created by her appearance as she murders her doting mother who once stated that 'You are my only joy' – the lines between right and wrong start to blur (108). The children are not innocent or good; rather they cleverly manipulate their father's guilt in their own power game: 'And how the three girls ruled the house – how they ruled! "To think of it", the father said. "To think I sold that witch her sparkling windows – and you three barely escaped"' (119). Meanwhile, the 'evil' stepmother is exposed as extremely vulnerable as she becomes a domestic slave to the children and her husband. She doesn't have a maternal impulse or any kind of affinity with them but is ruled by their every whim:

'The mother did everything she could to take care of their needs. Anything they wanted [...] It was such a joy to do this that she often wept while doing the dishes, or while helping them with their homework' – clearly the fairy-tale façade of 'happily ever after' is being mocked here by a series of red-herrings which continue to the story's conclusion: we are told that 'though she still wished to poison herself [...] She lives for her children. That's the beauty of things'.

(120, 122)

Having subverted fairy-tale morality through a disenchanting depiction of youth, Bernheimer warns us of the need to 'wean' girls from damaging fairy-tale influences. Just as *Cruel Pink* foregrounds the title colour as a critique of the cruelty of gender socialisation, *How a Mother Weaned Her Girl From Fairy Tales* is saturated with it, as it sickeningly seeps across the pages, pink literally constituting the form of an oath for two young friends in the tale 'Oh Jolly Playmate!':

Pink Chiffon
Pink Lace
Pink Lady's Slippers
Pink Daisies
Pink Lace
We the undersigned will write all our poems on
pink paper.
We the undersigned will write our poems on pink paper for
now and forevermore.
We the undersigned promise to think pink.
We the undersigned forever pink.
We will wear pink every Saturday.
We will wear pink every Monday.

> We will only write our poems on pink paper.
> We the undersigned:
> FOREVER PINK!

(54–55)

Bernheimer illustrates how such ideas drive young minds to the point of neurosis, with fairy tales being a major contributor to this problem. As she writes in 'Babes in the Woods', once the girls returned home,

> They were chain-smokers – those pastel cigars, the ones that come over from England in all the colors of the rainbow, tidily arranged in a small box. The colors matched a series of rainbow fairy tale books the girls had on their shelves.

(118)

Here, she illustrates how fairy tales are like nicotine: addictive, a bad habit, and once you start it is very difficult to stop. In her title story then, Bernheimer suggests that we must 'wean' ourselves from fairy tales and their damaging messages; we must break the cultural addiction. In this story, a young girl has two dolls that tell her stories, and on her fifteenth birthday, her mother wonders how she might wean her girl off them as she has become obsessed. That night a life-size doll visits and the mother explains that she will only be granted access to the house if she can tell stories, this is one of her daughter's regulations regarding dolls entering the house. Seeing that she must comply the big doll sets some rules: 'Yes, I will tell stories, but there must be no interruptions or I will tell no more stories to you' (84). Agreeing, the mother, daughter, and her two dolls settle into bed to hear the story:

> The doll began: 'An owl flew by a garden, sat on a tree trunk, and drank some water. An owl flew by a garden, sat on a tree trunk, and drank some water. An owl flew by a garden, sat on a tree trunk, and drank some water'. Over and over again, the doll repeated this sentence.

(85)

The young girl passively listens, but her two dolls interrupt to object: for them it is a break with the fairy tale tradition and does not follow the standard fairy-tale format so is deemed to be 'wrong'. Having broken the rules, the big doll leaves, taking the other small dolls with her to 'teach them how to behave' (87). Although she is saddened, we soon see that the scenario has taught the young girl to think critically and to question the motivations behind the stories: 'Maybe she was just lonely – maybe she needed some friends. It was worse for her, really. She didn't know how to tell a good story' (90). Before the doll's arrival, she passively listened to the same stories over and over without being capable of criticism, whereas now she has learnt, from the interactions of the three dolls, to analyse stories objectively, gaining a critical distance, while also becoming aware that alternative stories are possible. She knows that there is more than one way to think about the world and that she has freedom to contend with stories and their content. All in all, the young girl has now reached a deeper level of understanding and has been forced to use her own imagination, to create her own stories in her head: 'she might someday see them floating around in the dark sky, the big doll repeating her story over and over again while the small doll gently admonished, and the other berated, the tale' (90). Just to ensure that we've successfully grasped the pervasiveness of fairy tales, Bernheimer ends the story with a page repeating the doll's line over and over – 'An owl flew by a garden, sat on a tree trunk, and drank some water ...' (91). This emphasises our need to interrupt and question the stories that stick in young minds. It is in the last illustration of the collection that Bernheimer emphasises the importance of developmental stages in a child's life and the necessity of liberating youths from the chains of fairy tales and social ideologies in order to allow them to grow freely without the restrictive influences of such conditioning forces. She simultaneously highlights how youthful minds, although delicate and impressionable in one respect, are subversively strong and resilient too. If this collection has taught us anything, it is that appearances can be deceptive: youth is no guarantee of weakness and age, as we have seen, is no longer measurable by numbers but by experiences. The youths in this collection are as adept and knowledgeable as the adults. In essence, just as time is subjective, biological time/age is also relative, development evading any kind of linear or numerical measurement:

> I planted a garden I made sure to do it just right. It meant considering the angle of light. It meant taking things on – things you never intended. If things seem a bit gloomy, please don't be sorry. This is really a wonderful thing. Flowers are heavy, like boulders, when looked at just right. Because I am yours I am rosy – and trust me, I am quite strong. Everything dies: I'm not too young to know that particular story. I can hold the entire world up with my flowers. I love you. That is the beginning and end.
>
> (167)

There is 'no happily ever after' here – it is both the beginning and end – for growth is not static and there is no finish line as we continue to work towards change in both ourselves and society.

The 'Grey' Area of Feminism: The Politics of Ageing in Margaret Atwood's *Stone Mattress*

As Smethurst points out, the cruelty of time is predominantly associated with the 'irreversible time of ageing'.[12] Instead of progressing in our views and attitudes towards old age, this is one issue on which society actually appears to be regressing. Denial manifests in the form of botox and cosmetic procedures which haunt consumers on television screens daily and instruct us to 'fight the wrinkles'. Even Elaine Showalter aptly points out that,

> It's not easy to come out as an old person, especially as an old woman. While the coming-out process is usually seen as a public acknowledgement of an attribute that might otherwise stay invisible, such as being gay, and promises acceptance into a welcoming community, identifying yourself as old is to admit something everyone can see, and is thus somehow more shaming, carrying more of a stigma.[13]

In essence, nobody will admit to being old and there is, as a result, no community in which to find comfort or solace. Significantly though, as Nada Ramadan Elnahla states in the 2015 article titled 'Aging with Disney and the Gendering of Evil', it is not enough to point out how old age is scorned in our culture, rather 'the aspect of age intersecting with gender needs to be added' to current scholarship.[14] Certainly, Segal adequately surmises that ageing

> affects us all, and affects us all differently, but it is women who have often reported a very specific horror of ageing. It is associated, of course, with the place of the body, and fertility, in women's lives; above all, with what is seen as beauty, attractiveness, good looks, in defining the quintessentially 'feminine', however fleeting, however unattainable, this may prove.[15]

Certainly, Helen C. Andersen in the story of Bernheimer discussed earlier, is a modern and contemporary extension of the Queen from Snow White whose life is controlled by the mirror representing society's judgements of older women and their perceived aesthetic, and thus social, decline. After all, fairy tales are the ultimate vehicle for patriarchy in its perpetuation of negative portrayals of the ageing female. As Segal notes, there exists a clear and ludicrous double standard of ageing, and it is a very deliberate one:

> Fears of ageing are fed almost from birth by terrifying images in myth and folktale – the hag, the harridan, gorgon, witch or Medusa.

Such frightening figures are not incidentally female, they are quin-tessentially female, seen as monstrous because of the combination of age and gender. No such symbolic resonance trails through time from the male Gods of old – despite Cronus, for instance, being de-picted mythically as an old man with a sickle, who had castrated his father and would later eat his five children.[16]

This 'link between old age and villainy', and of course femaleness, domi-nates fairy tales and yet it is only very recently that fairy tale scholarship has begun to explore such depictions.[17] As Anita Wohlmann states in her paper 'Of Young/Old Queens and Giant Dwarfs: A Critical Reading of Age and Aging in *Snow White and the Huntsman* and *Mirror Mir-ror*', 'In the numerous readings and interpretations of "Snow White", the topic of age or ageism is occasionally discussed. Yet, in most cases, it is rather a supplement to the main argument and not the central element of analysis'.[18] Rebecca Sullivan, writing on the subject of fairy tales, also stresses that, 'ageing women lack a place in the discussion'.[19] This gap in fairy tale scholarship is surprising given the proliferation of ageing fe-male characters throughout the stories, and yet it is something which re-ally needs to be challenged. After all, Sullivan goes on to note that 'one of the longest-standing stereotypes of the Disney canon and the Western fairy and folk tale' is that 'older women with power have no place in soci-ety'.[20] Given Disney's vast cultural influence, this is a damaging trend that must be addressed, due to the social mirroring of such ideas where older women, like the Queen in 'Snow White', are expected to step aside and allow younger women, or Snow Whites, to take their place in an ongoing and vicious circle. As Barbara Walker points out, the result is that there are few older role models for young girls to look up to given that, though 'the law doesn't murder witches any longer, modern society does eliminate elder women in a sense. They are made invisible. They rarely appear on those mythic mirrors of our culture, movie and television screens'.[21]

However, there is an encouraging reason for this need to strip older women of power, and this lies in the fact that older women can be dan-gerously subversive. For example, Plato and Socrates equated old age with wisdom and it is true that older generations possess a wealth of experi-ences and knowledge that are potentially subversive if channelled in the right way politically.[22] The very invisibility of older women in our culture is radical in its own way as it gives them a kind of cover or vantage point from which to interrupt the dominant social order – if society does not value them and brushes them off to the side, then they can do and say what they like while on the fringes. Furthermore, in the words of Segal, 'over the centuries older women in particular have proved valuable as resisters, feared for their disobedience, anger, outspokenness and gen-eral non-conformity' and 'writer Carolyn Heilbrun, for instance, advised women to use any seniority they might have to take risks, make noise and become unpopular'.[23] Hence, like the assumptions about the naivety and innocence of youth that Bernheimer shattered in her collection discussed previously, old age is another category that has subversive tendencies lurking beneath the vulnerable and powerless exterior, with Judith Butler pointing out that 'ageing is not only a way of living on, but can be the focus of a strategy of resistance that is clear-eyed, even open to unexpected beauty'.[24] In addition, Segal's book *Out of Time: The Pleasures and Perils of Aging* posits that political activism is the dominant means of impacting upon the world and maintaining one's place, relevance, and meaning in a society that tries to exclude those who have crossed over the acceptable youthful threshold. Indeed, Elaine Showalter emphasises 'the enduring satisfactions of continued activism'.[25] Hence, the emerging field of age studies aims to point out these potentialities. While there has been some feminist work done on ageing (Simone de Beauvoir's *The Second Sex*, for example), the menopause, and loss and death, in the twentieth century, major feminist icons such as writers Sylvia Plath, Anne Sexton, and Angela Carter all died fairly young and the topic of ageing did not enter much into feminist discourse.[26] Segal was even 'cautioned' against writing her 2013 book on the subject, 'to avoid thinking of her generation as old', but she has pushed ahead in order to pave the way for 'a feminist sexual politics of ageing'.[27] As Showalter further points out in her introduction to Segal's text, 'she has written the big book we have been waiting for on the psychology and politics of ageing, for both women and men. The subjects that used to be unmentionable are now urgent and essential to discuss' (with longer life expectancies and a drastic rise in numbers among the older population) and 'we can be fairly certain that old taboos are already collapsing, often indeed that the floodgates are opening'.[28] The discussion is also being taken up in the literary world and, despite the pervasive stereotypes of fairy-tale witches and hags, Segal notes that there are 'endless stories that could be told and which, maybe today, are just a little more likely to be heard', and this focus on real age depictions is exactly what Atwood offers in her collection *Stone Mattress*.[29] Atwood's collection can be considered as part of the anti-tale genre in that it reads almost like a collection of fairy tales involving older people: we see ageing characters behaving like curious and naughty children (Hansel and Gretel-like in one tale), overcoming their own hurdles like the heroes of traditional stories, and finding love. One pensioner even resembles Prince Charming in rescuing his damsel-in-distress from a nursing home fire, though Atwood satirises his 'charm', showing it to be bound up in conservative chauvinism. In this way, Atwood's collection provides satirical subversions and is a play on traditional tales, shattering the myths and lies of fairy-tale idealism, showing the hardships and darkness in life that fairy-tale enchantment obscures, particularly for older people. Fairy tales favour the young, Atwood's anti-tales favour the old, and for these ageing characters, there is an acute awareness that life is not, and has never been, a fairy tale, but they nevertheless find their own sources of meaning and reconcile themselves to the disenchantments associated with old age, while recognising the fakery of their self-mythologised and idealised pasts, as they settle into their twilight years.

In *Stone Mattress*, as Justine Jordan summarises, 'Atwood is candid in her depiction of old age, which runs like a theme or warning through the book. Let's just say that no one here goes "gentle into that good night"'.[30] In the story titled 'Dark Lady', we follow the resistant defiance of two twins, Tin and Jorrie, who resemble an ageing Hansel and Gretel who playfully toy with death for their own amusement. We learn that they've defied social expectations their entire lives and have carried this trend into their twilight years:

> Gazing at their past selves, Jorrie and Tin feel a tenderness they seldom display to anyone in the present. They'd like to hug those scrumptious little scamps, those yellowing, fading echoes. They'd like to assure the pint-sized seafarers that, though their voyage through time is about to take a turn for the worse and will remain worse for a while, it will all work out in the end; which is, let's face it, where they are now.
>
> Because, voilà, here they are together again, full circle. A few inner wounds, a few scars, a few abrasions, but still standing. Still Jorrie and Tin, who'd rebelled at being nicknamed Marje and Marv, and who'd taken to using their last syllables as their real, secret names, known to them alone. Jorrie and Tin, in revolt against society's plans for them: no white weddings, for instance. Jorrie and Tin, who'd refused to knuckle under.[31]

These two have survived triumphantly into glorious old age with battle wounds to showcase their enduring strength. Also, their naming game here is rather childish – as we shall see, Atwood reveals, throughout the collection, that the ageing shells of bodies are no accurate indicators of the age of the selves hidden beneath the exterior. Even their mention of 'echoes' from their youth, and their ability to share and relive previous lifetime experiences together, once again endorses a view of ageing that challenges accepted notions of time as linear and irreversible, and links to Segal's idea that,

> As we age, changing year on year, we also retain, in one manifestation or another, traces of all the selves we have been, creating a type of temporal vertigo and rendering us psychically, in one sense, all ages and no age [...] the wayward temporality of psychic life.[32]

We see this too in *Cruel Pink* in Emenie's depictions of herself as a kind of age chameleon that looks like a child one moment and a pensioner the next as, through memories and traces of the past, we create 'our own everyday time-travelling'.[33] In essence, the inner lives of the characters in Atwood's collection are, as we shall see, prime examples of Segal's 'philosophical take on old age', in which 'the self never ages, although the body changes and the culture evolves. Ageing is also time-less, "not simply linear [...] in our minds we race around, moving seam-lessly between childhood, old age, and back again"'.[34] This disruption of the linear order of time, and refusal to give in to the process of ageing constructed by society, is conveyed rather morbidly in Jorrie and Tin's complacent and scathing defiance of illness and death, and the sense of superiority they achieve in reading daily obituaries and attending the funerals of their acquaintances who have 'given in' to their advanced years. Essentially, it is their willingness to confront the ultimate taboo for the elderly, to stare death in the face, that epitomises their ultimate means of resistance, their refusal to 'quietly wait their turn' as society expects. We learn that Jorrie 'wants to tap dance on the graves, figuratively speaking' and Tin reflects that he finds her:

> interest in such terminal rites of passage excessive and even morbid, and has told her so.
>
> 'I'm only being respectful', she says, at which Tin snorts. It's a joke: neither of them has ever made respectfulness a priority except for outward show.
>
> 'You just want to gloat', he replies; and Jorrie snorts in her turn because this is so accurate.
>
> 'Do you think we're brittle?' she's been known to ask him. *Terrific sense of humour* is one thing, but *brittle* is another.
>
> (70, 71)

As Elaine Showalter points out, 'attitude and humour are the strongest weapons in the armaments of ageing' and something that these two have in abundance.[35] Atwood here is sharp and satirical as always, however, there is a clear authorial respect for the characters' refusal to lie down quietly and accept their fate. Confronting ageing head on and with a scathing wit, Atwood brings taboos back into social discourse: for example, the confrontation of death (as above), sexuality among older generations (Jorrie joking that 'I know a lot of guys who wouldn't mind heaving their prostates out the window about now' but another character reflecting 'Who would have thought she was capable of having such an intense erotic dream, at her age?'), and also loneliness (one of her character's contemplating 'in her more extreme and lonely moments' leaving messages on the phone for her dead husband in case 'maybe he could listen to them through electric particles or magnetic fields') (72, 31, 13). In a society that refuses to acknowledge these subjects, even Atwood's willingness to address them constitutes a radical act.

Second, Jordan also describes the collection as

> a sly take on the memories and myth-making of old age. There are tales about tales – pulp horror, epic-fantasy, love poetry – with nearly all of the characters looking back from old age on a distant past that has become its own mythological landscape.[36]

Certainly, the first three interrelated stories that open the collection reflect on not just the past of the ageing characters but also their literary works, radically revealing the changes in attitudes towards women in both everyday society and the literary world within the characters' lifetimes. In essence, older characters provide Atwood with the chance to reflect upon both social and literary changes. In these three stories, we learn that the husband of an elderly lady, named Constance, has recently died and that she struggles to cope with her grief, believing he is still with her in the house, instructing her with his voice on how to survive the snow storm outside. Constance is not only a vulnerable ageing lady, however. She has her own extremely successful fantasy literature series called 'Alphinland' which gives us an insight into her vivid inner-life: 'Alphinland was hers alone. It was her refuge, it was her stronghold; it was where she could go when things with Gavin weren't working out' (22). Gavin is a poet, Constance's old egotistical and sexist lover from her youth, who scorned her work in the same manner as the male-dominated literary circles they were a part of:

> The poets and folksingers made fun of her Alphinland stories, naturally. Why not? She made fun of them herself. The subliterary fiction she was churning out was many decades away from being in any way respectable. There was a small group that confessed to reading *The Lord of the Rings*, though you had to justify it through an interest in Old Norse.
>
> (22)

And yet, Gavin's sexist poetry – one creation titled 'My Lady's Ass is Nothing Like the Moon' – is shallow and conceited in comparison to Constance's work which has much more integrity and authenticity; a creation that embodies her life in fantasy form (for example, in the heroine's mind, the cheating Gavin is locked in an Alphinland chest where he can no longer cause her any harm). Even Constance's small triumph over age in her ability to negotiate the treacherous icy pavements and get to the supermarket and home again, despite the news instilling fear in the elderly by warning television viewers to stay indoors ('Don't think you can brave the elements!'), constitutes a victory over social views of ageing – her refusal to 'become one of those statistics – old recluse, hypothermia, starvation' (2, 6). On a grander scale, her determination symbolises women's triumph over patriarchy, represented by Gavin in the story 'Revenant' in which he is, by contrast, 'a dysfunctional pet' for his much younger wife, is confined to a bed and lacks the determination that Constance has to keep active (36). The change in social attitude towards women and their literary works over the years is highlighted when Gavin is interviewed by a young woman about his poetry, only to discover that she is actually working on Constance's series. She is only interested in Gavin as a biographical note in Constance's life, whereas in their youth Constance had simply written to support them both economically while Gavin tried to write his masterpiece: 'Girls did that then – knocked themselves out to support some man's notion of his own genius' (21). Gavin watches in horror as Constance is interviewed on television and hailed as 'the grandmother of twentieth-century world-building fantasy':

> 'Didn't you feel very brave, writing what you did, back when you started? [...] That whole genre was a man's world then, yes?'
>   Constance throws back her head and laughs. This laugh – this airy, feathery laugh – was once charming, but now it strikes Gavin as grotesque. Misplaced friskiness. 'Oh, nobody was paying any attention to me then', she says. 'So you couldn't really call it brave. Anyway, I used initials. Nobody knew at first that I wasn't a man'.
>   (58–59)

Here, Atwood is able to contrast contemporary attitudes which praise her bravery in an era where women are asserting their right to a place in the literary and social world to those of the past in which 'nobody was paying any attention to me'. Gavin clings to the old attitudes, however, seeing Constance's new power as a disconcerting and emasculating 'misplaced friskiness' where once he found her charming. He even resorts to old stereotypes that were used to undermine women in the past, painting her as some kind of cackling witch from a fairy tale. Included in the list of women Gavin has hurt, we have Constance, whom he cheated on with Jorrie (from the 'Dark Lady' tale discussed previously), and Jorrie herself, who he got tired of and tossed aside. Atwood reconciles these female characters at Gavin's funeral where the two women meet and embrace, letting go of the pain of the past and making peace for their final moments on earth, putting an end to the female rivalry created by patriarchy. Contemporary feminism is also evident in Gavin's young wife, Reynolds, as she points out to him that 'Times have changed' (40). As Jordan notes, 'boho Toronto in the early 60s' is the past represented by the

> womanizing self-aggrandizing Gavin, whom we visit as a sulking elder statesman of literature, cosseted by a younger third wife who

berates him for his unreconstructed ways: 'You can't talk to women like that anymore!'. Gavin may be furiously sentimental about the past – watching a grainy video of a 60s poetry reading he begins to weep – but nostalgia, Atwood suggests, is just another form of male privilege.[37]

Certainly, Atwood solidifies this idea that nostalgia only exists for men, the older women in the collection often unable to look back fondly upon a past in which they were hurt and stunted by sexist oppression.

Atwood illustrates this through the heroine of the title story 'Stone Mattress', who struggles to come to terms with being raped in her youth. As Jordan notes, 'It's a revenge story, but also a hard-hitting account of sexual violence in a small town in the 60s, "so long ago it might be centuries", but thrown into sharp focus against the artic backdrop'.[38] Travelling on a cruise ship to 'shed worn skin', this is precisely what Verna does when she stumbles across Bob, who doesn't recognise her, though he's the man who raped her after their high school dance many years ago (201). Even his lack of recognition shows that, to him, she was 'Cheap. Cheap and disposable. Use and toss' (206). Atwood utilises Verna's age to critique, and to remind us of, the horrors of the patriarchal past and also to highlight how they still continue to cause damage in the present. As Verna states, in the past 'one false step and you fell, that's how life was. When it was evident that the worst had happened, she [her mother] bought Verna a bus ticket and shipped her off to a church run Home for Unwed Mothers' (207). Fortunately, Atwood reminds us that some change has taken place:

> Nowadays Bob would go to jail no matter what lies he might tell, because Verna was underage. But there were no true words for the act then: rape was what occurred when some maniac jumped on you out of a bush, not when your formal date drove you to the side of the road [...] told you to drink up like a good girl and then took you apart, layer by torn layer.
>
> (211)

Atwood shows how age is actually a strength for Verna. Atwood supports Ramadan Elnahla's idea that we, as a society, 'need to acknowledge mature beauty in women'[39] – with Verna refreshingly pondering, 'Does she really look different? Yes, she does. She looks better [...] "Though much is taken, much remains", she murmurs in the mirror' (208). But more than this she also moves beyond an emphasis on aesthetics, noting 'But the real difference is in attitude – the confident way she carries herself. It would be hard for Bob to see through that façade to the shy, mousy-haired, snivelling idiot she'd been at fourteen' (202). This supports Segal's endorsement of ageing's 'possibilities for reinvention and renewal'.[40] Seeking her revenge, Verna, like the rest of Atwood's characters, takes an active role and hits Bob over the head with a stromatolite while on a day trip off the boat. She uses her age as an innocent guise to dupe the guides. It is the perfect cover for hiding the murder weapon in full sight: "'May I take it back to the ship?" she asks sweetly. "For the rock table"' (221). The weapon is, of course, significant as it constitutes the title of the entire collection: as the guide states,

> What is a stromatolite? He asks rhetorically, his eyes gleaming. The word comes from the Greek *stroma*, a mattress, coupled with the root word for *stone*. Stone Mattress: a fossilized cushion, formed by layer upon layer of blue-green algae that created the oxygen they are now breathing.
>
> (216)

This may perhaps symbolise the layers of time and experiences older people have under their ageing exteriors, as it is with this weapon that Verna manages to 'shed the skin' of her past that has haunted her for years. Furthermore, as Meg Wolitzer points out,

> The stromatolite turns out to be an ingenious weapon. And since Atwood has titled the whole collection *Stone Mattress*, it may well be even more ingenious as a metaphor. She seems to be addressing, in these stories, the way we all roll around, generation after generation, on nothing more than a big slab of rock, doing various unspeakable human things to one another.[41]

In essence, although Atwood shows this revenge as a kind of cathartic release for Verna, and we condone her act of violence as readers, she also highlights how the layers of the past all constitute inhumane acts (especially towards women), and these are still haunting us and causing further brutality in the present. Atwood reminds readers that there is still much work to do to break this cycle of violence and oppression.

Finally, Atwood uses ageing to fight the 'generational warfare' mentioned previously. As Segal points out, 'age and ageing may appear elusive and complicated when looked at from any personal perspective, yet across society they are monotonously orchestrated in terms of a war of the generations, placing us within uniform and competing age cohorts'.[42] The media is complicit in staging this battle, and it is easy to see how these simplistic divisions are created. Tory MP David Willetts, for example, has published a book titled *The Pinch: How the Baby Boomers Took Their Children's Future – and Why They Should Give it Back*, which perpetuates the idea that generations are competing on an economic level for 'cherished resources'.[43] Even journalist

Neil Boorman is complicit in inciting anger in his book, provocatively titled *It's All Their Fault*, in which he writes that,

> This is a terrible time to be young. Graduates are joining the dole queue as soon as they leave university, while their parents retire on cosy nest eggs ... Young families are struggling to provide the basics as their grandparents embark on another cruise.[44]

And yet, as we have seen, the reality is very different: Verna, on her cruise, is a victim who has had to overcome horrific hardships of her own and Constance lives a secluded life, purchasing only the basic necessities required to survive. Not even the Brexit vote was immune from inciting generational warfare, with article headlines including 'EU Referendum Results: Young "Screwed By Older Generations"'[45] and 'Brexit is One More Example of the Older Generation Financially Bankrupting the Young'[46]. Society once again pits young women against their older counterparts, as in fairy tale narratives. It seems accurate then that Faludi sees the contemporary women's movement as 'fated to fight a war on two fronts: alongside the battle of the sexes rages the battle of the ages'.[47] Atwood exemplifies in her collection, through the past struggles of her female characters, that there is a need for cross-generational recognition among women: while the young try to forge new pathways, Atwood reminds them of the rights that have been won by the bravery of previous generations of women who fought for their place in the world. And with their 'layers' of knowledge and experience, the older generation has much to offer the young and they should begin to understand each other and work together to forge a better future. The collection makes an attempt at what Segal dubs an 'opening of doors to encourage more communication across the generations, which is more than enough sustenance for now'.[48]

These ideas are most explicit in the final story of Atwood's collection – 'Torching the Dusties'. In this story, we follow Wilma and Tobias, two elderly residents in a nursing home. Wilma has extremely blurred vision; however, she experiences visions of little people marching and dancing in front of her eyes, what is known as 'Charles Bonnet's Syndrome' (226). One day the nursing home becomes surrounded by a group of militant youths called 'Artern':

> 'They say it's their turn', says Tobias. 'That's why they put *Our Turn* on the signs'.
> 'Oh', says Wilma. Light dawns: *Artern. Our Turn.* She'd misheard. 'Their turn at what?'
> 'At life, they say. I heard them on the television news; naturally they're being interviewed all over the place. They say we've had our

turn, those our age; they say we messed it up. Killing the planet with our own greed and so forth'.

'They have a point there', says Wilma. 'We did mess it up. Not on purpose, though'.

(243–244)

This clearly mirrors contemporary debates about the economic divide among generations. Wilma's acknowledgement of responsibility points towards the potential for discourse among young and old and yet the youths refuse to acknowledge them at all. This is symbolised by the little people in Wilma's vision who are paralleled with the youths outside in her conversation with Tobias as he provides her visual details of the mob:

Stealthily she inches her hand across the table towards the dancers: if only she could catch one, hold it between thumb and forefinger like a beetle. Maybe then they'd acknowledge her, if only by kicking and biting. 'Do they [the protesters] have baby outfits on, as well?'
[...]
'No, just the faces [baby masks]', says Tobias. The tiny dancers won't give Wilma the satisfaction of allowing her fingers to pass through them, thus demonstrating their non-reality once and for all. Instead they curve their dance line to evade her, so perhaps they're aware of her after all [...] the little folk never acknowledge her; which is also – says the doctor – par for the course.

(246)

In this way, by evading one another, and allowing the perceived 'reality' of the arguments to remain unchallenged, the generations are able to continue using misconstrued and clichéd stereotypes. Tobias' old-fashioned ideas provide a case in point: while Wilma acknowledges responsibility for her generation's impact on the world on some fronts, she can also see through Tobias' archaic and absolutist ideas, which are an endorsement of the simplistic notions society holds up to keep the war raging on both sides:

He's of the opinion that all young people are lazy freeloaders and should get jobs. The fact that there are few jobs available for them doesn't register with him. If there are no jobs, he says, they should create some.

(237)

Anthony Cummins points out that this story 'reads as if Atwood feared her book featured too many OAPs. You feel her sympathy fork in two'.[49] In essence, she takes no side, but rather refocuses the blame on society and its perpetuation of this generational war. Atwood uses Wilma to showcase this middle-ground, her character providing a means for discussion and reconciliation. Wilma, although living in the upmarket Ambrosia Manor, is down-to-earth and human; she might have money, but she has never tried to deliberately hurt anybody else or to be greedy but simply attempts to maintain some meaning in a society that devalues the elderly. She points out that they are as powerless as the youths in the current social order, and it is a myth that they hold any position of influence or power: 'For heaven's sakes. It's not as if we can *do* anything. "They want us to make room. They want us to move over"' (244). By pitting the two generations against one another, those with real power can cause a distraction that defers attention away from genuine corruption. Through a conversation between Tobias and another resident, who believes they can get out through the gates before the mob burns the building, Atwood refocuses our attention on the fact that the source of this hostility is not to be found in the young or old generations but in the dominant social forces who serve their own interests:

> 'They will not let you through', says Tobias.
> 'But we'll all go together! The press will be there. They won't dare stop us, not with the whole world watching!'
> 'I would not count on that', says Tobias. 'The whole world has an appetite for ringside seats at such events. Witch-burnings and public hangings were always well attended'.
>
> (262)

The activism of these events inspires Tobias – 'this turn of events energized him' – and he becomes a kind of heroic fairy-tale prince who rescues Wilma from the burning building despite his age, and both, by their very survival, embody a radical resistance against a society that wishes to see them wiped out (241). However, despite the image of an ageing resistance posited by the story's conclusion, the overall message of the collection is a despairing one: generational warfare is yet another human cruelty carved into the layers of the big stone mattress we inhabit.

Overall, in her examinations of ageing, Atwood stresses the importance of women working together rather than in perpetuating the generational divisions between young and old that society endorses. The older women in her collection get the space to share their stories, marking the advances made in social and feminist change from the sexism and violence of the 1960s and the progress made in the present day. In this way, Atwood highlights how the older generation is valuable in a collaborative intergenerational effort as, in 'struggles for justice', they can 'cast their memory forward' and use their knowledge of old oppressions to serve in the war against current inequality.[50] As Segal points out, this is one way of facilitating the 'need to keep looking backwards, critically, to see the future'.[51] And it is only in a revaluation of the biological time of ageing, in which age is fluid and not decided by a number, that we can forge generational bonds and see the worth of those who still have a wealth of experience and wisdom to offer regardless of their advancing years.

'When the Skin Comes Off': Shattering Age-Related Fairy Tale Stereotypes in Nalo Hopkinson's *Skin Folk*

Nalo Hopkinson's Afro-Caribbean stories are worth discussing here, as, like Atwood and Bernheimer's tales, they perfectly expose the lies which fairy tales perpetuate in demonising ageing women and foregrounding the perceived goodness and naïve innocence of young, passive heroines.

Hopkinson's anti-tale awareness is evident in her recognition of the importance of writing tales that convey both her Jamaican ethnicity and her experiences as a woman rather than allowing her identity to be subsumed by the privileging of colonial and patriarchal Western European stories and contexts. Conservative, white, middle-class, male stories cannot be allowed to obscure alternative cultures, literatures, and ideologies: 'In my hands, massa's tools don't dismantle massa's house – and, in fact, I don't want to destroy it so much as I want to undertake massive renovations – they build me a house of my own'.[52] As I've said before, anti-tales do not reject the fairy tale genre entirely, rather, they take the traditionally accepted fairy tale model, contained in the collections of the Grimms and Perrault, and explode their restrictive structure from within in order to imagine new ways of seeing and being.

This is exactly what Hopkinson does with her story 'Riding the Red', an anti-tale revision of 'Little Red Riding Hood'. Hopkinson foregrounds the generational complexities of this fairy tale, reclaiming it as a stolen female oral folk story told as a warning to younger women in order to alert them to the dangers of the world, replacing the didactic voice of a patronising male author:

> Just as well they went home early that time, her and the little one. Leave me be, here alone with my cottage in the forest and my memories. That's as it should be. But it's the old wives who remember. We've been there, and we lived to tell them.[53]

Here, Hopkinson notes how younger generations often do not value the wisdom of their elders, ruing the seemingly patronising warnings as their social value declines with their increasing years:

> She never listens to me anymore. I've told her and I've told her: daughter, you have to teach that child the facts of life before it's too late, but no, I'm an old woman, and she'll raise her daughter as she sees fit, Ma, thank you very much.

(1)

However, by allowing the character of Granny to become the narrator of the story, rather than simply a snack for the wolf, Hopkinson foregrounds her wisdom and experience garnered from her own hardships in a patriarchal society, where she too was 'consumed' by the wolf (man) and left to weep. This anti-tale does not allow the fairy tale's dismissal of older woman to be maintained then, highlighting how the older woman holds the truth inside of her in a world unwilling to listen, and the story also refuses to allow Little Red Riding Hoods to be punished as disobedient young women in need of guidance. Rather, Granny points out how knowing she was as a young girl, willingly giving in to the wolf's advances:

> some say he even tricked me into it [...] but that's not the way the old wife remembers it [...] isn't wolfie a joy to see! His dance is all hot breath and leaping flank, piercing eyes to see with and strong hands to hold [...] That measure we dance together, wolfie and I.
>
> (2)

In essence, young women are not simply naïve and in need of control as patriarchal fairy tales would have us believe, rather, 'the red hood was mine, to catch his eye'; they consciously take control of their own sexual awakening (2). In addition, Granny notes, 'That's what my granddaughter has to know: It comes all right again', pointing out how life doesn't end just because they allow themselves to stray from the path of social conformity (3). Granny, as a symbol for the older generation, is not scornful or wanting to punish her daughter or granddaughter for their transgressions, she simply wants them to know it will be ok and she too did the same things – an intergenerational tie that binds them together in a harsh patriarchal world. On the contrary, Hopkinson hints that the real trap is the conformity that comes after the sexual transgressions:

> I grew up, met a nice man, reminded me a bit of that woodsman, he did, and so we were married. And wasn't I the model goodwife then, just like my daughter is now? And didn't I bustle about and make everything just so, what with the cooking and the cleaning and the milking and the planting and the birthing, and I don't know what all?
>
> (3)

Hopkinson foregrounds the cyclical nature of the fairy tale that ties women into a repetitious cycle of oppression: young and punished for indiscretions, middle-aged hardworking mother, followed by life as a silenced grandmother (fodder for the wolf); a cycle to be repeated perpetually. Hopkinson's story highlights how fairy tales undermine the young in assuming they are vulnerable and in need of rescue, obscure the powerful wisdom of older women who are killed off because of their knowledge and power, and that, by listening to stories of the past, we may be able to make sense of the present and bring about a different future, breaking out of the oppressive cycle.

Furthermore, as the epigraph to her collection implies, appearances can be deceptive, and in her tale 'Greedy Choke Puppy', we learn that wrinkly skin is not always the sign of an old hag nor the beautiful taught complexion of youth a symbol for innocence: 'Throughout the Caribbean, under different names, you'll find stories about people who aren't what they seem. Skin gives these skin folk their human shape' (1). In 'Greedy Choke Puppy', we encounter a young woman, Jacky, who is doing a thesis on 'Magic in the Real: The Role of Folklore in Everyday Caribbean Life', listening to her Granny's well-known stories, including one about 'a donkey with gold teeth, wearing a waistcoat with a pocket watch and two pair of tennis shoes on the hooves' (171, 167–168). It is significant here that Granny corrects her granddaughter's summary, Hopkinson keen to show how many cultural stories are westernised and lose their roots: 'Washekong, you mean. I never teach you to say "tennis shoes"' (168). In this tale, we follow Jacky's research into the myths of her grandmother and the death of her friend Carmen's newborn baby. The story is interspersed with italicised vignettes which the reader naturally assumes to be the inner-thoughts of Granny:

> *The first time, I ain't know what was happening to me. I was younger them times there, and sweet for so, you see? Sweet like julie mango, with two ripe tot-tot on the front of my body and two ripe maami-apple behind. I only had was to walk down the street, twitching that maami-apple behind, and all the boys-them on the street corner would watch at me like them was starving, and I was food.*
>
> *But [...] I get to find out that when you pass you prime, and you ain't catch no man eye, nothing ain't left for you but to get old and dry-up like cane leaf in the fire. Is just so I was feeling that night.*
>
> (170)

Told about Granny's greying braids and listening to her nostalgic reflections on the past, we assume that she is the 'Ol' Higue' Jacky is researching:

> the Guyanese expression for an old hag or witch woman. The soucouyant is usually an old, evil-tempered woman who removes her skin at night, hides it, and then changes into a ball of fire. She flies through the air, searching for homes in which there are babies [... and] sucks life from its body.
>
> (174)

We, therefore, are lead to believe that Granny's visit to Carmen's baby is the reason for the child's sudden death – Granny attempting to suck the youth into herself. Hopkinson cleverly tricks the reader, making us feel a strong sense of both surprise and guilt as Granny discovers that the witch is actually Jacky, who, despite her relatively young age, feels old because she is childless, not as beautiful and youthful as she once was. The raging ball of fire that Jacky becomes is a pitiable symbol for the rage that many women feel at their declining worth as they age; it literally consumes them, turning them into vengeful entities. Granny explains to Jacky that

> The soucouyant blood is in all of we, all the women [...] Even me. We blood hot: hot for life, hot for youth. Loving does cool we down. Making life does cool we down [...] When we lives empty, the hunger does turn to blood hunger. Love your work. Love people close to you. Love your life.
>
> (180)

Women feel like failures if they don't find a husband, get married, and have children at a young age, fairy tales teaching them that these things are gained through youthful beauty. As a victim of this indoctrination, Jacky fails to see the worth of focusing on her intellectual pursuits, seeing her 'failures' in love and family life to be detrimental. Granny, broken-hearted, is forced to cut Jacky's shed skin in half and let the Lagahoo take her life to stop her destructive impulses. However, like the grandmother from 'Riding the Red', she does not blame Jacky or her mother for giving in to their soucouyant impulses, knowing that the world and its ideologies are cruel and life-destroying for many women: 'I live to see the Lagahoo two time. Next time, God horse, you better be coming for me' (182). Overall, the interactions between the young and ageing characters in Hopkinson's stories shatter fairy tale stereotypes and combine to show readers that the hardships faced by women in the past are still lingering in the present, the older women watching with regret as the same tragedies play out, hurting the younger generations.

Conclusion

As this chapter illustrates, patriarchal fairy tales are responsible for instigating and maintaining generational tensions between young and old women as an attempt to eradicate the possibility of intergenerational cooperation and rebellion. Bernheimer deconstructs the fairy tale notion of youth as a time of naïve innocence, proving that the children in her stories are not to be patronised or underestimated, having their own power and wisdom. In this way, Bernheimer emphasises that we need to be careful not to patronise or preach at younger women but rather respect their ideas and unique perspectives; one way of relieving socially constructed generational tensions. Similarly, Atwood and Hopkinson revise old age and the idea that the elderly are worthless, proving that older people can be childlike, rebellious, and valuable in social protest. Debunking the notion that ageing is a linear and quantifiable process, they point out how we all move backwards and forwards in our minds and memories. Therefore, the elderly provide a radical and informed perspective, with the wisdom of their past experiences brought to bear on the present, often showing us that society has not changed enough.

Notes

1 Victoria Browne, *Feminism, Time, and Nonlinear History* (Hampshire: Palgrave Macmillan, 2014), p. 141. Hereafter, page references will be incorporated into the text.
2 Paul Smethurst, *The Postmodern Chronotope: Reading Space and Time in Contemporary Fiction* (Amsterdam: Rodopi, 2000), p. 176.
3 James R. Gapinski, 'Youthful Innocence and Sobering Realities: A Review of *How a Mother Weaned Her Girl from Fairy Tales* by Kate Bernheimer' in *Atticus Review* (12th February 2015) <https://atticusreview.org/youthful-innocence-and-sobering-realities-a-review-of-how-a-mother-weaned-her-girl-from-fairy-tales-by-kate-bernheimer/> [accessed 1st October 2016].
4 Kate Bernheimer, *How a Mother Weaned Her Girl from Fairy Tales* (Minneapolis: Coffee House Press, 2014), p. 1. Hereafter, page references will be incorporated into the text.
5 Gapinski, 'Youthful Innocence and Sobering Realities: A Review of *How a Mother Weaned Her Girl From Fairy Tales* by Kate Bernheimer' in *Atticus Review* <https://atticusreview.org/youthful-innocence-and-sobering-realities-a-review-of-how-a-mother-weaned-her-girl-from-fairy-tales-by-kate-bernheimer/> [accessed 1st October 2016].
6 Ibid.
7 Ibid.
8 Bacchilega, *Postmodern Fairy Tales: Gender and Narrative Strategies*, p. 144.
9 Gapinski, 'Youthful Innocence and Sobering Realities: A Review of *How a Mother Weaned Her Girl from Fairy Tales* by Kate Bernheimer' in *Atticus Review* <https://atticusreview.org/youthful-innocence-and-sobering-realities-a-review-of-how-a-mother-weaned-her-girl-from-fairy-tales-by-kate-bernheimer/> [accessed 1st October 2016].
10 Ibid.
11 Ibid.
12 Smethurst, *The Postmodern Chronotope: Reading Space and Time in Contemporary Fiction*, p. 176.
13 Elaine Showalter, 'Introduction' in Segal, *Out of Time: The Pleasures and Perils of Aging*, p. xi.
14 Nada Ramadan Elnahla, 'Aging With Disney and the Gendering of Evil' in *Journal of Literature and Arts Studies*, Vol. 5, No. 2 (February 2015), p. 114.
15 Segal, *Out of Time: The Pleasures and Perils of Aging*, p. 13.
16 Ibid.
17 Ramadan Elnahla, 'Aging with Disney and the Gendering of Evil' in *Journal of Literature and Arts Studies*, p. 117.

18 Anita Wohlmann, 'Of Young/Old Queens and Giant Dwarfs: A Critical Reading of Age and Aging in *Snow White and the Huntsman* and *Mirror Mirror*' in *Age, Culture and Humanities: An Interdisciplinary Journal,* Issue 2 (2015) <http://ageculturehumanities.org/WP/of-youngold-queens-and-giant-dwarfs-a-critical-reading-of-age-and-aging-in-snow-white-and-the-huntsman-and-mirror-mirror/> [accessed 3rd October 2016].

19 Rebecca Sullivan, 'Falling Short of Feminism: Why Modern Retellings of Fairy Tales Perpetuate Negative Stereotypes of the Aging Woman' <https://kb.osu.edu/dspace/bitstream/handle/1811/45697/Falling_Short_of_Feminism.pdf?sequence=1> [accessed 3rd October 2016].

20 Ibid.

21 Ibid., p. 23.

22 Segal, *Out of Time: The Pleasures and Perils of Aging*, p. 41.

23 Ibid., pp. 210, 211.

24 Ibid., Judith Butler's comments on review page.

25 Showalter, 'Introduction' in Segal, *Out of Time: The Pleasures and Perils of Aging*, p. xvii.

26 See for example the collection of responses by nearly 100 women in the edited volume by Dena Taylor and Amber Coverdale Sumrall, *Women of the 14th Moon: Writings on Menopause* (Toronto: Crossing Press, 1991).

27 Showalter, 'Introduction' in Segal, *Out of Time: The Pleasures and Perils of Aging*, p. xiii.

28 Ibid.

29 Segal, *Out of Time: The Pleasures and Perils of Aging*, p. 280.

30 Justine Jordan, '*Stone Mattress* Review – Margaret Atwood's New Collection of Short Stories' in *The Guardian* (10th October 2014) <https://www.theguardian.com/books/2014/oct/10/stone-mattress-margaret-atwood-review-short-story-collection> [accessed 3rd October 2016].

31 Margaret Atwood, *Stone Mattress: Nine Tales* (London: Doubleday, 2014), p. 76. Hereafter, page references will be incorporated into the text.

32 Segal, *Out of Time: The Pleasures and Perils of Aging*, p. 4.

33 Ibid.

34 Showalter, 'Introduction' in Segal, *Out of Time: The Pleasures and Perils of Aging*, p. xiv.

35 Ibid., p. xviii.

36 Jordan, '*Stone Mattress* Review – Margaret Atwood's New Collection of Short Stories' in *The Guardian* <https://www.theguardian.com/books/2014/oct/10/stone-mattress-margaret-atwood-review-short-story-collection> [accessed 3rd October 2016].

37 Ibid.

38 Ibid.

39 Ramadan Elnahla, 'Aging With Disney and the Gendering of Evil' in *Journal of Literature and Arts Studies*, p. 125.

40 Segal, *Out of Time: The Pleasures and Perils of Aging*, p. 27.

41 Meg Wolitzer, 'Margaret Atwood's *Stone Mattress* is Full of Sharp and Jabbing Truths' (24th September 2014) <http://www.npr.org/2014/09/24/348709868/margaret-atwoods-stone-mattress-is-full-of-sharp-and-jabbing-truths> [accessed 3rd October 2016].

42 Segal, *Out of Time: The Pleasures and Perils of Aging*, p. 39.

43 Ibid., p. 48.

44 Ibid., pp. 49–50.

45 Louise Ridley, 'EU Referendum Results: Young "Screwed By Older Generations"' in *The Huffington Post* (24th June 2016) <http://www.huffingtonpost.co.uk/entry/eu-referendum-results-age-data-young_uk_576cd7d6e4b0232d331dac8f> [accessed 3rd October 2016].

46 Ben Chu, 'Brexit is One More Example of the Older Generation Financially Bankrupting the Young' in *The Independent* (28th June 2016) <http://www.independent.co.uk/voices/brexit-eu-referendum-financial-economic-impact-older-generation-bankrupting-young-a7107666.html> [accessed 3rd October 2016].
47 Susan Faludi quoted in Segal, *Out of Time: The Pleasures and Perils of Aging*, p. 71.
48 Segal, *Out of Time: The Pleasures and Perils of Aging*, p. 280.
49 Anthony Cummins, '*Stone Mattress* by Margaret Atwood, Review: "Rich in Sly Humour"' in *The Telegraph* (25th August 2014) <http://www.telegraph.co.uk/culture/books/bookreviews/11035217/Stone-Mattress-by-Margaret-Atwood-review-rich-in-sly-humour.html> [accessed 3rd October 2017].
50 Adrienne Rich quoted in Segal, *Out of Time: The Pleasures and Perils of Aging*, p. 213.
51 Segal, *Out of Time: The Pleasures and Perils of Aging*, p. 213.
52 Nalo Hopkinson, 'Introduction' in *So Long Been Dreaming: Postcolonial Science Fiction and Fantasy*, eds. Nalo Hopkinson & Uppinder Mehan (Vancouver: Arsenal Pulp Press, 2004), p. 8.
53 Nalo Hopkinson, 'Riding the Red' in *Skin Folk* (New York: Warner Books, 2001), p. 2. Hereafter, page references will be incorporated into the text.

5 Embodying the 'Inbetween'
Subversive Bodies in Feminist Anti-Tales

Every choice I ever made, everything I did, my body kept a record. It tells me stories, and I have to remember to listen
— Betsy Cornwell, *Tides*[1]

And then there was pain. Every muscle burning. Every joint screaming. Her body in rebellion as it discovered what had been done to it
— Marissa Meyer, *Cinder*[2]

Introduction: 'Bodies That Speak'

Susan Bordo has pointed out how, 'through the organization and regulation of time, space, and movements of our daily lives, our bodies are trained, shaped, and impressed with the stamp of prevailing historical forms of selfhood, desire, masculinity, femininity'.[3] Having discussed their feminist revisions of time and space, I now intend to show how contemporary anti-tales also liberate and reclaim the female bodies that move within those temporal and spatial systems. Certainly, the body has become a text imprinted by culture and reading bodies can tell us a lot about power relations within our current society: even when observing what we eat or how we dress, the day-to-day rituals of our bodies provide a key medium in understanding the cultural rules, hierarchies, and ideologies that society etches on them. In this way, the body becomes a means of diagnosing or getting an impression of political and social life, while also being a direct means of maintaining power relations and social control. As the epigraphs from Betsy Cornwell and Marissa Meyer at the beginning of this chapter illustrate, contemporary anti-tale authors are encouraging readers to 'listen' to the bodies in their texts, to allow real female bodies to 'tell their stories' of oppression, to literally 'scream' out in rebellion against the torture to which they continue to be subjected. This analysis is timely considering Attila Kiss' assertion that today our society is in the midst of witnessing a renewed 'postmodern vogue of the anatomy'.[4] While the body has been fashioned as a prison for women within our patriarchal society, Kiss' statement refers to a more positive and emerging preoccupation with the hidden and subversive aspects of corporeality – the mystery of the body beneath its social, neat, and acceptable surface. Patriarchy may have historically used women's alignment with their bodies as opposed to their rational minds in a derogatory attempt to endorse the need for male control, but nevertheless, the unpredictability of the body and its mysteries below the exterior surface continually remind us of the positive potential inherent in its unruliness and refusal to be contained:

> The body has been held accountable not only for mortality, but everything which is beyond the capacity of the reasoning mind or the rationalizing ego to control – transgression, sexuality, heterogeneity, incalculable acts and thoughts of the subject. The body gets articulated, by the time the dominant discourses of Enlightenment settle in, as the ultimate target of social censorship.[5]

Patriarchy has always been paranoid about keeping the 'different', unruly female body straightjacketed and under control. Yet, the body continually refutes these attempts at mastery: as Kiss states, 'the body *is* [ultimately] a site of subversion'.[6]

Hence, this chapter will show how feminism is now embracing this leakiness of the female body, rather than rejecting its negative connotations and uses in male hands, as a means to get beyond social measures and to embrace its 'difference' as a way of gaining access to what Cornwell calls the 'inbetween' – a feminine conception of the world beyond the patriarchal binaries of man/woman, human/machine, and human/non-human animals. (This is a view that also embraces sexualities that seep outside of heteronormative frameworks.) This is done through first providing an outline of the different types of problems and oppressions women have faced throughout history in terms of their bodies and the restrictions placed on them, before highlighting how these patriarchal ideas and practices have been solidified and endorsed through traditional male fairy tales. Finally, an exploration of the challenge to these dilemmas, in the use of subversive bodies in twenty-first-century anti-tales, will be discussed. This includes the extreme bawdiness and hyperbolic violence done to women's bodies in the 2015 film *Tale of Tales* (which exposes the violence hidden beneath the enchanting surface of the traditional stories). The 'voiceless' protest of bulimic bodies, the radical 'otherness' of selkies (mythical women and seal hybrids), and the use of water as a radical force, will be outlined in relation to Cornwell's novel *Tides* and Han Kang's *The Vegetarian*. I will also explore the depiction of cyborgs as a challenge to patriarchal boundaries in Meyer's novel *Cinder*; and, finally, the use of transexual bodies as well as queer sexualities in conjunction with Butler's theory of 'gender as performance' will be discussed in relation to Tanith Lee's *Cruel Pink* in order to examine the continuously fluid and shape-shifting nature of bodies in their inherent rejection of fixed gender identities. This approach will illustrate, through an exploration of these 'bodies that do not fit', how patriarchal doctrines and systems are deconstructed: these outsiders finally embrace the freedom gained from their peripheral position in a space at once 'inbetween', and at the same time outside of, simplistic and socially constructed categories.[7] In essence, the bodies discussed here posit a feminine architecture which questions the very language, and structures, of social systems and knowledges in order to open up the possibility of forging a new world with a more complex and inclusive way of thinking and being.

'Women's Problems': The Female Body under Patriarchy

A brief examination of the central debates and problems concerning the female body under patriarchy provides a useful basis for this discussion and reveals the roots of the damaging acts and laws inflicted on women's bodies both historically and in our own contemporary society. As Bordo points out:

> Indeed, female bodies have historically been significantly more vulnerable than male bodies to extremes in cultural manipulation. Perhaps this has something to do with the fact that women, besides *having* bodies, are also *associated* with the body, which has always been considered woman's 'sphere' in family life, in mythology, in scientific, philosophical, and religious ideology [...] the social manipulation of the female body emerged as an absolutely essential strategy in the maintenance of power relations between the sexes.
>
> (143)

At the beginning of the sixteenth century, for example, a Platonic theme which saw the body as a distraction from the higher, intellectual pursuit of the mind, led to an emphasis on the Cartesian division of the mind and body. Bordo notes how 'that which is not-body is the highest, the best, the noblest, the closest to God; that which is body is the albatross, the heavy drag on self-realization' (5). It is not surprising then that women wore the millstone of irrational body association around their necks while men held the lofty position of mind-orientated rationality, legitimating the latter's feelings of superiority and mastery over women who needed to be controlled and protected from their own base urges and impulses. In the words of Bordo:

> The cost of such projections to women is obvious. For if, whatever the specific historical content of the duality, *the body* is the negative term, and if woman *is* the body, then women *are* that negativity, whatever it may be: distraction from knowledge, seduction away from God, capitulation to sexual desire, violence or aggression, failure of will, even death.
>
> (5)

These became dominant images in Western philosophy, with the genesis story of Eve eating the forbidden fruit providing much-lauded biblical proof of woman's inability to control her body and its appetites. Enlightened maleness was, therefore, pitted against the female body's mysterious nature, which could not be pinned down. In the words of Margrit Shildrick and Janet Price,

> The very fact that women are able in general to menstruate, to develop another unseen within their own body, to give birth, and to lactate is enough to suggest a potentially dangerous volatility that marks the female body as out of control, beyond, and set against, the force of reason.[8]

In this way, it seemed appropriate to put measures into place that would contain this threat to male security and knowledge. Because of these unique female bodily traits, women's 'difference' from the male body was emphasised as that which makes them 'other' and, once again, inferior. This difference from the male body was posited by Aristotle, among others, as proof that women were a defect of nature – female corporeality was labelled defective, and their bodies simply viewed as 'imperfectly formed versions' of the male model.[9] Even medicine throughout the centuries has been influenced by these ideas, with medical diagrams frequently constructed more from these gendered assumptions about the female body than from any kind of factual accuracy. For example, diagrams of maternal bodies often depicted women as nothing but empty containers without organs – women are absent and inconsequential to the development of the foetus, which uses their bodies only as a temporary home. As Shildrick points out, 'what the representations show is that where male bodies are all structure and solidity, women's bodies are dematerialised, and more often represented in terms of surfaces and internal spaces' – they are literally depicted as 'lesser' than men and as having little to no material significance.[10] In essence, woman is depicted as a non-entity.

These historical ideas are by no means resolved or left behind in some distant era, and it is important to stress the pressing relevance and urgency of body studies for women in our society. The cultural control of ideas surrounding the way society thinks about the female body is in fact now more prolific than ever before. Certainly, in our era of patriarchal capitalism, Bordo points out that 'body insecurity can be exported, imported, and marketed across the globe – just like any other profitable commodity', and one dominant means of controlling the female body today is in encouraging women to dislike – perhaps even hate – their forms, for the financial and ideological gain of those in power (xxiv). Indeed, our society, like the fairy tale, upholds beauty as a necessary goal that must be attained by all women. It abounds with advertisements that promise to liberate us, to make us feel beautiful, and to allow us to access the freedom of bodily autonomy for which feminists have fought tirelessly over the centuries. And yet, this language of liberation is a deliberate, and elaborately constructed, illusion that serves only the interests of patriarchal capitalism, keen on ideologically whipping women into submission through their vulnerabilities and in-securities (a response established by the fairy tales of our youth which depicted the beautiful as deserving of a 'happily ever after' while the ugly perished, unloved and unaccepted). In essence, far from being motivated to embrace our bodies, we are continuously encouraged to perceive their 'defects', to measure ourselves by the cultural ideals that continuously flash across our minds and television screens. Far then from retaining comfort in our post-feminist re-embodiment, we are more disembodied than ever before, forced to decorate our exterior shells according to soci-ety's demands. Our problem remains the same as that declared by Mary Wollstonecraft, unresolved since the eighteenth century: 'Taught from infancy that beauty is women's scepter, the mind shapes itself to the body, and roaming round its gilt cage, seeks only to adorn its prison'.[11] Certainly, as Bordo points out, women's obsession with beauty is 'bet-ter conceptualised as bondage rather than choice' (22). In this position, women's minds are distracted – solely focused on taming their bodies into submission – rather than directing their efforts towards the fight against patriarchy (as Naomi Wolf points out in her book *The Beauty Myth*).[12] Our culture's myth that we are free to design and forge our own bodies has now become one of the most elaborately constructed lies of our era and, disturbingly, even though Bordo points out that we are fully aware that the images in the media of celebrity bodies are fake, airbrushed to perfection, it makes no real difference:

> Are we sophisticated enough to know the images are not 'real'? Does it matter? There are no disclaimers on the ads: 'Warning: This body is generated by a computer. Don't expect your thighs to look this way'. Would it matter if there were? Who cares about reality when beauty, love, acceptance beckon? Does sophistication have anything to do with it? (xviii)

In the end, these images still create the concept society has of ideal wom-anhood, encompassing the standards we must strive for, in a futile and ongoing battle with our own bodies in which we are doomed to perpet-ual defeat. The ideal is conveniently unattainable in nature, so women spend more and more on surgeries to squeeze their forms into inhuman patterns (rather like the stepsisters in *Cinderella* cutting slices from their feet to fit the glass slipper, that ultimate symbol of social conformity).

From this brief overview of the problems for women and their bod-ies endorsed by patriarchy, we can see that the female body has, and remains, a social possession to be shaped by ideologies rather than a site of an individual self-determination. It is not difficult to understand then why many women, and even feminists themselves, have a troubled relationship with their bodies, consistently rejecting them because of the imposed associations and ideological chains that they are burdened with. It is not simply on the level of ideology that the female body is harmed; rather, these ideologies inform practical social regulations and laws. Jo Bridgeman and Susan Millns' book *Law and Body Politics: Regulating the Female Body* points out the implementation of laws that limit women's access to fertility and abortion services, that permit female circumcision, that problematise the cases of victims in domestic violence, as well as sexual assault cases, and a justice system that still caters for the 'legitimacy' of victim blaming.[13] In addition, we have seen here how contemporary restraints on the body are not new or unique, but that the age-old ideas have spiralled out of all control and are now dangerously couched in feminist rhetoric. It is up to feminists to pull back this veil of patriarchal 'backlash' (to adopt Susan Faludi's term) and to reclaim women's bodies once again.[14]

A 'Touchy' Subject: Feminism and the Body

In the previous section, I noted that the body is exploited as a tool in social control, with the female body's unruliness kept under the restraint of strict patriarchal laws and ideological practices. It was noted that women have, as a result, been conditioned to perceive their bodies as a fleshy cage from which they long to escape in order to dispose of their gendered associations, and feminists, in their turn, have also shared this suspicion of the body, considering it to be a touchy subject. Although the second wave of feminism saw a strive for sexual liberation and contraceptive rights, some feminists perceived discussions of the body to be dangerous to feminism's struggle in that it emphasised female difference – a potential barrier to gaining equality with men. Many second-wave feminists instead endorsed a rhetoric of sameness. As Judith Evans points out:

> Sameness feminists undoubtedly seek equality with men: they ask to be treated as men are, and justify this on the grounds of sameness, though 'likeness' might be a better term. So they ask, for example, for equal entitlement to consideration for jobs. To a suggestion of sex differences which ruled that out, they would reply that there are none, or rather that they are small in number and size, trivial in type, and irrelevant.[15]

In the words of Bordo then, 'Many feminists remain agnostic or ambivalent about the role of biology and sexual "difference"; justifiably fearful of ideas that seem to assert an unalterable, essential female nature' (36). However, surely it is damaging and highly problematic to reject our own femaleness (as patriarchy has done) and to condemn our bodies as outcasts rather than embracing and liberating them? For other feminists such as Irigaray, Cixous, Kristeva, and Beauvoir then, the importance of embracing female bodily difference was stressed, and Charlotte Bunch's 1968 'the personal is political' manifesto was central to their emphasis on the role politics plays in shaping the female body: Bordo asks,

> What, after all, is more personal than the life of the body? And for women, associated with the body and largely confined to a life centered *on* the body (both the beautification of one's own and the reproduction, care, and maintenance of the bodies of others), culture's grip on the body is a constant, intimate fact of everyday life.
> (17)

In essence, gender inequality in body politics cannot remain unchallenged – women must reclaim their right, not only to external spaces but also to their own very personal and internal space of the body from which they have been severed.

As Elizabeth Grosz states, the feminists who reject the 'difference' of the female body seem to 'presume that *only* anatomical, physiological, or biological accounts of bodies are possible, obscuring the possibility of *sociocultural* conceptions of the body and upheavals that may transform biological accounts'.[16] Their 'difference' need not be characterised as a weakness then, tying them into essentialist roles and behaviours (the idea that all women are maternal and naturally designed for motherhood, for example); rather, 'nonbiologistic, nonreductive accounts of the body may entail quite different consequences and serve to reposition women's relations to the production of knowledges'.[17] In short, the female body is more than just a fixed physical entity, it has many other cultural and ideological possibilities beyond gendered essentialism. No body is pure, it is always tainted by social forces and conditioning, but this is also a positive thing, in that its meanings are, therefore, ever-shifting and can be constantly altered or changed. In essence, the body can be viewed as a text, with postmodern feminism, in the words of Bordo,

> giving a kind of free, creative rein to *meaning* at the expense of attention to the body's material locatedness in history, practice, culture. If the body is treated as pure text, subversive, destabilising elements can be emphasised and freedom and self-determination celebrated.
> (38)

In this way, the female body need not be viewed as a grounded prison with a fixed set of associations but rather as the philosophical key to other ways of seeing and knowing. Feminine traits of leakiness, multiplicity, fantasy, 'otherness', and mystery can be embraced rather than vilified – a means of celebrating women's difference as opposed to rejecting it. As Shildrick asserts then, 'although intending to deconstruct the essentialism of the highly damaging historical elision between women and their bodies, postmodern feminists might see, nevertheless, the embodiment of the feminine as precisely the site from which new forms of knowledge could emerge'.[18] In this way, feminists can ironically embrace the feminine as a rejection of dangerous essentialisms due to its inherent fluidity and unbridled quality of not being easily pinned down to any one definition. The work of Luce Irigaray is foundational in this attempt to endorse 'the embodied feminine as radically "other"' as it provides an alternative conception of the world beyond a single, unified masculine outlook.[19] In the words of Grosz,

> Only through developing alternative modes of representation and inscriptional etching of female bodies can singular domination of the universal by the masculine be made explicit. Conversely, it is only through a careful reading of phallocentric texts and paradigms that the rifts, flaws, and cracks within them can be utilised to reveal spaces where these texts exceed themselves, where they say more than they mean, opening themselves up to a feminine (re)appropriation.[20]

This is the exact tactic that the anti-tales in this chapter adopt in their subversion of both the masculine fairy tale and social narratives, instead exposing those rifts in the armour of masculine reason in favour of a world of feminine plurality and multiple possibilities. To put it simply, the neat boundaries of masculine reason and order are threatened, with Shildrick noting that the subversive tactic she has in mind is the female body's 'putative leakiness, the outflow of the body which breaches the boundaries of the proper. Those differences – mind/body, self/other, inner/outer – which should remain clear and distinct are threatened by loss of definition, or by dissolution'.[21] These feminine qualities provide the subversive feminine form and ideas perpetuated in the anti-tale stories to follow. In essence, the negative terms used to describe female bodies in the previous section are now employed as the very means by which feminists seek to liberate them.

However, this postmodern approach must be tempered with an understanding that the body is also an irrefutably material entity with a locatedness in a specific time and place, vulnerable to real physical and practical manipulation. As Bordo affirms, they are not 'mere *products* of social discourse' otherwise 'they remain bodies in name only' (35). She also points out how an uncritical take on the aforementioned approach often leaves one wondering 'is there a *body* in this text?' (38). To see the body as simply a text, or set of ontological qualities, is to keep women

disembodied, out of touch with themselves and unable to find, or identify with, any sense of the self as an embodied subject. Therefore, the
postmodern feminist approach I take here acknowledges the materiality
of the female body, while at the same time embracing the fluid and liberating ontology that it produces beyond its own locatedness in the world.
This strand of postmodern feminism is one that I seek to endorse and is
described by Shildrick as an approach that

> insists on the significance of embodiment and turns away from the
> value-resistant and free-floating abstractions of an ultimately irre-
> sponsive postmodernism, and asserts that it is not all immaterial. To
> be committed to any agenda to valorise women entails, then, both
> the deconstruction of exclusive and essential identities and the move
> to re-evaluate the body beyond bio logistic, universalist and norma-
> tive presuppositions.[22]

Hence, the anti-tales in this chapter adopt the postmodern feminist
position in which there is an understanding of the 'feminine' as more
than an *abstract* theory; it is a philosophical perspective that provides
a temporary refuge for characters and readers on their journey towards
forming their own identity beyond the stifling remits of a worldview
shaped by the limited categorisations and essentialisms of a masculine
world. Following this, ourselves and the characters must return with
these new knowledges and transform them into a *practical* locus for social change – exposing the fragility of, and pushing ever wider, the limits
and boundaries of a masculine reality and society.

Assessing the 'Weight' of the Problem: The Female Body in Patriarchal Fairy Tales

As I will now illustrate, the anti-tales to be discussed here have a major
struggle on their hands in trying to liberate the female body from the
stifling stereotypes and ideologies contained within fairy tale narratives.
As Laurence Talairach-Vielmas notes, in

> fairy tales and fantasies, the emphasis is upon moulding, shaping, or
> framing the female body [...] From mere figures of speech, the wom-
> an's body is turned into a fiction, a tale promoted by society which
> little girls learn by rote from the moment they listen to them.[23]

As a result, the fairy tale is a major culprit in solidifying and endorsing
patriarchal conceptions of the female form mentioned earlier and pro-
moting the need for their containment and control.

Certainly, the dominant appeal of fairy tales for young girls is often
the beautiful princesses who are objects of desire to everyone around

them. For example, we are told that the Grimms' Sleeping Beauty 'was so beautiful, modest, good-natured, and wise, that everyone who saw her was bound to love her'.[24] Note that beauty is positioned first in this list, highlighting its importance compared to personality, intelligence or even moral stature, while the lexical choice of 'saw' indicates that her other characteristics are mere presumptions accorded to her because of her exterior façade only. She is a mere spectacle and object for both the male and female gaze. Fairy tales continually equate beauty with goodness. These heroines are mere images rather than fully fledged human beings. Sleeping Beauty and Snow White win their princes while displayed in comatose death-like states – they have only their looks to recommend them, but, in this society, it is enough. Indeed, the need for women to appear pleasing to men is foregrounded in the male gaze that saturates the following passage from the Grimms' 'Snow White': 'they had a transparent coffin of glass made, so that she could be seen from all sides, and they laid her in it [...] and one of them always stayed by and watched it'.[25] The pronoun 'it' betrays the fact that the girl is nothing but a nameless object without a complex identity – as her name, 'Snow White', suggests, she is only a visual sign. Talairach-Vielmas points out,

> what fairy tales foreground is the idea that femininity is closely linked to aestheticization, and that beauty is a feminine virtue which needs to be cultivated [...] these female characters all exemplify how much their own fate depends on their physical appearance, on their power to construct a self which matches male expectations.[26]

It is her beauty that ultimately saves Snow White from her fate in the forest 'as she was so beautiful the huntsman had pity on her'.[27] Without exception, all of the female protagonists in the traditional stories are beautiful, 'the fairest of them all', and, like the advertisements that pollute our billboards and television screens, the ideal images of perfect womanhood depicted are unattainable and beyond the remits of nature. Yet, like advertisements that advocate an ironic array of products to help us attain a 'natural' beauty, in the Grimms' story, patriarchy works in the same way to naturalise impossible beauty ideals by having Snow White's mother literally construct her daughter's image from nature, as observed outside her window, as if these extreme characteristics can be naturally bestowed on women at birth. After symbolically pricking her finger she states: 'Would that I had a child as white as snow, as red as blood, and as black as the wood of the window-frame'.[28] Furthermore, once beauty can no longer be utilised as currency in the social market, women are disposable and lose their power, like the vilified and ageing queen who is replaced by the younger woman, 'Oh, Queen, of all here the fairest art thou/But the young Queen is fairer by far as I trow'.[29] In this way, female competition is encouraged, with the Queen's 'weapons' – a comb and a corset – an explicit symbol for this vanity war that society continually perpetuates.

Unfortunately, beauty standards constitute only one of the problems posed for women's bodies in the traditional narratives, with fairy-tale enchantment watering down the full impact of the violence inflicted on bodies within the stories. For example, in Perrault's version of 'Sleeping Beauty', the princess wakes up only once her own child extracts the poisoned needle out of her finger – childless before the curse, the story says nothing about the obvious rape of the heroine while she has been asleep. Furthermore, the queen in 'Snow White' is murdered as entertainment for those at the ball, literally paralysed and unable to defend herself due to her loss of beauty, resulting in restrictions on her social mobility:

> 'she stood still with rage and fear, and could not stir. But iron slippers had already been put upon the fire, and they were brought in with tongs and set before her. Then she was forced to put on the red-hot shoes, and dance until she dropped down dead' – even her death is transformed into a visual spectacle.[30]

In another gruesome example, the stepsisters in 'Cinderella' are forced by their mother to slice off parts of their feet as an apparently 'logical' attempt to gain the prince's hand in marriage – an apt symbol for the pain, both physical and emotional, that social standards inflict upon women on a daily basis. As a final gesture of abhorrence for their ugliness, the story depicts the sisters having their eyes gorged out by birds while Cinderella rides off into the sunset with her prince – beauty having, of course, won the day.

It has been noted how the female body is constructed as a mere object for the male gaze, an image, or a source of entertainment, and, certainly, fairy tale narratives endorse bodiless heroines, celebrated for their complete lack of physical substance and their absolute modesty and neat containment. As Margaret Atwood sums up, women are not

> allowed to eat or shit or cry or give birth, nothing goes in, nothing comes out [... The fairy tale heroine is nothing more than] a seamed and folded imitation of a magazine picture that is itself an imitation of a woman who is also an imitation, the original nowhere [...] a captive princess in someone's head.[31]

Indeed, 'nothing goes in', with the regulation of food in fairy tale narratives symbolic of male attempts to control the female body once again: Hansel and Gretel's seduction by the appealing edible house of the witch almost leads to their demise; Snow White only has one bite of an apple and almost dies (the forbidden fruit subtext reminding women of their original sin and complete lack of corporeal control); and Lewis Carroll's

Alice, while in Wonderland, is forced to work out how much she must eat and drink to literally fit into her social situation at any given moment – she is consistently too big or too small for the spaces she inhabits until she learns to regulate her appetite by the end of the narrative.

The appetite is, of course, also a symbol for sexual desire, another aspect of female embodiment punished in the traditional stories. The most prominent example here is 'Little Red Riding Hood'. Originally a female folk story about a young girl's social initiation and development, it was transformed, by Perrault and the Grimm Brothers, into a moral tale chastising female promiscuity. The male authors even added the prolific element of the red cape as a clear symbol of the danger of burgeoning female sexuality. The ideological underpinning of the tale is implicit in the undertones throughout the Grimms' retelling. The adolescent heroine, for example, accepts the wolf's suggestion that she stray from the path (the metaphorical path of social conformity) to symbolically 'pluck' flowers:

> and so she ran from the path into the wood to look for flowers. And whenever she had picked one, she fancied that she saw a prettier one farther on, and ran after it, and so got deeper and deeper into the wood.[32]

This is a clear depiction of the idea that women cannot control their own bodies and desires, with the prettiness of the flowers enticing her to go further awry. Arriving late at granny's house, the wolf is already there to consume her (a thinly disguised rape scene), and it is only through the patriarchal policing force of the woodsman that she is cut free from the wolf's belly and learns her lesson. By the end of the story, female sexuality has been thoroughly restrained, Red noting that, 'As long as I live, I will never by myself leave the path, to run into the wood'.[33]

Having provided a brief overview of the damaging influence fairy tales have on women's relationships with their bodies, it is easy to see why anti-tale authors are now responding in an effort to liberate them from both these texts and from the oppressive forces of the wider society in which they were produced.

Twisted DNA: The Anti-Tale as a Subversive Bodily Form

Before moving on to the primary texts themselves, this study aims to assert for the anti-tale genre a quality that has often been overlooked: that the genre itself has a bodily form. This may sound odd; however, a few critics (including Kérchy in her study of Angela Carter's work) have started to note this trend in literature as a whole, with the emergence of ideas such as 'body-texts' and the application of the established feminist theory of 'writing the body' (*l'écriture féminine*), but it is becoming even more notable in anti-tales specifically. For instance Kiss, in her essay 'Postmodern Fantasies of Corporeality: Identity and Visual Agency in

Postmodern Anatomy Theatres', points out how the 'body is a territory of the fantastic', while also noting that, 'fantasy and the body, an inseparable pair in the history of civilisation, have their climactic thematicisation today in the re-emerging of anatomy'.[34] Essentially, she outlines how the mystery and fantasy elements of the body's interiority are projected onto the outer world, due to medical experiments which open up the body and reveal its inner recesses.[35] In essence, anti-tale writers utilise the mystery and 'otherness' of female bodies as a means to step out of restrictive realities in their texts into a world of fantasy in which anything is possible in order to expose the limited masculine view of the world. This is embodied perfectly in the clash between the fantasy world of the selkie heroine in *Tides* with the medical and 'rational' 'reality' of the scientist who attempts to bring the species under control through experimentation. In essence, anti-tale fantasy is often created through subversive bodies, which open up a world just out of joint with reality, and yet not entirely detached from it – creating a transformative magical realist strategy in which possibilities can be imagined for practical change in the real world. In addition, Schutz suggests a physical attribute of anti-tales and fairy tale revisions that links the genre to fleshy bodies quite literally. She does this through an analysis of the term 'palimpsest', defined as 'an artifact of medieval manuscript production: a piece of vellum or parchment (usually lamb or calf skin) that is scraped down a second or third time and re-used. Over time, the original writing can reappear beneath the second text'.[36] Schutz suggests that anti-tale re-imaginings are palimpsests due to the fact that they are saturated with links to previous fairy tales that continually evolve across time, the form using these shadows of old texts (which echo in the minds of readers accustomed to the original stories) in order to explode traditional patriarchal fairy tales from within. In this way, they fit Linda Hutcheon's adaptation theory where the reader is forced to confront this clash between outdated ideologies held in the traditional stories and his/her own contemporary reality portrayed in the new story.[37] Hence, we can see here how the anti-tale embraces the 'otherness' and fantasy elements of the body and that the very nature of the genre resembles a palimpsest with the various retellings showing through the surface of the text/skin of each new story.

However, perhaps the most explicit conception of the anti-tale's bodily form is to be found in Jack Zipes' book *The Irresistible Fairy Tale: The Cultural and Social History of a Genre*, in a section titled 'Memetics and Cultural Evolution'. Here Zipes highlights how tales 'assume a life of their own' becoming 'universal memes'.[38] He links the fairy tale form to DNA by quoting Richard Dawkins who states,

> Just as genes propagate themselves in the gene pool by leaping from body to body via sperms or eggs, so memes propagate themselves in the meme pool by leaping from brain to brain via a process which, in the broad sense can be called imitation.[39]

This links the fairy tale to the body through the idea of it as a reproductive process in which elements of each tale are passed down, almost like genetics, through the centuries. This idea is shared in Ella Price's story 'The Special Coil of Chemicals', where she shows how, like the fairy tale, the anti-tale shares some qualities of DNA; however, the anti-tale is a mutation, containing a subversive, 'twisted' molecule. Even the very structure and layout of the epigraph to the tale mirrors the ever receding and coiling shape of a DNA molecule diagram:

> Once upon a time there was a special coil of chemicals [...] It was a double helix of itself, a coil of creation with a bar code potential for swiping every twist and turn of every living thing you could possibly imagine into the hyper market of this hyper varied world [... But] therein lies the lovely loophole.
> This special coil of chemicals,
> after twisting its tale to me,
> went off merrily weaving its own DNA way.
> To live loopily ever after.
> Somehow.
> Someway.[40]

Containing three sections titled 'Fight', 'Fright', and 'Flight', Price uses bodily responses as the basic structure of her collection *Silicon Tales: Storytelling For the Digital Age*. 'The Special Coil of Chemicals' constitutes the initial adrenaline boost as the opening story. Being in the 'Fight' section might also symbolise the fight for feminist justice in this tale and indeed it is an impulse that is carried throughout the entire text. Referring once specifically to 'the special coil of chemicals' as 'weaving its own DNA way', we are also told that

> it may not have been called 'genetics', but ancient tales of mermaids with siren voices or donkey heads on characters in a Shakespeare play amount to much the same thing – blends and boggling mixes of the basic building blocks of life.[41]

This linkage of tales with DNA shares in Zipes' idea outlined above and Price uses it effectively in her critique of the digital age and her satirical attack on scientists in their search for rational advancement as a means to escape the untidy subversive quality of the body. She also critiques patriarchy ('God-man to rival the gods themselves') and its heroic masculine history: she does this in the assertion of

> master technicians who hoped to purify it [the special coil of chemicals ...] to be cloned whenever the world (or Herr und Frau Schmidt) needed a God to be born. A Godling of the purest double

loop, a genetic dream, a Man-god walking among us to rival all the faulty Gods of the ancient world, with their various pyrrhic victories and Achilles heels.[42]

Technological advancement is an attempt by these patriarch 'Gods' to bring subversive elements under control, but, as this chapter will illustrate, feminine bodies transgress any paranoid patriarchal attempt to create scientific and rationalised boundaries. For, as Sadie Plant has noted, 'in none of these things – science, machines, women – will form ever achieve the same completeness as it does in him [man], in the inner sanctuary of his mind. In them he has already exploded'.[43] (Meyer's cyborg heroine, Cinder, will provide a case in point). Man's attempt to control an uncontrollable reality, where a single 'truth' can no longer be captured, is a futile battle to maintain the illusion of grounded control in an increasingly feminine floating world with all its complexities and ambiguities. In this way, Price links biotechnology and genetics to the subversive impulse of the anti-tale by stating,

> Because this special coil of chemicals [the anti-tale] had a habit that it just couldn't break: of twisting, often in imperceptibly small ways. Such that whatever may have looked like a clone turned out to have some unexpected kink in it far, or sometimes not so far, down the line [...] This, then, seems to be the alchemy that eludes us: the full fakery of perfection.[44]

In essence, the anti-tale has a 'habit' of 'twisting' plots, performing like a cloned fairy tale but with subversive blood flowing through its veins and changing its genetic makeup, revealing the 'full fakery of perfection' in its politics of disenchantment and moral ambiguity: as Price states, 'Clever little coil – very twisty indeed!'.[45]

Similarly, while it was noted above that science is often used as a means of rationalising the body and keeping it under control, Suzanne Anker also points out in her essay 'The Extant Vamp (or the) Ire of It All: Fairy Tales and Genetic Imagination' that the new era of gene splicing and cloning opens up anxieties about the neatness of boundaries, species categories, and so on. As she points out, fairy tale revisions (anti-tales) resemble some of these developments in the scientific advances related to the body:

> Like cell samples or botanical specimens, fairy tales are also formed into collections. As stories from an oral tradition are retold and codified to produce volumes (as in the works of Hans Christian Andersen or the Brothers Grimm) [...] These volumes form a data bank, like all exemplars of symbolic matrices. Reuse of the extant, so prominent a feature of collage, montage, and appropriation, is

a framing device for these narratives as well. Currently, the Frankensteinian mashup in videos, web browsing, and music expands on such combinatory practices. Within the scientific realm, the ready-made has become a resource in xenotransplantation, tissue culturing, and reproductive technologies.[46]

In short, the recycling of fairy-tale elements from various sources (or data banks), and their mutation into something new, mirrors the subversive elements of genetic manipulation going on today – a practice that raises paranoia about the containment of categories, species boundaries, and masculine reason. As the collection of artworks and sculptures displayed in the freshly published book for the exhibition *Fairy Tales, Monsters, and the Genetic Imagination* attests, anti-tales are now seizing upon this paranoia of genetic manipulation and scientific advances in order to subvert the neat conservatism of the original stories.[47] Certainly, Meyer's cyborg, alien, and partly human, heroine provides a perfect depiction of such subversions in her feminist deconstruction of patriarchal frameworks and will shortly epitomise these ideas in practice. Having established the inherent bodily nature of the anti-tale genre as a whole, and having laid down the background, theoretical and contextual frameworks from which the anti-tales for this analysis emerge, this chapter can now proceed to look at the particular examples of subversive bodies within the selected texts themselves.

Flesh and Blood Bodies: Subversive Hyperbole and Excessive Violence in *Tale of Tales* (2015)

Matteo Garrone's 2015 *Tale of Tales* provides an apt starting point for an analysis of twenty-first-century anti-tales and their subversion of patriarchal fairy tale impacts upon the female body, due to the fact that the film foregrounds the extreme violence hidden beneath fairy tale sanitisation. Unlike the Disney films discussed so far, Garrone's adult-orientated art-house production is much more surreal and privileges highly symbolic imagery as the means of conveying the film's meanings. Garrone was clearly focused on how the film makes the viewer 'feel' through the bodily imagery and violence depicted – there are no explanations for the actions of each character, they simply exist in all of their raw humanity, encouraging critical engagement and interpretation rather than providing a neat and coherent plot that would safely guide the viewer through a passive viewing experience. In essence, unlike the fairy-tale moralising or neat conclusions at the end of Disney's films (even, to some extent, in those I deem to be anti-tales in the previous chapters), here *Tale of Tales* privileges complexity, and there is no neat way in which to moralise the actions, denying the viewer the concluding satisfaction that Disney privileges. The subversion of the film then is predominantly rendered through

Garrone's focus on the goriness and excessive bawdiness of the original folk renditions instead of allowing fairy-tale enchantment to cover these qualities over with a comforting surface layer, shattering the normalisation of violence in the traditional stories. Hence, Giambattista Basile's sixteenth-century collection of the same title provides the perfect source material for such an endeavour, with Nancy L. Canepa noting how his fairy tales are 'bawdy and irreverent but also tender and whimsical'.[48] Certainly, Basile has tended to be overlooked by critics and readers, due to the fact that his tales are much grittier, being labelled 'dark, violent and horrific' by Meagan Navarro, and they are also much closer to the oral folk style of the peasant storytellers he recorded rather than sharing the refined bourgeois conservatism of the collections by Perrault and the Grimms.[49] As Canepa notes, 'In general, Basile's characters exhibit more down-to-earth behaviour than many of their counterparts in later collections; they are flesh-and-blood creatures involved in fairy-tale adventures but also in the affairs of everyday life'.[50] Certainly, there are numerous references to 'diarrhoea', 'shit', and bodily excess.[51] For example, as he notes in one story, 'The Old Woman Who Was Skinned',

> it was lucky for the old woman that the king was wearing so much perfume, on account of which he wasn't able to smell the fumes coming from her mouth, the stink of her little tickly areas, and the stench of that ugly thing.
>
> (96)

There is nothing neat or contained about these bodies displayed in all of their fleshy squalor, and, in the words of Canepa, 'the collection is decidedly *not* for little ones'.[52] Having carefully selected only a trio of tales from Basile's hefty collection to frame his feminist revision, Garrone weaves a masterful narrative of three interrelated stories of women at different stages of their biological lives: a young woman, Violet, negotiating the perils of sexual maturity in a male world in 'The Flea'; the subversively powerful childbearing body of the nameless, middle-aged queen of the story, 'The Enchanted Doe'; and the two ageing bodies of sisters, Emma and Dora, in 'The Old Woman Who Was Skinned'. Instead of keeping the three stories neatly separated, Garrone allows them to unravel simultaneously – with the camera cutting constantly between one story and the next to establish the links – creating one unified vision of female bodily struggle. Most importantly, as Navarro states, Garrone's film

> connects with modern audiences because the problems faced by the film's characters are still just as relevant today as they were centuries ago [... They] still apply to the modern woman – feelings of inadequacy or jealousy in both love and lust, the yearning for motherhood

and the inability to let go, and the brutal sting of exposure to the outside world during the transition from childhood to adulthood.[53]

First, taking the tale 'The Old Woman Who Was Skinned', it is easy to see how, through a comparative analysis, Garrone transforms Basile's outdated sexism in his film's feminist revision. For it is true that, while Basile was subversive for his time, he was no doubt tarred with the same patriarchal brush as his contemporaries and Victorian successors. Basile opens the tale with the suggestion that vanity is a flaw intrinsic to the female species, with his narrator asserting that:

> The accursed vice, embedded in us women, of wanting to look beautiful reduces us to the point where to gild the frame of our forehead we spoil the painting of our face, to whiten our old wizened skin we ruin the bones of our teeth, and to put our limbs in good light we darken our eyesight, so that before it is time to pay our tribute to time we procure ourselves rheumy eyes, wrinkled faces, and rotten molars. But if a young girl who in her vanity gives in to such empty-headedness deserves reproach, even more worthy of punishment is an old woman who out of her desire to compete with young ladies becomes a laughingstock for others and the ruin of her own self, as I am about to tell you, if you will lend me a bit of your ears.
>
> (91–92)

The ridiculous image painted here supports the patriarchal notion of female irrationality, and, using 'us', the author naturalises their apparently base preoccupations with the body rather than the rationality of the mind. The blame is placed upon young girls who are ridiculed as having an 'empty-headedness', rather than there being an acknowledgement of society's role, and its expectations of female beauty, as the root cause of such neuroses. Basile also becomes a culprit here in demonising older women as enemies of the younger generation, as opposed to acknowledging their heightened vulnerability and powerlessness in a society that privileges beauty and youth. Even Basile's own distaste for the two old women ironically foregrounds the social pressures placed upon them to aesthetically defend themselves from such hurtful treatment and ridicule. They have no choice but to compete and to give in to vain preoccupations. Basile's words epitomise patriarchal oppression, which is merciless to those who fail to meet up to social standards:

> They were the summary of all misfortunes, the register of all deformities, the ledger of all ugliness: their tufts of hair were dishevelled and spiked, their foreheads lined and lumpy, their eyelashes shaggy and bristly, their eyelids swollen and heavy, their eyes wizened and seedy-looking, their faces yellowed and wrinkled, their mouths drooly and crooked; in short they had beards like a billy

goat's, hairy chests, round-bellied shoulders, withered arms, lame and crippled legs, and hooked feet. And to prevent even the Sun from catching a glimpse of their hideous appearance, they stayed holed up in a few ground-level rooms.

(92)

The excessive language used here highlights society's disdain for the body's raw state, and particularly the unruly female body and its refusal to be neat or tamed. Basile affords such women no redeeming qualities, equating their ugly exteriors with moral deficiency. In contrast, Garrone alters Basile's narrative by adorning one of the women, Emma, with a beautiful singing voice: it is through this genuine beauty that she attracts the king's admiration. In addition, Garrone emphasises the sisterly bond between the two women, which, despite their visually unnerving exteriors (with loose folds of hanging skin that gives the appearance of their bodies having been melted and tuffs of feathery hair that barely cover their heads), endears them to the viewer. However, their bond becomes fraught once patriarchy literally lands at their door in the form of the king and Dora jealously whips a necklace he has bestowed away from her sister once she sees her try it on – Emma is slightly younger in appearance and Dora feels jealous. This is Garrone highlighting how patriarchy cruelly breaks such profound female bonds in its manipulation of their insecurities.

Garrone strips back the veil of lavishness that Basile uses for the king's dialogue in the original stories, instead exposing his true sentiments by using the spectacle of cinema to showcase his despicable and sexist nature beneath the linguistic façade of Basile's writing. For example, in an added vignette, before he hears Emma's singing, he is depicted lounging drunkenly among the intoxicated bodies of sleeping prostitutes. Garrone shows him kicking one of them in drunken disdain, clambering over them, and trying to get them to satisfy him despite the women being practically unconscious. Angry at their rejection he splashes water from the fountain in their faces and stalks away. While Basile positions Emma and Dora as figures of ridicule, Garrone, given his contextual distance, is able to make their story a tragedy and visually illustrate the vulnerability and pain in their eyes which Basile's story fails to account for. Instead, in the film it is the king who is transformed into a bumbling clown. Arriving at their door shortly after the necklace delivery, Dora embraces the temporary power she holds over him and wields her powers of seduction by allowing only Emma's finger (which she has sucked smooth in a nervous habit over the years) to be exposed through a gap in the door. She relishes this position of superiority, but it is only temporary, with the king noting that: 'Now courtesy demands that I ask for something that I could freely take without any pretext. I am your king, don't forget'.[54] This statement is delivered in a stripped down form without

the flowery and decorative adornment of Basile's dialogue and foregrounds the oppression of female bodies in a rapacious culture in
which they are powerless to protest – all she can really do is delay his
advances. As Basile's text reads,

> The king, who as a practiced soldier knew that fortresses are won
> span by span, did not refuse this solution, hoping to conquer finger
> by finger the stronghold that he was keeping under siege, since he
> also knew that 'first take and then ask' was an ancient proverb.
>
> (93–94)

It is depicted as a battle of wills; however, really there is no battle, he
holds all of the artillery in a patriarchal world where, because of her
gender, her female body becomes something to be conquered. She must
use seduction to secure the best deal she can in life. Eventually agreeing
to sleep with the King in his chamber, permitting all of the lights are off
so he cannot gaze upon her, Dora asks her sister to assist in moulding
her flesh and sticking down the excess skin in order to make her body
feel youthful and taut (a clear reminder of contemporary cosmetic procedures that strike a chord with modern audiences). The King, after a night
of passion with Dora, breaks his promise and looks upon her. Horrified,
he orders his servants to throw her out of the window. Dora is found in
the forest below by a witch who makes her young and beautiful, with
the lustful king ironically falling in love with her again at first sight and
arranging their marriage. Emma, separated from her sister forever, falls
into despair and tries to discover how to be young again herself. It is not
jealously or envy that drive Emma to her demise (as Basile's original tale
suggests), but rather her love for her sister. Angrily refusing to tell Emma
how she obtained her youth, in the filmic remake Dora shouts that, 'I had

Figure 5.1 Emma's flayed body. *Tale of Tales*, dir. Matteo Garrone (Archimede
Film: 2015).

myself flayed!' and drags her out of the castle. Weeping and desperate, Emma finds a man and asks him 'Can you change my skin? Flay me?'. Suspecting her to be mad he still accepts her jewellery as payment and to the sound of horrifying screams he slices her skin from her body. The last we see of Emma is her bloody and dripping form walking through the streets, all of the skin gone, and her life draining slowly away – the ultimate victim of a society that will literally trade in female flesh.

Basile's tale of 'The Flea' concerns a king who keeps a flea as a pet, 'feeding it daily with blood from his own arm', and we are told that

> it grew so quickly that at the end of seven months, when he had to change its quarters, it was bigger than a lamb. On seeing this, the king had it skinned, and when the skin had been dressed he issued a proclamation: whoever was able to recognise to which animal the hide belonged would be given his daughter in marriage.
>
> (50)

Unfortunately, his arrogant toying with his daughter's fate means that she becomes the wife of an ogre who wins the fateful game. The original story ends, conventionally, with her rescue at the hands of seven miraculous brothers and their slaughter of the ogre. However, it is in his revisions of this tale in particular that the feminist impulse of Garrone's film is brought to the fore. Garrone adds numerous layers and levels of complexity to the story as well as foregrounding Violet and making her into a complex human being rather than a two-dimensional fairy tale heroine, as in Basile's story. The king patronises her from childhood into adulthood by making the same cooing pet noises at her as he does to the flea, feeding the flea Violet's food, and showering it with the affections he should be bestowing upon his daughter. Garrone, therefore, foregrounds Violet's repressed lifestyle and, while her female guardian reads her a fairy tale, she sits wide-eyed and attentive, asking 'can you just read the part where they kiss?'. Her favourite passage is highly erotic for a fairy tale narrative, and it clearly highlights her repressed sexuality in a society in which her father makes the decisions about her maturing body: 'and on the bed in warm embrace [...] now Lancelot has what he desires, the queen's embrace sets him on fire [...] such pleasure this if truth be told'. Despite being told that they must stop for the day, Violet begs 'could we read it again?'. Listening to this passage constitutes the sole outlet for her desires and she is very aware of her stunted development, alerting her father to the fact that,

> at my age a girl should already know what sort of gallantries men are capable of, she should be learning to distinguish whose heart is sincere and who instead tells lies. If I stay here, my head will always be empty and I fear my heart will be too.

The film makes clear the fact that she is desperate to find a suitor in order to escape the confines of the castle's four walls. Yet, women of the time were simply passed from one patriarchal prison (that of their fathers) to another (the abodes of their husbands). After she learns her fate, Violet's strong will surfaces as she undermines her father's patriarchal authority, both as a king and as a father:

> You're not a king, you're not even a man, not even a beast – beasts at least love their offspring! They try to protect them! But not you, I'm nothing to you. I wish that my mother had strangled me in my crib instead of leaving me in your hands.

The king is appalled by such a display of disregard for his authority, asserting that 'No-one has the right to question my will, least of all my daughter!'. In the end, Violet is powerless to refute the marriage. It is important to note that Garrone does not make a martyr of Violet. He shows her spoilt pettiness and sense of superiority over the ogre who tries to placate her with food, a bed and kindness, and her resolute coldness to this inferior 'monster'. It is implied that the ogre gets tired of her icy treatment and rapes her, yet he refuses to demonise him entirely, and despite depicting the ogre's savage murder of her rescuers (a diversion from the original story), he emphasises the ogre's softness towards the young girl as he prepares simply to carry her off back home without rebuttal. Violet, in the climactic scene, feigns tenderness towards him and asks him to carry her on his back. The ogre clearly softens at this sign of affection, relieved that her disdain appears to be lifting. In this way, Garrone undermines the black and white fairy-tale morality of good and evil and instead rejects binary thinking in favour of a feminine complexity and moral ambiguity. Pretending to climb on his back, Violet's expression changes to a determined and murderous glare – she has gone from screaming damsel in distress (allowing everyone to die defending her and passively accepting her own helplessness), now instead realising that she must seize her own power in a world that will not freely hand her any agency, and slits his throat. Walking back into her father's castle with the head of the ogre in hand, she reclaims her new position of power as queen.

Tellingly, the film ends with her coronation – all of the characters from the previous stories are present for the celebration – a final image of female ascendency and seizure of authority. Yet, the female characters of the other stories perish, and Dora's good looks start to return to their previous state at the ceremony's resolution and she is forced to sneak away. Thus, the final image of a human walking over a tightrope that is on fire and extends across the ceremony's roof highlights the fine line women are expected to walk: happiness appears to be fleeting for women in these circumstances.

Figure 5.2 Violet transformed from 'innocent persecuted damsel' to resourceful heroine. *Tale of Tales*, dir. Matteo Garrone (Archimede Film: 2015).

In essence, the various bodies in this film are subversive, shifting, and untidy. It is sufficient to note that even 'The Enchanted Doe', which I did not discuss in detail here, exemplifies this too as it contains the emasculating maternal body of a queen who is killed by her son. The men in her life struggle to cope with the power that childbearing and motherhood affords her. For as Shildrick points out:

> The indeterminacy of body boundaries [perpetuated by the leaky female body] challenges the most fundamental dichotomy between self and other, unsettling ontological certainty and threatening to undermine the basis on which the knowing self establishes control. I shall mark here that while women are represented as more wholly embodied than men, that embodiment is never complete or secure. And nowhere perhaps is female excess more evident and more provocative of male anxiety than in reproduction. The capacity to be simultaneously both self and other in pregnancy, which is the potential of every woman, is the paradigm of breached boundaries.[55]

As we have seen then, the three subversive bodies depicted all refute male attempts at rational coherence and control. Violet literally breaks the neatness and contained cleanliness of fairy-tale damsels when we are told, in Basile's story, about 'the tremors, the horror, the tightening of the heart, the runs, the fright, the worms, and the diarrhea that the poor girl experienced', and, in the film too, she is busy trying to get stains off her clothes before her escape.[56] Similarly, the tightrope walker evades neat closure, only getting halfway across the rope as the film ends, highlighting Garrone's rejection of any neatness in a happily-ever-after conclusion and instead favouring uncertainty: it is an ending poised halfway between happiness and sadness. Ultimately, the excessive bodies in the film – whether pregnant, decaying, bleeding, monstrous, deformed, or dirty – all refute masculine attempts at containment and control, the female body consistently transgressing these parameters. As Navarro states, 'these dark, violent, and horrific stories can allow for reflection of the past and potential course correction for the future': women can learn from these tales and refuse to accept the neat bodies and morals with which patriarchy and fairy tales attempt to chain them.[57]

The Bulimic/Anorexic Body as Feminist Protest in Betsy Cornwell's *Tides* and Han Kang's *The Vegetarian*

As Christopher Lasch states, 'Every age develops its own peculiar forms of pathology, which expresses in exaggerated form its underlying, unitary cultural character' and, as Bordo points out, 'In no case is this more strikingly true as in that of anorexia nervosa and bulimia, barely known a century ago, yet reaching epidemic proportions today' (141, 139). Importantly, she stresses that,

> Far from being the result of a superficial fashion phenomenon, these disorders reflect and call attention to some of the central ills of our culture – from our historical heritage of disdain for the body, to our modern fear of loss of control over the future, to the disquieting meaning of contemporary beauty ideals in an era of greater female presence and power than ever before.
>
> (139)

Certainly, dieting and appetite have always been central components of patriarchy's paranoia over the control of female bodies – food temptation being linked right back to the fall of Eve. Indeed, as Walter Vandereycken and Ron van Deth's study *From Fasting Saints to Anorexic Girls: The History of Self-Starvation* points out, self-starvation is not a new *social* phenomenon, rather anorexia and bulimia are only relatively new *medical* terms.[58] They have shown that self-starvation occurred in ancient societies (in the writings of Plato, for example) particularly in the form of religious fasts, resulting in the emergence of 'Miraculous Maidens' and 'Fasting Saints' (women praised for their rejection of food as a symbol of their moral purity and devotion to God).[59] It is not surprising that other rebellious or secular fasts by women were often linked to demonic possession and witchcraft. As we shall see this has clear links to Yeong-hye's treatment at the hands of the men in her life once she embarks on her vegetarianism, as she is deemed mad and punished for her disobedience. As Bordo points out, 'Anxiety over women's uncontrollable hungers appears to peak, as well, during periods when women are becoming independent and are asserting themselves politically and socially' (161). In the nineteenth century, for example, fear of the 'new woman' surfaced in the form of vampire narratives about unruly female appetites, both blood related appetites and sexual ones. In addition, women today are now a greater part of the public space, and control of their bodies through culturally instilled insecurities about weight loss literally restricts the amount of space they occupy – their bodies shrinking along with their power. As Bordo states, this marks 'a decisive male occupation of social space' and it is on 'the body of the anorexic woman that such rules are grimly and deeply etched' (171). Furthermore, advertisements frequently encourage thinness, equating slim exteriors with moral goodness and abstinence – like the fairy tales discussed earlier in their equation of beauty with moral superiority. Naomi Wolf shows how this is used explicitly in slimming organisations, where religious rhetoric encourages a feeling of guilt; fatty foods classified as 'sins', for example.[60] It is also a misconception that it is only those diagnosed with anorexia or bulimia that should be considered as having an eating disorder; rather, women's attitudes towards food are skewed across the board – our society has simply normalised these neuroses. Furthermore, today consumer capitalism is itself a bulimic system that encourages paradoxical lifestyles of indulgence and purging in equal measure; we are all bulimics in one sense or another, all victims of these psychopathological states. Bordo outlines this in the following passage:

> Whether or not the struggle is played out in terms of food and diet, many of us may find our lives vacillating between a daytime rigidly ruled by the 'performance principle' and nights and weekends that capitulate to unconscious 'letting go' (food, shopping, liquor, television, and other addictive drugs). In this way, the central contradiction of the system inscribes itself on our bodies, and bulimia emerges as a characteristic modern personality construction. For bulimia precisely and explicitly expresses the extreme development of the hunger for unrestrained consumption (exhibited in the bulimic's uncontrollable food binges) existing in unstable tension alongside the requirement that we sober up, 'clean up our act', get back in firm control on Monday morning (the necessity for purge – exhibited in the bulimic's vomiting, compulsive exercising, and laxative purges).
>
> (201)

This paradoxical mode is perfectly exemplified by Cornwell's bulimic character, Lo, who eats 'Sometimes only celery, sometimes whole batches of cookies' (59). In this way then, there is hatred directed towards the obese as they are seen as being indulgent, going beyond the restrictions that society, and patriarchy, has put into place and hence not abiding by the rules. This suggests that it is not often individual issues that are the primary cause of eating disorders; rather, it is a physical manifestation of wider social ills: the microcosm of the physical body symbolises the faults with the macrocosmic social body. In this way, the sick bodies of bulimic and anorexic women expose all that is wrong with society.

I now seek to explore how Betsy Cornwell's young adult novel *Tides* employs the bulimic body as a subversive one, a symbol for feminist protest exposing society's ills. I will draw links to Han Kang's 2007 novel *The Vegetarian*, which won The Man Booker International Prize in 2016, in order to exemplify that this idea of the protesting bulimic/anorexic body is emerging as a dominant trend across the spectrum of anti-tales in twenty-first-century literature and culture. For, while the immediate image conjured up by such bodies is one of fragility and weakness, for the individual with the eating disorder, their food refusal can become a voice or language of sorts – a form of feminist protest. Of course, the suffragettes used hunger strikes as one of their major forms of rebellion and, in their book, *Scenes of the Apple: Food and the Female Body in Nineteenth- and Twentieth-Century Women's Writing*, Tamar Heller and Patricia Moran note how women writers also 'relied upon images of feeding and starvation to explore the issues of female voice, identity, and authority'.[61]

Cornwell's novel *Tides* details the experiences of Noah and Lo, a brother and sister who stay at their grandmother, Gemm's, house for the summer on remote islands entirely out of touch with the mainstream world. Gemm lives in a lighthouse and Noah is there to take up an internship with marine scientists as he is a promising and successful student in that field, while Lo, by contrast, has been sent there by her parents because she is a social 'failure', struggling with body image and having developed bulimia. During their time on these remote islands, they meet Mara, a selkie (a human and seal hybrid) with whom Noah falls in love, and discover that their grandmother's outsider status within their wider family is due to the fact that she is a lesbian (her lover, Maebh, the selkie Elder), and so she herself is an outsider and subversive body. *Tides* explicitly draws parallels with and makes references to 'The Little Mermaid' within its narrative and retells it in an anti-tale revision that foregrounds the violence done to women's bodies, in particular the body of the 'other' (women and selkies). Yet the bodies in the text are subversive and scream out loudly in their suffering. This clash between the masculine reality from which the two siblings have arrived (which has damaged Lo's perception of herself and her female form) is, therefore, contrasted with the feminine world of the islands associated with the selkies (in particular, Mara, who marks out the fluidity of boundaries and embraces her body as strong, natural, and transformative, with Lo surprised at how she 'values function over form') (146). Significant to the overall message, Cornwell depicts Gemm and Maebh joking about the significance of Ovid's book *Metamorphoses* as an essential read for every selkie – with Lo and Noah undergoing their own transformations before returning to the mainstream world. The islands then become a kind of healing retreat from reality – a space for the two to grow and develop beyond social restrictions.

On the other hand, Kang's novel *The Vegetarian* charts Yeong-hye's journey from her resolve to become a vegetarian to its escalation towards her death-like state at the novel's resolution, where she attempts to become a plant in her rejection of all social and cultural ties. We watch as her family and husband fail to understand and limit her rebellious decision. They can only stand passively by and observe as she, a once invisible, demure and exploited wife, asserts her right to control both her body and her reality. The words of her husband are extremely telling:

> How on earth could she be so self-centered? I stared at her lowered eyes, her expression of cool self-possession. The very idea that there should be this other side to her, one where she selfishly did as she pleased, was astonishing. Who would have thought she could be so unreasonable?[62]

This novel's anti-tale status is not so explicit; however, the surreal dream sequences of Yeong-hye's inner turmoil that punctuate the perspectives of other characters, her starting position as fairy-tale-like damsel in distress, the constant references to the forest as an escape from society, the ecofeminist ideas that dominate the text, the feminine form of multiple points of view, and the step away from concrete reality into a world slightly detached from our own are all shared qualities of the anti-tale genre. The novel shares multiple affinities with the tales discussed throughout this book. References to Kang's text will be included then to enhance the idea of the subversive bulimic or anorexic body portrayed less explicitly in Cornwell's tale for a young adult audience.

First, taking Lo's bulimic body as the subject of analysis, Cornwell is able to highlight the damage our culture inflicts on women's perceptions of their bodies. Just as it is a male voice in the queen's mirror in 'Snow White' that casts judgement upon her appearance, it is significant to note that it is often a male will or voice that resides in anorexic women's heads telling them what to do, how to feel, what to criticise next. Certainly, Cornwell exposes this in her novel, with the text revealing the hold patriarchal attitudes have over her self-perception, both in Lo's sense that 'she could hear the mirror laughing at her' and the psychological torture of her father haunting her thoughts:

> 'How can it still be cold in June?' Lo asked. Noah laughed and tossed her the nubby blanket that hung over the couch's worn armrest. Their dad probably would have made a crack about Lo being insulated against the cold. She had been a skinny baby, he'd say. Was New Hampshire really so much colder than China that she had to get fat just to keep warm?
>
> (146, 10)

Not only does this expose male hostility towards otherness, both sexual and racial, but it also emphasises the fact that many women with eating disorders deliberately attempt to stay in an infantile bodily state due to the associations that accompany mature womanhood. In essence, anorexia and bulimia can be seen as a rebellion against one's own 'femaleness' (as dictated by culture), a protest against the hardships placed upon women. While Lo is naturally heavy and so cannot really cast off the curvy femininity of her shape, Kang's heroine Yeong-hye (in *The Vegetarian*) is able to utilise her extreme thinness to relinquish the chains of being a domestic and subservient woman in the contemporary world. This is made most explicit in her rejection of sexual objectification. The victim of a rapacious husband, Yeong-hye's increasingly skinny physique allows her to escape the objectifying male gaze that would castigate her as nothing but a sex object. Rather, in a photoshoot in which she willingly allows her brother-in-law to paint flowers all over her naked body, she holds all of the power and strips away the authority of the masculine gaze. As the photographer states:

> It called to mind something ancient, something pre-evolutionary, or else perhaps a mark of photosynthesis, and he realized to his surprise that there was nothing at all sexual about it; it was more vegetal than sexual [...] Only then did he realize what it was that had shocked him when he'd first seen her lying prone on the sheet. This was the body of a beautiful young woman, conventionally an object of desire, and yet it was a body from which all desire had been eliminated. But this was nothing so crass as carnal desire, not for her – rather, or so it seemed, what she had renounced was the very life that her body represented.
>
> (83, 85)

Yeong-hye's body successfully escapes the burden of female sexual objectification and even gender binaries altogether, managing to get back to a natural, pre-evolutionary state before cultural conditioning. Lo's heavier form, though not as successful at escaping its fleshy femaleness, also attempts to become that skinny infant her father could not criticise before she transformed into a womanly, and thus inferior, body – essentially, she is still using her body and its pain in an attempt to reject conventions and to speak out against her oppression. Above it was noted how women's shrinking bodies are literally and symbolically taking up less space in a male-dominated world. Cornwell captures this precisely in Gemm's story of when she was a young woman. A photographer from the mainland stole her away temporarily from her lover Maebh to be a model: we are told that this man, Roger, was 'leaning on the back of the couch and crossing one ankle over his knee, as if he meant to take up as much space as possible', telling Maebh that 'I've shot fashion models less striking than your friend, there. She could really make a name for herself on the mainland'. Maebh's response to him is telling: 'Dolores already has a name' (127). Certainly, Noah, noticing upon his arrival some of the old clothing advertisements featuring his grandmother, remarks how 'Gemm looked beautiful in every one, but blank somehow, as if she'd been white-washed too. There was something hollow in her brightest smiles'. Here, she is like the two-dimensional fairy tale heroines who are nothing but mere images, flat and waify, whereas she has now escaped the clutches of society, 'the mainland', and become a real and substantial human being (embracing also her true sexuality): 'Noah thought about how she looked now: strong and weathered, present, happy. He preferred this Gemm, the Gemm he knew' (9). It is also very revealing when Noah observes that, 'The women in the old advertisements had soft cheeks, curved waists, flaring hips' and yet, in our era, excessive thinness predominates, 'None of them would have made it into the modern fashion magazines his mother and Lo kept around the house' (61). Clearly, Cornwell exposes here how, in our society of greater female presence, shrinking women's bodies and compromising their vitality and health is one of the dominant means of keeping them under control, something Naomi Wolf also stresses in her study *The Beauty Myth*.[63]

With links to Hans Christian Andersen's 'The Little Mermaid', Cornwell's novel details the abduction of a girl selkie, Aine, by Noah's mentor, Professor Foster. It should be noted that male consumption in both texts is used as a metaphor for the violence done to women. Indeed, Professor Foster mutilates Aine's sealskin, cutting it up into grid-like pieces (these marks transferring into identical scars on her human form also). Carving her up, the Professor proceeds to literally consume her flesh:

> You've read my work on sealskin. This is a whole other level. I've done amazing things with the selkie skin already – I've had Hope's [he has renamed Aine as a symbol of his ownership] skin for years now. Just ingesting it makes me feel better – it's incredible.
>
> (236)

Clearly, women and the selkies, as 'others', are simply fodder for men, with Yeong-hye in Kang's novel also becoming a vegetarian because of the nightmares she has about animal suffering, suffering that she is clearly empathetic with, seeing direct parallels to her own treatment at the hands of patriarchy. Just as Aine's body is butchered because she is an inferior animal/human hybrid, Yeong-hye, as a female, responds to the violence inflicted on her with 'animal cries of distress' and 'growls': her dreams make this symbiotic animal and female suffering most explicit,

> Yells and howls, threaded together layer upon layer, are enmeshed to form that lump. Because of meat. I ate too much meat. The lives of all the animals I ate have all lodged there. Blood and flesh, all those butchered bodies are scattered in every nook and cranny, and

though the physical remnants were excreted, their lives still stick stubbornly to my insides.

(40, 49)

While Professor Forster relishes the flesh he eats, Yeong-hye recognises her position as a woman, a victim, and piece of meat in our society. Furthermore, by stealing Aine's sealskin, the Professor has absolute control over her (her selkie power is literally stripped away when she loses possession of it, and she is rendered powerless, having to follow the new skin's owner as her master, as well as losing her voice). The selkie skin is an apt symbol then of how women are controlled by patriarchy's manipulation of women's skins, its ownership of their bodies – they are literally puppets played by male hands. It is only when her skin is retrieved from Foster's house by Noah and Mara that Aine's voice suddenly returns – a clear symbol of how the body is itself a voice and a means of communication, because without it, 'For five years, even her screams had been silent' (246). This is a direct parallel to the original Little Mermaid who, separated from her natural mermaid body and given a conventional human form, can also no longer speak, having lost her sense of self in the process. Aine notes that, 'The worst was when he made her try to eat. He stuck his fingers down her mouth along with the food, just to make sure it got down her throat' (84). Here, he silences her voiceless protest, as she attempts to communicate through her rejection of food, and Kang's Yeong-hye also faces the wrath of a father who tries to force-feed her because of the shame she has brought in undermining his patriarchal authority: 'My father-in-law mashed the pork to a pulp on my wife's lips as she struggled in agony. Though he parted her lips with his strong fingers, he could do nothing about her clenched teeth' (40). The imagery here clearly enacts a rape.

Furthermore, using bulimia and vegetarianism as a language of rebellion, the two authors foreground the failure of men to understand each woman's behaviour. These men are only able to communicate in the conventional language of words, so fail to hear the female bodies voicing their pain. We are told that Lo keeps her reasons 'tucked deep in a locked chest of secrets inside her', and the book frequently references her brother's incomprehension of her actions, which constitute an alternative feminine language of protest (21). Similarly, Yeong-hye's baffled husband notes, 'I just couldn't understand her. Only then did I realize: I really didn't have a clue when it came to this woman' (15). Although he notes that, 'She hadn't said a single word on the way here, but I'd convinced myself this wouldn't be a problem. There's nothing wrong with keeping quiet; after all, hadn't women traditionally been expected to be demure and restrained?', in reality her body is speaking too loudly (21). Both Yeong-hye and Lo relentlessly foreground their cultural oppression, responding by making those around them uncomfortable and powerless to silence the bulimic or starving body and its continuing struggle to be heard: 'Never before had he set eyes on such a body, a body which said so much' (87). The body, therefore, becomes a kind of subversive art form, with Yeong-hye relishing the flowers her brother-in-law paints upon her body because it links her to the natural world and conveys her rejection of socially constructed masculine boundaries: 'Whether human, animal or plant, she could not be called a "person", but then she wasn't exactly some feral creature either – more like a mysterious being with qualities of both' (88). Her body communicates an alternative reality beyond masculine parameters and male language fails to pin down exactly what it is that her body represents precisely because of its formlessness. Similarly, Lo's body as subversive art is made explicit in her conversation with Gemm – the pivotal moment when she realises that her relationship and communication with her body has been severed by culture – when she recognises once again that it has the ability to alert her to its pain, record experiences, and tell her story:

> 'Ask your body. It will tell you'.
> She had to look at Gemm then. The idea of communicating with her body seemed as ridiculous as … as talking to a fish. A fish was a stupid creature, low and cold and ugly. Down in the muck, like her stupid fat body.
> [...]
> She guided Lo's hand to her left wrist and pressed the pads of her fingers down on the skin there. Lo felt her own heartbeat rushing too quickly, carrying oxygen to muscles too empty to do anything but tremble. Her throat still stung from her last wretch, though she hadn't even eaten yet today.
> [...]
> 'Every choice I ever made, everything I did, my body kept a record. It tells me stories, and I have to remember to listen [...] Make your body strong, Lo. Keep it sick and you might not live long enough for it to tell you stories'.
>
> (82–83)

In this way, Lo acknowledges the importance of her body and its role in her artistic sketches, which are both one and the same, harnessing truths that can help young women of the future:

> She imagined her great-granddaughter sifting through their pages, smiling when she recognized an expression, a setting, the feeling Lo preserved forever in the way she drew the curve of a lip or the sharp frill of a dry leaf. Her art was, in part, a gift for that unborn girl.
>
> (149)

Just as Gemm's stories of bodily struggle inspire Lo to heal, Lo plans to use her body's records of suffering to enlighten future generations of women.

As this discussion has shown, these two texts illustrate how bulimic and anorexic bodies can embody their own subversive form of feminist protest. However, as Bordo notes, despite the 'fantasies of absolute control' that coincide with the restrictions those with eating disorders place upon themselves, 'its most outstanding feature is often powerlessness' (151, 154). Certainly, while Lo's body is *symbolically* powerful, wanting to assist Noah in his rescue of Aine, Lo recognises her body's inability to respond and react *physically*,

> Lo had felt a hot surge of protective anger [...] But in the same instant, Lo had known that her body was too weak to fight, or even to scramble down the cliffs the way Noah had. Her aggression had leaked away. In that moment, Lo hated her body's weakness more than she'd ever hated its size. She'd felt ridiculous for ever thinking her body was *big*. She'd felt tiny and weak and helpless, watching her brother in danger and knowing she'd hurt herself so much that she couldn't help him.
>
> (209)

In this way, Aine and Lo are paralleled, sitting together on the dock as bodies that once spoke out in symbolic protest through starvation, but that now recognise their physical weakness and that it is time to heal – to take on the world, having used their bodies to symbolise their rejection of patriarchy. Their scars remain to tell their stories of oppression to other women and to record their new knowledges and strength:

> Lo looked at the girl next to her, and in spite of the sealskin on the dock, the little child's body, the scars that hinted at pain Lo couldn't even imagine, her heart leapt out and ached with recognition for the kindred spirit next to her.
>
> (278)

By contrast, Yeong-hye allows her body to waste relentlessly towards death. It is true that her determination and unwillingness to relent is admirable and subversive to the extreme. Her attempt to live like a hybrid of human, animal, and plant constitutes a beautiful rejection of the categories man has constructed to maintain the illusion of his superiority and right to rule the earth. Yeong-hye's struggle has been extremely powerful in shattering patriarchal binaries and species divisions (just as the selkies expose the fluidity of bodies and boundaries). As Yeong-hye's sister reflects:

> Now she was able to admit to herself what had really been going on. She was no longer able to cope with all that her sister reminded

her of. She'd been unable to forgive her for soaring alone over a boundary she herself could never bring herself to cross, unable to forgive that magnificent irresponsibility that had enabled Yeong-hye to shuck off social constraints and leave her behind, still a prisoner. And before Yeong-hye had broken those bars, she'd never even known they were there.

(142–143)

Yeong-hye functions as a martyr for her sister, releasing her from an unhappy marriage and forcing her to confront the illusory 'reality' that patriarchy has constructed for its own ends. However, despite the dark beauty of her bodily protest, Yeong-hye's fate, though not confirmed by the open-ended conclusion, appears to be hurtling towards an imminent death. Kang seems to be holding her up as a path-finder, a female we can use to shatter our limited and conditioned perceptions of the world and, therefore, be liberated from their constraints. Like Lo and Aine, we can read the pain of Yeong-hye's body, read its story, and symbolic emergence from social shackles. However, Kang is not advocating such physical extremism for the novel's readers, rather she is allowing us to learn from the heroine's pain, to absorb the new feminine perspectives and knowledges that it produces, and strengthen our connections with our own bodies, each other, and the natural world around us, unrestrained by the artificial barriers imposed by social systems. Instead, Cornwell's novel offers a compromise that combines the powerful symbolism of the bulimic body with the necessity for healing and finding a critical physical strength to apply their struggle in the material world: 'Noah thought back to what Lo's therapist had told their parents about eating disorders and about how she needed to be in control of something. She seemed to be starting to channel that need in better ways', not only claiming ownership of her body, but of her whole life (286).

Transformative Bodies: Kang and Cornwell's 'Bodies of Water'

As well as bulimic and anorexic bodies, the breakdown of boundaries is also constituted in the shape-shifting corporeality of the selkies, who live on both land and water and can be both seal and human. Referencing *Metamorphosis* within the novel, *Tides* utilises the transformative potential of these hybrid creatures. As Marina Warner states:

Relations with such enigmas, with monsters real and imaginary, call into play the very concept of metamorphosis, as both natural event and metaphorical transformation. Metamorphosis entails a fluidity of categories [...] In these stories, animal metamorphosis gives a character a way of facing fears about degradation, and of confronting in the process forbidden sides of experience, [...] open the human self to re-examination, and to search for human creatureliness; with characters like [...] the Little Mermaid, the genre of the monstrous allows an artist to move between make-believe and mythic symbol, between an imaginary animal and a psychological or ethical category of human being, between being a beast and being beastly or bestial, with the full range of qualities that implies.[64]

Certainly, it is Noah's interactions with the selkie, Mara, that brings about his transformation. Initially, as a male scientist, Noah's mentor is Professor Foster, who tries to dissect and experiment with the selkie skins in order to bring them under rational control, and Noah seems to share this fear of the 'other' that Mara represents: 'He forced himself to look at Mara, to pretend she was only the young woman he'd met a week ago, not some fairy-tale monster who had just shed her skin before his eyes', determined to see 'how human she was – even if she didn't fit the technical definition' (116, 117). Noah struggles with the breakdown of boundaries and reason that she represents and yet, through his relationship with her, he relinquishes masculine forms of knowledge in favour of uncertainty and fluidity, acknowledging, in contrast to Foster, that 'I kind of feel as if I don't know anything. But it's almost nice' (144). It is the selkies' watery bodies (both literal and symbolic) that represent the liberating power of the female body's subversive leakiness and advocate a feminine conception of the world. In her 2017 work, *Bodies of Water: Posthuman Feminist Phenomenology*, Astrida Neimanis provides a unique insight into the subversiveness of water, both its usefulness for feminism and its role in questions of embodiment. As she notes, 'To rethink embodiment as watery stirs up considerable trouble for dominant [masculine] Western and Human understandings of embodiment, where bodies are figured as discrete and coherent individual subjects, and as fundamentally autonomous'.[65] Indeed, as Neimanis outlines,

> as bodies of water we leak and seethe, our borders always vulnerable to rupture and renegotiation [...] Watery bodies are gestational milieus for another – and for others not at all like us. Our watery bodies' challenge to individualism is thus also a challenge to phallogocentricism, the masculinist logic of sharp-edged self-sufficiency.[66]

Certainly, water in Cornwell's text holds great significance and symbolises healing for all of the characters. This is most explicit in Aine's return to the sea after years of separation from it: 'Aine let out a wail, an uncontrollable babyish sound that embarrassed her even as she made it. She needed the water. She needed it' (262). Having been imprisoned and separated from her skin – just as women are severed from their bodies in our society – the return to the sea highlights her re-embodiment of her natural watery form and all of its fluid flexibility. The female body cannot be contained. Even Kang's heroine Yeong-hye's boundary subversions are symbolised through water – 'I need to water my body. I don't need this kind of food, sister. I need water' – as she becomes a 'hybrid of plant, animal and human', a watery body, both literally and figuratively (148, 113). Water takes on a major role then in the transformation of the self and renewed senses of embodiment in each of the texts. Cornwell opens her novel with Gemm talking about 'the inbetween', 'It's the space between light and blue, land and sea, where water is sometimes warm' (1). Certainly, the inbetween becomes an apt metaphor. Just as Noah could not comprehend Mara's watery fluidity at the beginning, Lo at the novel's exposition is also unable to access the 'inbetween', the space between binaries where nothing is neat or simple:

> she wanted to try to draw the inbetween, the not-quite ocean not-quite land, the thing that soaked through her memory of Gemm's story [...] As hard as she tried, though, she couldn't see into the space between the two – at least not enough to draw it.
>
> (28)

However, having both grown by the novel's resolution, Lo and Aine sit together in their 'inbetween', their bodies having undergone great pain but now beginning a process of healing, and Noah and Mara also find theirs on the island – a space where humans and selkies, man and woman, are indistinct, equal, one and the same, water representing a collective 'we' that flows on and on rather than stunted individualism that is advocated in masculine thought:

> Before this summer, he'd seen the land and the ocean as so different. He'd loved the ocean for how *other* it was. Here, though, everything mingled – water and rock, land and sea.
>   Mara tucked her foot under his, linking their dangling legs together. 'It's like Gemm's stories', she said. 'This can be our inbetween'.
>   'Gemm says nobody stays in the inbetween forever'.
>   'No. Not forever. But for now'.
>
> (291)

The inbetween is only a temporary place, one must use it to gain new knowledges and a renewed sense of self, before returning to the world and applying these lessons for practical change in society. Cornwell rejects permanent preoccupation in the abstract realm of ideas and advocates instead a material feminist intervention in real-world time and space.

Cyborgs, Aliens, and Adoptees: Exploding Bodies and Boundaries in Marissa Meyer's *Cinder*

When considering embodiment's challenge to boundaries, it is unsurprising that another subversive body appearing in anti-tale narratives is that of the cyborg. Mike Featherstone and Roger Burrows' definition refers to the cyborg as a 'cybernetic organism, a self-regulating human-machine system. It is in effect a human-machine hybrid in which the machine parts become replacements, which are integrated or act as supplements to the organism to enhance the body's power potential'.[67] It is no surprise that patriarchy has already attempted to impose sexist ideologies and practices onto the cyborg form, recognising the potential for corruption inherent in its redefinitions of the body. Anne Marie Balsamo notes this when she reflects upon an article in *LIFE* with images of the 'replaceable body' which labels all of the potential parts that may be found in a catalogue of the future.[68] She notes that while there is the 'inclusion of photographs of plastic penile implants and the plastic non-functional testicle', ironically the already existent prosthesis of the female breast is excluded – a clear biased gendering of the 'body of the future' as male.[69] Even more significant, the distinguishing feature for the future female noted in the article is an 'artificial uterus' and as Balsamo proceeds to point out, this is

> far from innocent. In this future vision, the male body is marked by the sign of a full-bodied person whereas the female body is marked only by an artificial uterus; such significations offer an ominous warning about the imaginary place of women in the technological future.[70]

Certainly, as we shall see, Meyer's cyborg Cinder, exemplifies this sexism when Dr Erland marvels most particularly at her remaining reproductive organs and their functionality, praising the surgeons who performed the surgery that transformed her into a cyborg, with this as their crowning glory. In reality, the surgery, despite saving her life, has left her in extreme pain. Yet, Donna Haraway's infamous essay 'A Cyborg Manifesto: Science, Technology, and Socialist-Feminism' introduced the more promising and radical potential inherent in the body of the cyborg. She points out:

> the relation between organism and machine has been a border war. The stakes in the border war have been production, reproduction, and imagination. This chapter is an argument for pleasure in the confusion of boundaries and for responsibility in their construction [...] So my cyborg myth is about transgressed boundaries, potent fusions, and dangerous possibilities which progressive people might explore as one part of much needed political work.[71]

The potentialities of the cyborg's confusion of divisions, boundaries and binary thought processes for feminists is made explicit here. As Anne Marie Balsamo points out, in this border war,

> gender, like the body, is a boundary concept. It is at once related to physiological sexual characteristics of the human body (the natural order of the body) and to the cultural context within which that body 'makes sense'. The widespread technological refashioning of the 'natural' human body suggests that gender too would be ripe for reconstruction.[72]

The birth of the cyborg, therefore, promises new possibilities and the potential to discover new ways of being in the world and hence new gender relations. Judith Halberstam makes the implications for patriarchal ideologies clear when she notes that 'the female cyborg exploits a traditionally masculine fear of the deceptiveness of appearances and calls into question the boundaries of human, animal, and machine precisely where they are most vulnerable – at the site of the female body'.[73] The female body has always represented that which is other and different and so it becomes the perfect embodiment of the cyborg's alien corporeality – that which is unknowable, deviant, and subversive. The cover of Meyer's novel, *Cinder*, exploits this subversiveness in that it features an image of a shapely feminine leg poised in a conventional red stiletto shoe. Yet, beneath the skin, there is a distinct metal (or prosthetic) structure replacing bones, symbolising how the text embraces the subversion inherent in the breakdown of surface appearances, notions of inside and outside, as well as boundaries and binaries, with the novel literally depicting a border war between Earth and Lunar (an alien planet). Even more significant is the fact this is, in particular, expressed through the cyborg, human, and alien body of its title heroine.

Revealing that Cinder's father died in an accident on his return from adopting her as a child, the novel details her struggle as she battles to escape the clutches of her reluctant adoptive mother. Told she was in this fatal traffic accident, Cinder survived only through heavy surgery that transformed her into a cyborg. Thus, already a machine and human hybrid at the exposition, Cinder is a figure of disgust and ridicule, as cyborgs are treated as inferior beings. We are even told that Adri, Cinder's adoptive mother, 'raved at how he could not leave her with *this thing*' (27). It is important to note, in the words of Deanna Stover, that, 'As a sixteen-year-old cyborg and Adri's ward, Cinder has no rights over her body or her life'.[74] Through Cinder, then, Meyer illustrates a young woman's struggle in a society that privileges patriarchal ownership of female bodies, against masculine institutions, both at the level of family (the head of the household, usually a father, but in this case, the masculine and power-hungry Adri) and the State (each citizen having been fitted with an I.D. chip for easy tracking). Meyer's alteration of the original 'Cinderella' story, by making her heroine an adoptee, is not a minor or trivial detail. Rather, as Stover notes, 'Set in a society with an emperor, consanguinity is key to the concept of family: heirs are assumed to carry royal blood. Lunar similarly functions under a monarchy. However, adoption challenges these assumptions about "blood", kinship, and relationality'.[75] Cinder is eventually revealed to be the rightful heir of the Lunar throne. It is worth noting how Stover's paper, 'Gold Slippers and Cyborg Feet: Comparing Adopted Bodies in the Grimms' 'Cinderella' and Marissa Meyer's *Cinder*' (2016), fails to link her analysis of the adoption narrative to feminist struggle. For, as Marianne Novy points out 'by living in border-crossing positions, adoptees have a better chance to get beyond our society's dichotomies' and their very presence challenges male institutions and knowledges.[76] Thus, Cinder's adoptee status constitutes one of the subversive aspects of her marginality and ability to remain on the fringes, fitting neatly into no category and questioning the patriarchal institutions of state, family, and monarchy that attempt to keep her under control. As an adoptee, Cinder becomes the perfect embodiment of Haraway's assertion that,

> the main trouble with cyborgs, of course, is that they are the illegitimate offspring of militarism and patriarchal capitalism, not to mention state socialism. But illegitimate offspring are often exceedingly unfaithful to their origins. Their fathers, after all, are inessential.[77]

Indeed, not only does Cinder literally fit this status of 'illegitimate offspring', and not only is her adoptive father dead (and therefore 'inessential' to her story), but we also discover as the novel progresses that she is a human, an adoptee, a cyborg, *and* a Lunar. Lunars are an alien race from a planet of the same name, which attempts to take over the earth by having its queen, Levana, marry Earthen Alliance's young prince, Kai, in order to prevent war. Having fallen in love with Kai, Cinder is definitely not faithful to her Lunar origins. She attempts to save him from a loveless marriage and discovers at the novel's resolution that she is, in fact, Princess Selene, the true heir to the Lunar throne. It was Levana who caused her to be made into a cyborg, by attempting to kill her as a baby in a nursery fire in order to take the throne for herself. The novel's challenge to boundaries then is extreme and relentless, taking multiple forms. However, these subversions are all encompassed in Cinder's body and self-discovery, as she attempts to find her sense of self despite failing to fit neatly into any one category, seeing herself instead as a messy entity, 'A girl. A machine. A freak' (126).

At the beginning of the novel, Cinder believes herself simply to be a human and a cyborg, and detests the cyborg part of herself for its perceived inferiority, constantly covering up her prosthetic leg and wearing gloves to shield her metallic hands, or what she calls her 'metal monstrosities' (32). It is apt then that Cinder's rejection of her body is accompanied by her lacking sense of self and belonging: her body is, therefore, easily manipulated by those who claim to own it. In essence, she is unwilling to claim ownership over her own body or selfhood because of her perceived inferiority and hatred of her form. Cinder is a victim of a society determined to forget about one's own human mortality (her cyborg form reminding them of her inhuman status) and society's fear of the body's untidy and subversive 'otherness' (of which she is also a persistent reminder). Certainly, fear and disgust of the cyborg is related to its breakdown of essentialist thinking: looking at scans of her body, Cinder recognises that she is 36.2% inhuman and this, in the words of Stover, raises anxieties about containment and leaves us wondering, 'At what point does a human being become not human? When technology becomes a part of our lives and our bodies, the archaic binaries between human and machine dissolve'.[78] The body is, therefore, revealed to be impure and tainted, rather than secure and containable. This fear of the body's uncontrollable nature and vulnerability to contamination is cleverly depicted at the beginning of the novel when Cinder observes children singing a nursery rhyme:

> Cinder's auditory interface dulled the noise [in the market] into a static thrumming, but today one melody lingered above the rest that she couldn't drown out. A ring of children were standing just outside her booth, trilling – 'Ashes, ashes, we all fall down!' – and then laughing hysterically as they collapsed to the pavement.
>
> A smile tugged at Cinder's lips. Not so much at the nursery rhyme, a phantom song about pestilence and death [...] But she did love the glares from passersby as the giggling children fell over in their paths. The inconvenience of having to swarm around the writhing bodies stirred grumbles from the shoppers, and Cinder adored the children for it.
>
> (4–5)

This links with the subversive and untidy bodies in Garrone's *Tale of Tales,* in which corporeality is reduced to its messy and fleshy baseness – something society likes to forget about or to, at least, rise above. It is fitting that disease (the plague) breaks out at the market on this very day; Meyer highlights how our bodies are not solid and predictable, rather, their boundaries are fluid, permeable, and beyond our control:

> The stench of excrement and rot reached out to her as she stepped into the warehouse. She reeled back, cupping her palm over her nose as her stomach churned, wishing her brain interface could dull odors as easily as it could noise.
>
> (145)

Control of the body in this society is essential, particularly the cyborg body, which becomes the projected site of these threats to rational security in its breakdown of neat ideas about embodiment. Indeed, Cinder's body is controlled as the property of Adri, who uses her as a domestic servant, and of the state, which utilises her in its investigations. After her sister Peony contracts the plague, Adri blames Cinder for taking her outside and signs her over to the state for experiments that aim to find a cure for the disease. Notably, these tests are only performed on cyborgs who are viewed as lesser beings:

> 'You will be going with these med-droids. Don't make a scene [...] Because we all have a duty to do what we can, and you know what a high demand there is for...your type. Especially now [...] They just need cyborgs to find the cure [...] Take her', said Adri. 'Get her out of my sight'.
> 'I didn't volunteer. You can't take me against my will!'
> The android was unperturbed. 'We have been authorised by your legal guardian to take you into custody through the use of force if necessary'.
>
> (66–67)

In this way, those in power, Adri and the State, cannot control her mind, but they can, quite literally, stifle her through control of her body. Even the State experiments are figured in rapacious imagery:

> She choked on the scream that tried to burble out of her. It was painless. Painless. But someone was in her head. Inside her. An invasion. A violation. She tried to jerk away, but the android held her firm.
> 'Get out!' The Scream echoed back to her off the cold walls.
> **SCAN COMPLETED.**
> The med-droid disconnected the prongs. Cinder lay trembling, her heart crushed against her ribcage.
> The med-droid didn't bother to close the panel in the back of her head.
>
> (81)

The problem here is that Cinder sees herself as inferior because she cannot accept her cyborg status and she even shares the prejudiced thinking of her society by refuting the Lunar race altogether, telling Dr Erland that, '"I am not one of *them*!" To be cyborg *and* Lunar. One was enough to make her a mutant, an outcast, but to be *both*? She shuddered. Lunars were a cruel, savage people' (178). Here, Cinder is still trapped in the prejudices of her society, unable to comprehend her increasingly hybridised identity. As Stover notes, 'already in a boundary position as an adoptee and a cyborg, Cinder's body further complicates her relationships because she is an intergalactic adoptee'.[79] Her body and its boundary-crossing challenges her to widen her perceptions and to reject masculine thinking, with its obsession over neat categories and defined boundaries. For it is only when she relinquishes the idea that she is one thing or another that she arrives at the recognition of her true self being a complex blend of different species, materials, and cultures. Cinder, therefore, becomes the ultimate subversive body. In her confrontation with Levana, her cyborg wiring intervenes in Levana's mental attack, resulting in her body exploding into a mess of blood, wires, and metal at the prince's ball. With her body literally opened up and revealed for the world to see, Cinder is confronted with her multifaceted biology and identity. Unable to accept her 'monstrous' form, Kai walks away from her and Levana has her thrown in jail. Yet, Dr Erland visits her, points out that her cyborg body saved her from Levana's attack as it shut down her system, helps her to understand and embrace her 'magic powers' as a Lunar to escape from the cell, and reveals her true identity as Princess Selene. In this way, by embracing her biology, Cinder has reached the point where she can embrace her multifaceted self and the radical potential it harnesses. By removing her chip, she unlocks her Lunar powers and casts off the false singular identity placed on her by a stifled society. Instead she can evade all attempts to contain and understand both her body and her self:

> Soon, the whole world would be searching for her – Linh Cinder. A deformed cyborg with a missing foot. A Lunar with a stolen identity. A mechanic with no one to run to, nowhere to go. But they would be looking for a ghost.
>
> (387)

'Curtain Call' For Gender Binaries: The Subversive 'Performances' of Queer and Transgender Bodies in Tanith Lee's *Cruel Pink*

The cyborg is only one form of postmodern embodiment with the potential to shatter the boundaries and binary structures of patriarchal masculine thought. Certainly, while the cyborg undermines cultural ideas of gender and sexuality – Cinder feeling like her boyish form does not fit social categorisation following her cyborg surgery – transgender and queer bodies also mount a subversive challenge to traditional ideas about the male/female dichotomy and heterosexuality, providing a means to liberate us from the established models which only offer polarised existences. In Judith Halberstam's book, *In a Queer Time and Place: Transgender Bodies, Subcultural Lives*, she notes how postmodern body theories have

> deepened, enriched, and complicated contemporary feminist understandings of the politics of the body; Judith Butler's *Gender Trouble*

is a striking example [...] to suggest how 'gender trouble' is culturally stirred up through 'subversive bodily acts' that exhibit the arti-
ficiality of gender.[80]

Similarly, Anna Kérchy stresses 'the body-political significance of the
trans-embodied self's insistence on "gender trouble" in a society governed by hierarchical dualisms and sexual taboos generated by the patriarchal, heteronormative reproductive economy'.[81]

Tanith Lee's *Cruel Pink*, discussed in previous chapters, once again asserts itself as a key text in this project (the title itself suggesting the cruelty
of rigid gender moulds, and the novel ironically repeating 'blue for a boy,
pink for a girl' throughout each character's narrative). Similar to Meyer's
Cinder, *Cruel Pink* fits into Halberstam's idea of artwork that 'concep-
tualizes embodiment in Butlerian terms as a repetitive series of gestures
that in these instances, depict identity as process, mutation, invention,
and reconstruction'.[82] The very premise of *Cruel Pink* is the multiple
personality disorder of an elderly lady, Dawn, whose various personae
are not only enacted mentally but also physically in her cross-dressing
performances of each different character in public and private settings.
My study has noted to date how her performances cross the boundaries
of masculine definitions of time and space, but they also cross body
and gender boundaries too: none of the personae fit neatly into any one
gender category. For example, Klova plays the obsessively feminine role
of sex object and ends up a slave to her lipstick with its symbolically engraved initials of 'C. P.' (Cruel Pink); Irvin is a bisexual actor who quite
literally performs his sexuality according to the individual he pursues;
Rod was born biologically male but raised as a girl until his parents died
and the horror of his new guardian forced him once again into what he
calls 'the straitjacket of maleness'; and, finally, Emenie is a lesbian serial
killer who describes herself as a chameleon, able to mutate into different ages at will.[83] Dawn's seamless shifts between genders, sexualities,
ages, beings, times, and spaces utilises Judith Butler's 'gender as performance' theory to foreground what Kérchy asserts to be a 'questioning
of dualisms, hierarchies, and centers, and a reconception of meaning,
identity and body as social construct and dynamic act', coinciding with
'the major projects of poststructuralist cultural critical investigations'.[84]
Certainly, as the actor, Irvin, states, 'It is all actors' moves, I find. Life,
that is. Or most of life' (105). Certainly, Rod harbours a wardrobe full of
female clothes which he permits himself to indulge in twice a day as his
'fix' – however, this time relishing femininity does not constitute his true
cross-dressing moments, I would argue. Rather, his male business-suit
façade, which he is forced to adopt every day in order to do his mundane
job, is his real performance. Here Lee is certainly foregrounding the
'cruelty' of limited conceptions of gender, Rod reminiscing that, after
his parents' deaths, 'On went the strait-jacket of maleness. On went the

shackles of *learning*, all over again, what *not*, and *what* to do, to want, to hate' (125). Lee's emphasis here on 'learning' exposes masculinity and femininity to be constructs, guises, or costumes that we put on to act the socially acceptable part. As Bordo points out, 'In imitating gender, drag implicitly reveals the imitative structure of gender itself – as well as its contingency'.[85] Gender is as fluid as a dress or suit that can be changed, swapped, or exchanged at any given moment; as Rod notes, our bodies are 'cast in a new mould' for every occasion (121). Dawn is the ultimate postmodern body par excellence, and fits, in the words of Bordo, 'the body of the mythological Trickster, the shape-shifter: "of indeterminate sex and changeable gender...who continually alters her/his body, creates and recreates a personality ... and floats across time" from period to period, place to place' (227). Certainly, after Dawn's death, the academic, James Pinkerton, charged with finding out her incredible story, records his draft article for the reader. Here we see his conventional and patriarchal paranoia surface when he states:

> My name is James Pinkerton, which I'm afraid, besides sounding very Gilbert and Sullivan, has earned me among my colleagues the dubious nickname of *Pinky*, or *Pink*. The last is a slang term too for a certain part of the female anatomy, a wonderful part, true, but I've not been that keen on its being applied to me. As a bloke, I'm not, in any way aside from name, PINK.
>
> (195)

We are immediately alerted to the fact that he may be aligned with the title *Cruel Pink*, in that his masculine logic is cruel and harmful to the lives we have just watched unfold and perish – he attempts to interview locals to find out about Dawn's personae, viewing them all as mere ramblings in a crazed old woman's mind. However, her gender-bending performances and her evasion of all neat summations (Pinkerton is unable to get a straight or easy answer from anybody, as each interviewee is simply left confused by her complexity), ultimately shatters his limited patriarchal mindset. We can even see this mirrored in his writing, with the structure breaking down entirely. Trying to write up the article, it starts to collapse into:

> OK.
> Yes.
> OK.
> How did I get started on all this?
>
> (211)

In the end, Pinkerton recognises that we are all actors, our identities are a series of performances and that Dawn's personae are not any less real because of that fact – she was all of these people, just as we are all different versions of ourselves every day. Ultimately, limited masculine rationality or patriarchal thinking cannot contain our fluid gender identities:

> Split personality. Multiple personality. Classified terms for a particular form of certifiable madness.
>   But.
>   You know, we all do it – don't we? – one way or another. I mean, of course, we lead many different lives inside our one.
>   One personality for work, and one for your sexual partner, another for the kids, if you have any. Another when you're really elated, when you're angry, and another when you're scared shitless. Every seven or ten years, too, you seem to grow into another skin as the old one shreds itself off.
>
> (220–221)

Refusing to confine Dawn to a simplistic summary now, Pinkerton refuses to do the article, asserting that 'I may just hand over my three hundred pounds to Dimble. And suggest to D.C.W. he find another patsy. Rest in peace. Let it go' (221). In this way, Lee points out that our society's conception of 'bodies that matter' must be widened to include those outside of established categories, and, as Butler states,

> it may be precisely through practices which underscore disidentification with those regulatory norms by which sexual difference is materialised that both feminist and queer politics are mobilised. Such collective disidentifications can facilitate a reconceptualisation of which bodies matter, and which bodies are yet to emerge as critical matters of concern.[86]

Pinkerton, then, starts his article as the symbol of 'the masculinist hubris of the Cartesian ideal of the magisterial, universal knower whose privileged epistemological position reveals reality as it is', and this is contrasted to the novel (as well as Dawn herself) which embodies, in the words of Bordo, 'the postmodern ideal of narrative heteroglossia [...] celebrat[ing] a "feminine" ability to enter into perspectives of others, to accept fluidity as a feature of reality' (228). Dawn's five lives, without exception, exist outside of patriarchal categorisations in 'a queer time and place', with Irvin noting that 'They are a queer parcel of citizens that dwell in the building, and where I have glimpsed them [...] they seem dressed in a diverse and bedlam manner' (111). And yet, they are also lives which matter (even though history and society excludes them), Lee highlighting their humanity and illustrating to the reader that, despite their status as performances, they are still real selves, real identities, just as we ourselves, as conglomerations of performances, recognise our own humanity. As Butler notes, we are forced to consider,

> What challenge does that excluded and abjected realm produce to a symbolic hegemony that might force a radical rearticulation of what qualifies as bodies that matter, ways of living that count as 'life', lives worth protecting, lives worth saving, lives worth grieving?[87]

Conclusion

To conclude, this chapter illustrates how the body has been reclaimed by feminist anti-tale authors in the twenty-first century and transformed into a subversive feminine conceptual and textual architecture in their narratives, which shatters (like the revisions of space and time in the previous chapters) masculine logic and patriarchal boundaries. Embracing difference, these feminist authors are able to utilise the female body's radical otherness as a means of envisioning alternative realities and societies. This chapter illustrates how Garrone's *Tale of Tales* emphasises the extreme violence done to female bodies in traditional patriarchal fairy tales and embraces the fleshy baseness of the body as messy, uncontrollable, and marks its resistance to neat containment by restrictive rationality or social measures. Similarly, I show how Cornwell's *Tides* juxtaposes the restrictive masculine forces of 'the mainland', and the scientists who try to bring the selkie body under rational control, with the shape-shifting nature of the selkies which evade any attempts at categorisation or mastery. They are literally slippery bodies, with water emphasised as a major metaphor in capturing the liberating fluidity of feminine bodies and knowledges. In addition, the anorexic and bulimic bodies of Cornwell's Lo and Kang's Yeong-hye, in *Tides* and *The Vegetarian*, express not their individual maladies, but rather society's own ills and neuroses – their bodies loudly voicing their stories of pain and oppression. Meyer's cyborg-alien-human heroine in *Cinder* also shatters the boundaries of Enlightenment notions of the body and the binaries of inside and outside, human and non-human, male and female. The discovery of her identity's hybrid complexity even liberates Cinder's own mind from the confines of its prejudiced patriarchal thinking in favour of the subversive power inherent in her real identity, established in an understanding of her body's complexity, fluidity, and its ability to breach boundaries. Finally, the queer sexualities and transgender bodies in Lee's *Cruel Pink* highlight how gender is a performance, identity ever shifting, and the sense of a stabilised self nothing but a fantasy. Each of Dawn's various personae are bodies that are excluded from the dualistic and heteronormative structures sustained by patriarchy, and yet, Lee marks out the need for this patriarchal logic to be deconstructed (Pinkerton unable to sustain his masculine impulse towards simplicity and neatness after investigating Dawn's story). The novel, therefore, widens the umbrella of 'bodies that matter'. While these analyses are highly theoretical, and often used metaphorically in the stories, they also have real practical application, opening our minds, and shattering patriarchal masculine knowledges and structures, so that new solutions and existences can be imagined and forged in real time.

In essence, the project of these anti-tales is aligned with that of Shildrick in the following proclamation:

> What a feminist project might aim to do is to uncover the mechanisms of construction, flaunt the contradictions and transgressions which destabilize the binaries, and insist on a diversity of provisional bodily identifications. The move towards embodied selves need not entail a new form of essentialism nor a covert recuperation of biological determinism. Rather it celebrates embodiment as process, and speaks both to the refusal to split body and mind, and to the refusal to allow ourselves to be either normalized or pathologised. At the same time to stress both particularity *and* substantiality for the female body challenges the universalized male standard and opens up for us new possibilities of (well) being-in-the-world.[88]

I do not dangerously advocate a mere text in the place of the body in this chapter, rather the ideas are intended as a process – offering us an 'inbetween' space outside of essentialist and dualistic thought – in which new bodies and new knowledges can emerge, allowing for a greater diversity of beings to be accepted and integrated into social life, in order to demand both recognition and equality. In essence, this chapter's textual bodies aim to liberate material bodies in the real world, rather than denying the body's fleshy reality.

Notes

1 Betsy Cornwell, *Tides* (New York: Houghton Mifflin Harcourt Publishing Company, 2013), p. 83. Hereafter, page references will be incorporated into the text.
2 Marissa Meyer, *Cinder* (London: Puffin Books, 2012), p. 101. Hereafter, page references will be incorporated into the text.
3 Susan Bordo, *Unbearable Weight: Feminism, Western Culture and the Body* (London: University of California Press, 2003), pp. 165–166. Hereafter, page references will be incorporated into the text.
4 Attila Kiss, 'Postmodern Fantasies of Corporeality: Identity and Visual Agency in Postmodern Anatomy Theatres' in *Postmodern Reinterpretations of Fairy Tales: How Applying New Methods Generates New Meanings*, ed. Anna Kérchy (Lampeter: The Edwin Mellen Press, 2011), p. 264.
5 Ibid., p. 251.
6 Ibid., p. 259.
7 Anna Kérchy, 'Bodies That Do Not Fit: Sexual Metamorphosis, Re-embodied Identities and Cultural Crisis in Contemporary Transgender Memoirs' (2009), p. 1

<https://www.academia.edu/5432781/Bodies_That_Do_Not_Fit_Sexual_
Metamorphoses_Re-embodied_Identities_and_Cultural_Crisis_in_
Contemporary_Transgender_Memoirs?auto=download> [accessed 7th April
2017].

8 Margrit Shildrick and Janet Price, 'Openings on the Body: A Critical Introduction' in *Feminist Theory and the Body: A Reader* (Edinburgh: Edinburgh University Press, 1999), p. 3.

9 Margrit Shildrick, *Leaky Bodies and Boundaries: Feminism, Postmodernism and (Bio)Ethics* (London: Routledge, 1997), p. 28.

10 Ibid., p. 37.

11 Mary Wollstonecraft, *A Vindication of the Rights of Women & A Vindication of the Rights of Men* (New York: Cosimo, Inc., 2008), p. 53.

12 See Naomi Wolf, *The Beauty Myth* (London: Vintage Books, 1990).

13 Jo Bridgeman and Susan Millns, *Law and Body Politics: Regulating the
Female Body* (Hants: Dartmouth Publishing Company Limited, 1995).

14 See Susan Faludi, *Backlash: The Undeclared War Against Women* (London:
Vintage, 1992).

15 Judith Evans, *Feminist Theory Today: An introduction to Second-Wave
Feminism* (London: SAGE Publications, 1995), p. 3.

16 Elizabeth Grosz, *Space, Time and Perversion: Essays on the Politics of Bodies* (London: Routledge, 1995), p. 31.

17 Ibid.

18 Shildrick, *Leaky Bodies and Boundaries*, p.10.

19 Ibid., p. 102.

20 Grosz, *Space, Time and Perversion*, p. 38.

21 Shildrick, *Leaky Bodies and Boundaries*, pp. 16–17.

22 Ibid., p. 216.

23 Laurence Talairach-Vielmas, *Moulding the Female Body in Victorian Fairy
Tales and Sensation Novels* (Hampshire: Ashgate Publishing Limited,
2007), p. 8.

24 Jacob & Wilhelm Grimm, 'Sleeping Beauty' in *The Complete Fairy Tales of
the Brothers Grimm* (Hertfordshire: Wordsworth Editions Limited, 2009),
p. 248.

25 Grimms, 'Snow-White and the Seven Dwarfs' in *The Complete Fairy Tales
of the Brothers Grimm*, p. 270.

26 Talairach-Vielmas, *Moulding the Female Body in Victorian Fairy Tales and
Sensation Novels*, p. 5.

27 Grimms, 'Snow-White and the Seven Dwarfs' in *The Complete Fairy Tales
of the Brothers Grimm*, p. 263.

28 Ibid., p. 261.

29 Ibid., p. 271.

30 Ibid.

31 Margaret Atwood, *Surfacing* (London: Virago Press, 1972), p. 194.

32 Grimms, 'Little Riding-Hood' in *The Complete Fairy Tales of the Brothers
Grimm*, p. 144.

33 Ibid., p. 146.

34 Kiss, 'Postmodern Fantasies of Corporeality: Identity and Visual Agency in
Postmodern Anatomy Theatres' in *Postmodern Reinterpretations of Fairy
Tales: How Applying New Methods Generates New Meanings*, ed. Kérchy,
pp. 259, 253.

35 Ibid., p. 259.

36 Schutz, 'Monsters Beneath the Skin: Angela Carter's "The Courtship of Mr
Lyon" as Palimpsest in Snow Patrol's "Absolute Gravity"' in *Postmodern
Reinterpretations of Fairy Tales: How Applying New Methods Generates
New Meanings*, ed. Kérchy, p. 203.

37 See Linda Hutcheon, *A Theory of Adaptation* (New York: Routledge, 2006) where she also notes that adaptations are not inferior or secondary to the original material but must be considered as original works in their own right.

38 Jack Zipes, *The Irresistible Fairy Tale: The Cultural and Social History of a Genre* (Oxford: Princeton University Press, 2012), p. 17.

39 Richard Dawkins quoted in Zipes, *The Irresistible Fairy Tale*, p. 17.

40 Ella Price, 'The Special Coil of Chemicals' in *Silicon Tales: Storytelling for the Digital Age* (Bristol: Silver Wood Books, 2013), pp. 15–18.

41 Ibid., p. 16.

42 Ibid., p. 17.

43 Sadie Plant, 'The Future Looms: Weaving Women and Cybernetics' in *Cyberspace, Cyberbodies, Cyberpunk: Cultures of Technological Embodiment*, eds. Mike Featherstone and Roger Burrows (London: SAGE Publications, 1995), p. 62.

44 Price, 'The Special Coil of Chemicals' in *Silicon Tales: Storytelling For the Digital Age*, p. 17.

45 Ibid., p. 17.

46 Suzanne Anker, 'The Extant Vamp (or the) Ire of It All: Fairy Tales and Genetic Engineering' in *Fairy Tales, Monsters, and the Genetic Imagination*, ed. Mark W. Scala (Nashville: Vanderbilt University Press, 2012), p. 37.

47 See Mark W. Scala, ed., *Fairy Tales, Monsters, and the Genetic Imagination* (Nashville: Vanderbilt University Press, 2012).

48 Nancy L. Canepa, 'Introduction' in *Tale of Tales* (New York: Penguin Books, 2007), p. xxxv.

49 Meagan Navarro, 'The Dark Need For Modern Fairy Tales' in *Birth Movies Death* <http://birthmoviesdeath.com/2017/01/12/the-dark-need-for-modern-fairy-tales> [accessed 7th April 2017].

50 Canepa, 'Introduction' in *Tale of Tales*, p. lix.

51 Giambattista Basile, *Tale of Tales* (New York: Penguin Books, 2007), pp. 53, 55. Hereafter, page references will be incorporated into the text.

52 Canepa, 'Introduction' in *Tale of Tales*, p. liv.

53 Navarro, 'The Dark Need For Modern Fairy Tales' in *Birth.Movies.Death* <http://birthmoviesdeath.com/2017/01/12/the-dark-need-for-modern-fairy-tales> [accessed 7th April 2017].

54 *Tale of Tales*, dir. Matteo Garrone (Archimede Film: 2015) [on DVD].

55 Shildrick, *Leaky Bodies and Boundaries*, pp. 34–35.

56 Basile, 'The Flea' in *Tale of Tales*, p. 53.

57 Navarro, 'The Dark Need For Modern Fairy Tales' in *Birth.Movies.Death* <http://birthmoviesdeath.com/2017/01/12/the-dark-need-for-modern-fairy-tales> [accessed 7th April 2017].

58 See Walter Vandereycken and Ron van Deth, *From Fasting Saints to Anorexic Girls: The History of Self-Starvation* (London: The Athlone Press, 1994).

59 Ibid.

60 See Naomi Wolf's, *The Beauty Myth* (London: Vintage Books, 1990).

61 Tamar Heller and Patricia Moran, eds., *Scenes of the Apple: Food and the Female Body in Nineteenth- and Twentieth-Century Women's Writing* (Albany: State University of New York Press, 2003), p. 5.

62 Han Kang, *The Vegetarian* (London: Portobello Books, 2007), p. 13. Hereafter, page references will be incorporated into the text.

63 See Wolf, *The Beauty Myth*.

64 Marina Warner, 'Metamorphoses of the Monstrous' in *Fairy Tales, Monsters, and the Genetic Imagination*, ed. Scala, p. 24.

65 Astrida Neimanis, *Bodies of Water: Posthuman Feminist Phenomenology* (London: Bloomsbury Publishing Plc, 2017), p. 2.
66 Ibid., p. 3.
67 Mike Featherstone and Roger Burrows, 'Cultures of Technological Embodiment: An Introduction' in *Cyberspace, Cyberbodies, Cyberpunk: Cultures of Technological Embodiment* (London: SAGE Publications, 1995), p. 2.
68 Anne Marie Balsamo, *Technologies of the Gendered Body: Reading Cyborg Women* (London: Duke University Press), p. 6.
69 Ibid.
70 Ibid., pp. 6, 9.
71 Donna Haraway, 'A Cyborg Manifesto: Science, Technology, and Socialist-Feminism in the Late Twentieth-Century', pp. 1, 3. <http://www.labster8.net/wp-content/uploads/2015/11/Haraway-Cyborg-Manifesto2.pdf> [accessed 7th April 2016].
72 Balsamo, *Technologies of the Gendered Body*, p. 9.
73 Judith Halberstam, 'Automating Gender: Postmodern Feminism in the Age of the Intelligent Machine' in *Feminist Studies*, Vol. 18, No. 1 (Spring 1992), p. 440.
74 Deanna Stover, 'Gold Slippers and Cyborg Feet: Comparing Adopted Bodies in the Grimms' 'Cinderella' and Marissa Meyer's *Cinder*', p. 1 <http://s3.amazonaws.com/academia.edu.documents/41571309/Stover.MLA2016.pdf?AWSAccessKeyId=AKIAIWOWYYGZ2Y53UL3A&Expires=1491645940&Signature=tzsAryuNUXHwox6N4be%2BkyzQAyk%3D&response-content-disposition=inline%3B%20filename%3DGold_Slippers_and_Cyborg_Feet_Comparing.pdf> [accessed 7th April 2016].
75 Ibid., p. 3.
76 Marriane Novy quoted in Stover, 'Gold Slippers and Cyborg Feet: Comparing Adopted Bodies in the Grimms' 'Cinderella' and Marissa Meyer's *Cinder*', p. 3.
77 Haraway, 'A Cyborg Manifesto: Science, Technology, and Socialist-Feminism in the Late Twentieth-Century', p. 2.
78 Stover, 'Gold Slippers and Cyborg Feet: Comparing Adopted Bodies in the Grimms' 'Cinderella' and Marissa Meyer's *Cinder*', p. 3.
79 Ibid., p. 4.
80 Judith Halberstam, *In a Queer Time and Place: Transgender Bodies, Subcultural Lives* (London: New York University Press, 2005), p. 289.
81 Kérchy, 'Bodies That Do Not Fit: Sexual Metamorphosis, Re-embodied Identities and Cultural Crisis in Contemporary Transgender Memoirs', p. 2.
82 Halberstam, *In a Queer Time and Place: Transgender Bodies, Subcultural Lives*, p. 110.
83 Tanith Lee, *Cruel Pink* (Stafford: Immanion Press, 2013), p. 125. Hereafter, page references will be incorporated into the text.
84 Kérchy, 'Bodies That Do Not Fit: Sexual Metamorphosis, Re-embodied Identities and Cultural Crisis in Contemporary Transgender Memoirs', p. 4.
85 Judith Butler quoted in Susan Bordo, 'Postmodern Subjects, Postmodern Bodies' in *Feminist Studies*, Vol. 17, No. 3 (Autumn 1991), p. 170.
86 Judith Butler, 'Bodies That Matter' in *Feminist Theory and the Body: A Reader*, eds. Shildrick and Price, p. 237.
87 Ibid., p. 234.
88 Shildrick, *Leaky Bodies and Boundaries*, pp. 60–61.

Feminine Conclusions
New Architectures, New Futures

As Elizabeth Grosz points out,

> conceptions of spatiality and temporality have rarely been the explicit object of feminist reflection: they have always appeared above the more mundane concerns of day-by-day politics, too abstract, too neutral and self-evident to take as an object of critical feminist analysis.[1]

However, as my textual analysis in this study demonstrates, spatio-temporality is, in fact, deeply enmeshed in the practical and formal construction of social, political, and cultural relations and, as such, presents a critical topic for feminist discussion. Focusing on the spatial, temporal, and corporeal aspects of twenty-first-century anti-tales, it is evident from my research that this triad is a generic component and trend within the anti-tale genre. Anti-tales appear to be contributing to Grosz's project as set forth in my introduction, suggesting that 'the links between corporeality and conceptions of space and time' *are* proving 'to be of major significance in feminist research' and that 'if bodies are to be reconceived not only must their matter and form be rethought, but so too must their environment and spatio-temporal location'.[2] The feminisation of space by the texts discussed in Chapters 1 and 2, and their revision of time as feminine and complex discussed in Chapters 3 and 4, provides greater scope for the feminine bodies considered in Chapter 5 to search for a self beyond the restrictions of established masculine frameworks and simplistic, heteronormative knowledges. This fulfils Luce Irigaray's assertion that,

> In order to make it possible to think through and live [sexual] difference, we must reconsider the whole problematic of *space* and *time* ... The transition to a new age requires a change in our perception and conception of *space-time*, the *inhabiting of places* and of *containers*, or *envelopes of identity* [bodies].[3]

Thus, this book shows how anti-tales today are taking up the postmodern feminist project outlined by feminists such as Irigaray and Grosz, in reconceptualising established forms of constructing space, time, and bodies in order to liberate women from the restrictive architecture of patriarchal ways of seeing and being.

The concept that has consistently emerged as the key to the subversive anti-tales' space, time, and body revisions across the chapters is the idea of the feminine: from the multifaceted and ever-shifting feminine city in Chapter 1, which subverts the simplistic, exclusionary, and rationalised urban space constructed by the male *flâneur*; to the use of nature as an alternative feminine space beyond the artificially constructed binaries and divisive architectures inherent in male philosophy; to the feminisation of time in Chapters 3 and 4, which deconstructs the orderly and stifling regime of the patriarchal clock and undermines stereotypes about youth and ageing; and finally, to the use of feminine bodies in Chapter 5, which shatters the illusion of bodily containment and neatness held up by paranoid social forces keen to keep unruly bodies under control. In this way, their revisions of spatial, temporal, and corporeal architectures, both practical and ideological, allow for alternative, fluid, more complex, and inclusive feminine architectures and perspectives to emerge: whether that be in the form of feminine urban and natural spaces that refute any attempts at male mastery; polytemporal, subjective, and fluid feminine times as opposed to the simplistic mechanical time of clock; or the emergence of subversive forms of other/feminine bodies that defy any neat labels or rationalisation. These provide a feminine architecture that creates greater freedom and scope for constructing alternative societies and futures built on inclusivity and favouring diversity. Therefore, as stated in my introduction, my conception of the feminine is not essentialist, but rather refers to a multitude of fluid and marginal presences. For example, the analysis of feminine knowledges and positions in Tanith Lee's *Cruel Pink* does not exclude male or transgender characters. Rather, Rod, Klova, Irvin, Emenie, and Dawn all constitute subversive feminine positions as outsiders, existing in spaces, times, and bodies that seep beyond, and into, the gaps left by simplistic masculine modes of understanding.

Hence, as all of the chapters ultimately foreground the idea of feminised spaces, feminine bodies, and feminine time as the subversive radical edge of the stories, I suggest that the anti-tale itself is a feminine form. In the introduction, I foregrounded Grosz's idea that the 'architecture' (or power structure) of patriarchy is centred around space, time, and bodies; however, I also noted that this term also has greater significance for this study. I suggest that space, time, and bodies constitute the subversive feminine architecture of the anti-tale that allows the genre to subvert the rigid structure, or architecture, of the patriarchal fairy tale. Just as a feminine conception of the world shatters masculine social and logistical frameworks, it also shatters the masculine form of the fairy tale and its rigid formal conventions. Indeed, the fairy tale's absolutist black and white morality is subverted by the breakdown of male binary logic through the use of feminine nature in both *Maleficent* and *Into the Woods*, as shown in Chapter 2. *Maleficent*'s narratological displacement,

in privileging the story of a character who is on the margins of the traditional story, constitutes a greying of good and evil, while the transmu-
sicality of the baker's wife and her closing song in *Into the Woods* also
narratologically subverts the binary fairy-tale framework and its limits
on interpretative responses. Rather, we can be many things, villains *and*
heroes, allowing us to question 'Is it always "or" is it never "and"?'.[4]
In addition, the fairy-tale dependency on the binary of youth (equated
with innocence) and old age (innately linked to villainy) is shown to
be subverted in Kate Bernheimer's stories where youth is depicted as a
time of power and corruption while Margaret Atwood's *Stone Mattress*
highlights an innocence and childlike quality in her older characters. In
addition, both authors (alongside Nalo Hopkinson) advocate an intergenerational bond between young and old, highlighting their similarities and
shattering the perceived boundary between the two categories. The om-
niscient narration of conventional fairy tales and its apparent neutrality
is also shown to be subverted in Chapter 1, where the authoritative male
flâneur is deconstructed in favour of a diverse plurality of perspectives
embodied in the feminine figure of the *flâneuse*. The smug male voice of
Lee's academic character, Pinkerton, for example, crumbles to nothing
as he attempts to sum up Dawn's multiple personalities into a neat and
coherent narrative in *Cruel Pink*. This *écriture féminine* style of employ-
ing multiple and overlapping narrative strands is used to deconstruct the
simplicity and exclusionary tendencies of patriarchal fairy tales throughout the anti-tales in this study, from Lee's novel, to *Into the Woods*, the
Maddaddam trilogy, and *Stone Mattress*, among others. Meanwhile,
the similarly detached neutrality of the fairy tale's 'Once Upon a Time'
trope is deconstructed by the anti-tales examined in Chapter 3, which
reveal all temporalities to be inherently subjective and political, the fairy
tale's motif allowing outdated ideologies to appear timeless and carrying
across centuries. In Chapter 1, Karen Best's 'Blizzard Season' was shown
to subvert this too, illustrating how fairy-tale ideologies and morals can
no longer be allowed to appear universal through this 'Once Upon a
Time' motif; rather, once her fairy-tale Snow Whites find themselves in
a twenty-first-century city, they are shown to be outdated, out-of-time,
and ridiculous. Even the neat 'happily ever after' ending of fairy tales is
subverted by these feminine anti-tales which refuse closure: whether it
be Noah and Lo's uncertain anticipation of the future as they leave the
'inbetween' space of their grandmother's remote abode in *Tides*; Cinder's
new beginning with a reinvigorated sense of self at the end of Meyer's
novel; or Alison's fear of an uncertain future for her adopted little girl
in a masculine city at the conclusion of *Alison Wonderland*, all of these
anti-tales shatter the myth of stability, closure, and stasis at the end of
the story, favouring instead the feminine leaks and rifts that flow beyond
the pages. It should also be noted that Alison's story actually begins after
her marriage to 'Mr. Wonderland' has broken down, the 'happily ever

after' fairy-tale ending of marriage being completely debunked, with life continuing beyond the conventional story's closure.

Thus, anti-tales not only contribute to the feminine subversion of masculine reality by shattering its established, foundational spatial, temporal, and corporeal architecture – endorsed by the postmodern feminist projects outlined earlier – but use this radical femininity as a structural means of subverting the patriarchal form of the fairy tale genre too. It is apt then that Grosz links the significance of space, time, and body revisions to literature when she states,

> Conversely, it is only through a careful reading of phallocentric texts and paradigms that the rifts, flaws, and cracks within them can be utilised to reveal spaces where these texts exceed themselves, where they say more than they mean, opening themselves up to a feminine (re)appropriation.[5]

This coincides with Catriona McAra and David Calvin's suggestion that the anti-tale is a 'shadow' of the fairy tale genre, with the genre's feminisation and complication of fairy tales allowing them to work within the older genre in order to 'explode' it.[6] However, instead of the anti-tale simply being labelled feminist, I suggest that the label of 'feminine' should also be added to McAra and Calvin's existing definitions. After all, the radical feminine architecture of the anti-tale that this study identifies not only supports Calvin and McAra's definitions of the term but rather encompasses all of the elements in their table detailing the differences between the fairy tale and the anti-tale. So while the fairy tale is indeed patriarchal, set 'Once Upon a Time', has a black and white morality, and the anti-tale *is* feminist, no longer ahistorical, and contains a grey morality, I propose that it is these features (along with other spatial, temporal, and corporeal elements) that mean the patriarchally fossilised fairy tale is a masculine form, while the anti-tale can be defined as a radical feminine one. The anti-tale then has a feminine architecture both literally in its material construction and conceptually in its advocacy of feminine forms of knowledge. It is this feminine (and feminist) architecture that I believe paves the way for a more concrete definition of the anti-tale genre and which distinguishes it from fairy tale retellings.

Having proven conclusively that space, time, and bodies constitute the feminine, and hence feminist, architecture of the anti-tale form, this study aims to provide foundations for future study and there is great scope for further projects. As I have stated within this work, many of the analyses in my chapters are based on areas which are in need of greater scholarly interest and further research: for example, the concept of time is an entirely neglected area of fairy tale and anti-tale scholarship, the city in fantasy literature is a now part of a newly emerging genre of 'urban fantasy', and ecofeminist ideas are currently pervading both popular and literary works, with my study suggesting that the feminist fear of ecofeminism's perceived essentialism needs to be overcome in order to appreciate the potential and radicalism of these works. In addition, neglected authors such as Tanith Lee, Nalo Hopkinson, Ekaterina Sedia, and new authors Betsy Cornwell and Helen Smith have been given a space in this monograph for consideration, and by highlighting the richness and complexity of their works, I hope to pave the way for further interest and investigation into these writers. This study selects only certain, relevant aspects of temporality, two different types of space (the urban and natural environments), and a selection of subversive bodies in order to suit the scope of the project, with plenty of material having to be side-lined for future work. Each of the three concepts – space, time, and bodies – contains many different ideas and strands, all of which could be explored further in relation to postmodern anti-tales and, indeed, a book could and perhaps should be written on each theme individually. This study also poses the much broader question: is this feminine revision of spatio-temporality and corporeality indicative of a wider trend across postmodern feminist literature in the twenty-first century as a whole? For now, however, I have demonstrated that the anti-tale is a feminine form and have illustrated how the selected texts are successful in contributing to postmodern feminism through their reconfigurations of space, time, and bodies. In doing so, these anti-tales aid in showing us alternative architectures for the future, disenchanting established spatio-temporal laws and structures, as well as limited ideas surrounding the body, ultimately liberating us from the shackles of a single-minded and simplistic masculine reality currently upheld by dominant social forces and patriarchal fairy tales themselves. This is particularly pertinent in this era of Brexit and Trump, with dominant features of our age being a growth in discrimination; increasing paranoia and fear of the 'other'; and the conservative need to uphold binary logic and establish neat boundaries in order to sustain notions of patriarchal power and control. It is only when these masculine tales and social architectures are deconstructed that new, more inclusive realities and futures can be brought into being.

Notes

1 Elizabeth Grosz, *Space, Time and Perversion: Essays on the Politics of Bodies* (London: Routledge, 1995), p. 120.
2 Ibid., p. 124.
3 Luce Irigaray, *An Ethics of Sexual Difference*, trans. Carolyn Burke and Gillian C. Gill (London: Athlone Press, 1993), p. 7.
4 *Into the Woods*, dir. Rob Marshall (Walt Disney Studios Home Entertainment: 2015) [on DVD].
5 Grosz, *Space, Time and Perversion: Essays on the Politics of Bodies*, p. 38.
6 Catriona McAra and David Calvin, eds., *Anti-Tales: The Uses of Disenchantment* (Newcastle upon Tyne: Cambridge Scholars publishing, 2011), p. 4.

Bibliography

Primary Texts

Alice through the Looking Glass, dir. James Bobin (Walt Disney Studios Home Entertainment: 2016) [on DVD].

Atwood, Margaret, *Maddaddam* (London: Virago Press, 2013).

—— *Oryx & Crake* (London: Virago Press, 2003).

—— *Stone Mattress: Nine Tales* (New York: Nan A. Talese/Doubleday, 2014).

—— *The Year of the Flood* (London: Virago Press, 2009).

Basile, Giambattista, *Tale of Tales* (New York: Penguin Books, 2007).

Bernheimer, Kate, *How a Mother Weaned Her Girl From Fairy Tales* (Minneapolis: Coffee House Press, 2014).

Best, Karen, *A Floating World* (Orlando: Beating Windward Press LLC, 2012).

Carter, Angela, *The Bloody Chamber and Other Stories* (London: Vintage Books, 1979).

Cornwell, Betsy, *Tides* (New York: Houghton Mifflin Harcourt Publishing Company, 2013).

Faber, Michel, *Under the Skin* (Edinburgh: Canongate Books Ltd., 2000).

Grimm, Jacob and Wilhelm Grimm, *The Complete Fairy Tales of the Brothers Grimm* (Hertfordshire: Wordsworth Editions Ltd., 2009).

Hairston, Andrea, 'Griots of the Galaxy' in *So Long Been Dreaming: Postcolonial Science Fiction and Fantasy*, eds. Nalo Hopkinson and Uppinder Mehan (Vancouver: Arsenal Pulp Press, 2004).

Hopkinson, Nalo, *Skin Folk* (New York: Warner Books, 2001).

Into the Woods, dir. Rob Marshall (Walt Disney Studios Home Entertainment: 2015) [on DVD].

Kang, Han, *The Vegetarian* (London: Portobello Books, 2007).

Lee, Tanith, *Cruel Pink* (Stafford: Immanion Press, 2013).

Maleficent, dir. Robert Stromberg (Walt Disney Studios Home Entertainment: 2014) [on DVD]

Meyer, Marissa, *Cinder* (London: Puffin Books, 2012).

Price, Ella, *Silicon Tales: Storytelling for the Digital Age* (Bristol: Silver Wood Books, 2013).

Sedia, Ekaterina, *The Secret History of Moscow* (Canada: Prime Books, 2007).

Smith, Helen, *Alison Wonderland* (Las Vegas: Amazon Encore, 2011).

Tale of Tales, dir. Matteo Garrone (Archimede Film: 2015) [on DVD].

Willingham, Bill, *Fables: Legends in Exile*, Vol. 1 (New York: DC Comics, 2012).

Secondary Texts

Alaimo, Stacy, *Undomesticated Ground: Recasting Nature as Feminist Space* (London: Cornell University Press, 2000).

Alcoff, Linda andElizabeth Potter, eds., *Feminist Epistemologies* (London: Routledge, 1993).

Andermahr, Sonya and Phillips Lawrence, eds., *Angela Carter: New Critical Readings* (London: Continuum International Publishing Group, 2012).

Anonymous, 'Anti-Fairy Tale' on *Wikipedia* <https://en.wikipedia.org/wiki/Anti-fairy_tale> [accessed 18th June 2017]

Anonymous, 'Book Review: *Alison Wonderland* by Helen Smith' in *Read in a Single Sitting* <http://www.readinasinglesitting.com/book-review-alison-wonderland-by-helen-smith/> [accessed 26th January 2015]

Apter, Emily, '"Women's Time" in Theory' in *Differences: A Journal of Feminist Cultural Studies*, Vol. 21, No. 1 (2010), pp. 1–18.

Augustine, Jane, 'From *Topos* to Anthropoid: The City as Character in Twentieth-Century Texts' in *City Images: Perspectives from Literature, Philosophy and Film*, ed. Mary Ann Caws (Pennsylvania: Gordon and Breach, 1991), pp. 73–86.

Bacchilega, Cristina, 'An Introduction to the "Innocent Persecuted Heroine" Fairy Tale' in *Western Folklore*, Vol. 52, No. 1 (January, 1993), pp. 1–12.

——— *Fairy Tales Transformed?: Twenty-First Century Adaptations and the Politics of Wonder* (Detroit: Wayne State University Press, 2013).

——— *Postmodern Fairy Tales: Gender and Narrative Strategies* (Pennsylvania: University of Pennsylvania Press, 1997).

Balsamo, Anne, *Technologies of the Gendered Body: Reading Cyborg Women* (London: Duke University Press).

Bandyopadhyay, Debarati, 'An Ecocritical Commentary on the Posthuman Condition in Margaret Atwood's Fiction' in *The Criterion: An International Journal in English*, Vol. 1, No. 1 (April, 2011), pp. 1–14.

Beckett, Sandra L., ed., *Transcending Boundaries: Writing for a Dual Audience of Children and Adults* (New York: Garland Publishing, 1999).

Bell, David, et al., eds., *Pleasure Zones: Bodies, Cities and Spaces* (New York: Syracuse University Press, 2001).

Bell, Elizabeth, et al., eds., *From Mouse to Mermaid: The Politics of Film, Gender, and Culture* (Bloomington: Indiana University Press, 1995).

Benczik, Vera, 'Review of Margaret Atwood's *Maddaddam*' in *Americana*, Vol. IX, No. 2 (Fall, 2013) <http://americanaejournal.hu/vol9no2/benczik-rev> [accessed 22nd February 2016]

Bennett, Barbara, *Scheherazade's Daughters: The Power of Storytelling in Ecofeminist Change* (New York: Peter Lang publishing, Inc., 2012).

Bennett, Michael and David W. Teague, eds., *The Nature of Cities: Ecocriticism and Urban Environments* (Tucson: The University of Arizona Press, 1999).

Benson, Stephen, 'Angela Carter and the Literary *Märchen*' in *Angela Carter and the Fairy Tale,* eds. Danielle Roemer and Cristina Bacchilega (Michigan: Wayne State University Press, 2001), pp. 30–58.

Bernheimer, Kate, *Mirror, Mirror on the Wall: Women Writers Explore their Favourite Fairy Tales* (New York: Anchor Books, 2002).

Bettelheim, Bruno, *The Uses of Enchantment: The Meaning and Importance of Fairy Tales* (London: Penguin Books Ltd., 1976).

Blau du Plessis, Rachel, *Writing beyond the Ending: Narrative Strategies of Twentieth-Century Women Writers* (Bloomington: Indiana University Press, 1985).

Bloch, Ernst, 'The Fairy Tale Moves on its Own in Time (1930)' in *Breaking the Magic Spell: Radical Theories of Folk and Fairy Tales*, ed. Jack Zipes (London: Educational Books Ltd., 1979), pp. 133–135.

Bondi, Liz and Damaris Rose, 'Constructing Gender, Constructing the Urban: A Review of Anglo-American Feminist Urban Geography' in *Gender, Place and Culture: A Journal of Feminist Geography*, Vol. 10, No. 3 (2003), pp. 229–245.

Bordo, Susan, 'Feminism, Foucault and the Politics of the Body' in *Feminist Theory and the Body: A Reader,* eds. Janet Price and Margrit Shildrick (Edinburgh: Edinburgh University Press, 1999), pp. 246–257.

—— 'Postmodern Subjects, Postmodern Bodies' in *Feminist Studies*, Vol. 17, No. 3 (Autumn, 1991), pp. 159–175.

—— *Unbearable Weight: Feminism, Western Culture and the Body* (London: University of California Press, 2003).

Bottigheimer, Ruth B., 'Tale Spinners: Submerged Voices in Grimms' Fairy Tale' in *New German Critique*, Vol. 27 (Autumn, 1982), pp. 141–150.

Boyne, R. and A. Rattansi, *Postmodernism and Society* (London: Macmillan, 1990).

Bridgeman, Jo and Susan Millns, *Law and Body Politics: Regulating the Female Body* (Hants: Dartmouth Publishing Company Limited, 1995).

Brooks-Bouson, J., 'A "Joke-Filled Romp" Through End Times: Radical Environmentalism, Deep Ecology, and Human Extinction in Margaret Atwood's *Maddaddam* Trilogy' in *The Journal of Commonwealth Literature* (13th April, 2015), pp. 1–17 <http://jcl.sagepub.com/content/early/2015/04/13/0021989415573558.full.pdf> [accessed 8th November 2015]

—— 'We're Using up the Earth. It's Almost Gone': A Return to the Post-Apocalyptic Future in Margaret Atwood's *The Year of the Flood*' in *The Journal of Commonwealth Literature*, Vol. 46, No. 1 (March, 2011), pp. 9–26 <http://jcl.sagepub.com/content/46/1/9.full.pdf> [accessed 22nd February 2016]

Browne, Victoria, *Feminism, Time, and Nonlinear History* (Hampshire: Palgrave Macmillan, 2014).

Buda, Agata, 'Destructive Power of Gothic Time and Space in the Postmodernist Fiction by Michel Faber' <https://www.pulib.sk/web/kniznica/elpub/dokument/Bila2/.../Buda.pdf> [accessed 22nd February 2016]

Butler, Judith, 'Performative Acts and Gender Constitution: An Essay in Phenomenology and Feminist Theory' in *Theatre Journal*, Vol. 40, No. 4 (December, 1988), pp. 519–531.

Caws, Mary Ann, ed., *City Images: Perspectives from Literature, Philosophy and Film* (Pennsylvania: Gordon and Breach, 1991).

Chu, Ben, 'Brexit Is One More Example of the Older Generation Financially Bankrupting the Young' in *The Independent* (28th June, 2016) <http://www.independent.co.uk/voices/brexit-eu-referendum-financial-economic-impact-older-generation-bankrupting-young-a7107666.html> [accessed 3rd October 2016]

Cixous, Hélène, 'Castration or Decapitation?' in *Signs*, Vol. 7, No.1 (Autumn, 1981), pp. 41–55.

————— 'Difficult Joys' in *The Body and the Text: Hélène Cixous, Reading and Teaching*, ed. Helen Wilcox, et al. (Hertfordshire: Harvester Wheatsheaf, 1990), pp. 5–30.

————— 'The Laugh of the Medusa' in *Feminist Literary Theory: A Reader*, ed. Mary Eagleton (West Sussex: John Wiley & Sons, Ltd., 2011), pp. 311–313.

Collin, Robbie, '*Into the Woods*, Review: "Pure Pleasure"' in *The Telegraph* (7th January, 2015) <http://www.telegraph.co.uk/culture/film/filmreviews/11298668/Into-the-Woods-review-Meryl-Streep-Emily-Blunt-Anna-Kendrick.html> [accessed 5th November 2015]

————— 'Maleficent, Review' in *The Telegraph* (30th May 2014) <http://www.telegraph.co.uk/culture/film/filmreviews/10858663/Maleficent-review.html> [accessed 22nd February 2016]

————— '*Under the Skin*, Review' in *The Telegraph* (13th March 2014) <http://www.telegraph.co.uk/film/under-the-skin/review/> [accessed 22nd February 2016]

Connor, Steven, ed., *The Cambridge Companion to Postmodernism* (Cambridge: Cambridge University Press, 2004).

Cornell, Sarah, 'Hélène Cixous and Les Etudes Féminines' in *The Body and the Text: Hélène Cixous, Reading and Teaching*, ed. Helen Wilcox, et al. (Hertfordshire: Harvester Wheatsheaf, 1990), pp. 31–40.

Coverley, Merlin, *Psychogeography* (Herts: Pocket Essentials, 2006).

Cummins, Anthony, '*Stone Mattress* by Margaret Atwood, Review: "Rich in Sly Humour"' in *The Telegraph* (25th August, 2014) <http://www.telegraph.co.uk/culture/books/bookreviews/11035217/Stone-Mattress-by-Margaret-Atwood-review-rich-in-sly-humour.html> [accessed 3rd October 2017]

De Mylius, Johan, '"Our Time Is the Time of the Fairy Tale": Hans Christian Anderson between Traditional Craft and Literary Modernism' in *Marvels & Tales*, Vol. 20, No. 2 (2006), pp. 166–178.

Dillon, Sarah, '"It Is a Question of Words, Therefore': Becoming-Animal in Michel Faber's *Under the Skin*' in *Science Fiction Studies*, Vol. 38, No. 1 (2011), pp. 134–154.

Dobrin, Sidney I. and Kenneth B. Kidd, eds., *Wild Things: Children's Culture and Ecocriticism* (Michigan: Wayne State University Press, 2004).

Dowling, William C., *Ricoeur on Time and Narrative: An Introduction to Temps et récit* (Indiana: University of Notre Dame Press, 2011).

Duff, David, ed., *Modern Genre Theory* (Harlow: Pearson Education Ltd., 2000).

Dunlap, Allison, 'Eco-Dystopia: Reproduction and Destruction in Margaret Atwood's Oryx and Crake' in *The Journal of Ecocriticism*, Vol. 5, No. 1 (January, 2013), pp. 1–15.

Edgerton, Teresa, 'The Object of Desire: Our Interview with Tanith Lee' in *Chronicles: Science Fiction and Fantasy Community* (14th May, 2012) <https://www.sffchronicles.com/threads/536440/> [accessed 26th January 2015]

Eagleton, Mary, ed., *Feminist Literary Theory: A Reader* (West Sussex: John Wiley & Sons Ltd., 2011).

Eagleton, Mary, 'Finding a Female Tradition', in *Feminist Literary Theory: A Reader* (Oxford: Blackwell Publishing, 1996), pp. 1–8.

————— 'Genre and Gender' in *Modern Genre Theory*, ed. David Duff (Harlow: Pearson Education Limited, 2000), pp. 250–262.

—— 'Introduction: Writing, Reading, and Difference' in *Feminist Literary Theory: A Reader* (West Sussex: John Wiley & Sons Ltd., 2011), pp. 266–274.

Easton, Alison, *Angela Carter: Contemporary Critical Essays* (London: Macmillan Press Limited, 2000).

Eisfeld, Conny, *How Fairy Tales Live Happily Ever After: The Art of Adapting Fairy Tales* (Hamburg: Anchor Academic Publishing, 2014).

Faludi, Susan, *Backlash: The Undeclared War against Women* (London: Vintage, 1992).

Featherstone, Mike and Roger Burrows, eds., *Cyberspace, Cyberbodies, Cyberpunk: Cultures of Technological Embodiment* (London: SAGE Publications, 1995).

Festa McCormick, Diana, *The City as Catalyst: A Study of Ten Novels* (London: Associated University Presses, Inc., 1979).

Foundas, Scott, '*Into the Woods* Review: "Be Careful What You Wish for"' in *Variety* (17th December 2014) <http://variety.com/2014/film/reviews/film-review-into-the-woods-1201381097/> [accessed 22nd February 2016]

Freeman, Mark, 'Mythical Time, Historical Time, and the Narrative Fabric of the Self' in *Narrative Inquiry*, Vol. 8, No. 1 (1998), pp. 27–50.

Front, Sonia, *Shapes of Time in British Twenty-First Century Quantum Fiction* (Newcastle upon Tyne: Cambridge Scholars Publishing, 2015).

Frow, John, *Genre* (London: Routledge, 2005).

Gaard, Greta, 'Ecofeminism Revisited: Rejecting Essentialism and Re-placing Species in a Material Feminist Environmentalism' in *Feminist Formations*, Vol. 23, No. 2 (Summer, 2011), pp. 26–53.

Gaard, Greta and Patrick D. Murphy, 'A Dialogue on the Role and Place of Literary Criticism within Ecofeminism' in *Interdisciplinary Studies in Literature and Environment*, Vol. 3, No. 1 (1996) <isle.oxfordjournals.org/content/3/1/1.full.pdf> [accessed 22nd February 2016]

—— eds., *Ecofeminist Literary Criticism: Theory, Interpretation, Pedagogy* (Chicago: University of Illinois Press, 1998).

Gaard, Greta and Patrick D. Murphy, 'New Directions for Ecofeminism: Toward a More Feminist Ecocriticism' in *Interdisciplinary Studies in Literature and Environment*, Vol. 7, No. 4 (2010), pp. 643–665 <http://isle.oxfordjournals.org/content/17/4/643.extract> [accessed 5th November 2015]

Gapinski, James R., 'Youthful Innocence and Sobering Realities: A Review of *How a Mother Weaned Her Girl from Fairy Tales* by Kate Bernheimer' in *Atticus Review* (12th February, 2015) <https://atticusreview.org/youthful-innocence-and-sobering-realities-a-review-of-how-a-mother-weaned-her-girl-from-fairy-tales-by-kate-bernheimer/> [accessed 1st October 2016]

Gibbons, Joan, 'Mapping and Memory: Contemporary Psychogeographies' in *Public Space: The Battlefield for Public Art*, No. 10 (September, 2007), pp. 37–41.

Gilbert, Sandra and Susan Gubar, *The Madwoman in the Attic: The Woman Writer and the Nineteenth-Century Literary Imagination* (London: Yale University Press, 2000).

Glazer, Jonathan, *Under the Skin* (Seventh Kingdom Productions Limited, Channel Four Television Corporation and the British Film Institute, 2014).

Goldstein, Dina, 'Snowy' in *Fallen Princesses* <http://www.fallenprincesses.com> [accessed 7th September 2016]

Greenhill, Pauline and Jill Terry Rudy, eds., *Channeling Wonder: Fairy Tales on Television* (Detroit: Wayne State University Press, 2014).

Grosz, Elizabeth A., *Architecture from the Outside: Essays on Virtual and Real Space* (Massachusetts: Massachusetts Institute of Technology, 2001).

—— *Becomings: Explorations in Time, Memory, and Future* (London: Cornell University Press, 1999).

—— *New Materialisms: Ontology, Agency, and Politics* (London: Duke University Press, 2010).

—— *Space, Time, and Perversion: Essays on the Politics of Bodies* (London: Routledge, 1995).

—— *Time Travels: Feminism, Nature, Power* (Crows Nest: Allen & Unwin, 2005).

—— *The Nick of Time: Politics, Evolution and the Untimely* (Durham: Duke University Press, 2004).

Haase, Donald, 'Children, War, and the Imaginative Space of Fairy Tales' in *The Lion and the Unicorn*, Vol. 24 (2000), pp. 360–377.

—— *Fairy Tales and Feminism: New Approaches* (Michigan: Wayne State University Press, 2004).

—— 'Yours, Mine, or Ours? Perrault, the Brothers Grimm, and the Ownership of Fairy Tales' in *The Classic Fairy Tales,* ed. Maria Tatar (London: W. W. Norton & Company, 1999), pp. 353–363.

Halberstam, Judith, 'Automating Gender: Postmodern Feminism in the Age of the Intelligent Machine' in *Feminist Studies,* Vol. 18, No. 1 (Spring, 1992), pp. 439–460.

—— *In a Queer Time and Place: Transgender Bodies, Subcultural Lives* (New York: New York University Press, 2005).

Haraway, Donna, 'A Cyborg Manifesto: Science, Technology, and Socialist-Feminism in the Late Twentieth-Century' <http://www.labster8.net/wp-content/uploads/2015/11/Haraway-Cyborg-Manifesto2.pdf> [accessed 7th April 2016]

Harries, Elizabeth Waning, *Twice Upon a Time: Women Writers and the History of the Fairy Tale* (New Jersey: Princeton University Press, 2001).

Haut, Mavis, *The Hidden Library of Tanith Lee: Themes and Subtexts From Dionysos to the Immortal Gene* (London: McFarland and Company Inc., 2001).

Hawkes, Jean, trans., *The London Journal of Flora Tristan* (London: Virago Press Limited, 1982).

Heller, Tamar and Patricia Moran, eds., *Scenes of the Apple: Food and the Female Body in Nineteenth- and Twentieth-Century Women's Writing* (Albany: State University of New York Press, 2003).

Hengen, Shannon, 'Margaret Atwood and Environmentalism' in *The Cambridge Companion to Margaret Atwood,* ed. Coral Ann Howells (Cambridge: Cambridge University Press, 2006), pp. 72–85.

Howell, Philip, 'Crime and the City Solution: Crime Fiction, Urban Knowledge, and Radical Geography' in *Antipode*, Vol. 30, No. 4 (1998), pp. 357–378.

Huehls, Mitchum, *Qualified Hope: A Postmodern Politics of Time* (Ohio: The Ohio State University Press, 2009).

Hutcheon, Linda, *A Theory of Adaptation* (New York: Routledge, 2006).

Irigaray, Luce, *An Ethics of Sexual Difference*, trans. Carolyn Burke and Gillian C. Gill (London: Athlone Press, 1993).

—— *This Sex Which Is Not One* (New York: Cornell University Press, 1985).

—— 'When Our Lips Speak Together' in *Feminist Theory and the Body: A Reader*, eds. Janet Price and Margrit Shildrick (Edinburgh: Edinburgh University Press, 1999), pp. 82–90.

Jordan, Justine, '*Stone Mattress* Review – Margaret Atwood's New Collection of Short Stories' in *The Guardian* (10th October, 2014) <https://www.theguardian.com/books/2014/oct/10/stone-mattress-margaret-atwood-review-short-story-collection> [accessed 3rd October 2016]

Kérchy, Anna, *Alice in Transmedia Wonderland: Curiouser and Curiouser Forms of a Children's Classic* (Jefferson: McFarland, 2016).

—— 'Ambiguous Alice: Making Sense of Lewis Carroll's Nonsense Fantasies' in *Does It Really Mean That? Interpreting the Literary Ambiguous*, eds. Kathleen Dubs and Janka Kaščáková (Newcastle upon Tyne: Cambridge Scholars Publishing, 2011), pp. 104–120.

—— 'Bodies That Do Not Fit: Sexual Metamorphosis, Re-embodied Identities and Cultural Crisis in Contemporary Transgender Memoirs' (2009) <https://www.academia.edu/5432781/Bodies_That_Do_Not_Fit_Sexual_Metamorphoses_Re-embodied_Identities_and_Cultural_Crisis_in_Contemporary_Transgender_Memoirs?auto=download> [accessed 7th April 2017]

—— *Body Texts in the Novels of Angela Carter: Writing from a Corporeagraphic Point of View* (Lewiston: Edwin Mellen Press, 2008).

—— 'Feminist Psychogeography and Jeanette Winterson's Passions' in *She's Leaving Home. Women's Writing in English in a European Context (European Connections)*, eds. Nóra Séllei and June Waudby (Oxford: Peter Lang, 2011), pp. 131–149.

—— 'Narrating the Nervous, Bulimic Body-Text in Angela Carter's *The Passion of the New Eve*' in *Gender Studies*, No. 5 (2006), pp. 84–110.

—— *Postmodern Reinterpretations of Fairy Tales: How Applying New Methods Generates New Meanings* (Lampeter: The Edwin Mellen Press, 2011).

—— 'Wonderland Lost and Found?: Nonsensical Enchantment and Imaginative Reluctance in Revisionings of Lewis Carroll's *Alice* Tales' in *Anti-Tales: The Uses of Disenchantment*, eds. Catriona McAra and David Calvin (Newcastle Upon Tyne: Cambridge Scholars Publishing, 2011), pp. 62–74.

Kristeva, Julia, 'Women's Time' in *Signs*, Vol. 7, No. 1 (Autumn, 1981), pp. 13–35.

Ku, Chung-Hao, 'Of Monster and Man: Transgenics and Transgression in Margaret Atwood's Oryx and Crake' in *Concentric: Literary and Cultural Studies*, Vol. 32 (2006), pp. 107–133.

Labudova, Katarína, 'Paradice Redesigned: Post-Apocalyptic Visions of Urban and Rural Spaces in Margaret Atwood's *Maddaddam* Trilogy' in *Eger Journal of English Studies*, Vol. XIII (2013), pp. 27–36.

—— 'Power, Pain, and Manipulation in Margaret Atwood's *Oryx and Crake* and *The Year of the Flood*' in *Brno Studies in English*, Vol. 36, No. 1 (2010), pp. 135–146.

Lee, Tanith, *A Different City* (Stafford: Immanion Press, 2015).

—— *Disturbed by Her Song* (Maple Shade: Lethe Press, 2010).

Lieberman, Marcia R., 'Some Day My Prince Will Come: Female Acculturation through the Fairy Tale' in *College English*, Vol. 34, No. 3 (December, 1972), pp. 383–395.

Little, Jo, Linda Peake and Pat Richardson, eds., *Women in Cities: Gender and the Urban Environment* (London: Macmillan Education Ltd., 1988).

Lurie, Alison, 'Fairy Tale Liberation' in *The New York Review of Books* (December 17th, 1970) <http://www.nybooks.com/articles/1970/12/17/fairy-tale-liberation/> [accessed 18th June 2017]

Maitland, Sara, *Gossip from the Forest: The Tangled Roots of Our Forests and Fairy Tales* (London: Granta Publications, 2012).

Mărginean, Alexandra, 'Deconstructive Angles in *Maleficent*' in *Communication, Context, Interdisciplinarity* (Romania: Petru Maior University Press, 2014).

McAra, Calvin, David Catriona, eds., *Anti-Tales: The Uses of Disenchantment* (Newcastle Upon Tyne: Cambridge Scholars Publishing, 2011).

McNamara, Kevin R., ed., *The Cambridge Companion to the City in Literature* (New York: Cambridge University Press, 2014).

McRobbie, Angela, *The Aftermath of Feminism: Gender, Culture and Social Change* (London: SAGE Publications Ltd., 2009).

Minh-ha, Trinh T., 'Write Your Body and the Body in Theory' in *Feminist Theory and the Body: A Reader,* eds. Janet Price and Margrit Shildrick (Edinburgh: Edinburgh University Press, 1999), pp. 258–266.

Moen, Kristian, *Film and Fairy Tales: The Birth of Modern Fantasy: From* the Blue Bird *to* Harry Potter (London: I.B. Tauris & Co. Ltd., 2013).

Nanni, Giordano, 'Time, Empire and Resistance in Settler-Colonial Victoria' in *Time & Society*, Vol. 20, No. 1 (2011), pp. 5–33.

——— 'The Colonisation of Time: Ritual, Routine and Resistance in the British Empire' <http://www.worldhistory.pitt.edu/documents/Nanni.pdf> [accessed 26th July 2017]

Nast, Heidi and Steve J. Pile, eds., *Places through the Body* (London: Routledge, 1998).

Navarro, Meagan, 'The Dark Need for Modern Fairy Tales' in *Birth.Movies. Death* <http://birthmoviesdeath.com/2017/01/12/the-dark-need-for-modern-fairy-tales> [accessed 7th April 2017]

Nead, Lynda, *Myths of Sexuality: Representations of Women in Victorian Britain* (Oxford: Basil Blackwell Ltd., 1988).

Neimanis, Astrida, *Bodies of Water: Posthuman Feminist Phenomenology* (London: Bloomsbury Publishing Plc, 2017).

Orenstein, Catherine, *Little Red Riding Hood Uncloaked: Sex, Morality, and the Evolution of a Fairy Tale* (New York: Basic Books, 2002).

Osterweil, Ara, '*Under the Skin*: The Perils of Becoming Female' in *Film Quarterly*, Vol. 67, No. 4 (Summer, 2014), pp. 44–51.

Parsons, Deborah L., *Streetwalking the Metropolis: Women, the City, and Modernity* (Oxford: Oxford University Press, 2000).

Perrault, Charles, 'Little Red Riding Hood' reprinted in Catherine Orenstein, *Little Red Riding Hood Uncloaked: Sex, Morality, and the Evolution of a Fairy Tale* (New York: Basic Books, 2002), pp. 19–21.

Pinkola Estés, Clarissa, *Women Who Run with Wolves: Contracting the Power of the Wild Woman* (London: Rider, 1992).

Plumwood, Val, 'Ecofeminism: An Overview and Discussion of Positions and Arguments' in *Australasian Journal of Philosophy*, Vol. 64 (1986), pp. 120–138.

Preston, Peter and Paul Simpson-Housley, eds., *Writing the City: Eden, Babylon and the New Jerusalem* (London: Routledge, 1994).

Ramadan Elnahla, Nada, 'Aging with Disney and the Gendering of Evil' in *Journal of Literature and Arts Studies*, Vol. 5, No. 2 (February, 2015), pp. 114–127.

Redington Bobby, Susan, ed., *Fairy Tales Reimagined: Essays on New Retellings* (London: McFarland & Company Inc., 2009).

Reynolds, Kendra, 'A Rude Awakening: Sleeping Beauty as a Metaphor for the Slumber of Post-Feminism' *Journal of International Women's Studies*, Vol. 16, No. 1, pp. 34–46.

Ridley, Louise, 'EU Referendum Results: Young "Screwed By Older Generations"' in *The Huffington Post* (24th June, 2016) <http://www.huffingtonpost.co.uk/entry/eu-referendum-results-age-data-young_uk_576cd7d6e4b0232d331dac8f> [accessed 3rd October 2016]

Robey, Tim, '*Alice through the Looking Glass* Makes Wonderland Look Good Enough to Eat' in *The Telegraph* (26th May, 2016) <http://www.telegraph.co.uk/films/2016/05/26/alice-through-the-looking-glass-makes-wonderland-look-good-enoug/> [accessed 25th September 2016]

Romney, Jonathan, '*Maleficent* Review: "Messy Live-Action Retelling of Sleeping Beauty"' in *The Guardian* (Sunday 1st June, 2014) <http://www.theguardian.com/film/2014/jun/01/maleficent-review-messy-derivative-live-action-sleeping-beauty> [accessed 22nd February 2016]

Roper, Caitlin, 'Book Reviews: *Maddaddam* by Margaret Atwood' in *Transnational Literature*, Vol. 6, No. 2 (May, 2014) <http://dspace.flinders.edu.au/xmlui/bitstream/handle/2328/27600/Maddaddam.pdf?sequence=1> [accessed 22nd February 2016]

Rowe, Karen E., 'To Spin a Yarn: The Female Voice in Folklore and Fairy Tale' in *The Classic Fairy Tales,* ed. Maria Tatar (London: W. W. Norton & Company, 1999), pp. 297–308.

Sage, Lorna, 'Angela Carter: The Fairy Tale' in *Angela Carter and the Fairy Tale,* eds. Danielle Roemer and Cristina Bacchilega (Michigan: Wayne State University Press, 2001), pp. 65–82.

———— *Angela Carter* (Plymouth: Northcote House Publishers Ltd., 1994).

Sargisson, Lucy, 'What's Wrong with Ecofeminism?' in *Environmental Politics*, Vol. 10, No.1 (2001), pp. 52–64.

Scala, Mark W., ed., *Fairy Tales, Monsters, and the Genetic Imagination* (Nashville: Vanderbilt University Press, 2012).

Segal, Lynne, *Out of Time: The Pleasures and Perils of Aging* (London: Verso Books, 2014).

Sellers, Susan, ed., *Feminist Criticism: Theory and Practice* (Hertfordshire: Harvester Wheatsheaf, 1991).

———— *Myth and Fairy Tale in Contemporary Women's Fiction* (Hampshire: Palgrave, 2001).

Sheets, Robin Ann, 'Pornography, Fairy Tales, and Feminism: Angela Carter's "The Bloody Chamber" in *Journal of the History of Sexuality*, Vol. 1, No. 4 (April, 1991), pp. 633–657.

Shildrick, Margrit, *Leaky Bodies and Boundaries: Feminism, Postmodernism and (Bio)Ethics* (London: Routledge, 1997).

Shildrick, Margrit and Janet Price, eds., *Feminist Theory and the Body: A Reader* (Edinburgh: Edinburgh University Press, 1999).

Shoard, Catherine, 'Into the Woods Review: Trees Fall in the Forest, Making One Hell of a Sound' in *The Guardian* (17th December, 2014) <http://www.theguardian.com/film/2014/dec/17/into-the-woods-review-meryl-streep-rob-marshall-stephen-sondheim> [accessed 19th November 2015]

Showalter, Elaine, 'A Literature of their Own: British Women Novelists from Brontë to Lessing' in *Feminist Literary Theory: A Reader*, ed. Mary Eagleton (West Sussex: John Wiley & Sons, Ltd., 2011), pp. 11–15.

——— *A Literature of their Own: British Women Novelists from Brontë to Lessing* (Princeton: Princeton University Press, 1977).

Smethurst, Paul, *The Postmodern Chronotope: Reading Space and Time in Contemporary Fiction* (Amsterdam: Rodopi, 2000).

Stein, Howard F. and William G. Niederland, eds., *Maps from the Mind: Readings in Psychogeography* (London: University of Oklahoma Press, 1989).

Stover, Deanna, 'Gold Slippers and Cyborg Feet: Comparing Adopted Bodies in the Grimms' 'Cinderella' and Marissa Meyer's *Cinder*' <http://s3.amazonaws.com/academia.edu.documents/41571309/Stover.MLA2016.pdf?AWSAccessKeyId=AKIAIWOWYYGZ2Y53UL3A&Expires=1491645940&Signature=tzsAryuNUXHwox6N4be%2BkyzQAyk%3D&response-content-disposition=inline%3B%20filename%3DGold_Slippers_and_Cyborg_Feet_Comparing.pdf> [accessed 7th April 2016]

Sturgeon, Noël, *Ecofeminist Natures: Race, Gender, Feminist Theory and Political Action* (London: Routledge, 1997).

Sullivan, Rebecca, 'Falling Short of Feminism: Why Modern Retellings of Fairy Tales Perpetuate Negative Stereotypes of the Aging Woman' <https://kb.osu.edu/dspace/bitstream/handle/1811/45697/Falling_Short_of_Feminism.pdf?sequence=1> [accessed 3rd October 2016]

Talairach-Vielmas, Laurence, *Moulding the Female Body in Victorian Fairy Tales and Sensation Novels* (Hampshire: Ashgate Publishing Limited, 2007).

Taylor, Dena and Amber Coverdale Sumrall, eds., *Women of the 14th Moon: Writings on Menopause* (Ontario: Crossing Press, 1991).

Thacker, Andrew, *Moving Through Modernity: Space and Geography in Modernism* (Manchester: Manchester University Press, 2003).

Thrift, Nigel, 'Cities without Modernity, Cities with Magic' in *Scottish Geographical Magazine*, Vol. 113, No. 3 (February, 2008), pp. 138–149.

Vakoch, Douglas A., ed., *Feminist Ecocriticism: Environment, Women, and Literature* (New York: Lexington Books, 2012).

Vance, Carole S., *Pleasure and Danger: Exploring Female Sexuality* (London: Routledge, 1985).

Vandereycken, Walter and Ron van Deth, *From Fasting Saints to Anorexic Girls: The History of Self-Starvation* (London: The Athlone Press, 1994).

Walker, Alice, 'In Search of Our Mothers' Gardens' in *Making Sense of Women's Lives: An Introduction to Women's Studies*, eds. Michèle Plott & Lauri Umansky (Oxford: Collegiate Press, 2000).

Walker, Nancy A., *The Disobedient Writer: Women and Narrative Tradition* (Austin: University of Texas Press, 1995).

Walton-Lange, Lucy, '*Alison Wonderland* by Helen Smith (Interview)' in *Female First* (Website: 28th January, 2013) <http://www.femalefirst.co.uk/books/alison+wonderland-275631.html> [accessed 26th January 2015]

Wandor, Michelene, ed., *On Gender and Writing* (London: Thorsons, 1983).

Williams, Raymond, *The Country and the City* (Herts: Granada Publishing Limited, 1973).

Wilson, Elizabeth, ed., *The Contradictions of Culture: Cities, Culture, Women* (London: SAGE Publications Ltd., 2001).

Wilson, Sharon Rose, *Margaret Atwood's Fairy Tale Sexual Politics* (Jackson: University Press of Mississippi, 1993).

Wohlmann, Anita, 'Of Young/Old Queens and Giant Dwarfs: A Critical Reading of Age and Aging in *Snow White and the Huntsman* and *Mirror Mirror*' in *Age, Culture and Humanities: An Interdisciplinary Journal*, Issue 2 (2015) <http://ageculturehumanities.org/WP/of-youngold-queens-and-giant-dwarfs-a-critical-reading-of-age-and-aging-in-snow-white-and-the-huntsman-and-mirror-mirror/> [accessed 3rd October 2016]

Wolitzer, Meg, 'Margaret Atwood's *Stone Mattress* Is Full of Sharp and Jabbing Truths' (24th September, 2014) <http://www.npr.org/2014/09/24/348709868/margaret-atwoods-stone-mattress-is-full-of-sharp-and-jabbing-truths> [accessed 3rd October 2016]

Wolf, Naomi, *The Beauty Myth* (London: Vintage Books, 1990).

Wollstonecraft, Mary, *A Vindication of the Rights of Women & A Vindication of the Rights of Men* (New York: Cosimo, Inc., 2008).

Zipes, Jack, 'Breaking the Magic Spell: Politics and the Fairy Tale' in *New German Critique*, No. 6 (Autumn, 1975), pp. 116–135.

—— *Breaking the Magic Spell: Radical Theories of Folk and Fairy Tales* (London: Educational Books Ltd., 1979).

—— *The Irresistible Fairy Tale: The Cultural and Social History of a Genre* (Princeton: Princeton University Press, 2012).

—— *The Trials and Tribulations of Little Red Riding Hood: Versions of the Tale in a Socio-Cultural Context* (London: Heinemann Educational Books Ltd., 1983)

Zipes, Jack, Pauline Greenhill and Kendra Magnus-Johnston, eds., *Fairy-Tale Films beyond Disney: International Perspectives* (London: Routledge, 2016).

Zoller Seitz, Matt, '*Maleficent*: Movie Review' (29th March, 2014) <http://www.rogerebert.com/reviews/maleficent-2014> [accessed 19th November 2015]

Index

Notes: *Italic* page numbers refer to figures and page numbers followed by "n" denote endnotes.

For Product Safety Concerns and Information please contact our EU
representative GPSR@taylorandfrancis.com
Taylor & Francis Verlag GmbH, Kaufingerstraße 24, 80331 München, Germany

www.ingramcontent.com/pod-product-compliance
Lightning Source LLC
Chambersburg PA
CBHW071507110726
47908CB00003B/758